Harry Cole was born and brought up in Bermondsey, south London. He left school when he was fourteen, during the war, and became a cricket-bat maker, soldier, stonemason and, in 1952, a policeman. For thirty years, until his retirement in 1983, he served at the same police station in London.

He is a qualified FA coach, a referee and a keen cricketer but his main sporting interests now are swimming, bowls and watching his grandson play cricket and football. The author of the popular *Policeman* books about life on the beat ('Harry Cole is the police's James Herriot' *Sunday Express*), he has also written two volumes of autobiography.

In 1978 Harry Cole was awarded the British Empire Medal for voluntary work. Since leaving the force, in addition to writing, he has taken up after-dinner speaking.

Also by Harry Cole from Headline

Queenie

Billie's Bunch

Harry Cole

KNIGHT

Copyright © 1995 Harry Cole

The right of Harry Cole to be identified as the Author of
the Work has been asserted by him in accordance with the
Copyright, Designs and Patents Act 1988.

First published in 1995
by HEADLINE BOOK PUBLISHING

First published in paperback in 1996
by HEADLINE BOOK PUBLISHING

This edition published 2000 by
Knight an imprint of Caxton Publishing Group

10 9 8 7 6 5 4 3 2

ISBN 1 84067 194 7

Printed and bound in Great Britain by
Mackays of Chatham PLC, Chatham, Kent

Caxton Publishing Group
20 Bloomsbury Street
London
WC1B 3QA

To Barbara Garrett for her help and support.

ACKNOWLEDGEMENTS

With special thanks to:
Derek Blake for his advice on Spain.
Barbara Coker for her general advice regarding nursing.
The twelve police pensioners for their memories of the
Mosley marches.

1

'What!' exclaimed Miss Billie Bardell. 'No newspapers? I can't possibly start my day without my *Daily Mirror*. Excuse me, Alice, whilst I sulk.'

Alice Giles, her gentle, slightly rounded, fortyish-something maid, gave a little frown. 'Well, your bath is ready, Miss Bardell . . . Oh dear,' she almost whimpered, 'I don't like telling you this – but there's no milk or post either. Not only that—'

'Oh, Gawd, you mean there's more?' interrupted Billie with a heartfelt groan.

''Fraid so,' continued the maid. 'There's also more than a possibility that the lights will go out, the taps dry up and the gas go off. It's the general strike, y'see.'

'Quick then, girl,' Billie replied, leaping naked from her bed. 'Do me a large fried breakfast whilst I have a quick dip. Once I've washed me intimates and knocked back a couple of fried eggs, I shall be more than ready to cope with a bloody strike.' Within seconds she had slipped her feet into a pair of pink fluffy slippers and practically skipped into the adjoining bathroom.

The maid watched her mistress with her usual admiration. Familiarity did not breed contempt in Alice's case. She had served Billie Bardell, the former queen of the music halls, for some two years now. During that time she had been a personal maid, friend, confidante, cook and general dogsbody. In spite of all that had passed, she was as in awe of her now as she had been that raw November day in 1924 when

1

she had arrived, penniless, for the interview. At the time, her own fortune had been at its lowest ebb. When Alice had entered that large house, clutching the hand of her fourteen-year-old daughter Julia, she could not see her future beyond the next few days. All of that was behind her now and had been from the moment the two women had met. Billie Bardell had not just taken her into her house but had also given her warmth, hope and employment to young Julia. These two years had easily been the happiest of Alice's life.

'I'll get you a warm towel, Miss Bardell,' she called from the airing cupboard.

'Three fried slices would be more acceptable, Alice. By the way, if you haven't cooked my breakfast before the gas is cut off, you do realise you're out on the streets again, don't you?'

The maid looked at her fondly. There was no doubt about it, though she had been on the halls for the best part of thirty years, Billy Bardell was an astonishing-looking woman. In fact, until her widowhood a few years earlier, she had hardly altered from her earliest photographs that had plastered every music hall in the country since 1900. Since her retirement from the halls she had certainly put on a little weight, yet even this did not detract because, apart from being blessed with an astonishingly clear and line-free complexion, the pounds had spread themselves evenly over her well-proportioned frame. Alice Giles had no definitive impression of Boudicca but she suspected that Billie Bardell could easily have played the role. In olden days her torso would probably have provided a figurehead for a sturdy man-o'-war. Her proud head, broad shoulders and deep full breasts, would have provided sanctuary for half a medieval fleet. In short, Billie Bardell was truly magnificent.

As Alice raised the large white towel to accommodate her voluptuous mistress she said, 'I'd better warn you, I think you're due to receive a works deputation.'

'What!' exclaimed Billie. 'From whom, and why?'

'At the moment, only from Julia, but she could well be accompanied by Duncan.'

'What's this then? A bloody workers' council? D'you realise those two comprise two-thirds of my workforce? They're not joining the general strike as well by any chance, are they?'

'Wouldn't surprise me,' sighed Alice. 'For a sixteen-year-old girl, she can be politics mad at times. God knows where she gets it from, certainly not me.'

'Perhaps it was from her dad?'

'I very much doubt that,' said Alice, shaking her head. 'He didn't even vote.'

'Well, how about young Duncan?' persisted Billie. 'He's not into politics, is he?'

Alice shook her head ruefully. 'I don't know if he's into politics but given half a chance I think he'd be into my Julia. Being the only two youngsters on the premises, they are thrown together a lot, which doesn't help.'

'Oh, come on, Alice,' reproved Billie. 'I've got eyes, y'know. Your Julia is nuts about him. Though I don't blame her for that. I've watched them from the window many a time. No wonder my shrubbery is in such a state when me bloody gardener keeps getting accosted by your daughter.'

'Don't get me wrong, Miss Bardell. If I could pick out a son-in-law for myself, Duncan'd be top of my list, but she is still only sixteen and even though she seems to take things like politics very seriously, she's still quite daft in other matters.'

'Alice,' said Billie, wrapping the towel firmly around herself, 'I'm a million light years from sixteen but I'm *still* daft. Why don't you just let the thing work itself out naturally? If they're together often enough they could well wind up hating each other. I mean, Duncan is so relaxed about everything that I'm sure such a serious and tidy-minded lass as your Julia will eventually want to throttle him – and speaking of "throttling" have you started my breakfast yet?'

It was a little over an hour later that, with great satisfaction,

Billie pushed away a crust-wiped plate and glanced gratefully up at Alice who was pouring tea. 'Alice Giles,' she announced formally, 'eggs, bacon, tomatoes and fried bread, as cooked to perfection by you, is one of the great dishes of the world and I don't give a jot what those ignorant Frogs say about our cooking.' She turned to face the window and called to no one in particular, 'Okay, workers, do your worst and on with the strike! I'm now fit for anything.'

'Well, two of the workers are outside,' said Alice, gathering up the plates and nodding towards the door. 'They've been waiting for you to finish your breakfast. Shall I show them in?'

'Of course! But sharpen the guillotine loudly. I want them to know the sort of person they're dealing with.'

As Alice stood at the door with an armful of crockery, her daughter entered followed by the gardener. Each time Billie saw the girl she could not fail to be impressed. She was obviously Alice's daughter, of that there could be no question, yet she was truly beautiful in a way that Alice could never have been. Her slim dark looks appeared to have been carved for another life, as if in the rush to be born, someone had mixed the ingredients. Young as she was, she exuded a sensuality that should only be radiated by self-assured women twice her age.

On the other hand, Duncan Forbes, the gardener who followed her in, was as relaxed as the girl was intense. Though two years her senior, he was usually content for her to take the lead. Yet, in spite of this, it was difficult to avoid the feeling that he treated everything she said with amused indifference. Occasionally the girl would sense it and this would ignite her anger but with his cool informality and his classically good looks, she found it impossible to be angry with him for long.

'Well, workers,' said Billie, looking directly at Duncan, 'what's the moan today?'

The young man gave the merest nod towards Julia. Then,

4

as if his part in the proceedings was complete, he turned his head to the window and gazed out idly at his garden.

'Er – well, Miss Bardell,' the girl said softly, 'we wondered if we could have some days off to go to town to show support for the general strike . . . We both feel quite strongly about it,' she added as a quick afterthought.

Billie resisted the urge to question the likelihood of Duncan feeling strongly about anything and instead replied, 'I don't get it. Are you telling me that because there's a general strike, my gardener and my deputy maid are downing tools? What on earth will that achieve?'

At Billie's words, Duncan came about as close to anxiety as he had ever been. 'Good heavens, *no*, Miss Bardell,' he exclaimed. 'That's definitely not the idea. Tell her, Julia.'

'Er – he's right, Miss. We've got no complaints about you at all. It's just that being stuck here . . . well, we don't feel part of it. I mean, in years to come when everyone is talking about what they did in the general strike, we won't be able to say anything.'

'Let me get this straight,' responded Billie calmly. 'You want *me* to pay *you* to partake in a strike which is nothing to do with *me*, so in forty years' time you can boast to your grandchildren. I have got that right, haven't I?'

'Well, er – it's not really *quite* like that, Miss Bardell,' protested the girl.

'Oh, I'm not so sure,' said Duncan thoughtfully. 'Come to think of it, it does sound a mite that way, y'know. I mean, whatever way you look at it, we don't want to be *here*, we want to be *there*, but we only get our wages for being *here*, and we don't propose to *be* here, do we? Here, tell y'what we could do,' he switched his gaze quickly from one to the other. 'We could go off-pay. How about that?' he asked proudly.

The girl shot a dagger-like glance at him. 'Off-pay' was hardly what she wanted to hear, particularly from her own side, but she knew he had now committed them well and truly. 'That's what I was going to say,' she said unconvincingly.

'Well, that's all right then,' agreed Billie, barely able to hide a grin. 'Providing you've nothing outstanding in the garden you can go with my blessing.'

'Garden's fine,' said Duncan, nodding in agreement with himself. 'Bedding plants are warming up nicely in the greenhouse, wallflowers are still blooming, daffs have at least another couple of weeks before they can be cut down and I trimmed all the lawns yesterday. Even the calendar is on our side!'

'So, when do you propose to be back?' asked Billie. 'Tomorrow? Friday? Not at all?'

'Well, today's Tuesday,' said the girl thoughtfully. 'How about Saturday?'

'Saturday it is then,' agreed Billie. 'Eight o'clock sharp, minus pay and don't give this address if you wind up nicked because I won't be bailing you out.'

'Thanks, Miss Bardell,' said the girl warmly. 'I'll not forget this.'

'No, and apparently neither will your grandchildren, poor little perishers.'

When she was sure the interview had completely finished, Alice spoke for the first time. 'Duncan, you will look after my Julia, won't you?'

'O'course, Mrs Giles,' he assured.

The pair were as good as their word and within the half-hour had waved their goodbyes as they strode out briskly down the gravel drive.

'Their first test is about a hundred yards away,' said Alice quietly. 'And my Julia will be back about two minutes after that.'

'What test? And why will she be back?' asked Billie curiously.

'It's the test that says there are no trains or buses running into central London and she realises she can't walk there in those heels . . . There, what did I tell you?' She pointed to the grass verge at the side of the drive where an exasperated Julia was already sprinting a barefoot return with her shoes in her hand.

Billie watched with an amused smile as Alice met her daughter at the door with more sensible footwear and within a few seconds the girl had rejoined the youth and set off once more on the six-mile hike to town.

It was shortly after midday when the pair approached a dingy café just off the Tottenham Court Road.

'I'm still not quite sure what we're supposed to be doing here?' said Duncan. 'It hardly looks impressive.'

'You should never take things at their face value,' reproached Julia. 'You should always make a point of searching for the truth, then pause and think deeply before jumping to any conclusion that you may afterwards regret.'

For a moment he looked at her in disbelief before breaking out into a laugh of derision. 'Who told you that? A parrot?' he leaned forward and peered through the steamy window of the café. 'These friends of yours we're supposed to be meeting don't all spout tripe like that, do they?'

'Listen, don't you *dare* show me up in front of them! They will be taking this strike very seriously indeed and if they hear you talk like that they'll think I'm not trustworthy. Now, don't forget, they will almost certainly refer to you as "brother" or possibly "comrade", so please don't try to be clever and make a stupid joke about everything or I'm disowning you.'

She pushed the door and entered a dim crowded room where condensation ran in rivulets down planked walls. Crowded lines of bench seats and tables ran at right angles from the left wall, leaving only the narrowest of gangways between the end of the benches and the café counter. The smell of strong tobacco, tea and stale cabbage water hung heavy in the stifling air.

'We're going to be in here long?' Duncan grizzled. 'I can't breathe.'

'Good! Perhaps then you might shut up!' Julia hissed through a forced smile.

'Ah, Julia! At last!' came a cry from the far table. 'And you've fetched a friend. Good! If we're going to win this battle we need everyone we can get.'

'Good God!' exclaimed Duncan, making little attempt to disguise his reaction. 'It's Lenin himself. Ouch!' He winced as Julia's left elbow struck deep into his ribs.

Angry as the girl was, she couldn't avoid a sneaking similar thought. Since she had last seen the newcomer at a political meeting some four months earlier, he had taken to wearing a cap, spectacles and sprouted a beard. Comrade Nathaniel Moses Sprigg had taken to the strike in a wholehearted way.

'You are very late, my dear,' he reproved. 'We were really expecting you some time ago. Many comrades have been out there since the first hours of the strike.'

'I know, I'm very sorry,' she murmured, 'but we had trouble getting away.'

'From your employer, I suppose? How typical!' Sprigg snarled bitterly.

The girl, embarrassed, looked for help towards Duncan. For what seemed an eternity, he made no move to rescue her. Just as she was about to open her mouth to blurt out some ill-thought-out excuse, Duncan finally interjected.

'No, 'fraid it was from me, mate. I'm a gardener, y'see, and I wanted to tuck up my plants all nice and snug afore I left them. All you need is a late frost in May and it'll slaughter your summer beds overnight.'

'I take it we are speaking here of your own garden?' queried Sprigg.

'Nah,' he replied, shaking his head vigorously. 'Belongs to the lady I work for.'

'The lady you . . .' began an incredulous Lenin. 'Let's get this straight; once this battle has been won, we will be the masters. Considerations such as you have just put forward are inconsequential and not worth thinking about. They

8

must therefore be disregarded entirely.'

'I should bloody say not!' exploded Duncan. 'Have you ever tried growing begonias and geraniums from seed? I've spent all winter nurturing twenty trays of the buggers. They're my kids, they are. I wouldn't dream of leaving them to fend for themselves.'

The answer was not what his interrogator expected to hear and the man thought quickly for a moment. 'Look, tell you what, comrade,' he said, taking hold of Duncan's arm, 'why don't you sit here and have a cup of tea and a bacon sandwich or something – it's all paid for out of party funds – whilst I take this young lady to meet the committee. I promise we won't keep you long.'

The long walk had sharpened Duncan's appetite and if the committee were to be anything like Nathaniel Sprigg, then a bacon sandwich had infinitely greater appeal. 'Done!' he agreed, rubbing his hands together. 'See you later, girl.'

The 'girl' was led away by Lenin as Duncan made his way to the food counter.

Four bacon sandwiches and two teas later, a solemn-faced Julia returned. Sliding in alongside him, she immediately noticed the pile of bacon rinds piled high upon his saucer. 'How many sandwiches have you had?' she demanded suspiciously.

'Er – three, or it might have been four.'

'Four! You – you – you PIG, you!' she stamped her foot and gestured around her. 'Don't you know these comrades have been putting their pennies in a fighting fund for the last twelve months for such a day as this?' She shook her head despairingly. 'And a gannet like you comes along and eats *four* of their bacon sandwiches!' She raised her eyes to the ceiling and spread her arms wide in penance. 'And to think I'm the one who brought you here!'

'I couldn't help it, you were such a long time,' he protested. 'Anyway, what's the master plan that's going to put little Nathaniel in Number Ten Downing Street?'

She leaned slowly forward and with hands on hips and legs slightly parted, she stared at him furiously. 'You're not taking this thing seriously, are you? You think it's all a joke, don't you? I guessed you would, because that's so bloody typical of you, Duncan Forbes. Comrade Sprigg saw through you right away; he said he didn't think your heart was in this and he's already been proved right!' She had leaned so far forward that her nose was just inches away from his face. Before she could react, he moved swiftly forward and kissed the tip of it.

'Well, while we're swapping confidences, I think Comrade Sprigg is a randy old sod who's after your cherry. But if he's not,' he shrugged and opened wide his palms, 'then he's a bit the other way, 'cos you look sensational when you're furious.'

By way of reply, she swung a tremendous slap towards the side of his head, but to incense her further, he parried it with ease.

'Now, now, comrade,' he chided, 'our battle is out there with the oppressors, not in here with each other.'

As he slowly released her hand she was aware that everyone in the café was staring at them. 'You've shown me up in front of my friends, you have, you – you bastard! I'll never forgive you for this,' she hissed.

He slowly relinquished his hold on her wrist. 'Aw, c'mon, girl,' he pleaded, 'you ask me along to keep you company and that's what I intended to do. Now all of a sudden you tell me I'm a spy! If you want me to do something constructive for your cause then bloody well tell me what it is. I'm new to this game, y'know.'

'D'you really mean that?' she asked, verging on tears of frustration. 'Because I'm not sure if I can ever rely on you again.'

'Scout's honour,' he said, drawing a finger across his own throat. 'Of course, I mean it; what would I be doing here otherwise?'

She turned and looked towards a doorway where Sprigg

had been watching the whole confrontation with no little interest. 'He still insists he wants to help, Comrade Sprigg,' she called.

At first Sprigg made no reply but walked thoughtfully to their bench. 'Then let's all sit down and stop behaving like drunken proletariat.' He motioned towards the two seats across the bench-table. He stared straight at Duncan. 'It has been decided that Comrade Julia has an important role in our overall strategy. As a newcomer, you are obviously on trial. However, we do have an almost equally important task for you. Are you prepared to undertake such an assignment?'

'Well, I don't know what it is yet,' protested the young man. 'But if I'm with Julia, it'll be okay.'

'No,' snapped Sprigg irritably, 'it will *not* be with Comrade Julia. Instead, you will be our eyes and ears out there on the streets. We will give you a couple of areas of which our knowledge is scant and you will report directly back to us if anything is happening.'

'Such as?'

'Such as, are there any blacklegs working on the public services and where would be a suitable place for more demonstrators? General intelligence of that sort.'

'How do I contact you?'

'From a public telephone box, of course. We'll give you three shillings and sixpence in coins and the telephone number of this café and turn you loose.'

'Where would you like me to start?'

'Westminster, I think. Though we probably are fairly thick on the ground there already; that's where most of the newspaper and newsreel reporters will be so that's where we'll attract most publicity. Your job will be to search out anything that may be happening down the lesser roads near the Admiralty.'

'What time do I finish work and where do I collect my three and sixpence?'

'You get it from me now by signing for it. That's the easy

11

bit but as regards finishing work, forget it,' replied Sprigg sharply. 'We are working for as long as this strike takes bu we do have access to Bender's old warehouse at the Londor Bridge end of Tooley Street. You can't miss it, most of th windows are broken. It has lavatories, running water and ; few blankets. But we don't want to see anyone there unti they are totally exhausted. No one's going to change th world by sleeping all day. So it's at the forefront where I'l expect you to be most of the time, understand? If you agree make your move now, time's getting short.'

Smuggling another bacon sandwich into his pocket, anc being refused a kiss by Julia, Duncan said his goodbyes anc made his way slowly towards Westminster. Having walkec many miles that day, he soon found himself waiting at a bu: stop before remembering it was the absence of buses tha accounted for his presence.

His knowledge of London was minimal and after takin; several conflicting directions he finally saw an interesting looking crowd at the rear of the Foreign Office opposite S James's Park. As he neared, he realised the crowd actuall consisted of small orderly queues that stretched back som twenty yards from a line of camping tables. Though peopl seemed to be enrolling, it looked far more professional anc very different from Nathaniel Sprigg's crowd. On the fringe: of the crowd stood two men with notebooks who appeared tc be asking questions of anyone showing interest befor directing them to a table. Having given his brief backgrounc to one man, he was directed to table number five. Here ar attractive tweed-suited, ash blonde woman of some thirt years sat with a welcoming smile and an opened register 'D'you know anything about tramcars, young man?' was her surprising opening remark.

'Er – no,' he replied. 'Only that they run on rails and yor can drive them from either end,' he said hopefully.

'You sound eminently suitable.' She beamed. 'Would yor like to know more about them, enough to drive one, I mean?

'DRIVE ONE!' he exclaimed. 'Hell's bells! Wouldn't I just!' He had by this time fully realised that somehow he had blundered into the opposition's recruiting centre. He felt a quick twinge of apprehension at the thought of explaining his actions to Julia, but that soon passed. Anyway, how could anyone in their right mind offset that with the chance actually to drive a tram! A real proper double-decker bright red London Transport TRAM! It was something he had wanted to do since he was two years old! He guessed he would be expected to return old Sprigg's three and six but even that failed to dismay, though it did manage to remind him of the bacon sandwich in his pocket.

'How about accommodation?' the woman said. 'Will you require a bed for the night?'

His heart jumped before he realised she was reciting the questions from a form and not from any sexual preference. He then took all of two seconds to weigh up Julia's probable reaction before blurting, 'Yes, please.' After all, he had never really fancied recuperating at Bender's Warehouse. Still, God only knows what old Lenin would have to say about it.

'Right, I'll give you a pass for the Guards Barracks over there in Birdcage Walk. They'll put you up there free for the remainder of the strike.' She slid a small officially stamped piece of paper towards him. 'Do you know where the Kingsway tram tunnel is?' He nodded. 'Good. Go there as early as you can in the morning, take this pass with you and they will give you your first practice on a tram.' She looked at her watch and added with a beautiful wide smile, 'I would now suggest you get yourself a good night's sleep because I'd say you are going to have a very interesting day tomorrow. Oh, by the way, you are over twenty aren't you?'

'Of course, I am!' he lied.

With the pass clutched tightly in his hand, he was more or less off duty until he reported to the Kingsway tunnel in the morning. He was suddenly indecisive – to whom did he owe allegiance? For a moment he thought about placating his

13

conscience by working for Spriggs until midnight then for the government from the stroke of twelve, but then that seemed needlessly complicated. He would buy himself a pint and have an early night just as the woman had suspected. Passing one of the men with a notebook, he asked directions to the nearest pub. It seemed that Lenin's three shillings and sixpence was suddenly burning a hole in his capitalist pocket.

Three hours, four pints, two pies and three shillings and sixpence later, Duncan Forbes, traitorous turncoat and tram driver apparent, fell into his bunk to sleep the sleep of the just. At that precise moment, a confused Julia Giles had roused herself from what seemed a dozen layers of sleep to find a bespectacled, bearded little impersonator of Lenin, already into her blankets and busily running both hands up the inside of her warm thighs.

Kingsway tunnel was not exactly well lit. It had been built a quarter of a century earlier to pass under the Strand and enable the tramcars to avoid traffic congestion. However, many of the latest trams were already proving too tall and the tunnel had been closed for many months in order to be heightened. With the rails still in place, it was a good central location to start a crash course in tram control.

'The good fing about trams, boy,' said the old pipe-smoking instructor, 'is yer don't 'ave ter steer 'em. Yer stops 'em, yer starts 'em and yer dings a bell from time ter time. Yer also trys not ter run over old ladies, traffic coppers an' the 'ousehold Cavalry. An' that's about all there is to it.'

The team of prospective drivers looked dubiously at each other. Though their enthusiasm was boundless, they strongly suspected the task was being oversimplified. But within a few hours and in spite of these doubts, most had learnt the rudiments and were ready for the practice runs near Mitcham Common.

By the fifth day of the strike, Duncan Forbes was relishing every minute, but Julia Giles was finding that being a part of a revolution was less to her liking than she had imagined. She had visualised being arm in arm with Duncan and striding valiantly at the head of flag-waving hordes along the centre of the capital's thoroughfares whilst singing suitably revolutionary songs. All this would be done to the cheers of thousands of pavement-lining supporters. Instead, Duncan had disappeared with three shillings and sixpence of the party's funds and the people who should have been cheering on the footpath did not give a toss who won the fight as long as their own lives weren't interrupted. Meanwhile, Comrade Sprigg appeared to be under the impression that he was the wolf, she a promiscuous Red Riding-Hood who was desperately in need of a seeing-to. In addition, she was almost out on her feet and would have killed for a good soak in a bath, something to eat and a bedroom door that would lock.

She had deliberately arrived late at the daily briefing in order to pick a seat as far away from Sprigg as possible.

'Ah, you're here at last, Comrade,' he greeted her from across the table. 'I was beginning to think you'd been captured by the same scoundrels that appear to have ensnared your friend, Comrade Forbes. Still no news of him, I suppose?'

By now, almost too weary to speak, she just shook her head in response. 'Right, Comrades,' Sprigg continued, 'has anything arisen out of yesterday's intelligence that we should be made aware of?' He looked around him. 'Yes, Comrade Faversham?'

Comrade Faversham was a large fat man with badly trimmed beard and odd shoes. Exactly why he wore odd shoes, no one knew. He had an intimidating presence and spoke very little, so few people were inclined to take the risk of asking him. 'Number twelve trams,' he boomed.

'Er – yes,' said Sprigg. 'What about them – could you be more explicit, Comrade?'

'They're getting away from us, you know. Look, I'll show you.' He swiftly assembled an assortment of cutlery and condiments and arranged them across the table. 'We've been dwelling on Westminster, London and Blackfriars bridges, but the number twelve trams have been stopping short of Southwark Bridge and discharging their passengers who then walk over the bridge a quarter-mile away. They've been doing it every day and this is the first we've known of it.'

'So what are you suggesting, Comrade?'

'I'm suggesting we ambush a tram at the five-road junction of St George's Circus. There are masses of little streets nearby. With a couple of spotters in the Circus, we could all emerge before they knew what was happening. If we can derail just one tram there, it could seriously affect a dozen or so routes, three of which feed the bridges.' A murmur of approval ran throughout the café.

'Is there a time which you think appropriate, Comrade Faversham?' asked one.

'Yes, this afternoon,' said Faversham.

'But why this afternoon?'

'Because they'll be more tired than in the morning. If these blackleg scum who persist in going to work suddenly find it's their trip back that's most dangerous, they may think twice before even leaving home in the morning.'

'That's good reasoning, Comrade Faversham. How d'we all feel about this?'

There was a unanimous roar of approval and so plans were made.

Duncan's tram, with twenty city-bound evening office cleaners on board, had just turned from the Albert Embankment into Lambeth Road when he saw a solitary but massive bearded police constable pedalling laboriously towards him. Easing from his cycle, the constable signalled him to stop. Now well into his routine, Duncan managed to accomplish this feat without causing everyone on board to respond with a nod. On his first day, his sudden braking had achieved a degree of notoriety with every passenger swaying forward and nodding each time he touched the brake. Now he was well past that stage and, though some way from perfection, there had certainly been an enormous improvement.

'Yes, mate?' he asked the constable.

'I'm yer escort,' puffed the copper, lifting up his cycle and sliding it aboard. 'Me name's Drake, Reuben Drake. I think yer might 'ave a bit o' trouble at St George's Circus. There's a group of 'em lying in wait.'

'Who else is coming with us?' asked Duncan as he moved the tram forward again.

'Just thee an' me,' replied the copper, casually lighting a pipe. 'They'll probably want to overturn your tram or such like. As soon as yer find yer have ter stop, I suggest yer leg it as quick as yer can.'

'Not sodding likely,' said Duncan defiantly. 'This is my tram, this is, and no bunch of layabouts are going to get their mitts on it, I can tell you.'

The copper shrugged. 'Well, if they're a mob of them I can't see how yer gonna have any choice, mate. But please yourself.' He sat down on the steep stairs that led up to the top deck and, puffing contentedly, soon closed his eyes. 'Personally, I'd sooner 'ave a good kip,' he muttered wearily.

A few minutes later, any doubts Duncan may have had about the policeman's warning were dispelled as he saw a large group of people swarming into the road at his approach. 'They're here!' he yelled. 'About twenty-five of them dead ahead.'

'Slow down and try to edge through 'em,' ordered the constable sharply.

'And if they come aboard, what then?'

'Well, if they do manage ter get aboard,' said Reuben philosophically, 'they won't be disposed to be too friendly towards you. So if yer thinks they're goin' ter belt yer, piss off quick or belt the buggers first.' So saying, he tapped out his pipe and drew his truncheon from his pocket and laid it tidily in his lap.

'Blackleg! Blackleg!' came the chant and several of the office cleaners raised their heads from their knitting.

'Will yer be goin' any fur'ver, mate?' asked one.

'I'd like to say Southwark Bridge, luv,' replied Duncan, 'but who can tell?'

He slowed the tramcar to a crawl and edged forward as Drake had directed. Immediately a cascade of sticks, stones and cans hit the tram with several landing on his platform.

'I order you to stop this tram at once in the name of the workers,' called a short bespectacled and bearded man.

'I'm a bloody worker!' yelled the stoutest of the cleaners. 'An' I'm tellin' yer ter sod orf.'

'Madam!' began the little man, 'as a member of the working-class proletariat, you do not seem to understand . . .'

'I understand your sort right 'nuf,' yelled back the woman. 'We never see a sign o' you bleeders until there's trouble, then yer turns up like flies on 'orse shit.'

Further verbal exchange was halted by a concerted rush to the tram platform. Duncan realised to drive on was hopeless, so he applied the brake and stopped the vehicle. He had scarcely done so when he was overwhelmed by a dozen or so protesters. Within seconds, he had sustained several blows to his head and numerous punches to the face and body. Fighting back, he saw four men and two women easing a long steel pole beneath the tramcar, presumably to overturn it. Instantly a blinding rage overtook him and he fought like a cornered animal.

'That's my bloody tram, you bastards,' he cried. But in spite of his fury he was still losing the fight. Suddenly his fortunes changed as most of the cleaners surged to his assistance with at least four of them wielding the most ferocious-looking hatpins. He was also vaguely aware of Reuben Drake battling away, truncheon in hand, on the rear platform. As soon as he thought the women could deal with the remnants, he leaped from the tram and tore into the group with the pole. 'You dare damage my tram!' he almost screamed. 'You just fucking dare.' His furious attack took them completely by surprise and within moments he had seized the pole and to an accompaniment of screams and yells, began wielding it around his head like an enormous claymore. A clanging from the tram's bell suddenly drew his attention back to the vehicle where the triumphant cleaners had finally repelled the intruders and Reuben Drake was relighting his pipe. The battle had not been waged without casualties – several windows were broken and at least two of the cleaners had cuts and bruises. As he inspected the damage, the last four attackers staggered groggily from the tramcar and onto the road.

'You'd better get those cuts on your bonce seen to, son,' Reuben Drake advised, pointing at Duncan's head with the stem of his pipe. 'They look nasty an' there's no knowin' the last time them buggers washed themselves.'

'There's one of 'em still 'ere,' exclaimed a cleaner, pulling the sole survivor to her feet. 'She's a bit groggy but she's only young, silly little bitch.'

'Smack 'er arse an' send 'er 'ome to 'er muvver,' suggested another.

'I might have guessed!' snorted Duncan as he wiped a wisp of bloodstained hair from the girl's face. 'How'd you get yourself in this state?'

'HOW DID I GET!' exploded Julia 'HOW-DID-I-GET?' she repeated. 'I'll tell you how I bloody GOT! I bloody "GOT" because my bloody escort, not satisfied with running away with the petty cash, changed bloody sides and tried to kill me by charging into me with a tram! A TRAM mark you, a bloody TRAM! He then has me beaten up by a bunch of old witches and thrown on the floor. And this after Lenin, that randy old red, tries to get in my knickers every night.' She stepped towards him and wagged her finger almost into his face. 'And you're the bloke who promised my mum you'd look after me!' Suddenly most of her anger vanished as she stared at his head. 'My God, Duncan, look at you!' she

19

exclaimed. 'Your skull's almost split open! You'll have to go to hospital with that.'

'Oh, I'll survive,' he assured her. 'You don't look too wholesome yourself.'

'I think both of yer should go ter Guy's 'ospital,' suggested Reuben Drake. 'That way yer can both claim an 'onourable draw.'

'Well, I can't very well take me tram to the hospital,' pointed out Duncan. 'There ain't no rails, but if we give the policeman back his bike and drop these good ladies off at Southwark Bridge, I can leave it at the terminus and we can go home and lick our wounds. What d'you say to that, girl?'

'Well, if you stop calling me "*girl*", I'll agree it was a draw, but if you value your life, you'd better steer well clear of my mum for a while . . . Come on, you embezzling bloody traitor, I'm going to roast you all the way back to Hampstead.'

2

The summer of 1930 had been a good one and though 'Wonky' Lines, was reluctant to tempt fate, he was drifting to the conclusion that life was looking up for him at last. It was a state of mind that affects many who work a long-term fiddle. To paraphrase his friends, Wonky, or Claude, as his mother would have him called, 'was well at it'.

Mark you, his employer, Sidney Grechen, was hardly a paragon of virtue. Sid had made enough capital to open a small haulage business by a series of petty, mean little crimes, all of which had generated more misery to the victims than reward to himself. Still, that was never a factor to inhibit Sid. It was strange that, of all businesses available for purchase, he should have chosen a haulage firm. After all, he knew nothing about lorries. Come to that, he knew little of anything mechanical. But in the slump of 1930, a small haulier's could easily be purchased from the proceeds of a couple of decent burglaries and a swindle or two. It was to counteract his ignorance that his first instinct had been to avoid employing regular personnel. He prophetically reasoned that long-term workers could mean long-term fraud. 'They'd nick anything, some of 'em,' he would genuinely complain. Yet constant staff changes for a fleet of four trucks proved to be more trouble than it was worth. In an uncharacteristic rush of compromise, he settled for one full-time employee (Wonky) and two other part-time drivers. This plan was partially forced upon him by the mechanical state of three of the trucks, two of which had been cannibalised from the 1914–18

21

War and the third had the mobile reliability of a lethargic clam.

Sid had known Wonky for many years and considered the stuttering, limping, shy ex-rifleman to be thick enough to manipulate yet bright enough to rely upon. To be fair to Sid, this was not a rash assessment. Wonky, as his nickname implied, was certainly no intellectual, but the German mortar that had given him both stutter and limp, had not impaired his native cunning. It had simply masked it. Being the only employee at a yard where the frequently absent owner had difficulty working a can-opener, had given the ex-soldier scope he could only have dreamed of. Sturdy, pleasant, despite his limp, he was a bachelor of some forty-five years and lived contentedly in a ground-floor Waterloo tenement with Pieshop, his beloved dog and companion. He had found the brown-and-white mongrel abandoned on the mudflats near Southwark Bridge eighteen months earlier and in the absence of any other family of his own, it had been an instant and mutual attraction. Since then, no matter how heavy or large the load, Wonky always found room on a lorry for Pieshop. The dog was small and wiry enough to wriggle in and out of the broken windows at the rear of each of the driver's cabins and onto the rear of the lorry. This could be invaluable in slow-moving traffic when young boys clambered onto the tailboard for a ride. Over the previous twelve months the animal had developed a partiality for the flavour of small grimy fingers as many a tearful urchin could testify.

That morning Wonky was scheduled for an early start and left home just after midnight to collect the old Commer lorry from the nearby yard. Both master and animal had a long day ahead but each had the ability to doze at any given opportunity. The first call was to a market garden near Rainham in Essex to collect produce for Rawlinson's Vegetable Wholesalers at the Borough Market near London Bridge.

Wonky enjoyed this run. Traffic would be light and at the small Rainham farm he would find the produce neatly stacked awaiting him. Though he would need to load the truck himself, he enjoyed the feeling of remoteness pervading the reclaimed land on the still warm autumn nights. At such times he felt both he and Pieshop had the world to themselves. That is, of course, with the exception of the rabbits. The problem with rabbits is that they run – and run damn fast. To one who had never seen rabbits before, they were a phenomenon that would bewilder any dog. Pieshop would chase cats in town and expect them to find sanctuary by climbing up, or into, some structure or other. But there was no 'structure' in the market garden so the rabbits simply ran and Pieshop simply chased. Yet, try as he might, he never got near one of them. It was all too bewildering for a poor city dog.

On Pieshop's return, and once the vehicle was loaded, Wonky would drive the creaking swaying lorry across the deep muddy cart ruts that led to the distant road. The exhausted Pieshop would then doze comfortably with his head on Wonky's shrapnel-torn thighs without a care in the world. An hour or so later, the bright lights and confusion of a busy night-time market would stir the weary dog into opening one eye. Despite his reluctance, Pieshop knew it was worth it because there would be a pint of porter for the driver and biscuits for himself.

As Wonky rolled the last potato sack from the rear of the truck and onto the squat shoulders of the market porter, he gingerly straightened his back. Closing his eyes, he rested both hands on his kidneys and gave each a deep and penetrating massage. Puffing his cheeks, he exhaled a long sigh. 'That's all the s-spuds f-for today, Jock,' he panted. 'S-see you t'morrow?'

'Aye!' nodded the gnarled old Scot as he thudded the final sack onto a barrow. 'Are ye nae havin' breakfast afore ye go?'

Wonky glanced up at the ugly old Victorian clock that hung suspended from the cast-iron beams of the vast draughty arcade; it showed two minutes after 3 a.m. 'Not t'day, ole s-son,' he replied. 'I'm collecting s-some hop-pickers as s-soon as I leave here and I want to be down the f-fields by a little after f-five o'clock, s-so I can be back in the yard afore the g-guv'nor arrives at nine. Th-that is o'course if he a-arrives at all. S-some days he does and s-some days I s-see n-neither hide nor hair of him.'

'So who actually runs yer yard?'

'I d-do, really. I'm f-far happier that way. As l-long as he p-pays me, he can s-stay away for ever if he l-likes.'

The informality was apparently too much for the tidy-minded Scot. Giving a disapproving sniff, he changed the subject. 'Anyway, who are these hop-pickers, ye go on aboot? I'd nae heard aboot them afore I came to London.'

'Oh, they're f-families who go to K-Kent for th-three or f-four weeks each S-September when the h-hops ripen. While th-they're th-there, th-they l-live in little t-tin h-huts near the hopfields. It's a r-rough ole l-life, I'll t-tell you, but it's about the only t-time most of th-them will b-breathe some decent air. I take 'em there and fetch th-them back, usually in about th-three or f-four weeks' time.' He shook his head philosophically. 'M-mind you, I've g-got a right b-bleedin' tribe of 'em today. The W-Wilkinsons, they are. If you were to s-see 'em on the l-lorry, you'd think there were th-thousands of the b-buggers. God only knows how sh-she manages. I've never seen a b-bloke with her yet but s-someone obviously comes round and b-bungs her in the p-pudden club every twelve months or s-so. Sh-she's knocking on a bit now th-though, s-so perhaps her b-breeding s-season's over. Still, you h-have to give her credit, she takes every one of her k-kids hopping every y-year. R-rumour has it her n-neighbours give her the m-money to go s-so they can have a month's p-peace and quiet.'

'She's nae husband, ye say? Ye could be all right there then, laddie. Sounds just what ye need. Ye could *really* git yer feet under the table. Just think, a ready-made family!'

'Gor b-blimey, no!' exclaimed Wonky in genuine horror. 'She l-looks l-like a l-little h-hippo in a b-big f-frock and all those k-kids would send me m-mad!'

'I take it Sid doesna know?'

'You take it r-right,' Wonky winked knowingly. 'What the e-e-eye doesn't s-see . . .'

'Aye, aye! I know,' Jock cut in as he reached for the greasy cigarette stub that lodged above his right ear. 'Spare me the wee homilies and gi' me a light, there's a good fellah.'

Wonky carefully struck the slim Swan Vestas match and cupped it delicately until the flame flickered bright. Like many of his friends, he would use odd moments to razor matches lengthwise, thereby doubling the box's usual content of fifty. It made good economy but lousy matches. He quickly ignited the Scotsman's stub and just managed to light his own roll-up before the dying flame caressed his thumb. 'B-Bugger it!' he spluttered, flicking the charred sliver to the ground.

Jock chuckled. 'It nivver fails. I've yit ter see yer matchstick splitters withoot a scorched thumb, an' they say Scotsmen are tight!'

'At l-least I d-did *have* a b-bloody match,' muttered Wonky, ruefully licking the burn.

'That thumb's nowt to what that wicked hellion Sid'll be doin' ter ye if he finds ye usin' his lorry tae run yer own business oot o' hours. Does he nae check the mileage?'

'He c-can't,' murmured Wonky, still preoccupied with his singed thumb. 'Three of the trucks are t-too old to have a m-mileometer and the fourth can easily be turned b-back with a s-screwdriver. I do b-buy me own p-petrol, though,' he added defensively.

'Well, if ye'll take a tip from an ould chum, ye'll nae smoke in yon cabin 'cos the way ye sling matches aboot, sooner or later Sid's best lorry's gonna be a smouldering wreck an' when he finds oot ye did it, ye'll be smouldering too.'

'Don't w-worry,' Wonky cheerfully assured him as he

climbed back in his cabin. 'If it *does* go up in flames I'll tell him it was struck by the devil's own l-lightning. After the life he's led he'll probably believe it. Anyway, I can't s-sit 'ere talking to you all d-day, I've got h-hoppers to pick up.'

If it was difficult entering the market, it was a nightmare leaving. Trucks, barrows, horses-and-carts, ponies-and-traps and porters with baskets piled high on their heads competed to block his route. After blasts on the horn, barks from the dog and a torrent of stuttering swear words, the old truck finally rolled out into the Borough High Street en route for Canal Lane near Southwark Bridge.

'Well, P-Pieshop,' whispered Wonky, as he ran the back of his fingers lightly down the dog's spine, 'y'd better make the m-most of the next f-few minutes 'cos the W-Wilkinsons h-have h-hordes of bleedin' k-kids.'

On the journey to 15 Canal Lane, it was apparent that the Wilkinsons were not the only family with 'hordes of bleedin' kids'. In spite of the early hour, streams of women of all ages accompanied by children from babes in arms to teenagers, all scurried in the same direction with their huge wheeled boxes, perambulators, pushchairs and handcarts all determined to catch the next 'Hopper's Special' from London Bridge station. 'Hopper's Special' was the rather grandiose name given to the trains that would leave the station regularly between 2 a.m. and 6 a.m. each day, bound for the Kentish hopfields. With the exception of the menfolk, many streets and tenements would be like ghost towns for the next few weeks as upwards of sixty thousand pairs of London feet set off for the countryside.

A few minutes later the old truck rattled its way to a halt outside the Wilkinsons' basement residence. This was an end-of-terrace house with the basement entrance secreted beneath fifteen whitened stone steps that led up to the spotless front door. True he was five minutes early, but the place was still in darkness. Considering at the last count there were at least six children still at home in the family, they would certainly have appeared to have cut it fine. As he alighted from the cabin, he realised that, contrary to his first impression, the place was alive with kids.

'Ma! The lorry's 'ere!' came the excited cry from the gloom. As Wonky's eyes adjusted, he suddenly saw children everywhere. In fact, not just children but chairs, a small pram and several rugs, all stacked on the basement steps. The bulky figure of Lillian Wilkinson emerged from the hidden door.

'Micky, Danny, Mary, pick up those chairs and the rugs. Nuuala, you take the pram and the budgie. Terry, you take the puppies and the dog, and you, Teresa, you carry the baby . . . and don't drop her this time!'

'Baby?' exclaimed Wonky to Pieshop. 'W-what b-bleedin' b-baby?' There had been no baby last year! The immediate thought that occurred to him was: Who on earth is the phantom father who keeps finding the motivation to put Lilly Wilkinson in the family way? 'P-poor s-sod must b-be b-bloody b-blind,' he muttered, shaking a disbelieving head.

Lillian Wilkinson, dark and fiery, short of height, of unknown weight and indeterminate age, gave a cheery wave in the direction of the lorry. 'All ready fer yer, Mr Lines. If yer don't mind stopping orf at Newington Causeway, we can pick up me two eldest girls and their kids.'

Wonky bravely hid his dismay as he answered the woman. 'Of c-course, Mrs W-Wilkinson, but why are you in the d-dark? I can hardly see a th-thing.'

'The gas ran out last night, Mr Lines. Seemed silly ter put a tanner in the meter when we were gonna be away fer nearly a mumf, don'tcha fink?'

'You mean to s-say, you g-got all those k-kids ready in the d-dark?' he asked incredulously.

'O'course not,' she sniffed indignantly. 'We 'ad a candle, didn't we, kids?'

The idea of organising seven kids, one budgie, four puppies

and a dog for a month-long absence by the light of a solitary candle, almost turned Wonky's mind. 'Er – d'you m-mind if we get going, Mrs W-Wilkinson, only I've got a l-lot to do t'day.'

'Course not, Mr Lines, o'course not. OKAY, KIDS! Start loadin'!'

With the encouragement of a few sharp cuffs to a few small heads, the load was soon in place. During this loading, great care was taken to leave space for every hopper's most essential item, namely the 'Hopping Box'. This box had a dual role; apart from being an excellent container, it was also the family table for the duration of their stay. It needed to go on the lorry last because it would be the first piece to be unloaded. It was a huge made-to-measure wooden receptacle with a detachable wheel at each corner. Most stored items would be those that were soonest needed. With such a large family, this ranged from a mattress cover, through pots and pans to newspaper squares for the lavatory. All except the youngest two children surrounded the hopping box and, with a series of exaggerated grunts and groans, slowly eased it off the ground. Once it was at a sufficient height, Lill Wilkinson wriggled beneath it and, with her solid back, heaved it level with the platform of the lorry, whereupon it was seized quickly by Wonky and slid smoothly into one of the few spaces left on the vehicle. After a couple of ropes were thrown across the load, the children sat in whatever recesses they could find and cuddled into each other or one of the bewildered puppies. Once all were settled, Lill took her latest addition to her bosom and climbed into the driver's cabin alongside a nervous Wonky and a resentful Pieshop.

'Number eleven Newington Causeway, if yer please, Mr Lines,' requested Lill as she wriggled her ample bottom across three-quarters of the bench seat. Once settled, she added to Wonky's further discomfort by promptly breast-feeding the baby.

'Er – where are your two eldest d-daughters and g-grandchildren goin', Mrs W-Wilkinson?' asked Wonky staring rigidly ahead.

'Wateringbury 'opfields. Same as us, Mr Lines,' she replied. 'Didn't I tell yer?'

'N-nunno, Mrs W-Wilkinson. I mean, where are they g-going to sit on this l-lorry?' he bleated. 'Th-there's not a l-lot of room left on it, you see.'

'Oh, don't worry, they'll squeeze on board somewhere, Mr Lines, you'll see. That's wot 'opping's all about, ain't it? My old mum used ter say if yer can't rough it yer shouldn't be goin' in the first place. S'all a question of making do and mendin', Mr Lines. I bet you're enjoying this, ain't yer, yer little terror!'

Wonky assumed, indeed prayed, the last remark was addressed to the gulping tot and not to himself, though with Lillian Wilkinson one could never be sure.

Wilkinson junior was only halfway through his breakfast when 11 Newington Causeway came into view. The newcomers, in the shape of two young women and two toddlers were waiting patiently at the door and, to Wonky's instant relief, appeared to have little other luggage than what they could carry in a couple of sacking bags.

'Lovely gels, ain't they, Mr Lines? Not married, yer know. Two bleedin' sailors it were wot put 'em in the club. Gawd knows where the pair o' blighters are nah, though. We did try ter check but the navy covers for 'em yer know; they deliberately cover for the wicked bar-steds. They 'ad their bit o' fun then scarpered, typical bleedin' men. Present company excepted o'course, Mr Lines. Still, worse fings 'appen at sea – or they will if there's any bleedin' justice.' She gave a fearsome chuckle before turning her attention to her driver. 'I should fink a nice bachelor like yerself really looks forward ter a little country trip like this, 'specially with three unattached females, eh?' To reinforce her supposition she elbowed him so violently that her massive and bare right breast didn't stop wobbling until he braked outside the address.

To Wonky's pleasant surprise, the two girls, Esther and Evelyn, were really quite attractive. But then, the more he thought about it, the more he realised that all of big Lill's brood were pleasing to the eye. Strange that. With an assorted variety of fathers, the gene must presumably come via the mother, though exactly how it manifested itself in the nine end products was difficult to perceive. Even at this stage, both elder girls were showing early signs of their mother's proportions but it could not be denied they were fine-looking wenches.

'D'yer fink we could squeeze 'em both in this cabin, Mr Lines?' asked Lill.

Intriguing though the appeal first sounded, Wonky suddenly had visions of the lorry bumping across the tramlines at New Cross whilst the three of them breast-fed their offspring. 'N-no, I'm s-sorry, Mrs Wilkinson, we'd get p-pulled up by the p-police. It'll h-have to be the b-back of the l-lorry, I'm afraid, but you s-sit tight and I'll help them on b-board.'

Wonky, who was ever partial to a plump rounded thigh, would be the first to admit a certain sensual satisfaction in assisting both young women scale the tailboard. But after two minutes, their screeching voices cleared up more questions about the vanishing matelots than an hour's conversation with big Lill ever could.

Having ensured the latest two passengers, together with their children, were more or less secure, Wonky hurried to his cabin to resume his journey – a journey which was already running an hour late and one which he had almost yet to start. He already had a foot on the running board when a shout caught his attention.

'Wonky! Hang about! I want a word with yer!'

Wonky swore under his breath, for it was a tone he knew only too well and one which he could have well done without. For a brief moment he considered pretending he had not heard, but Police Constable Reuben Drake was not a man one could ignore. He turned towards the sound and saw the massive, bearded, pipe-smoking figure on a creaking old cycle emerging from the shadows beneath a distant railway bridge.

'How are yer, me son?' boomed the voice from a good hundred paces.

'Wot sorta damn-fool question is that?' demanded the irate Lillian. 'Tell 'im ter wait till yer come back if 'e wants ter speak ter yer. We're all supposed ter be pullin' 'ops in a few 'ours, not sittin' on our arses spouting to bleedin' coppers!'

'I-I'd b-better not, luv,' replied the apprehensive Wonky. 'Old Reub don't t-take kindly t-to that sort of thing. Let's just wait and s-see what he wants.' Wonky was reluctant to admit it, even to himself, but he always had the gut feeling that Reuben sensed his duplicity with the trucks. He also knew Reuben Drake hated Sid and would like nothing better than to nail the old crook permanently.

'Now then,' smiled Reuben as he joined Wonky with one foot on the running board and the other on his cycle pedal. 'That's better, ain't it? We can hear each other now.' The policeman made no move to inspect the lorry but relit his pipe and just glanced pointedly over the load and quickly into the cabin. As much to prove her indifference to the newcomer as to satisfy her infant, Lill Wilkinson had now exposed her other breast and deliberately transferred the child to it.

'Don't 'appen to know the time do yer, Constable?' she asked pointedly.

'I never looks at me watch when I'm on night duty, luv, I find it makes the time go slow.' He gave a long sniff and nodded towards her. 'But still, seeing as yer asked me, I'd say it was time yer buttoned yer coat; yer don't want ter get a chest cold through this chill night air, now do yer? Those old hopping huts ain't the best places to treat consumption, yer know.' Turning to Wonky, he added, 'Where's Sid these days? Ain't seen him around for some time.'

Wonky opened his palms helplessly. 'D-dunno, Reub, he c-comes and g-goes. S-sometimes I don't see h-him for a week or more. There ain't no t-telling. D'you w-want me t-to give him a message when I do s-see him?'

The constable gave a great shrug. 'No, it's not that important. Just tell him his ole mate Reuben Drake was inquiring after his welfare, that's all. That'll cheer him no end I'd say. Off yer go now.' Leaning forward, he opened the cabin door and gestured graciously for Wonky to enter. 'Meanwhile, mam,' he said, turning to Lillian, 'you enjoy yer hop-picking, and don't forget to keep yer chest wrapped up nice an' warm. It's bad enough that poor Wonky's got bad legs, we don't want to bugger up his eyesight as well, do we?'

To Wonky's ill-disguised relief, the old motor started up first time and seconds later they were heading at a lumbering fifteen miles per hour for the Old Kent Road.

'Wot was that all about?' asked Lillian. 'I didn't like that copper one bit. Right bleedin' pig 'e was.'

'Not a b-bad description,' agreed Wonky. 'B-but he's not usually m-much harm to the l-likes of us. It's my g-guv'nor, S-Sid Grechen, he's really after. He likes to keep him on the hop; that's why he asked about him. He just d-does it to make S-Sid n-nervous or angry . . . w-works too.' He laughed.

'So wot does this Sid usually say when yer tell 'im the copper was askin' after 'is welfare?' persisted Lillian.

'He d-don't s-say anything, usually because I d-don't tell him,' he gave a mirthless chuckle. 'I learnt my lesson early. If old R-Reuben wants to g-get at S-Sid he can d-do it himself and not th-through me. S-Sid can be a vindictive b-bastard when he's upset and R-Reuben Drake *always* upsets him.'

'Yer still ain't told me why?'

'I honestly d-don't know wh-why, but it's s-something way back in their p-pasts. Anyway, let's not t-talk about it any more; it makes me nervous.'

The old truck engine had now begun to warm up again and, much to the relief of all its passengers, this clearly showed in a much brisker ride.

Pulling the cuff of her coat over her wrist, Lillian leaned

forward and wiped clear a little circle in the centre of the moist screen. Squinting, she peered into the misty distance. 'This is wot I really love about 'opping, Mr Lines.'

'You mean the ride down to K-Kent?'

'The ride?' she echoed. 'Good Gawd, no, Mr Lines! I'd sooner travel in an 'orse and cart any day.'

'S-so what're you t-talking about?'

'I'm talkin' about this time of year. Yer can't beat it, it's so romantic like.'

Wonky gave a nervous little laugh. 'F-first t-time I've ever heard anyone s-saying September in the Old Kent Road is romantic, Mrs W-Wilkinson.'

'Not the bleedin' *road*, Mr Lines – the 'opfields! It's the 'opfields I'm talkin' of. Y'see, when yer wake up in the mornins an' yer throws open the 'ut door, the ole mist will be swirlin' everywhere an' the grass'll be damp and the smells – oh the *smells*, Mr Lines – unless you've been 'opping you've never smelt anyfing like it. It makes the rest o' the year bearable. Better than any o' that Paris perfume muck, I'll wager. An' then yer takes a walk up the slope ter the lavatory an' in the distance yer can see the sun just beginning ter peek thru' the mist, oh it's so bloody wonderful and peaceful, Mr Lines, I luv it. I absolutely bloody luv it!'

Big Lill craned her neck forward and peered as if she could already see the fields that were still a good thirty miles distant. She then bit her lip and lapsed into a moisty-eyed silence.

Wonky's initial reaction was to laugh. The idea of this burly woman feeling romantic about the thought of climbing a misty hill on a dawn visit to a hopfields lavatory could only be nonsensical. The idea was too ridiculous for words. Then suddenly he was almost overcome by sadness for her. She had an outward demeanour that was as tough as old boots, but then with nine kids, four pups, one dog, a budgie, a generous share of poverty and no husband, that exterior could only be expected. He said nothing, but slid his left

33

hand from the huge old steering wheel and gave her still cuffed wrist the faintest of squeezes.

Half-a-mile away in Trafalgar Avenue, a taxi had drawn to a halt outside a small block of private flats and the driver gave a gentle toot on the horn. The curtains at a first-floor window were briefly parted and a man's arm waved a quick acknowledgement. Seconds later, a couple hurried from the block into the taxi.

'You know where to go, driver?' asked the man.

'Usual address, sir?'

'If you would be so kind,' replied the man politely.

Bertram Franks congratulated himself on his good fortune that his last destination of the night should be less than two minutes' drive from his own home. Didn't often work out like that, as Bert would never tire of telling. As he glanced in his inside mirror, he lapsed into his usual practice of trying to guess the relationship between the man and woman. It was obviously an affair, that was for sure. The furtive way the couple had left the man's flat, the tight embrace in the back of his taxi and the regular destination to deliver the woman made that very clear. They had obviously been at it for most of the night, lucky buggers. He was intrigued to know just who they were. The man was no problem; he had seen him several times, in fact he looked familiar from somewhere. He was middle-aged and, as far as Bert could judge, fairly handsome. Furthermore, if tips were anything to go by, he was not short of a few bob. The woman, however, was a very different matter. Of excellent figure, he had never once seen her face. It had always been dark and she had always been veiled. By the way she kept her head down, there was no doubt of her desire for anonymity. He found himself wondering what her husband (he was convinced she had one) did for a living. Did he work away? Was he on shifts? Did he even care? Perhaps not – after all, it takes all sorts. Wouldn't mind a pop at that meself, he thought, as he moved his attention reluctantly back to the road. One blessing about working at this time of night, there was little other traffic to worry about. He hadn't seen another vehicle for ages. His original intention had been to cut through the back streets of Walworth, but at this time of night the main road would be his best bet, yes the Old Kent Road would do nicely.

Just as he was about to swing the cab into the main thoroughfare, a quick movement in the corner of his mirror diverted his attention. Blimey, something happening and he nearly missed it. The woman had suddenly pulled herself from the man's embrace and turned away as if in annoyance. Funny creatures, women, he thought. Bet before we get to the Elephant and Castle she'll be back around his neck like a lovesick python. He'd have to watch for that, he enjoyed seeing a bit of groping, did Bert.

Smiling to himself, he tightened his grip on the wheel and decided there was just time to take one quick tantalising glance in the mirror before making the turn. Cor, look at them now! With his imagination running riot he was almost beside himself with excitement! If the truth were known, Bert never even saw the old Commer truck. One thing was sure, if he never saw it then, he would never see it again. The steering wheel, the one he had held so excitedly a split second before, ensured that the very last thing Bertram Cyril Franks saw on this earth was a lover's tiff.

3

The 'doll's eye' disc on the switchboard at Rodney Road police station clattered down and the warning bell that accompanied it cut deep into the concentration of Station Sergeant Bill Barclay. The sergeant had been unusually quick to answer the telephone, which had less to do with dedicated policing and more to do with the fact he was losing tenpence at cribbage to his assistant PC David Diamond.

'Where you say? . . . Old Kent Road outside the Dun Cow pub? . . . I see . . . How many? . . . Just the one? Southwark mortuary? . . . What's that . . . *SEVEN!*' He glanced up at the old wall clock. 'So what're all those kids doing up at this time of the bloody morning? . . . Oh, I see, hoppers, are they? I might have known . . . Okay, I'll get the duty officer to attend as well, I always enjoy giving him bad news and this is going to please him no end. Get as many witnesses as you can. You never know, you *might* find one somewhere . . . Yes, okay.'

He replaced the receiver and neatly stacked his cards whilst giving a smile of smug satisfaction to his opponent. 'Sorry, lad,' he announced with reeking insincerity, 'game's over. Get your bike out and take a run up to the Dun Cow. That was Poshie Porter, he's on patrol up there. He woke the landlord of the pub to use his telephone. I bet right now the crafty bastard's trying to wangle a pint. He reckons there's one dead taxi driver and a horde of soddin' kids swarming all over the place.' The sergeant yawned and walked over to the door to the inspector's room. 'Isn't that bloody predictable? Quiet all night and just when you're thinking of your bed, along comes a bloody fatal. You'd think people'd be more considerate than to get themselves killed twenty minutes before knocking-off time. Typical contrary cabbie by the sound of it.'

'What, another one, Sarge?' queried the young constable, shaking his head. 'That's our fourth fatal this week! The Old Kent Road's getting more dangerous than the Khyber Pass. Still, until drivers are licensed, what can we expect?'

Barclay nodded in agreement. 'I was looking at the accident circulars only last night; d'you know there have been over three hundred people killed in London alone in the last three months. And I wouldn't mind betting half the buggers have done it thirty minutes before going-home time.'

Protocol, to say nothing of respect, dictates that sergeants should knock at the door of the inspector's room before entering, but Barclay was not a man who laid store by such requirements. Whenever in the presence of junior ranks, he would pay the inspector due deference, in private he felt no such heed. To be fair to the sergeant, he was not alone in this attitude. It was accepted throughout the station that Inspector Percival Marsh was slimy, indecisive and weak but must be tolerated until his selection board, when they all hoped he would be promoted elsewhere. Marsh made no attempt to hide his disdain for his colleagues nor the area and its inhabitants. He clearly considered he was meant for grander things than policing such places as the Old Kent Road and its surroundings.

Throwing open the door, Barclay gazed scornfully down at the slumped inspector. He was reminded of a collapsed deckchair. Everything about Marsh was skimpy and thin, his build, moustache, hair and personality. As he stared, Barclay suddenly remembered Reuben Drake's words. 'Sarge, if a door opens and no one comes in, then it's that creepy bastard Marsh.' Though he had been obliged to reprimand the constable at the time, he had understood his meaning only too well. He reached across the slouched figure and picked up the empty hip flask that lay flat on the table. After sniffing it quickly, he thrust it roughly into the inspector's partially opened hand. 'Gin,' he muttered to himself. 'How can you trust a man who drinks gin?'

The movement finally roused the sleeping duty officer. 'There's been a fatal accident in the Old Kent Road – cab driver, apparently,' grunted Barclay. 'Porter is already up there and I've sent Diamond to give him a hand. I thought you might wish to attend.'

Marsh blinked rapidly and for a moment gazed panic-stricken about him. He gave a cold shudder as, suddenly aware of the flask in his hand, he thrust it quickly into a trouser pocket. After several attempts, he managed to clear his throat, sat up straight and tugged down the front of his jacket. 'N-no, sergeant, they're two competent enough men; I'm sure they'll cope admirably and . . .'

'That's not in doubt,' cut in Barclay, 'but I seem to remember seeing a memo from the superintendent stating that duty officers should at least check the circumstances of any "accidental" death. PC Diamond reckons we've had four fatals in the district this week. For all we know, it might be another Jack-the-Ripper tearing around smacking into people. Don't reckon the superintendent would be too thrilled if you just left it to a couple of PCs to deal with, especially if it turned out to be some mass murderer. D'you?'

The sergeant was beginning to enjoy himself and Marsh's alcoholic haze had cleared sufficiently for him to realise he was cornered. All it now needed was the accident to be classified as 'suspicious' and Barclay to state he had made his duty officer aware of the fact and he could kiss promotion goodbye for another five years. He nodded a reluctant agreement before reaching for his cap and making his way unsteadily to the door.

'And drive carefully, sir,' called the sergeant pointedly. 'Remember, we've had four fatals already, we don't want a fifth now, do we?'

To Marsh's relief, the old Vauxhall started first time and, as he drove past the trickle of early-morning office cleaners, his head slowly cleared. It was on his approach to the scene of the accident that he registered his first surprise. The damage to the vehicles appeared negligible for such a fatality. The front offside wheel of the taxi had certainly been crushed and so had both offside windows. It also was easy to see the point of impact and to understand how the steering column would have buried itself in the unfortunate driver's chest, yet the truck was barely marked. But then for two years it had served as an old Flanders battle wagon. If it could survive shellfire in France, a rickety London cab wouldn't present much of a challenge.

Turning his head to mask the scent of gin, Marsh approached the constable who was engrossed in a notebook. 'How's it going, Porter? Any problems?'

'No, sah,' responded the constable without looking up. Douglas Porter, alias Poshie, was the beanpole son of a well-to-do financier who had fallen on hard times. His education had been abruptly cut short and after a brief and unsuccessful flirtation with the army, he had finally arrived in the metropolitan police. With such a background and accent, the Rodney Road station should have been a disaster for him, but he had taken to it superbly and was a great favourite amongst his less articulate colleagues.

'Driver was in something of a mess, I'm afraid, sah.' He nodded towards an ambulance. 'They are putting the poor chappie in there now, but other than the odd bruise, everyone else seems fighting fit. Fact, if truth be known, I think all the little kiddywinks have quite enjoyed it. Bloodthirsty little bunch, if you ask me, sah!'

'Do you have any witnesses?'

'I do, sah, but I'm afraid they are of an indeterminate nature. They are a couple of early-morning milkmen but they were rawther distant to be of use. They claim the taxi swung out into the main road straight into the side of the truck. The position of the vehicles seems to bear this out.'

'I'm surprised at the lack of damage to the lorry.'

'Well, yes, sah, I suppose so.' The constable rubbed his chin thoughtfully. 'But then there is a lot of weight on that vehicle doancha know, sah. Funny thing is, with all that junk on board, they didn't lose as much as a chamber pot.'

'How does the driver explain such a load?'

'He said PC Drake spoke to him just after he loaded up. Bu. he claims Drake failed to mention anything about the truck being overloaded. By virtue of that conversation, he thought it was okay, sah.'

'So what does he have to say about the accident?'

'Precious little, really. He says the first he saw of the cab was when it came out of the side turning and was about to swing into him. He reckons he distinctly saw the driver lift his head and stare into his mirror. If true, sah, it means the cabbie wasn't looking where he was going.'

'But why would this cabbie want to do a thing like that, particularly when entering a main road? After all, he was a professional driver, wasn't he?'

'Well, there is one rawther peculiar thing, sah. Lines, the lorry driver, reckons the couple who were in the back of the cab disappeared.'

'DISAPPEARED! What d'you mean DISAPPEARED? Are you telling me there were two passengers in the cab and you haven't found them?'

'That's exactly so, sah. PC Diamond's having an old scout round at this very moment.'

'Good heavens, man, they could be injured somewhere! There'd be a right stink if we didn't find them – and I've got a promotion board coming up!'

'There's only a smear of blood in the cab, sah. Looks like one of them cut themselves when the window broke. If you ask me, sah, I reckon they've simply gone to ground. I'd say they were indulging in a little hanky-panky and didn't want to be caught. I mean, if we were in their position, we'd probably do the same thing, wouldn't we, sah?'

'No, *we* damn well wouldn't!' exploded Marsh. 'And d'you often ride in cabs in the early hours whilst fornicating with other men's wives then, Porter?'

'Heavens above no, sah! Well, not currently anyway. It's just that I was placing myself in their situation, hypothetically speaking, that is, of course, sah. I mean, if the accident *was* nothing to do with them, I'd say the last thing they'd wish to do is make a witness statement.'

The inspector shook his head in despair. 'I take it you did obtain a description of them?' he asked acidly.

'Not much of a one, I'm afraid, sah. A tallish middle-aged man, smartly dressed with a bowler hat and rolled umbrella. He was accompanied by what appeared to be a rather good-looking woman or girl, and that's about it.'

'What do you mean by "appeared to be" and what d'you mean by "woman *or* girl". That's hardly a concise description.'

'Well, it was quite dark, sah, and the man was obstructing the witness's view. Also the female was wearing a dark coat, dark hat and what could probably have been a dark veil. All the witness could really see, sah, was that she was somewhat tall for a female and she looked a bit – well – in the local vernacular, "tasty", I think was the word used.'

'How could she be "tasty" when the witness said it was dark and he could hardly see her?'

'I think he was speaking sexually rather than aesthetically, sah.'

'In *this* borough,' snapped the inspector irritably, 'they speak no other way. They're animals, damned animals.'

'I say! There's PC Diamond just returning, sah,' interjected the constable, hoping desperately to deflect Marsh's wrath onto someone else. 'Davy, old chap, over here,' he called, through cupped hands. 'Mr Marsh wants to have words with you!'

Dave Diamond slowly freewheeled towards them and swung his right leg backwards from the pedal before neatly hopping off. 'Sir?' he acknowledged.

'Did you find any sign of them, Diamond?'

'No, sir.' He waved an arm generally towards the direction he had come from. 'There're a score of alleyways and streets within five minutes' walk of here. They could be in any of 'em. The only thing I found was this.' He slipped his hand into his pocket and pulled out a crumpled white linen handkerchief.

'Well, if it's theirs, then that narrows the field considerably,' snapped Marsh, 'because for a start they're obviously not local. Most people in this damn pigsty wouldn't know a handkerchief if it was stuffed down their throat. The educated ones blow their noses on their sleeves and the rest snort it out onto the pavement.'

'It's not the *handkerchief* I'm referring to,' said David tersely. 'It's what's *in* it. And by the way, me and my family live in this "damn pigsty", as you call it, SIR. Furthermore, with all due respect and for your information, SIR,' he persisted, 'we neither blow our noses on our cuffs nor on pavements. What I'm talking about is this, SIR!'

Before Marsh could reply, the constable unfolded the white linen to reveal a small but elegant blue pendant inscribed with a pair of twining roses attached to a delicate but broken gold chain.

'Pretty piece,' grunted the inspector grudgingly. 'Where'd you find it?'

'On the kerbside by the offside passenger door.'

'D'you think it came from the occupants of the taxi?'

David Diamond shrugged. 'We can never be sure, but I can't imagine it lying on the kerbside very long if it didn't. The Old Kent Road never sleeps; there's always someone or other moving about.'

'Very well, give Porter a hand to finish taking statements and measurements. I'm going back to the station. And I want to see Drake before he goes off duty. I want to know why he allowed this lorry to make this journey. Meantime, I'll circulate what little description we have of the two passengers and get someone to trace the cabbie's next of kin. Incidentally, I think I'll put that pendant in the safe in case it's of any value.'

'Yessir,' replied David, handing over the pendant. 'But Lilly Wilkinson wants to know if they can continue to the hopfields? What with all these kids and animals, I think it might be a good idea, guv! After all, though it's a big load, it's quite secure and if we take both vehicles back to the nick it'll take up half the space in our yard, and where are we going to keep seven kids, five dogs and a budgie, to say nothing of Lilly and her pair of randy daughters?'

David saw instantly his suggestion had confused the inspector. On the face of it, it was a sensible request. On the other hand it would have meant making a serious decision and serious decisions are not popular with inspectors waiting for promotion boards.

'Er—' began Marsh.

Having put his duty officer neatly on the spot, David saw no reason to let him off. 'Still, if you're going to tick off PC Drake for not stopping the lorry, sir, perhaps you'd prefer them all to come back to the nick? If so, would you mind explaining that to Mrs Wilkinson? I think it might come better from you, sir. You see, she's quite a belligerent lady who fucks-and-blinds a lot and I don't think she'd take it too kindly from me or PC Porter. Oh, look, there she is now, sir. Shall I call her over?'

'Er—' the inspector began again, 'er – perhaps you're right, Diamond. It certainly seems secure enough. Yes, yes, come to think of it, that's not a bad idea at all. We'll let the lorry go on its way but we'll get the early-turn shift to tow the taxi into our yard.' He rubbed his hands together in the gesture of a task well done. 'Now, I think I'll leave you both to it. I'm sure you'll cope admirably.' Acknowledging their salutes, the inspector hastened to his car and drove swiftly away.

'Thank heaven for that!' sighed the relieved Porter. 'If

we'd taken this legion to the station, we wouldn't have got home till Michaelmas.'

'Yes,' agreed David. 'And it's my boy Ben's third birthday today.' He mopped his brow in mock relief. 'I tell you, my missus would never have believed me. She'd have sworn I'd forgotten.'

'Okay,' replied Douglas Porter. 'Let's wrap this up jolly quick, or else we'll never finish here. I think our first priority is to get rid of these hop-pickers and their blasted lorry as soon as possible. Because when Marsh arrives back at the station, dear old Sergeant Barclay's going to take a fiendish delight in informing him he should have towed in *both* vehicles. He'll be in such a state when he discovers that little gem, that he won't know if he's on his jolly old arse or his elbow. So come on, Davy, old chap, chop chop!'

Ninety minutes later, Wonky Lines still couldn't believe his luck. He knew he was not out of the wood by any means, but as the village of Wateringbury came into view he at least felt he was making progress. 'Wh-where to now, M-Mrs W-Wilkinson?'

'Go over the level crossing, Mr Lines, and you'll see a gate. Go fru' the gate, up the hill and yer in paradise, Mr Lines, absolutely bloody paradise.'

Wonky had never had a real image of paradise but he knew if he had, it would be somewhat removed from those black corrugated hovels on that misty hillock. Still, there was no denying big Lill's infectious enthusiasm. The excited chatter also told clearly how it had spread to her entire brood.

The lorry creaked to a halt at the closed five-barred gate.

'See that, Mr Lines? Over there t'wards Maidstone, see it? It's the *sun*, Mr Lines, the *sun*! Always comes up there it does. Give it an 'our or so an' it'll clear all this mist away an' then you'll be able ter see the river, the orchards, the 'opfields, the gipsy caravans an' oh, just about everything anyone could ever wish ter see.' Lill turned away from him and put her head out of the open window.

'Terry! Micky! Open the gate for Mr Lines, please, there's good lads.' The cart ruts were so deep that the lorry almost steered itself as it followed them slowly up the incline towards the huts. 'Okay, gang!' called Lill, 'it's unloading time. Everybody off!' She turned her attention back to her driver. 'Yer will stay an' 'ave a bit o' breakfast wiv' us, won't yer?'

'N-No, I can't, Mrs W-Wilkinson, honest,' apologised Wonky as he helped her from the cabin. 'I've got t-to get back and see m-my guv'nor as s-soon as p-possible. H-He's going to h-have the right hump w-with me I can tell y-you and the sooner I get it over w-with the better.'

'I've an idea, Mum,' chimed in Esther, the darker of the two elder daughters as she clutched the old soldier's right arm. 'Why don't he come down and stay with us at the weekend?'

'That's a great idea!' shrieked her sister Evelyn, promptly seizing his other arm.

'Didn't I say they were lovely gels, Mr Lines. Didn't I?' exclaimed Lillian proudly. 'And bright as buttons as well! Fancy me not finkin' of that idea meself! No doubt about it, I must be slippin'. Still, why don'tcha do that, Mr Lines? Arfa London comes visitin' to the 'opfields at the weekends. They come on bikes, trains and carts. You'll love it, you'll see; it's just like a big party.'

Wonky scratched his head thoughtfully. It was certainly something to consider. After all, he had no idea how Sid was going to take his indiscretions and he hadn't had a holiday since he had left the army twelve years earlier. Who knows, it could be a good rest or even a safe bolt hole. In fact, if he was lucky, it could prove to be both. It was true he did not know how long he could stand the family; it was equally true he did not know how long he could stand their voices, but then London was only forty miles away and, if the worst came to the worst, he could always do a runner.

'Well, I'm making no promises, mind . . .' he began but

before he could utter another word both girls screamed with delight and planted a great wet kiss on his cheek. 'He's coming, Mum, he's coming!'

'W-Wait a m-minute, w-wait a m-minute!' he protested, tugging both arms free. 'W-What I was going to s-say is, I'll do my b-best, but before I do I just w-want to make sure it'll be all right if I f-fetch m-my dog?'

'Mr Lines!' exclaimed Lillian, nudging him sharply in the ribs. 'If it's goin' ter make me gels as 'appy as that, yer can fetch the entire Berkshire 'unt! Yer see, that's the one big problem with 'op-picking, there's 'ardly any blokes about an' that makes life so difficult fer my gels. Them bein' such a fine and 'ealthy pair o' lasses an all that.'

Though Wonky was not too sure how 'fine and healthy' translated into his personal phraseology, he did have a suspicion. Because of this, he found himself echoing weakly, 'Fine and healthy, Mrs Wilkinson?'

'That's right,' whispered Esther as she tiptoed up to his ear. 'We're as fine an' healthy a pair of gels as you're ever likely to find. Ain't that right, sis?'

'Dead right, sis!' came the predictable reply.

During a three-second assessment, Wonky balanced up an hour with Sid Grechen as opposed to a hop-picking weekend with the Wilkinson sisters. It was really no contest. After all, whatever the outcome with the girls, it would never result in a disembowelment and that was more than a possibility with Sid.

'Okay, I'll b-be here as s-soon as I can on S-Saturday,' he agreed. 'N-now if you d-don't mind, it's t-time I was on my way, the p-police haven't finished with me.'

To a chorus of goodbyes, he turned the old lorry on the slippery grass before rolling gently down to Wateringbury station.

Both Poshie Porter and David Diamond had long given up thoughts of a 6 a.m. finish. Dave guessed he would be lucky to see his family before they left for shopping, and even luckier to fall into bed before ten o'clock. Still, at least he lived within a few minutes' cycle ride of the station, whereas poor Poshie lived two bus rides away at Rotherhithe. The only cheerful spot in their morning was the fact that Sergeant Barclay had smugly spent a good hour making it clear to Inspector Marsh – with all necessary respect, of course, that 'a twenty-two carat balls-up had been made, *sir*!' In an effort to correct the error of releasing the lorry, Marsh was, again to quote the sergeant, 'tearing around with his arsehole making buttons before the superintendent arrives at nine o'clock.' As each minute passed his desperation increased and as each weary member of the night duty returned, they were promptly about-turned and sent back on their beat to search for Wonky and his wagon.

Marsh had not totally given up hope of laying the blame for his mistake at someone else's door. At first he considered denying he had ever given permission to the two constables to release the hopping party. The main problem with that was the pair of them would then doubtless support each other. No, the best bet would be to go straight on the attack against Reuben Drake. It's true that still didn't excuse the release of the lorry but at least it clouded the issue. Besides, he had never been happy with Drake; the man was insolent and always skirted round the force's strict discipline code. Yes, that was it, he would interview Drake in the privacy of the inspector's office and away from all nosy parkers.

'Sergeant Barclay!' he called from the open office door. 'Send Drake to me when he returns.'

The station sergeant had just begun the process of handing over the reins of the front office to his early-turn successor who had arrived a few minutes early. Unfortunately, it was not the moment when sleep-starved station officers are at their most tolerant, particularly to frivolous interruptions. Barclay, therefore, gritted his teeth and assumed total deafness. The inspector made to repeat his request but, thinking better of it, decided to search for someone a mite more cooperative. To his great delight, the first person he saw was Drake himself, who had entered the back gate of the station on his creaking old cycle a full ten minutes before dismissal time. Matters were looking up at last!

'Ah, PC Drake,' he called. 'Just the man. Come into my office. I'd like a word.'

'Sir,' acknowledged the constable as he parked his cycle lovingly against a wall.

Marsh led the way across the front office, past the desk where Barclay and his relief were still engrossed in the intricacies of changing shifts and into the tiny brown-painted room. The inspector sat down but made no offer to the constable to do the same. 'Shut the door after you, Drake,' he requested icily.

'Sir,' the reply came in a quiet respectful tone.

'Drake, I understand that you had a conversation a few hours ago with a—' Marsh glanced down at some notes, '—a man named Lines. Is this information correct?'

'It's correct, sir.'

'This Lines, was he in possession of a motor vehicle at the time?'

'Was indeed, sir.'

'A *laden* motor vehicle?'

'Laden with goods *and* folks an' bound for the hopfields. Leastways, it would'a bin if it hadn't clobbered Bertie Franks's cab on the way.'

'You knew the deceased then?'

'There ain't much I don't know about this manor, sir. I understand that's what the commissioner pays me for. Bertie Franks is – or rather was – a late-night cabbie. Didn't get on with his missus all that well – she is a bit of a dragon. He reckoned if he worked most of the night and slept most of the day, he'd find her a whole lot more tolerable.' The PC paused and shrugged his shoulders before adding, 'In my experience of women, sir, I'd say he was probably right.'

'Leave the cab driver and your expertise on women aside for the moment, Drake. Let's go back to the truck. You said it was laden with goods and folks and it was bound for the hopfields. I've got that right, have I?'

'That's what I said, sir,' replied the constable slowly.

'But that lorry was dangerously overloaded. Why did you not prevent it from being driven? You not only compounded an offence but, by your sheer negligence, you may well have been responsible for a fatal accident.'

For a moment or so Drake made no reply but almost imperceptibly nodded his head. 'I thought this might be a-coming,' he finally murmured.

Marsh rose to his feet and pointed dramatically. 'And is that *all* you have to say about it, man? From my understanding you will be very lucky if your punishment is only dismissal. I think at the very least you should make a written statement admitting your negligence.'

The constable's eyes narrowed. 'Well, now, I'll tell you something, shall I, sir?' he almost whispered. 'I'm not very good with all these motor vehicles. I'm more a horse-an'-cart man meself. Mechanical matters bewilder me and the force ain't done nothin' to improve my ignorance. After all, sir, they say you can't make a silk purse outa sow's ear, don't they? So I can't see as I can be held to ransom over that little matter, d'you?'

'This is crass insubordination, Drake. I am therefore obliged to report you for . . .'

'Hang on, sir, hang on a minute. There's a bit more to this little discussion than Wonky Lines's lorry. After all, you've had your say, perhaps now I'll give yer mine. Y'see, even though it may have been a big load, it was also a safe one. Now as far as I understand from Poshie Porter, nothing fell off. Not even a piss pot, he reckons. Therefore, I don't think we should concern ourselves too much with that aspect, d'you?'

'I hate to agree with you, Drake, but you're right. By your

own actions you have taken this talk into a whole new realm.
I shall therefore require your . . .'

Reuben Drake's whole demeanour suddenly changed and,
for the second time in as many minutes, he cut across the
inspector's preaching. Leaning forward, he grasped Marsh by
the neck of his tunic. 'Listen to someone else for a change,
will you, you pompous prick. I've been here on this manor
now for twenty years. I've caught almost as many thieves as
the rest of the nick put together. When I'm out there,' he
gestured with his thumb over his shoulder, '*I'm* the guv'nor,
not them. No tuppenny-ha'penny little tin-pot fuckin' squirt
is goin' to have the last word with me. And if that goes out
there then it also applies in *here*.' With the slightest of effort he
dumped the inspector back into his chair. 'I know who *really*
made the fuck-up tonight, it was YOU! You let that lorry go,
not me, not Diamond, not Porter but YOU! You let it go and
now your arsehole's pouting because you've got some fuckin'
promotion board coming up where you think they're goin' to
make you chief inspector! Hah! Well, I've got news for you. If
they find out you let that lorry go, you can kiss promotion
goodbye for another five years and if you start trying to dump
your disasters on my shoulders, I'll grass you up for the
weasling little shit that you are. I've got nine more years to
serve in this job and quite frankly I don't much care where I
serve it. Remember this, I *know* why we're alone in here; it's
because you were hoping you could intimidate me with all
this discipline tripe. It just goes to show you haven't the
remotest idea about me or any other man who works here,
you fuckin' fairy.'

Marsh, now white-faced, tried to rise from his chair.
'D'you know what you're saying, man?' he cried. 'It's not just
discipline now, it's – it's – arrestable!'

'Oh, no, it ain't,' corrected Drake. 'It's not arrestable
because you daren't make it so. If this little conversation
comes out – even if they sacked me – they'd laugh you out of
the force because you're as weak as piss. And don't you

forget one other matter. It don't bother me what side of the fence I'm on. I could probably earn a better living out there as a villain than as a copper. But you –' he looked disdainfully down at the now terrified officer, 'you've got sod all to offer and you've only got this far because everyone'll be pleased to see the back of you. Well *I* want to see the back of you as well. I'm quite content to forget this little chat, but at the same time it don't bother me one way or the other.' The constable slid his old turnip watch from an inside pocket. 'It's now ten minutes past my bedtime. I'm going home and I expect to sleep the sleep of the just. I suggest you do the same. When we're outa this office, I'll pay you all the respect regulations demand but don't you ever threaten me again – SIR!' Reuben Drake turned on his heel and left the room, closing the door quietly behind him.

4

The voice David Diamond heard was so tiny and distant it could have been from another planet. All his senses were being dragged reluctantly through layer after layer of warm woolly sleep and there were still dozens to go. The supreme effort of whimpering 'Go away!' exhausted him as he slipped back into oblivion. Yet slowly the voice took on an increasing clarity.

'Daddy, Daddy, wake up, wake up. Mummy said your-tea's-poured-out-and-Grandma-is-coming-and-it's-my-birthday.'

He opened one eye and for a moment stared confusedly at the white haze that seemed to envelop the world before remembering he always covered his head with a sheet when he slept during daylight. Before he could pull back the cover it was removed for him as three-year-old-to-the-day Benjamin Samuel Diamond stared excitedly down. David eased a thick arm from the rumpled covers and pulled the eager-faced child to him.

'Hullo, mate,' he greeted in a sleep-thick voice, 'give us a birthday smacker before you get too big to kiss your old dad. Mmn, smashin' kiss that! Happy birthday, Ben, where's my tea?'

He raised his eyes beyond the tousle-haired boy to where his wife Grace stood clutching the blue china cup and saucer. It was at moments like this – sudden unexpected moments – that he remembered just how stunning she was. Even the tatty old overall she wore around the house could not detract from her beauty. Her tall lithe figure always seemed strangely out of place in the seedy two-roomed Victorian tenement grandly named 'Queen's Buildings'. He grinned up at her. 'What's the chances of a second birthday kiss?'

'If it was your second birthday you'd be quite entitled to it, but peculiar men who're twenty-two if they're a day don't qualify, I'm afraid.'

'Who *said* I'm peculiar?' he asked in mock dismay. 'I'm not peculiar, am I, boy?'

'If you could only have seen yourself with that sheet wrapped around your face you'd be the first to admit you were *very* peculiar. Now drink that tea before it gets cold. Your mother will be here soon and, for a brand new three-year-old, your son has been very patient. Let's not push our luck.'

He folded his arms and clamped his lips tightly together. 'I don't care. I'm on strike until I get a wake-up kiss.'

She gave an exaggerated sigh. 'What d'you think, Ben?' she whispered. 'D'you think he deserves one?'

'I've done Daddy one, Mum,' complained the lad. 'I'm too big now fur anuver one.'

'Sensible lad!' concurred his father, as he leaned forward from the bed and wrapped his arms around his wife's curving hips and buried his face deep into her soft warm belly.

'Just because I have a cup and saucer in my hand, Constable Diamond, you are taking advantage of a poor girl. Typical copper if ever I saw one.' Balancing the saucer carefully in one hand, she bent forward and, lifting his head with the other, planted the warmest of kisses on his lips. 'Now will you please *move* yourself, and don't you *dare* spill that tea, or else . . .'

'Okay, girl,' he yawned as he stretched out and swung his feet to the floor. 'Do we have any birthday cake? Don't forget I've had no breakfast this morning.'

'Seeing as it was almost lunchtime before you arrived home, I'm not surprised. Why so late? You did mutter

54

something but you were so tired you were practically incoherent. Seriously though, Dave, you've only been to bed for a few hours. You sure you want to go to your mother's so soon?'

'What! And disappoint my son? To say nothing of his grandma! By the way, she is feeding us, I hope?'

'Of course, she is. We're going for "high tea" as she calls it. She's picking us up in about twenty minutes. The kettle is on and you've just got time for a good strip wash before she comes. Just think, though, your old mum's driving a new Morris Six! Isn't that impressive?'

'It'd be more impressive if she'd passed a test. Anyway, it's the old man's car. He only lets her drive it because he's frightened of the bloody thing.'

Leaving his wife to change, he made his way sleepily out of the bedroom and, after ducking a washing line and a hanging fly-paper, took a route somewhere between the kitchen table and a freshly laden clotheshorse. 'D'you want me to save any hot water for you?' he called.

'No fear! It's a big treat for me today, my friend. Your mother's promised I can use her bathroom. Ooh, such luxury!'

'That's an idea! Perhaps she'd let us both use it at the same time? D'you know I've not washed your back since that bed-and-breakfast weekend at Canvey Island. You were eight months pregnant at the time, so you weren't in much danger.'

'*David*! What a thing to say! I'd be too embarrassed to ask her; she's a middle-aged woman!'

'Well, that don't make her a nun, y'know. According to what I hear from my grandmother, Billie Bardell, my old mum was a bit of a sensation in her younger days.'

'Huh!' exclaimed Grace, untying the tatty overall. 'With your gran's record, *she* should be the very last one to talk! Besides, you're referring to your mum and she's over forty years of age. For heaven's sake, she's not a young flapper, y'know!'

'Mummy!' cut in a little voice excitedly from the bedroom window, 'Grandma's here!'

David wrapped a towel around his waist and trotted into the bedroom to confirm the sighting. 'Yup!' he agreed as he glanced quickly down to the street. 'But she's still got ninety-six stairs to climb, so . . .' He pushed his wife back playfully onto the bed, 'it just gives us time for a little . . .' he made to peel back the overall, but she suddenly fought him like a tigress. 'Okay! Okay!' he yelled. 'I'm on your side! Take it easy, I've just woken up and I'm fragile.'

'David, we haven't time! Besides, your mother's here.' She snatched back the overall tightly around her. 'Will you please let me up? Apart from your mother, you're confusing your son. You don't want him crying on his birthday, now do you?'

He gave her a quick peck on her forehead and raised himself from the bed. 'I was only having a little look,' he said in a mock hurt tone.

'Davy, darling, I'm sorry,' she murmured, with a swift change of mood, 'but things have been hectic today and your mother is only about four flights down. Open the door for her. Please?' As an incentive she puckered up for a quick kiss.

'Of course, sweetie,' he said, briefly brushing her lips. 'It's all this night duty, it plays havoc with your sex life.'

Readjusting his towel, he opened the door and listened as the nearing footsteps increased in volume but faded in tempo as each new flight was faced. When the newcomer was still two flights away even the breathing could be heard.

'It's easy to see the good life has softened you up, Mother,' he called down. 'When you used to live here, you were up and down those stairs like a gazelle. Now, look at you! You look as if you could do with a week's convalescence.'

'When I – used to live here – young man,' she panted, 'it was my blasted inconsiderate son – who was – mainly responsible for my dozen daily climbs. He gave me leg muscles – like – a bloody kangaroo!'

'Nonsense, Mother, I kept you fit and you know it.'

'Listen, I'm not standing here talking to you in that indecent outfit. Get yourself dressed. Anyway, where's my grandson? I want to give him a big birthday kiss.'

Brushing past her son, Queenie Forsythe hastened to the bedroom door and swept up her grandchild in one all-embracing movement. With her arms locked around him she hugged him tightly and swung round in a circle before deliberately falling back onto the large feather bed. The child's chuckles and the woman's laughter filled the whole flat for minutes before David reached out and assisted them both back to the floor.

'Now, come on, Davy,' his mother scolded, 'I thought you were supposed to be ready when I called. Look at you. You haven't even shaved!'

'You must forgive him, Mum,' cut in Grace as she finished dressing behind the bedroom door. 'He didn't get to bed till nearly noon and he's only been awake for a few minutes.'

'I'm so sorry, m'dear,' replied Queenie, reaching for her daughter-in-law's arm. 'Now Jim's a superintendent, I sometimes forget all these maddening frustrations. It seems like another lifetime since I sat in this room waiting for Sam to come home and staring at the clock for hours on end.'

With the sudden mention of David's dead father, each of them realised these words had changed the whole mood.

Queenie was the first to break the silence. 'Hey!' she exclaimed, lifting her grandson onto her knee, 'I've got a surprise for you all. Now, if my good-for-nothing son ever gets around to washing and dressing, where d'you think we're all off to?'

With a razor in one hand and a face covered in lather, David turned away from the small mirror. 'Well, seeing as I haven't yet eaten today, I was hoping we were going to your place. I need a good meal and Grace needs a good bath and . . .'

'*David!*' exploded the girl. 'What a thing to say!'

Queenie burst into laughter. 'It's all right, luv,' she assured. 'He gets his diplomacy from his father.' She turned again to her son. 'No, we're not going to my place. As it's a special birthday, I've had an urgent request. Your glamorous grandmother requests the pleasure of seeing you all. Now, how about that!'

'Billie?' cried Grace. 'Billie Bardell? Oh, that's wonderful! Come on, Davy, speed yourself up! It looks like we're *all* getting a birthday treat.'

'Woah, just a minute,' said David raising a hand. 'And just how do I get back in time for work tonight? Billie lives miles away in Hampstead, doesn't she?'

'Does indeed,' agreed Queenie. 'And that's the reason I've brought the car. Don't worry, son. I'll get you back in plenty of time.'

'I just wish someone had told me,' muttered David as a trickle of blood ran from his neck. 'There! See what you've made me do!' Yet in spite of his protestations he was secretly as thrilled as his wife. Billie Bardell, maternal grandmother, man-eater extraordinaire and very rich widow of Sir Cedric Claude Hathaway, had been a great favourite of his since his childhood.

'How about Jim?' asked Grace. 'Is he coming?'

'Yes, but not until later. He has to attend some conference or other at Scotland Yard and he's not sure what time he'll be able to escape.'

David was not too upset at that news. For a street constable to have a police superintendent as a stepfather could be difficult, to say the least. The fact that it *wasn't*, said volumes for the easy-going nature of Jim Forsythe. In spite of this, the idea of making family small talk over a meal was not something he particularly enjoyed. The problem would not arise from the two policemen themselves but from one or other of the family, who would usually bring the conversation to a point where each of them took opposing views. For this reason, only the closest of David's friends were party to his relationship.

As the quartet descended the stairs to the street, the sound of young Benjamin intermittently counting the steps swept Queenie back a score of years to her own toddlers doing the same thing. So much had changed since then, so much tragedy and so much happiness. Her husband and sister-in-law, Jane, had both suffered violent deaths, whilst her only daughter and granddaughter had died in the flu epidemic. She had thought nothing could compensate for these losses. Yet Jim Forsythe had emerged to transfer her from the cold grinding poverty of Queen's Buildings to a warm loving haven where she woke each morning in bewildered disbelief. It seemed strange that her son should move into the very same flat she had vacated on her marriage, but, in such hard times, a ten-shilling rent had a lot to be said for it. There were certainly occasions when she pondered the future for her grandson, yet she was secretly proud that David had refused every offer of help from her. She was sure his pride and determination would eventually see him through. Like his father, he needed to stand on his own feet. If she had a worry at all, it was for Grace. The girl had seemed destined to be a beauty since the day she was born and she had now fulfilled that promise. Yet for a girl to be young, desirable and *poor* could be an insoluble mixture. Cool heads can turn when poverty rules. Her meditations were suddenly interrupted by a serious complaint from her grandson.

'Oh, Grandma,' he sulked almost tearfully, 'I fort you were helpin' me. I've forgot how many I counted now.'

'Don't worry, darling,' she soothed, taking his hand. 'When your daddy was little he never got it right once.'

The two of them emerged into the street in time to see Grace in conversation with a short bubbly blonde girl and David trying hard to shoo away a dozen or so children who had gathered curiously around the car.

'They don't see many of these in Queen's Buildings, Ma,'

he explained. 'But with such an attentive audience, you'd better make sure you start it first time, or by God, they'll give you some stick!'

'That girl, David, the one Grace is speaking to. I know her, don't I?'

'Probably,' he nodded. 'Her maiden name was Sheila Bowen. We were all kids together and she now lives next door to us. She lost her husband in the diphtheria outbreak in the buildings a couple of years back – she and about two dozen other poor things! – she and Grace have now become very close. Remind you of anything?' he asked casually.

As she stared at the two young women, equally happy in each other's conversation, she instinctively bit her lip. After a few moments she whispered sadly, 'Of course they do! Jane and me.' After a quiet sigh, she continued, 'I still miss her, you know. Hardly a day goes by without her coming to mind. When you're a young wife and you're trying to raise a family in a place like this, a good female friend is almost as essential as a good husband. In fact, frequently more so. At least girl friends don't knock you about.'

Unlocking the car door, she reached across and pushed down the nearside interior handles and David and Ben both slid eagerly aboard.

'I think Sheila's a bit more scatterbrained than Aunt Jane was, though, Mum. I'm sure at times she's bloody certifiable.' He leaned across and pulled back his mother's sleeve and glanced at her wristwatch. 'Come on, Ma, give her a blast on that horn. Once those two get talking they can be there all night.'

Queenie left it as long as possible before she slowly reached out of the car and squeezed the large bulbous horn. The bellow caused distress to Ben and alarm to everyone else. That is, with the exception of the two women still chattering on the pavement, though even they heard the second blast.

'Good heavens!' exclaimed David. 'Sounds like something

salvaged from the *Titanic*! If every car had one of those, it'd halve the accident rate. People would be too scared to leave their homes. Look! Even Grace has heard it this time!'

With a laugh and the quickest of touches, Grace had obviously said goodbye to her friend and was sprinting towards the car. 'Oh, I'm so sorry, Mum. But I just had to hear about Sheila's new boyfriend. She reckons he's got twelve toes, six on each foot! You know, I've never known that girl to have a normal bloke. Even her husband was seven feet tall. Sometimes I think she collects them from circuses.'

To cheers from neighbours and jeers from urchins, the gleaming black car rolled smoothly out into Southwark Bridge Road and turned north for the river and Hampstead.

Though Grace and Ben sat oohing and aahing in the rear of the car, David's attention hardly moved from his mother. His early apprehension gave way to increasing admiration. 'Mum, you're not a bad driver,' he said without a trace of rancour.

'Praise indeed!' she marvelled, 'coming from a son. Actually I have to thank Jim for this. He hates driving and he's hired a retired chauffeur to teach me. The government keeps talking about bringing in licensed driving tests so I thought I'd better get in quick. Incidentally, I hope you know the way to your grandma's house, because north of the Thames is about as familiar to me as Norway.'

'Don't worry, it's fairly central but I must say even after all this time, I still can't get used to calling Billie "Grandma". You are supposed to associate grandmas with your pram and your potty, not satisfying some horny git who's not much older than you are yourself. Anyway, she's never looked like a grandma to me; she's far too glamorous. Was she as good as they say? On the stage, I mean!' he added hastily.

'Oh, yes,' replied Queenie. 'Even when we were enemies I had to admit that. In fact, there were none better. She could captivate, torment or hold an audience for just as long as she wished. She was easily the hit of at least two Royal Command

Performances and the sailors of the Home Fleet adopted her as their own in 1916.'

'And what about – well, you know. The other side to her. She was a bit famous for that as well, wasn't she? You've always seemed to have made a point of avoiding the very mention of it to me and I'm a big boy now. I can cope with these things.'

Queenie gave a quiet smile and for a moment or so made no reply. 'Well, she *is* your grandmother; let's just say she was unusual in her choice of men, shall we?'

'If she was so unlucky, why did she eventually make such a good marriage?' he persisted. 'After all, she seems to want for very little nowadays.'

Queenie suddenly steered the car into the kerbside in Regent's Park and switched off the engine. She turned to her son and also gave her daughter-in-law a quick embracing glance. 'Look, I'll tell you this much, because it could affect you one day, then we'll discuss it no more. Understand?'

'If you're asking for our confidentiality, you've got that without question,' David said for both of them. 'Go ahead.'

Queenie gave the deepest of sighs before continuing. 'You're very wrong about one thing, Davy. It was not a "good marriage". Well, not in the accepted sense, anyway. It was more a marriage of convenience. As you know, he was much older than her, but he was a great collector of paintings, treasures and such like. Your grandmother was, still is, in fact, quite an impressive-looking woman. Some would even say stunning. For years she hardly changed and—'

'Oh, come on, Mum!' David chided. 'Leave it out. She's not a blushing virgin, y'know, she's a great-grandmother!'

'True,' nodded Queenie. 'But you're not taking into account the ages of both her and me when we became mothers. We were *very* young – unfortunately, much, much, too young,' she added sadly.

'And me!' interrupted Grace. 'Don't forget me. I was barely eighteen.'

'Okay, okay,' conceded David holding up his hands in surrender. 'So you were all child brides. Go on.'

'She was also very generous, in fact, at times she could be quite silly with money. Whilst everyone thought she was rolling in cash she was almost bankrupt. The music halls were dying and the demand for big stars was fading fast. To cut a long story short, I suppose you could say she was "collected". Sir Cedric Hathaway had recently lost his wife who was a former society beauty and he needed another to take her place very quickly. Billie was simply in the right place at the right time. The arrangement suited them both; it was a mutual collection. He had collected another glamorous wife that he could show off on suitable occasions and she collected security. He was even happy for them to live their own lives. He made no demands on her and she made no demands on him, except a monthly allowance. He even agreed she could keep her own name.'

'Why would she want to do that?'

'I don't know. Pride perhaps. After all, when they hear her name people still come up to her and say things like, "I saw you once at the Palladium and you were marvellous." She thinks that wouldn't happen if she was just Billie Hathaway, and I daresay she's right,' Queenie shrugged.

'You said it could affect us one day. What did you mean by that?' asked Grace.

'Well, strictly speaking, me and Davy are her only two living descendants. When she eventually dies – mark you, she'll probably outlive us all – one or both of us could expect to inherit at least some of her estate. Well, the fact is she has none. A legal contract was drawn up and she was given a generous monthly allowance for the rest of her life. This was to protect Sir Cedric's children. There are five of them and they weren't very happy about any part of it, I can tell you. Especially when the poor old sod died a year after the marriage! Anyway, she now lives in a fair degree of luxury but she has to mind her manners – and God knows *that* was never her strong point – for fear of incensing the family, as if they weren't incensed enough! They allow her to live comfortably in Sir Cedric's old house with her maid Alice and her young gardener, Duncan.'

'Didn't I once hear something about her adopting a daughter?' asked David.

'Well, it wasn't what you'd call an *official* adoption,' his mother said. 'The girl would have been too old for that anyway. Apparently her maid was widowed during the war and eventually found the task of bringing up a young girl and doing a twelve-hour-a-day munitions job impossible. Billie was always a pushover for a good sob story, so when she decided to employ the woman she just sort of took the child on as well. She probably did it for company as much as anything else.'

'How old is she?' asked Grace.

Queenie shrugged. 'Somewhere around her mid-teens. Anyway,' she glanced down at her wristwatch, 'if we don't get moving, poor Ben won't have time for his party.'

Soon they had crossed Hampstead Heath and, just off Hampstead Lane, stood an impressive red-brick dwelling in its own grounds and surrounded by a high brick wall and large open iron gates. The car rolled into the gravel drive and Grace immediately let out a little whistle.

'You're right. This *is* a "fair degree of luxury". I can well understand the old man's children being a bit miffed. Especially if they don't even like her! I should think they cry themselves to sleep every night. I know I would.'

Queenie stopped the car in front of a pillared portico and the wide-eyed young couple alighted. As David turned to assist Ben, Grace continued to indulge herself in admiration of the house and its grounds.

Her attention was caught by a tall athletic figure in light blue overalls who could be seen rising to his feet and gazing at them from amidst a cluster of rhododendrons. 'Oh! He's so handsome!' she whispered. 'He's like Rudolph Valentino!'

'That's Duncan the gardener,' replied Queenie. 'He comes with the house.'

'He must suit your mother a treat,' grinned David as he alighted from the car.

Queenie suddenly found herself crimsoning with embarrassment at David's words and Grace's stare. 'Oh, don't be stupid!' she snapped in a fluster. 'He's just a boy.'

'He might *look* like a boy,' murmured Grace with an exaggerated sigh, 'but there's a lot more than snakes, snails and puppy dogs' tails moving around in those overalls, I can tell you. From here he looks edible.'

Queenie wriggled uncomfortably at the turn in the conversation. 'I always expect, even prepare, for this sort of thing from your grandmother, but I certainly didn't foresee it from her grandchildren.'

'So!' came a quiet but penetrating voice from behind them. 'You're here at last! I was looking forward to seeing you an hour ago.' They turned to see a regal blonde figure in a blue-trimmed, three-quarter-length white silk dress and matching bolero striding out from the shade of the portico. 'I was becoming concerned. By the way, young woman, the young man you are staring at open-mouthed is my gardener. So it's hands off, you hussy. Duncan comes with the house. Isn't that right, Duncan?' she called.

Duncan, who had only heard part of the conversation, nodded an agreement and resumed his battle with the shrub roots whilst Grace exploded into laughter.

Billie Bardell looked sharply from one to the other.

'It's a private joke. Having said that, Grandma, you look an absolute knockout! How on earth do you do it?'

'One of the ways it's done,' she replied, 'is to forget I am anyone's "grandma". Especially anyone who is old enough to be a policeman and a father. The word "grandma" is therefore taboo in this house, young man. Anyone using it will have their mouth washed out with carbolic.'

'And how about *great*-grandma?' David persisted.

'With cyanide,' she ruled.

'Then, will you just tell me what name I should use to preface the sentence ". . . and I think you are still a beautiful woman"?'

'Ah, well, close friends are allowed to use the name Billie.' She held out her arms and both David and Grace fell happily into them. Meanwhile, Ben, somewhat undecided, clung to his grandmother's dress and watched proceedings with only the mildest of interest.

Grace had been prepared to acknowledge the fact that Billie would always have a certain glamour but she had wondered if it would stand close scrutiny. Her doubts were instantly resolved by raising her glance to the woman's profile. The neck was as smooth as her own, with just the hint of a crease around her top lip and eyes and, if she was dyeing her hair, it was expertly done because the soft ash colour suited her perfectly.

'Grand— I mean Billie!' said Grace, 'I think the nearer I get to thirty, the more maddening I'm going to find you.'

'Enough of this flattering bullshit,' said Billie dropping her arms and pushing the pair away. 'How's my little Benjamin?' She held out both hands. The child, like generations of admirers before him, forgot his previous reservation and ran to meet her. She swept him up and planted a great smothering kiss on his nose, leaving an equally great smothering lipstick mark in its wake. 'Come on!' Billie urged, leading the way, 'you must be starving. Alice, my maid, has done a wonderful birthday spread for us and I'm dying to hear all your news.'

The chattering group entered the house and were greeted by the smiling maid.

'This is Alice Giles,' said Billie. 'She's the world's best maid and an absolute gem and I don't want anyone upsetting her. Clear?'

Though undoubtedly pleased at the compliment, the maid reddened and said in a shy whisper, 'You mustn't believe everything Miss Bardell says. This way, please.'

She led them into a rug-lined, stone-paved entrance hall and on through a door in an oak-panelled wall and finally into a lavishly furnished room with a large limestone fireplace at the far end. To the left and set before the long French windows was a table extensively laid with sparkling cutlery and gleaming bone china.

'If you wish to use the bathroom,' said the maid, 'there's one just across the hall and two more at the top of the stairs.'

David gave Grace a quick smile but received an angry glare and a muttered, 'Don't you dare!' in return.

Billie, who was balancing her great-grandson on her knee, raised her eyebrows. 'Something wrong?' she asked.

'Not really,' David assured her. 'It's just that my wife claims she is desperately in need of a bath, and I must say both the sanitary inspector and myself agree,' he continued with the straightest of faces. 'We had planned to give her a hose down at Mother's, but . . .'

'*David! You pig, you!* How could you possibly say that again?' Grace punched her husband's arm in frustration before turning in anguish to her hostess. 'Oh, Miss Bardell!' she pleaded, 'don't believe him! Please, don't believe him!'

'Don't worry, love,' comforted Billie, slipping an arm round her. 'He seems just about as tactful as his old man.'

'I'm sorry,' said Queenie. 'I'm afraid I'm responsible for this. I did promise them the use of my bathroom. As you know, they have none of their own. On the other hand, I hardly expected my son to be quite such a—'

'There's a Mr Forsythe outside, marm,' Alice interrupted at that moment. 'He's just arrived in a taxi. Shall I show him in?'

'Please do,' responded Billie. 'And if he doesn't come at once, club him and drag him in.' She then turned her attention to Grace and added, 'You can use all three bathrooms if you wish, my dear, and for just as long as you bloody well like, and, if this husband of yours dares to set foot in any of them, I'll personally drown him.'

'Er – I trust this is the place?' chuckled a tall smartly suited man with a neat clipped moustache and fluffy grey hair. 'Only I thought it was my grandson's birthday party, but it sounds like the Three Ferrets at closing time.'

'Jim Forsythe!' exclaimed Billie. She slid back her chair and quickly transferring the bewildered Ben to his mother's lap, rushed forward to greet him. 'No wonder your wife has been keeping you hidden! It must be years since I've seen you and you look bloody marvellous!' She threw her arms tightly round his neck and kissed him passionately on the lips. On releasing herself she added, 'But still no one has told me why you're all so late. I was expecting you ages ago.'

'I've had a boring meeting at Scotland Yard,' pleaded Jim, looking expectantly at Queenie, 'but I've no idea what excuses the rest of the gang have to offer.'

'I'll put my hands up to that one,' pleaded David, 'but only if someone gives me something to eat. I was told I was coming to a binge but as yet no one's even tossed me a bun.'

'A thousand apologies, and you're right, of course,' Billie agreed as she turned to Alice. 'Can you get young Julia to give you a hand and feed these refugees from south of the river? Then perhaps I'll hear their boring excuses.'

Alice nodded and glided from the room, leaving the conversation to gather momentum. Within minutes she returned, together with daughter Julia and a trolley laden with an assortment of cold meats, pies and pastries. In addition, partly hidden at the bottom of the trolley, was an ice-bucket and a magnum of champagne.

'By the way, everyone,' said Billie, preparing to do battle with the cork, 'this young lady, as you've doubtless guessed, is Julia, Alice's daughter. Isn't she a beauty?'

'She most certainly is,' said Queenie emphatically. 'And she more than does you credit, Alice.'

Neither man spoke, but in spite of the newcomer's tender years, both were instantly aware of a sensuality about the girl that made them feel uncomfortable.

Their work done, Alice and her daughter finally left the room, allowing the conversation to resume its former volume and after an hour or so, the subject of their late arrival was yet again raised by Billie.

'You still haven't told me why you were late!' she complained. 'I'm not letting it go. Is it a state secret or something?'

'We simply had a fatal accident in the Old Kent Road just before knocking-off time,' explained David. 'There was a bit of a mystery about it and, as a result, I was several hours late getting to bed.'

'So?' persisted Billie. 'You don't expect to leave it there, surely? What *was* the mystery?'

David recounted as much of the tale as he knew and even some that he didn't know, but was then more than relieved to hear Jim interject, 'I know a little about that, myself. I sat opposite your superintendent at the meeting today. Quite a mystery, wasn't it? Like you, he seems to think it was nothing more than a liaison. Still, it does leave an untidy gap in a fatal accident report.'

'But surely the police are not going to waste their time searching for such a couple?' queried Billie. 'According to what you say, they have enough evidence from the two milkmen and the lorry driver. I'd be peeved if I was in that taxi and appeared in the newspapers because some idiot was so bloody nosy that he killed himself! They're all the same these peepers. They're the soul of virtue on the outside but love having a good leer on the inside. Dirty old men, all of 'em! If I had my way, peeping would be a castrating offence.'

'A posthumous one in this case, I assume?' smiled Jim. 'Anyway, no one knows for sure he was peeping this time.'

'This time?' echoed David. 'You said "this time" – why?'

'Ah, yes, you wouldn't know, would you; it never emerged until later in the day. He had a couple of convictions for breach of the peace. Both of them for peeping. I admit it must be a bit distressing for the victims, but nevertheless, having your chest stove in is a bit severe, don't you think, Miss Bardell?'

She responded with a rueful smile. 'I'm sorry, but I do get worked up about it, it's a hobby horse of mine. They are usually sanctimonious little creeps who wouldn't say boo to the vicar. God knows I've experienced enough of them.'

'But surely,' interrupted Grace quietly, 'the fact that a man was killed changes things. Doesn't it?'

'Not in my book, it don't,' announced Billie obstinately. 'Look, the possibility is that one or other of these two was married. Yes?' Without waiting for an answer she continued, 'But we don't know – no one knows – exactly *why* a bloke, or a girl for that matter, should be in that position. It's therefore nothing to do with anyone except themselves.'

'Do you have any idea who this couple are?' asked Queenie.

'Up to the time I left this morning,' answered David, 'not the faintest. All we know is she was tall, reasonably dressed and could possibly have cut herself. Oh, yes, she may have lost a pendant at the scene and the two milkmen thought she was "tasty". That's about it.'

'What qualifies as "tasty"? In a milkman's vocabulary, I mean,' queried Billie.

David shrugged. 'Depends entirely on his needs – or his fantasies.'

'Where on her body d'you think this girl, or woman, was cut?' asked Queenie.

'Hard to say,' mused David. 'But if the couple had no warning of the crash and therefore didn't duck or take any other avoiding action, then it was probably on her hand or arm, her right arm. But that's a pure guess.' His last words had been interrupted by distant church chimes. 'Hey!' he said anxiously. 'What time is that?'

'Eight thirty,' said Billie. 'But you don't have to worry. Young Ben is asleep.'

'Young Ben, as you call him, has a father who will be looking for another job if he doesn't make tracks home this

70

very minute.' David slid back his chair. 'Sorry, Mum, but we must get going very soon.'

'But how about poor Grace's bath?' protested Billie. 'After all, I did promise it to her. You must make time for that, surely? Tell you what,' she added saucily, 'you help her, it'll be done twice as quick that way.'

'He'll do nothing of the kind,' said Grace firmly. 'We'll be here all night if he starts that game.'

'Look, I know!' exclaimed Billie. 'How about a shower? It won't take a fraction of the time. Come on,' she ordered, rising to her feet and seizing Grace's hand. 'I'll show you.'

'Listen, you've got fifteen minutes at the most,' called David at the fleeing pair. 'If you're not ready in that time we're going without you and you can put on a long wig and ride home naked on the back of a horse.'

'God, but the boy's well read,' muttered Queenie.

As the child slept and Billie returned, the two men spoke more freely than Queenie had ever known before. She had always been aware of the gulf that David had erected between them but here at last was real conversation. True, most of it was 'trade' but it was animated and not just an exchange of polite responses. Billie, on the other hand, had opted out of boring male chat and sat dozing in a winged armchair. In fact, the men were so engrossed that it was only Queenie who realised the minutes were racing by. It was definitely time to hurry along her daughter-in-law's toilet. With a reassured glance at the sleeping child, she crept from the room whilst the two men heatedly discussed the merits of the current commissioner.

The first bathroom was in darkness and the door ajar. Climbing the stairs to the next landing, she saw a light shining under an oak-panelled door. Without thinking, she knocked and entered at the same time. The opening of the door caused the naked Grace to wheel anxiously around from the mirror clutching a blood-stained wrist. Her right wrist.

5

Though he enjoyed an occasional pint, Wonky Lines was not a drinking man. Which was more than fortunate because the state in which he found himself was unquestionably conducive to intoxication. To say he was between the devil and the sea, was a gross understatement. There were the lusty sisters on the one hand and Sid Grechen on the other. For two nights he had hardly slept a wink. Even the three visits he had made to Rodney Road police station he had taken in his stride. After six months on the Somme, a fatal road accident didn't bother him at all. It was Sid Grechen that bothered him. As he lay awake for the third night he made a decision: he would see Sid and have it out with him. To run away without finding out if Sid even knew of the accident would serve no purpose. After all, he could be running away for nothing. No, there was only one thing to do and he would do it on Friday night – see Sid.

Of course, there was always the possibility that in spite of this brave decision, nothing would be resolved. Sid did not always visit the yard on a Friday but if there *was* a time when he was more likely to than any other, Friday evening after closing time was the best bet. Comforted at last by his decision, he punched a sizeable dent in his pillow and crashed out for the next nine hours. The strength and weakness of Wonky's decision were exactly the same -- when he woke in the morning it would *be* Friday. If he was still determined to see Sid, he would have a little over twelve hours to change his mind. If he did change his mind, he would have a little over twelve hours to be overcome with remorse and change it back again.

In his eventual wish to see Sid Grechen, Wonky Lines was by no means alone. Police constable Reuben Drake had been seeking him for far longer. It was not for any specific offence but more a cat-and-mouse game for Reuben. Basically he hated everything Sid stood for and Reuben would have no qualms at all in incarcerating his foe for as long a time as possible by whatever means possible. Yet even this was not enough for Reuben. He also wanted Sid, as he quaintly called it, to simmer. There was no doubt of the success of this approach, certainly as far as the nerves of Sid Grechen were concerned. That gentleman was not even sure if Reuben had enough evidence to charge him, or indeed even any evidence at all. Yet such was his fear of the man, that Sid's appearances on the Rodney Road manor were becoming more and more infrequent.

Wonky's slumbers might well have gone on far longer than nine hours, but he was rudely disturbed by a crashing double bang on his door and a predictably noisy response from Pieshop. The time he took to rouse himself was obviously longer than the patience of the caller and a second double knock shook the household, followed by another canine outburst.

'I'm c-coming! You d-don't have to knock the s-soddin' house down.' Wonky slid back the bolt and peered into the glare of the late morning as the tiny trilby-hatted figure of Albert Mendoza materialised.

'Ah-ra, Mr Leens, sah,' greeted Albert, raising the trilby. 'I'va missed-a you for a coupla months or so.' The caller had a book already opened in one hand and a pencil licked and poised with the other.

'Accordin' to-a my accounts, you owe-a da firm six-a shillings and-a freepence.'

'S-six shillings and wh-what–' began Wonky. 'Oh, n-no, you're r-right, you're r-right. C-come in, I'll s-see

74

if I can f-find some ch-change.'

The call had its origins in a particularly rewarding delivery he had carried out two months back when he had felt so affluent that he had rashly bought himself an eight and ninepenny fireside rug. He had paid half-a-crown deposit but had not kept up instalments. 'I've already b-burnt a h-hole in it,' complained Wonky. 'D-does that in-invalidate the g-guarantee, d'you th-think?'

Such a word as 'guarantee' taxed Albert's English beyond its limitations, so he adopted his customary routine when he sensed a potential protest; he just smiled and held his hand out expectantly.

'Okay,' sighed Wonky, tilting the chipped china jug he kept on the dresser. 'H-how much d-d'you s-say?'

Minutes later, the still smiling Albert once more tipped his hat and disappeared into the morning bustle of the Blackfriars Road. Wonky suddenly began to wonder if this was going to be an omen for the day. It was bad enough to have his sleep disturbed without having to pay six shillings and threepence into the bargain. Perhaps, after all, there was something to be said for working long hours – at least you were never at home to callers.

After a shave, Wonky took Pieshop for a leisurely stroll in the park in the warm autumn sunshine. He could not remember the last time he had a day off and found it thoroughly enjoyable. Even the thought of Sid Grechen was becoming less daunting as he spread himself on the grass, pushed his cap over his eyes and eased his brain into neutral. The distant sound of a bicycle bell roused a half-hearted response from Pieshop but it was only a token gesture and the dog quietened as the cycle faded from view. Funny that, thought Wonky beneath his cap, the dog had always hated cyclists. Come to that, Wonky did not much care for them himself. Dangerous idiots most of them who hung onto the tailboards of lorries and swung violently off course in their endeavours to avoid tramlines. Still, shouldn't be too hard;

he was a cyclist himself once. In fact he still had it somewhere in his cluttered backyard under a canvas sheet. Should get rid of it really, it was taking up room and he would probably never ride it again. Suddenly he sat bolt upright. If his plan was to see Sid Grechen and, if things went badly, seek refuge at the Wilkinsons' hopping hut, how was he to get there? Sid was hardly likely to offer him unlimited use of his trucks and the hoppers' specials only ran for the mass exodus of the first couple of days of the season. After that, the timetable for the Kentish countryside reverted to normal – 'normal' in this context meaning a scanty service on tiny branch lines that ran between Sevenoaks and the river Medway. Besides, if he did a runner, Sid would guess he would be bound for London Bridge station. So what was the alternative? He could try thumbing a lift – with the number of weekend visitors going to the hopfields, there would be no shortage of transport on the roads – but then how would Pieshop manage? He now knew he needed an alternative plan should his chat with Sid go wrong. He was also trying desperately to avoid the conclusion that the best answer would be to dig out his old cycle. There was a fairly sizeable basket on the front, though whether Pieshop would sit in it was quite another matter. If he didn't like cyclists in the first place he was hardly likely to take kindly to a tour to the hopfields squatting in a basket on a bike. So what was to be done? At first Wonky tried his usual system for difficult dilemmas. He closed his eyes, lay back and tried to forget them. He gave this up after half-an-hour and rising to his feet ruffled his old friend's coat and said, 'Come on, boy, you're not going to like this but we've got a little practising to do.'

Sid Grechen was not a happy man. He had a few gambling debts and needed to pay off a west London mob, particularly as they had already indicated payment was overdue. This oversight had actually exposed a flaw in his finances that he had always believed could never happen. Prior to this he had

had an excellent summer working with a north London compatriot, he had been making one of his occasional and very profitable 'on the knocker' forays to the West Country and returned to find a trusted employee had been short-changing him, probably for years. Sid liked to do these forays every few months; they were an easy source of revenue and difficult to classify as crime. Two of them would chat their way into an elderly widow's house and whilst one kept the old girl talking, the other was sizing up anything of value. An offer, always a fraction of the articles' true worth, would be made and with surprising frequency a deal would be done. Sid could therefore placate his conscience, not that he actually had one, with the thought that the whole thing had been nothing but a smart stroke of business. Now, after all that euphoria he had returned to find several notes from the collectors asking for immediate payment and one from the local police asking him to attend Rodney Road station to clear up a few points such as insurance and vehicle ownership. If Sid hated police stations, he hated them even more if Reuben Drake was present. There was something about the man that made Sid go cold. It was getting very close to the time when he would need to take some action there. Anyway, now was not the time – there were too many other matters that needed his attention. After all, there was no sense in dealing with him unnecessarily. He reached for the telephone and dialled Rodney Road police station. Composing himself for a moment he then put on his best possible accent.

'Could Hi speak with Police Constable Drake, please? . . . Hi see . . . so when his 'e next on duty? . . . Tonight? . . . Hat ten o'clock, you say? . . . Very well, Hi'll call again then . . . No, no, the hofficer was very 'elpful to me once and Hi was seeking 'is 'elp once hagain . . . No, no, hit can wait, thank you hall the same. Goodbye.'

He glanced at his watch; eight thirty, eh? Good. That left him a full hour-and-a-half to get to the station and get matters sorted before Drake arrived for duty. He strode briskly into his yard and climbed into his new Ford. As he expected, at that time of day there was very little traffic. In fact, it was a completely uneventful journey, except for having to swerve to avoid some nutty bloody cyclist who was wobbling along Blackfriars Road in the dark with a stupid dog in a basket. Shouldn't be on the road, some people!

The front office desk at Rodney Road station was cluttered with the usual evening clientèle. There were precious few telephones on the manor and any query or information required would need to be dealt with by physical presence. In addition to these routine visitors, there would be a few customers who had returned home from work to discover they had been burgled and finally the latter group would include those reporting on daily bail, many of whom were directly responsible for the visit of the former. Sidney Grechen found the whole thing particularly distasteful. All these pseudo Bill Sykeses lying around the waiting room and being given precedence over him made him despair of the country's present state. No wonder there was a slump.

After a twenty-minute wait he was finally ushered into an interview room by an official-looking constable with an official-looking book tucked firmly under his arm. After a brief study, the officer said it appeared there were no apparent driving offences but a certificate of insurance and proof of ownership would be required before the inquest took place, probably about a week hence. Though Sid was confident he had the insurance details somewhere around his office, his confidence did not run to the same certainty as regarded ownership. The vehicle certainly did not belong to anyone else, but whether it *officially* belonged to Sid was a completely different matter. Probably the last official owner had been the Royal Artillery and they would doubtless have had three different registrations for what was now one vehicle. As the constable droned on, Sid was thinking ahead and deciding that if a registration offence was all that could be laid at his door, he would not be losing much sleep. He had always believed it was possible to get out of most little difficulties by paying up and a five-quid fine was not going to distress him too seriously. Besides, he still had two weeks of Wonky Lines's wages in his wallet. The swindling rogue was hardly likely to show his face in the yard again and Sid had no intention of sending them to him. With luck, he could even make a profit on the deal and, with even more luck, it might even be possible to shove the whole registration offence onto Wonky. Perhaps something like: 'My transport manager, Mr Lines, had been instructed by me to register the lorry but had patently failed to do so and had clearly kept the money instead. Now, smitten by guilt, he has left the yard and gone away, heaven knows where.' Yes, Sid was quite pleased with that, it had a nice efficient ring to it. The constable took such details as there were and Sid finally left the station. He was certainly much happier than when he entered, after having signed a witness statement concerning the malpractice of one Claude Clement Lines and promising faithfully to search for the insurance certificate.

Sid's original plan had been to go home to Hoxton and rummage around the office the following morning for the insurance certificate. But he suddenly realised the route of his homeward journey took him past his yard, so after a quick Scotch at the Jolly Miller he was unlocking the yard gates at around ten thirty. His first action was to fill the kettle and put it on the burning gas ring, whilst his second action was to kick a very familiar dog that had just followed him in.

'Y-you ain't got no c-call t-to do th-that,' admonished Wonky.

Sid wheeled sharply. His fury was instant.

'Oh 'aven't I? You've got some front, boy, you 'ave. You've bin robbin' me fuckin' blind munf in, munf out an' nah you've got the fuckin' brass neck ter complain that I've kicked yer scabby mongrel!' He almost flew across the office and launched himself at Wonky. Seizing him by the throat, he pulled him back onto a torn old horse-hair, three-legged sofa that lay propped up next to the gas ring. His aggression easily quelled Wonky's token protest.

'That's not 'alf yer worries. Before I knock seven buckets of shit outa yer, I want ter know just wot you've been up to?' Gritting his teeth in anger, he secured a hold on Wonky's shirt collar with both hands and bounced his head back several times against the brick wall above the sofa. 'I've just spent the best part of two 'ours down that fuckin' nick – and why? I'll tell yer! I've bin there because good ole reliable Wonky Lines 'as 'ad 'is hand in *my* till right up ter 'is fuckin' armpits! You've bin takin' more fuckin' transport jobs than the Royal Army Service Corp! Shall I tell yer wot you've done? You've destroyed my trust, mate, that's wot you've done. There I was, finking that I can go away an' leave the firm in safe an' reliable 'ands an' there was you, larfin' yer dick orf while me back was turned. That's right, *larfin*'! Well, I'll tell yer this much, Wonky Lines, yer won't be larfin' agin fer a while.' Tightly twisting his prisoner's shirt collar with one fist, he reached up towards the near-boiling kettle with the other hand.

Whether two hours in the basket had slowed Pieshop's reactions or whether he was sulking and just wanted to prove a point will never be known but the situation was fast becoming perilous before the dog finally sank six teeth into Sid Grechen's left ankle. Of course, this did nothing to hinder Sid's right ankle which then rocketed over to lift the yelping animal clear across the room. Resuming his stranglehold on Wonky, Sid renewed his attempt to reach the kettle.

Up to that moment, Wonky's nervous protests had all been verbal which was hardly his strongest point. But as Sid finally gripped the kettle handle, the same feeling of entrapment erupted in Wonky that had first shown itself on a terrible July day in 1917 when his trench had been mortared then overrun by the Germans at Passchendaele. It was a day of which he had been the sole survivor. On that dreadful morning, he had the strange feeling he was no longer in command of himself. Someone or something had totally taken him over. Whatever it was, caused him to fight, claw and tear his way from that pit of hell in a display of such mindless violence that he had long since erased it from his mind. Well, now it was back.

Sid Grechen was a powerful man in anyone's eyes. He may not have been fit but he was tall, heavy and ruthless. His round pudding face was topped by oily sleek hair with a parting so straight it could have been made by a meat cleaver. Yet, as Wonky finally raised his fingers to the fist that was choking him, he pulled it aside with astonishing ease. He then chopped a hand down so ferociously on Sid's other arm that every sinew and muscle in it ceased to function. Sid's fingers slid uselessly from the kettle handle and down its scorching side. They then carried on limply through the flames that licked its base until they reached the side of their horror-struck owner. Wonky lifted himself from the sofa and, with the minimum of effort, threw off his opponent who rolled wide-eyed and screaming to the floor. Wonky then kicked open Sid's legs and picking up the bubbling kettle, glared down and tilted the spout slowly towards Sid's unprotected genitalia.

'NO! NO! PLEASE NO!' screamed Sid. 'FOR GAWD'S SAKE, NO!'

As fast as the mood had enveloped the ex-soldier, so it vanished. He lifted his glance to see that Sid's eyes were screwed tight shut in expected agony. Moving the angle of the kettle back slightly, he let it spatter its boiling contents harmlessly onto the frayed floor linoleum between Sid's knees and feet. As the last drop finally plopped onto the floor, Wonky realised he had a further problem, namely what should he do now?

One thing was sure; he had put the fear of hell into Sid but the mood had now passed. On the other hand, if Sid became aware of this, his own life would not be worth a toss. As he looked down at the whimpering man he almost wished he had the nerve to kill him. It would certainly make his own life a little easier, but he knew he could not do it now, not in cold blood. Only twice in his life had he been in fear of his own life and on both occasions he had reacted the same. Twice in forty-five years is hardly habit-forming. In addition to that, there had been an interval of thirteen years between the first and second occasions. Who knows, perhaps with luck, he might never experience it again. If that was the case, then all he now had left to offer was bluff. He turned out the gas and replaced the kettle on the now dead gas ring. Meanwhile Sid, not knowing what to expect next, lay motionless with the burning sensation searing his left fingers.

Wonky slowly sat down on the sofa and placed one foot on Sid's chest. If he was going to convince Sid of his determination then he had to sound determined. That might be difficult with a pronounced stutter. He knew he must try to keep his stammer to a minimum. Taking a deep breath, he slowly exhaled, then began. 'Now get this straight, Mr Grechen. You're only alive now because I've allowed you to . . .' He suddenly faltered – there was no stammer! But why? No never mind why, he must continue '. . . I've allowed you to be. But if you ever threaten me or my dog again, you're a dead man, Mr Grechen. Understand?'

Sid did not even make an attempt to reply but gave a slight head movement that Wonky quickly deciphered as an agreement.

'Now,' continued Wonky, 'if you'd just like to pay me the two weeks' wages you owe me, Mr Grechen, then I'll be on my way.' This time Mr Grechen made not the slightest move that could be interpreted as compliance. 'In here, you say, Mr Grechen?' asked Wonky, bending over the prostrate figure and sliding his hand into an inside pocket and removing a well-stocked wallet. 'Two weeks at four pounds a week is – let me see – eight pounds exactly, I believe, Mr Grechen. Well if I charge you ten bob for tearing my shirt and a further thirty bob for kicking my dog, that'll be ten pounds exactly. Here you are, sir. As you can see, I've removed two fivers but I'd be careful if I was you, sir, walking about with all that money. There are some very dishonest people about. Goodnight to you, Mr Grechen, you needn't see me out.'

In spite of an almost overwhelming desire to run, Wonky brazenly sauntered out with Pieshop at his heels and closed the gates shut behind him. As they clicked together he had difficulty sorting out his thoughts – at best they were a confusing jumble of contradictions. He had been frightened, yes, even petrified would not have been too strong a word, but then his fears had given way to fury. A fury where nothing else mattered other than wreaking vengeance on his tormentor. The problem with that was Sid would now be the one looking for revenge and next time he would certainly have help. Yet even that paled into insignificance beside the disappearance of his stammer and, of course, the small matter of his now being unemployed.

His thoughts were suddenly interrupted by a familiar creaking noise and a booming 'Hullo there! Given up drivin', 'ave we? Not surprising with your record.' Reuben Drake was cycling slowly along the opposite side of the road and gradually easing over to Wonky's section of pavement. He braked to a halt and, placing one foot down on the kerbstone, folded his arms and leaned back on the saddle. 'Not working tonight, then?' he persisted.

'Er – n-no n-not t-ternight,' answered Wonky closing his eyes in frustration at the return of his handicap.

'How's your guv'nor? Seen 'im lately?'

'My g-guv – oh, you mean Mr G-Grechen, I s'pose? Er – n-no, I ain't s-seen him for some little time n-now. Why d'you ask? Everything all r-right?'

'It's just that I understand 'e was down at the nick tonight. I like to keep abreast of such matters, yer know. I mean fer all anyone knows 'e might be in need of desperate 'elp.'

Little do you know, thought Wonky, that for once, you've

actually got it right! Still, the fact that Reuben Drake was about the streets was at least reassuring. If, by chance, Sid should make a swift recovery and come rushing out with daggers drawn, it was nice to know he would have to deal with the old constabulary blackguard first.

'D'you know, you r-remind me of s-someone from a book, Mr D-Drake,' said Wonky impulsively and with no little daring.

'Well, now,' said Drake rubbing his chin thoughtfully. 'Lemme think – some kind benevolent soul, no doubt, hmmn? No, you've got me there, boy, I ain't that well read, I'm afraid. Is it someone from the Bible – Samson p'raps?'

'Well, I was th-thinking more of Peter P-Pan. You s-see, with your b-bike s-squeaking all th-the t-time, it reminds me of the c-crocodile. Y'know, where he c-creeps around with an a-alarm c-clock ticking away in h-his b-belly or somewhere and keeps putting the f-fear of C-Christ up C-Captain Hook. You and your b-bike are just like th-that with Mr G-Grechen.'

Reuben Drake stared at him for a moment or two before exploding into a gale of raucous laughter. 'Yes, mate, I think you're dead right. I quite like the idea of creeping around scaring the shit outa old Grechen. Especially with an alarm clock up my jacksy. It appeals to my artistic nature, as yer might say.' With that he pressed down on his pedal and creaked slowly away towards the Old Kent Road, still laughing uproariously.

Wonky stood watching until he was long out of sight. The idea of relying on anyone as capricious as Reuben Drake, delighted to be compared to a crocodile with an alarm clock up his rear, struck Wonky as cockeyed to say the least. 'C'mon, b-boy,' he muttered to Pieshop. 'We'll go home the other w-way in case he ch-changes his m-mind and k-kills me.'

As Wonky let himself into his dingy flat, he fell over the cycle which he had left propped against the passage wall. As he picked himself up, serious reservations began to creep in about the whole idea of a forty-mile bike ride to Wateringbury. His plan, which had seemed eminently sensible during the warm lazy afternoon, had been to make the journey overnight. With clearer roads, it would have been a leisurely ride and he would have arrived in time for the Wilkinsons' breakfast. With Lillian's assurance that the warm sun rises regularly over Maidstone fresh in his mind, the whole idea had seemed almost romantic. But now, with a damp heavy mist and a considerable fall in temperature, the open road had lost its allure.

'T-tell you w-what, Pieshop,' he announced, 'we'll have a g-good sl-sleep and l-leave first th-thing in the morning, just before the s-streets are aired. That's a b-better idea, don't you th-think?' Pieshop, having no desire to waste thoughts on such an obvious move, ignored the question and wearily curled up on his blanket at the foot of the bed.

Wonky would not have been so keen to have revised this timetable, if he had been aware of Sid Grechen's plan of revenge. Almost before he had risen from the linoleum, Sid had telephoned two freelance thugs with an immediate scheme for the removal of Wonky and dog. Yet before the hired hands arrived in their black limousine, the burns on his hand told him a postponement was inevitable.

'Okay,' Sid snarled at them, shaking his fingers as if playing an invisible banjo, 'take me to hospital, I'll get a dressin' on it an' we'll call on the rat first thing in the mornin'. You two can kip 'ere fer the night.'

'We'll do it fer yer now, guv,' offered one of them generously. 'You just tell us where 'e lives an' yer needn't come. You stay 'ere an' look after yerself. We'll do a real tidy job fer yer on our own.'

'Not likely, mate!' snapped Sid. 'I've got the address on a piece of paper somewhere but I wanna be there. If I'm payin' ter finish the barsted, I wanna watch. He owes me that much entertainment!'

Showing surprising care, the two potential executioners

led Sid to their car and, within minutes, up the casualty steps at Guy's Hospital.

The casualty doctor, who soon became the target of Sid's verbal abuse, derived no little joy from the first-aid hint that had been given to Sid by one of his companions. 'Cover it up in butter, guv,' had been the advice. 'My old lady swears by it, she does. Takes all the sting out of it, she reckons.'

'Well, you see, Mr Grechen,' explained the doctor, after pulling back the filthy hand towel that had also been applied, 'before we can actually treat your burn, we'll need to remove the gauze and bits of cotton which are stuck to it from the hand towel, to say nothing of the vast covering of butter with which someone seems to have smothered your wound.' Showing not a hint of satisfaction, the doctor then looked up into Sid's worried face and added disconcertingly, 'Of course, Mr Grechen, you may experience a certain amount of discomfort.'

'Discomfort!' repeated Sid again and again as he sat in the back of the car some two hours later. 'Fuckin' *discomfort*? That's 'ospital code fer we're gonna kill yer.' He turned angrily to one of his companions. 'That doctor enjoyed that, yer know. They're not proper doctors there, not at Guy's they're not. Butchers, that's what they are, fuckin' butchers. I tell yer what, though, when we git 'old of that barsted, Lines, 'e's goin' ter pay fer this little lot, you see if 'e don't.'

Four hours later Sid was still making brave attempts at sleep but each time he moved his hand the pain drove him to distraction. It was a pity really, because when he finally gave up all thoughts of sleep for the night, Wonky Lines had just persuaded Pieshop into a basket for a forty-mile ride into a misty Kentish dawn.

6

Jim Forsythe folded up his evening paper and gave a stretching yawn. After a glance at the mantelpiece clock, he turned to his wife who sat knitting on the sofa and shook his head in a gesture of faint disbelief.

'I must be getting older quicker than I realise,' he sighed. 'D'you see the time? Ten thirty! Ten thirty, and I can hardly keep my eyes open! I don't know how I'd cope if I was still a street copper instead of being a nine-to-five Scotland Yard warrior. I think a week's night duty now would just about kill me.'

'Well, you're not a boy any more, Jim,' Queenie pointed out. 'And if the slump worsens you could easily find yourself back in the front line of street demonstrations and riots again. Have you given any more thought to retiring?'

'Yes, I have. I was approached early this week by a detective agency in Bloomsbury, but I'm not sure if that's what I want to do. I don't much fancy the idea of being the one who creeps around spying on some poor unsuspecting blighter in order to provide evidence for a divorce. It seems sordid somehow.' As he finished speaking, his mouth gave the merest hint of a smile.

'So what's tickling you?' she asked.

The smile gave way to a light laugh. 'As I said that, I instinctively thought of your mother. I bet her adventures of a few years ago could have kept a dozen detective agencies in full-time work for years.'

'I'll thank you to keep your thoughts about me mother to

87

yourself, Jim Forsythe,' Queenie said with mock severity, but then added in a much more pensive tone, 'I just hope the same thing will never be said about your daughter-in-law, that's all.'

'My daughter-in-law? Good heavens, woman, what are you saying? Are you talking about Grace?'

'Seeing as she's the only daughter-in-law you've got, that's a fair assumption.'

'I don't understand. What do you mean? She's a great girl and they're a very happy couple, surely?'

'Are they? Are they really?' she asked. 'If you think that perhaps you'd better listen to this.'

All traces of tiredness vanished from even the remotest recesses of his mind as he sat up straight and stared at her.

'I'd better warn you first, Queenie,' he murmured quietly, 'I've got a lot of time for that girl.' He raised his hand to forestall any objection that might have been forthcoming but there were none. 'And I certainly don't want to hear any cheap tittle-tattle about her. She's a beautiful girl and some folk are bound to be small-minded and jealous and . . . Oh, I'm sorry, love!' he added quickly, 'I didn't mean that to sound quite the way it came out.'

She gave a wry smile. 'I know that, Jim, but then you always were a pushover for a pretty face and a good figure and I have to admit that lass certainly has both.'

'Oh, come on, Queenie,' he replied defensively. 'There's far more to her than that, as you of all people know. She grew up in your shadow. If I might remind you, you were like a lioness with a cub and you were even prepared to kill for her once. That can't have escaped your memory surely?'

'Jim, you must listen to me. Say nothing until I have finished, but don't make your mind up until then. Agreed?'

'Very well,' he nodded. 'But I simply wanted you to know where I stood, that's all.'

Queenie began by telling him of her discovery of the girl's cut forearm.

'So, how'd she explain it?' he asked impatiently.

'She said she was rearranging her plant pots on the balcony and one suddenly fell. She said she was terrified it might have fallen onto some children playing in the square four floors below, so she made a grab for it. Instead of catching it cleanly, she banged it against the wall and it disintegrated and a sharp piece cut into her arm. I asked her if David knew of this and she said he'd been asleep at the time and she didn't want to disturb him. I asked her why she hadn't gone to hospital to have it stitched and why she hadn't mentioned it to David subsequently. She said that would have been a great fuss over very little.' Queenie stared at her husband for a moment, then added pointedly, 'Jim, it wasn't very *little*. It was a bad cut that merited several stitches.'

'Is that all?' he protested. 'I think you've made a mountain out of a molehill. Surely you remember what it was like when Sam was on night duty? There were all sorts of things you meant to mention but, because he wasn't there at the time, or perhaps was asleep, you'd forget. Happens all the time to shift-working families, you must know that.'

'A cut like that doesn't. But in any case, there's more, much more. You remember the pendant David said was found at the scene?' He nodded. 'Well, I clearly remember Grace wearing a set of earrings that matched that very pattern at her wedding. I remember thinking at the time how unusual they were.'

'But, Queenie!' he protested. 'Earrings are earrings and pendants are pendants. No manufacturer ever makes just one set. There are probably hundreds if not thousands in circulation.'

'But if they were hand-made they would be much rarer,' she argued.

'If they *were* hand-made, then Grace would not have been wearing them,' he countered. 'Those two kids have not had two ha'pennies to rub together since they first started courting. I know you think she's a bit immature at times but I can't see

even Grace spending a fortune on earrings for her wedding
when there were so many other things she needed.'

'Someone could have given them to her?' Queenie said
pointedly.

'Queenie, for God's sake! You're putting two and two
together and making a dozen!'

'Okay, so you've obviously dismissed my second point. So
what do you say to this one? Five days ago, when we had all
that rain and you'd gone to Birmingham for that conference,
I found a toy motor of Ben's that had dropped down between
the seats in our car. I almost posted it to him – I now wish to
God I had. Instead, I took it round to him. Because of the
time, it was seven o'clock in the evening, I thought I would
also see David before he left for work. Anyway, David wasn't
there. He had finished night duty a few days earlier and was
on a four-to-midnight shift.' She stopped for a moment to
ensure her words had sunk in before continuing. 'But not
only was David absent, so was his wife.'

'What!' exclaimed Jim rising to his feet. 'You mean young
Ben was there on his . . .'

'No, no. He had someone with him all right – a young
woman – you may remember her as Sheila Bowen. She's a
widow now and I don't know her married name. She doesn't
seem a bad girl, but she's not the brightest brain in the
buildings. I asked her where Grace was. At first she tried to
tell me she didn't know. She gave me some rubbish about her
popping out to the shops for a few minutes. When she saw I
didn't believe her, she said Grace had gone dancing at the
Elephant and Castle Palais and she soon admitted that it was
a regular occurrence whenever David was on that late shift. I
asked if David knew of this and she said no because Grace
was always back home well before midnight and she thought
he might not approve . . . Might not approve!' she echoed. 'I
don't suppose he would! Whilst my son's at work, his wife
leaves his only child while she goes off dancing! He'd hardly
be likely to approve of that!'

'Well,' faltered Jim as he sought desperately for a possible defence, 'she's still a young girl, and you know how young girls can be? She sees poverty all around her and probably feels she must occasionally break away from it, if only for an evening. I recall how restless you were at her age. If I remember rightly Sam went round to Max's club and dragged you out.'

'Okay! You want more? Sit tight, I'll give it you. I pretended to drive away but simply did a circuit and parked so I could see the entrance to their staircase. At quarter past eleven, a black delivery van pulled up at the end of the street. It was pouring heaven's hard and all I could see was a young fellow kissing a girl in the front of it and subsequently a tangle of arms as they embraced. The girl then got out and ran into Queen's Buildings doing up her coat and blouse. You don't need me to tell you who it was, do you?'

'So you're implying that your daughter-in-law was not only in a cab with a middle-aged bloke at four in the morning when some poor sod was killed, but also that she is regularly out with a younger man in another vehicle at a different time of the night? Does sound like our Grace is putting herself about in a big way. Have you spoken to her?'

'No, but I very much intend to,' Queenie said emphatically. 'I'm going to pick my time, that's all. I want to do it when it will have the least effect on David and Benjamin.'

'So how about forty years hence?' Jim rose to his feet and crossed to the sofa and sitting alongside his wife, placed a comforting arm round her shoulders. 'Look, love, if you cast your mind back to our younger days, we had some pretty bleak moments between us, didn't we?' She made no direct answer but stared at him. 'Well, between us we sorted them out and that's what those two kids need to do. If David ever finds out about this, it must never come from you, d'you understand? Because the way things are at the moment, you could well be losing a daughter-in-law, but if you are the one that blows the whistle, it's odds on you'll also lose a son *and* a grandson too and we don't want that, do we? I love being both a grandfather and a father, so don't take that away from me, please.'

'So what are you saying? I should keep it to myself?' Queenie asked.

'That's about the strength of it, yes.'

'But don't you realise that every time I speak to her I shall be biting my tongue? I shall be visualising her in that van knowing she is betraying my son.'

Jim slipped his arm from around her shoulders and turned to face her direct. 'Queenie,' he said quietly, as he deliberately stared into her eyes, '*why* do you think I asked you to marry me?'

'I don't honestly know. I s'pose we were always good friends and circumstances had thrown us together. If truth be known, we probably needed each other. After all, you'd lost Jane and I'd lost Sam. To that extent you could say it was inevitable.'

Jim gave a little false laugh. 'Whatever it was, it certainly wasn't inevitable. You see,' he reached out and took both her hands, 'when Jane was killed I thought my own life had fallen apart, but then, one way and another, I knew I was falling in love with you. When that first happened it could easily have been an emotional reaction. Jane was dead and I needed someone to take her place. But that was not the case. After Jane died, I had quite a few years before you were widowed. During that time I met several women, yet after knowing each of them for a short time, I knew I would never marry again unless you were free. Of course, you were still a beautiful woman but so were several of those others. What they didn't seem to have was your dedication, consideration and loyalty. The Queenie I fell in love with would never take the action you're proposing now.'

'Are you saying I am no longer the woman you married? Is that it?'

'No, I'm not. What I *am* saying to you, though, is that

what you are proposing would have been unthinkable to the woman I fell in love with.'

'You spoke of loyalty,' Queenie said defensively. 'Am I not showing loyalty to my son who has been betrayed by his own wife?'

'Forget the phrase "his own wife" for a moment, because it is very convenient and enables you to distance Grace from your own conscience. Instead, let's substitute "daughter" because that is what she virtually was to you. Once she had lost her parents, you and Sam practically raised her. She became almost as much a part of your family as your own two children. *She* didn't choose that; *you* did. So don't you think you owe *her* a little loyalty?'

'No, I don't!' Queenie snapped angrily, wrenching her hands free. 'There's a limit to everything and that includes my tolerance. I think that young lady has now gone beyond those limits and it's time it was pointed out to her.'

Jim's eyes narrowed. For a moment he looked placid enough but she was by now too aware of his mannerisms not to know that his thoughts were racing.

'I was hoping I wouldn't have to say this, Queenie, but desperate times call for desperate measures. Can you tell me then what Grace has done – not what you *suspect* she has done but what you actually *know* she has done – that you never did when you were her age? Think about it carefully before you answer. You're blaming her for being in the taxi, but you have no proof. You are saying she went out to a dance hall without her husband knowing, but you went night after night to a club that was littered with half the cut-throats and whores of south London! You saw her kissing, perhaps even embracing, a fellow in a cab. Well, that's doubtless true. But how about me? Didn't you kiss me when you were still married to Sam? Oh, for God's sake, Queenie, can't you see? I'm just about clinging on to this family – my family – by my fingertips. I want that family to remain intact. I need that family. Don't cut us adrift, I beg you!'

93

'Have you had these thoughts simmering for long?' Queenie said quietly.

'Ten minutes, I'd say. I haven't been harbouring them for months if that's what's worrying you. Come on, love, give it a try, eh?'

She turned her head away quickly but not before he glimpsed a solitary tear escape from the corner of her eye. 'Okay, but I can't say how long we have before the thing blows up. I'll try to be good, but I can't sit on this keg forever; it's dynamite. So don't get too close to it or you might get caught in the blast.'

Jim placed one finger under her chin and slowly turned her head back to face him. Leaning forward he kissed the single tear that by now had trickled halfway down her cheek. 'C'mon, old girl,' he whispered. 'I've still got faith in that lass. It will be all right, I know it will. I can feel it.'

Queenie gave a wry smile. 'Like I say, Jim, you are *so* gullible for a pretty face and a good figure.'

Jim paused for a moment before replying thoughtfully, 'Well, I'm not so sure about that. Perhaps you should take me to bed and demonstrate your theory. After all, you still fit that particular role perfectly. But I warn you, I shall resist bravely.'

'Shame on you, Jim Forsythe!' she reprimanded. 'And you nearly a pensioner!'

A few minutes later, whilst Queenie was in the bath and before Jim's bravery could be put to the test, the telephone rang. Queenie heard Jim give their number but could not make out his replies. She then heard the receiver being placed on the table and the bathroom door suddenly opened.

'It's Grace,' Jim said quietly. 'She's in a call box. She wants to know if you'll be at home tomorrow afternoon. She wants to talk to you.'

Leaving a trail of water in her wake, Queenie raced from the bathroom with the towel barely covering her shoulders. She snatched up the telephone. 'Hullo . . . Yes . . . Of course.

No, Jim won't be here . . . Yes, certainly . . . Okay . . . About four thirty. Will you be fetching Benjamin? . . . I see. Okay . . . Till then . . . 'bye.' She replaced the receiver and stared at it for a few moments, and only then was aware that Jim had adjusted her towel.

'You'll catch your death running about like that when you're wet,' he said quietly. 'C'mon, either dry yourself or get back into that hot water.'

'I think I might already be in it,' Queenie muttered. 'That is judging by the tone of my daughter-in-law's voice.'

'I think I got the gist of it,' Jim said. 'I take it she didn't want me here, right?'

'She not only didn't want you here but she didn't want anyone else, and that includes my grandson. As soon as David goes on duty, she's going to leave their flat and hopes to arrive here well before you come home. Well, Jim, love. It looks like you won't have to wait very long for the explosion now.'

'So what's happening to Ben?'

'Her friend Sheila is having him,' Queenie replied, stepping back into the bath.

'So, how d'you feel about it? Her coming here I mean?' Jim asked.

'I feel quite relaxed about it now. I know you meant well, Jim, but it's something that needs to be faced and the sooner the better. I'm only pleased for our sakes that it was her who actually suggested the meeting. It's time it was aired.'

Jim prefaced his reply with the deepest sigh she had ever heard him give. 'Women!' he finally lamented. 'I'll never bloody understand them as long as I live.'

'By that, do I take it you are now no longer interested in my face-and-figure theory?'

'You take it damn right!' he snapped, as he wheeled away from her and slammed the bathroom door. She watched him go with a rueful glance as she blew his retreating figure a silent kiss.

Next morning, Jim was in no better humour and, after a silent breakfast, the dry, forehead-brushing kiss came as no great surprise to Queenie. 'D'you want to tell me what time you'll be home?' she asked, as he picked up his briefcase and made for the door.

'Dunno,' he grunted. 'But certainly not before the inquisition has made its final judgment.'

As the door slammed behind him, Queenie glanced up at the clock. 'Seven thirty!' she muttered. 'Is that all? Still nine whole hours to go! It'll seem like an eternity.' She closed her eyes and, not for the first time, wished fervently she had never stumbled into Billie's bathroom that night.

Within the first hour of that 'eternity', Jim had reached his office on the fourth floor at Scotland Yard. As he sat in his chair, he stared hypnotised at the shiny black telephone standing on the corner of his desk. Finally breaking the spell, he reached out, unhooked the receiver and dialled Rodney Road police station.

'Chief Inspector Fanshaw, please, Superintendent Forsythe here.' He drummed his fingers as the line went quiet for a few seconds. 'Hullo, George? Oh, Jim here. Wonder if you can do me a personal favour? You remember the fatal accident in the Old Kent Road last week? . . . Yes that's right. Well, there was a lady's pendant with a broken chain found at the scene . . . Yes, yes, that's the one. Has it been valued by a jeweller yet? . . . It has? Oh, good. And what was the verdict? . . . It's *unique*? So, how much did he say it was worth? . . . Ye gods! As much as that? Thanks, George, thanks a lot. Gladys and the kids okay? . . . Yes, thanks, she's very well. Okay, George, much obliged. See you soon.' He replaced the receiver thoughtfully and resumed drumming his fingers on the desk top. 'Well,' he muttered, 'that's theory number one down the drain. So where to now?'

Queenie Forsythe stared at the clock for what seemed to be

the hundredth time. Only minutes to go. She had known the day would be long but even so, she had still not been prepared for such a tortuous wait. At first she could not understand her own anxiety. After all, she had already experienced more tragedy in her life than any normal woman could expect. She had taken deaths, poverty, rejection, violence, gangsterism and a war almost in her stride. Why then was her mouth so dry and foul-tasting simply at the thought of her son's wife knocking at the door? Before she could ponder further, there it was, just one fairly ordinary everyday knock. She entered the hall and paused at the mirror long enough to smooth her dress and straighten an imaginary strand of loose hair. The words she had rehearsed a score of times had totally vanished from her mind.

Slipping the catch, she eased back the door. The pale face she saw almost stunned her by its delicacy and perfection. That the girl was a beauty was never in doubt, yet that pale unpainted complexion above a dress entirely of black, should have portrayed a ghostlike quality. Instead it radiated such a vulnerable little-girl-lost look, that Queenie's first instinct was to gather the girl in her arms, tuck her up in bed and tell her Santa would come in the night. The older woman tried desperately to reassemble her thoughts as if a spell had been cast. Meantime, Grace stood immobile at the door as if waiting for an instant verdict. Can this be the same girl? thought Queenie. Can this be the one who was almost a whore before she was married? And who, since she has married, lies, cheats and fornicates? Surely not? 'Come in,' she invited, before adding almost as an afterthought, 'my dear.'

She led the girl through the hall and into the large comfortable room where she and Jim had so painfully argued the previous evening. 'I've got the kettle on,' said Queenie, 'so tea won't be long.'

'I don't want any tea, thank you,' said Grace politely.

'Well I jolly well do,' responded Queenie, the spell suddenly broken. 'My mouth's tasted like a farmyard since I woke up this morning.'

A few minutes later, with the tea-tray between them, the combatants sat on either side of the fireplace and faced each other.

'As you were the one that phoned,' began Queenie, 'I assume you're the one with something to say. The floor's yours.'

The girl gave a wan smile. 'I can't believe you won't also have something to say, Queenie, but I take your point. I obviously know from Sheila that you called when I was out.'

'When you were out?' echoed Queenie. '*Out?* D'you mean when you were making love with a fellow in a van until almost midnight? Is that what "out" means nowadays?'

'If you're going to pick up every word I say without really listening to me, Queenie, then this visit will be a waste of time surely?'

'Well you're the one who wanted it, dear, not me,' Queenie retorted.

'That's not really true, is it? You and I know each other fairly well and I'd say if I didn't come to visit you, you'd soon have been knocking on my door with all the risk that entails. Can I continue?' Queenie gave a tight-lipped nod. 'I know exactly what you're thinking and believe me you couldn't be more wrong. You were first suspicious of me when you saw the cut on my arm, yes?' Again Queenie nodded. 'Then, to your mind, your suspicions were confirmed when you discovered that I was out when you called. Right?'

'No, wrong. In fact totally wrong. The fact that you were out was nothing compared to the fact that your own friend admitted that you were frequently out when David – your husband, mark you – was working four till midnight. In other words, it was a long-standing deception.'

'No, Queenie, no,' Grace replied. 'It just wasn't like that at all! I swear it wasn't. Look, I honestly love David, but as I look to the future, I can't see anything changing in my life. The years are slipping by and before I know where I am, I'm going to realise my life is over and I've been nowhere and done nothing.'

'You and millions of others,' said Queenie. 'Surely you gave this a thought when you agreed to marry him.'

'Of course, I did! But I was barely eighteen! Nevertheless, I made those vows and I will stand by them. But marriage, even in Queen's Buildings, should not be a lifetime penance, surely? I love to dance, you know that. Everyone who knows me knows it. David can't stand dancing, so twice a week I go to the Palais where I dance and I love it. It's glamour, it's sparkle, it's everything that I do not have when I'm sitting at home watching the bed bugs climb the wall whilst my husband is at work. I can only do this when David is four-to-midnight and he only does that particular shift twice every six weeks. Oh, I know I should have told him, and that's worried me. But supposing I did tell him and supposing he said I can't go, or we can't afford it. What then?'

'So, how *do* you afford it?' Queenie asked.

'I go free. The manager pays me just to go there and dance with the customers who are there on their own.'

'You mean you are a hired dance-hall trollop?'

'If you want to put it like that, yes, I suppose I am.'

'What other way *is* there to put it? And this money. How much is it and how do you explain it to David?'

'It's five shillings a night and I don't have to explain it because I don't keep it. I give it to Sheila for sitting with Benjamin. It's a convenient situation. She's saving up to get married and earns herself five bob each evening and I get four hours' free dancing.'

'So how about the fellow – and before you say *what* fellow, I'll tell you – the one in the black van. The one who kissed you and managed a quick romp with you about half past eleven the other evening when the rain was coming down in stair rods. How about him?'

'But I had to cadge a lift home because the rain was torrential,' Grace said.

'So that's okay then, is it? If it's raining, anything goes? Kisses, gropes or whatever happens to be on the menu in the old van for that particular evening?'

'Look!' sighed Grace. 'If only you'd been closer, you'd have seen what happened. Yes, I certainly let him kiss me. He'd been waiting for me for almost an hour and I thought it was the least I could do. But having done that, he thought he had carte blanche to do anything else. He had his hand inside my coat and two buttons off my blouse before I drew breath. If you'd seen the scratches I left on his face, you might have formed a different opinion.'

Queenie stared at the girl in silence for a minute or so, obviously choosing a careful reply.

'Grace, are you trying to tell me that the cut on your arm, the dancing, the kiss, or whatever you like to call it in the car, plus the woman in the taxi in the Old Kent Road, are all one bloody great coincidence?'

'Not at all. I'm telling you that the cut most certainly is a coincidence but I'm telling you that you have taken all the rest and made it fit your theory. In any case, as far as I understand, the accident in the Old Kent Road was about four in the morning, so that lets me out surely?'

'Not really,' replied Queenie. 'Because David was on night-duty and he would not have been home until six thirty at the earliest, and I'd like to ask you one other important question. Did you ever have a blue pair of earrings with a pair of entwined roses embossed on them?'

'Yes, I did. I had them at my wedding, as a matter of fact.'

'Did you have any other jewellery that matched them and if so, where is it now?'

'No, that was the only piece I had and I lost both earrings ages ago when Benjamin had just begun to crawl. I could only guess that he hid them somewhere. Anyway, I've not seen them since. Why'd you ask?'

'Something similar was found by the cab door in that fatal accident.'

'Well, don't look at me,' Grace replied.

'Grace,' said Queenie, rising from her chair and walking to the window, 'the main purpose of your visit today is that David should not know about these excursions of yours, right?' The girl nodded. 'So what would happen in future – about these free dance evenings, I mean, if I promise to let the matter rest?'

'I would give them up, of course.'

'Willingly?'

'Anything but willingly,' the girl shrugged philosophically. 'But then, you know what they say about beggars?'

'Very much so!' replied Queenie sharply. 'I've been one! But that's not the point we're discussing. *That* point is, everything you say *could* just about be right. In addition to that, as I listen to you speaking about your frustrations at home, I heard myself saying much the same words twenty-odd years ago. I do hope you weren't aware of that, because if you were, I would smell a very big rat indeed. But until I actually get a whiff of the creature, I'll keep my peace. That is, of course, unless I find you're lying to me, then the roof really would fall in.' She nodded towards the tea-tray. 'The pot's cold, shall I put the kettle on again?'

Grace's pale face broke into its first delicate smile. 'Yes, I think I'd like that very much now, thank you.'

As Queenie bent to gather up the tea-tray, she asked casually, 'And how is the cut on your arm? You're taking good care of it, I hope?'

'Yes,' said Grace somewhat unconvincingly. 'When you saw it at Billie's, it was only bleeding because I'd moved the dressing accidentally.'

'Well, actually,' responded Queenie. 'I never did see it that clearly; you were a bit coy as I remember. May I look at it now? I shall only worry about it unless I can be sure it's not infected.' With that, she reached out to slip back the sleeve of the black dress. Although the words appeared to have been formed in the nature of a polite request, there was a harshness in the tone that Grace knew would be impossible to resist. Almost trance-like, she offered her arm and, by raising the sleeve, the soggy stained dressing was revealed.

'But, Grace!' exclaimed Queenie anxiously, 'it's still weeping! Come into the kitchen, I've some clean dressings in there.'

The girl followed her without a word and within a few minutes, Queenie had eased off the encrusted lint to reveal an angry deep straight cut that was weeping a messy discharge. Queenie looked at her daughter-in-law with concern. 'Grace, dear, this needs a doctor. You must know that, surely?'

Grace hastily slipped down the sleeve. 'No,' she said defensively. 'It'll be all right with a clean-up, you'll see. I don't want to bother any doctor with it. They have enough to do as it is.'

'Grace,' insisted Queenie firmly, 'let's have no argument, please. We're going to the hospital *now*!'

Thirty minutes later a young Irish doctor turned up a rather sensitive nose as he removed the temporary dressing. 'And ye say ye did this on a flower pot, me darlin'?' As the girl nodded nervously, he said, 'Ter be sure, me lovely, the Little People must have been livin' in it an' ye no doubt upset them. It's a nasty infected cut to be sure but ye'll nae be dying. But I'd be a touch more careful in the future if I were ye.' He lifted his gaze from the wound and shot a quick disbelieving glance up at Queenie. 'I'll clean it and stitch it for ye an' ye'll need to come back an' see all us good people agin in a week or so. Is that all right wi' ye?'

The girl hesitated, but Queenie was quickly in to confirm. 'Of course, she will, doctor, I'll make sure of it.'

Twelve stitches and two hours later, Queenie stopped her car at the entrance to Grace's building. 'Are you sure you don't want me to come up with you?'

'Positive, Mum,' said the girl as she leaned forward and

kissed the older woman warmly. 'And thank you for everything you have done today. I'll not forget it.'

'And David? What will you tell him?'

'The truth, Mum, just the truth.'

As Queenie watched the girl disappear into the dark recesses of the building, she glanced at her watch. Though she had no idea of the time of Jim's return, she knew he could not remain angry for long and she suspected he would be home already. As she drove her car into her driveway some thirty minutes later, she could see through the curtains that her guess was not wrong.

Putting down his paper as she entered, he looked up. 'Well, how'd it go? Am I still a father and grandfather, or have you made me an orphan?'

'No, you don't have to worry any more. You're still loved, you don't have to seek adoption.'

'And you're totally convinced your daughter-in-law is not a loose woman?'

Queenie gave wry smile. 'Stupid, yes. Even unthinking, but loose? No, not loose.'

'And the late nights and the capers in the van, all that's now to your satisfaction?'

'More or less,' Queenie nodded.

'Wow!' he exclaimed. 'All I need to hear now is that you accept that she didn't cut herself in the taxi and I'll be a fully fledged grandad once again.'

'In that case, you'll be delighted to know she definitely did not cut herself in that taxi. Nor indeed on the balcony with the plant pots.'

'Good,' he replied. 'So where did she do it then?'

'Oh, that?' said Queenie as casually as she could. 'She did it in her flat when she was attempting suicide.'

7

In the early stages, the hour of Wonky Lines' departure from Blackfriars had stood him in good stead. In fact, until he reached Sidcup, there was little in the way of traffic to concern him, but by the time he approached Swanley, the sound of horns, the fumes of exhausts and the jeers from the windows of passing traffic, constantly filled the air. His pedalling, sweating figure on his wobbling, creaking bike, seemed to present a verbal magnet for every idiot between London and Maidstone. 'Git orf an' milk it!' seemed to be the popular phrase of the day.

For the first mile or so, Pieshop had shown signs of agitation but, philosophically, he had soon settled down in his basket and left the worrying to Wonky. Mentally, Wonky had set aside six hours to complete his journey and it was therefore late morning as, with aching legs and burning buttocks, he pushed his bike over the level crossing at Wateringbury station. Once clear of the railway lines, he had intended to resume his ride but his limbs rebelled so much that the mere thought of squatting on that saddle again filled him with horror. Besides, in the distance, he could see the lines of huts that were ranged around the misty hillock. Once through the gate Pieshop was easily persuaded out of his basket.

In the hopfields, there was always a carnival atmosphere about Saturday mornings. Picking would cease at one o'clock and everyone would return to the huts in jubilant mood to prepare to face the swarm of visitors who would be descending later in the day. There was shopping to be done, beds to be aired, wood to be cut and water to be drawn, fires to be built and the hillside lavatories to be cleaned out and fumigated.

Most hopfields could be reached by train from London Bridge, with motorcycles and sidecars, vans, lorries, cars, ponies-and-traps and tandems filling the Maidstone and Tonbridge roads. Though many of these visitors would be the cause of great excitement, others would cause some heart sinking. To spend a weekend with friends anywhere can be stressful but with an average of a dozen people of mixed ages in a one-bedded twelve-by-fourteen hut without lavatory or running water, could tax nostrils and friendship to the borders of insanity.

Even if visitors were not expected, there were still chores to be carried out. With nine children, three adults, four puppies, one dog and a budgie in the Wilkinson family, a hut could become fairly pungent by the end of the week. It was therefore customary for one adult plus a couple of the older children to remain at the hut on Saturday morning to make a start on the weekly tasks. Easily the most unpopular of these was the drawing of water. Wateringbury, unlike many other hopfields, drew its water from a spring. This necessitated carrying two empty buckets for a quarter-mile to the edge of the woods and two full buckets back. At least this was the theory, but though the buckets may have been full on leaving the spring, they would be best-part empty by the time they returned to the huts. Of the remainder, half would be slopped along the pathway and the rest into the Wellington boots of the poor infant deputed to carry it. Water carrying, as opposed to fire lighting, was considered a child's task as other than trench foot, there was little damage even the most careless of youngsters could inflict with a bucket of water.

Outside number thirty-two in a row of huts, a head-scarfed, coarse-aproned, ragged-jerseyed, slightly smudged Esther Wilkinson had draped an enormous straw mattress over four chairs to catch the first rays of the morning sunshine.

With nine young children and three adults sleeping on it nightly, a good airing was the most urgent task of the day. By virtue of their position on the top of the hill, these huts were the first to emerge from the morning mists. Meanwhile, Terry and Teresa Wilkinson were raking over the cold ashes from the previous day's fire to salvage any dry sticks for kindling.

'Essie!' called Teresa, pointing down the hill, 'ain't that the dog that fetched us 'ere?'

'Dog that fetched . . .' Esther began. 'Oh, no, it's Mister Lines! Oh!' Panic-stricken, she looked frantically about her. 'I won't be a minute, kids.' With that she rushed into the hut and closed the squeaking door quickly behind her.

At first, even though both children stared at him, Wonky could not remember which hut housed the Wilkinsons. After all, Wilkinson kids simply looked like everybody else's. Besides, being stared at proved nothing – most kids stared at him. It was when the pair of them called out to Pieshop that the mystery was solved. 'H-hullo, you t-two,' he greeted. 'Are your m-mum or s-sisters about?'

The hut door was suddenly flung open and Esther Wilkinson stood posed with one hand on her broad hips and the other pointing dramatically at a couple of empty buckets. 'Teresa! Terence! Would yer please fill these, there's good children.'

In the short time since she had first seen Wonky approach, Esther had managed to divest herself of her coarse apron and jersey and had changed into a tired short-sleeved blouse with a hanging bra strap and a pleated skirt that had lost most of its pleats. She had probably wiped her face with a licked handkerchief, because though the smudges had not fully gone, they were certainly diluted. 'Why, Mr Lines!' she exclaimed girlishly as she tried tucking her bra strap unobtrusively back into her blouse, 'what a surprise! It's naughty of yer not to tell us you were comin' because I would have changed into somethin' a bit more suitable. Still,' she said, smoothing down her eyebrows with a licked finger, 'Mum'll be pleased to see yer. Are yer staying with us? I'm sure yer'd be very welcome; we have no other guests this weekend.'

'Er w-well,' began Wonky as he realised in his quest for sanctuary that he had completely forgotten the grating tone of the Wilkinsons' voices. 'Y-yes, that w-would be very n-nice, if you're s-sure your m-mum wouldn't m-mind. I'm afraid I h-haven't much b-bedding, though.'

'Bedding's no problem, Mr Lines,' she laughed. 'Once all of us are tucked up tight fer the night, there ain't really a call for it. But how did yer get here – yer didn't bike all the way surely?'

'I d-did indeed, miss, and w-while I th-think of it, might I h-have a w-wash or s-something?'

'Oh, of course, Mr Lines, of course.' She turned to the two children who had been watching the peculiar antics of their sister with open mouths. 'Now, Terence, now, Teresa, what have I told yer? Run along now and get Mr Lines some water.'

Giving each child a persuasive nudge, she set them in the general direction of the spring and turned her attention once more to her guest.

'They won't be long, Mr Lines, but unless yer can wait for the fire to build up, I'm afraid it'll have to be cold water.'

'C-cold water'll do just f-fine, Miss W-Wilkinson, just f-fine.'

'I hope yer don't mind me saying so, Mr Lines, but don't yer think it's time we used our Christian names? I mean, I can't keep calling yer "Mr", now can I? And I'd certainly like yer to call me Esther. Or, as yer're now already a friend, perhaps Essie?'

'W-Well, most people c-call me W-Wonky,' he offered.

'Oh, I couldn't possibly be so forward,' she murmured shyly. 'What's yer proper name?'

'C-Claude, I'm afraid.'

108

'*Claude?* Oh, how wonderful!' Esther screamed. 'I should think it's probably Roman, isn't it? Those dignified names usually are. But look, yer've biked all the way down here and I've not even offered yer a mug of tea, and not only that, yer must also be starvin'. Now I've got the fire going again I can put the kettle on. We also have some bread and cheese if that's any help?'

Whilst Wonky was most certainly thirsty, the mention of food also reminded him just how hungry he was. 'I'd g-give away me s-soul for s-some bread and cheese, Essie, I really w-would.'

Dropping her eyes, Esther nudged him with her hips. 'Perhaps yer'd throw it in my direction in that case, Claude, eh?' she giggled.

Wonky suddenly looked at the whole scene with mixed emotions. He knew he needed food and drink, he suspected he needed a wash, but by the way this lass was acting, he might well be in for a third option, but he wasn't sure if he was strictly ready for it. No, he must be firm, it was the only way. 'W-Well, it ain't m-much of a s-soul, Essie,' he said. 'So I don't th-think you'd b-be gettin' a v-very good b-bargain.'

'S'all right, Claude,' Esther said, clinging to his arm. 'It ain't much of a sandwich.'

'B-But I'm so exhausted with h-hunger,' he pleaded, 'th-that I need tea and a s-sandwich before I'd be f-fit f-for anything.'

Before she could make a reply, the sound of approaching children's voices reminded them that the water was on its way.

'Sit yerself down on that log by the fire then, Claude,' Esther said. 'I'll do yer a sandwich and find some biscuits for yer dog.'

Whether it really was the best sandwich he had had in his life is debatable but he certainly spent enough time claiming that it was. But after a forty-mile ride on the instrument of torture that had almost wrecked his manhood, most things would have tasted memorable. If the sandwich had been debatable, the tea certainly wasn't. He found the strong sweet smoke-tinted liquid a pure elixir.

'I know,' she agreed as she edged alongside him, 'it's the wood smoke that does it. Only known it to fail once.'

'When was th-that?' he muttered into the big china mug.

'Last year, when Danny and Mickey had an accident.'

'An accident? W-was it b-bad?'

'Well, it was all right for them, but it wasn't for us. Y'see, if yer want to use the lavatory, yer have to walk up that hill to the little shed on the top. Well, it gets pitch black here at night and yer can't expect the kids ter walk up there in the dark by themselves, so they all share a little potty. But they're supposed to be very careful where they empty it. Well, the little sods weren't. Yep,' she nodded, 'that's right. According to Mickey, Danny tipped in the lot and the little buggers never mentioned a word about it until everyone thought they'd been poisoned at their first mouthful. There are times I hate my brothers, Claude. I really hate the disgustin' little sods.'

Having demolished a second sandwich and a further two mugs of tea, Wonky slowly felt life ebb back. 'D'you th-think I could h-have me w-wash now, p-please?'

'Of course!' Esther replied leaping to her feet. 'If yer just want a quick wash, we have the big basin there on the table, but if you want ter do all yer joints, you can carry the table into the hut and strip off. I think the water's hot enough now anyway.'

'I th-think I'll take it into th-the hut, if you d-don't m-mind?'

'Good!' she exclaimed, 'I'll give yer a hand with the table and show yer where everythin' is.'

. Lifting one end of the table, Wonky entered the hut backwards as Esther directed from the other end. His first surprise was the floor. It was uneven and consisted entirely of pressed soil with the odd sacking mat scattered casually around. The lime-washed wooden walls were mainly covered by several lengths of wallpaper which, in turn, were affixed by a generous line of drawing pins. Wedged tightly in one corner of the room was a huge wooden box with the caged budgie perched in its centre. Alongside, were four chairs, each in various stages of disrepair but just about capable of taking a moderate weight and a dirty white dog together with four puppies in a basket. On the opposite side of the room was a full-size green-painted dresser displaying an assortment of ill-focused family snapshots, two rows of chipped plates, a dozen mugs and a large brass oil lamp. But three quarters of the space in the hut was taken up by the base of the massive bed. This consisted of many bundles of long sticks, or faggots, as they were usually called. These faggots served two purposes – they could be used for the bed base with the huge straw-filled mattress draped over them or they could be used for fuel. There was usually an enormous stack of them at the rear of each row of huts that would be replenished from time to time by the farmer.

'But wh-where d'you all s-sleep; you've only one b-bed?'

'There can only ever be *one* bed at hoppin',' she explained. 'There's not a hut on this hopfield that's got room fer two beds.'

He looked around him. 'S-so where d'you all s-sleep?' he persisted. 'Th-there's a b-bloody dozen of y-you?'

'I've just told yer!' Esther cried, and pointed to the bed. 'In there; we top an' tail. Half at the bottom, half at the top. Everyone does it that way.'

'Wh-what! You mean like s-sardines?' he asked incredulously.

'Just like sardines – but without the oil of course. Though when yer've spent a warm night with someone's foot stuffed under yer nose, yer do begin ter wonder.'

'B-But how about—' he faltered, hardly able to bring himself to mention the word, 'v-visitors?'

'Them as well,' Esther answered cheerfully. 'The more the merrier!'

111

He shook his head and stared around him. The dividing walls between their hut and the huts on either side did not quite reach the corrugated-iron roof. 'Does anyone l-live over th-there?' he whispered, nodding to the partition.

'O'course,' she replied. 'Every hut's full, didn't yer notice?'

'Yes, b-but . . .' he began, '. . .b-but, well, wh-what about pr-privacy?'

Esther burst into a peal of laughter. 'Privacy? At hop-picking? Bless yer, Claude, there's no such thing!' She pointed to the bed base. 'What with sticks underneath and straw on the top, yer can hear 'em turn over in bed three huts away!'

'But wh-what happens when someone sleeping in the c-centre of the bed want t-to get out – say in the m-middle of the night?'

She shrugged. 'Then they either wait till mornin' or they climb over everyone. There's no such thing as a weak bladder at hop-picking, Claude. That'd be very unpopular. Anyway, if yer care ter start undressin' I'll get yer a towel and fetch in yer hot water. We usually stand it in the bowl on the big hopping box there in the corner.'

'Er—' he looked around anxiously.

'Like I say, Claude,' she said with a sly wink, 'there's no such thing as privacy at hop-picking, though if yer under six, the Salvation Army will bath yer fer a penny on Sundays. Anyway, speakin' of bathin', I could do with a good wash-down meself. Still, if it makes yer less shy, I'll send the kids away down the orchards to swipe some apples; they always enjoy that.' The door squeaked as she quickly left the hut and called to the children. 'Terry, Teresa, go down to the orchard on the other side of the hopfields, we could do with some apples for pudden. But don't go past the farmhouse, y'understand? Go the long way round so no one sees yer, okay?'

'Can we take Pieshop?'

'Providin' he wants ter go, yes.'

However, in spite of the children's persistent invitation,

Pieshop's refusal to open even one eye indicated the complete canine indifference to green apples.

Wonky had just removed his sweat-soaked shirt and was sitting on the faggots to ease off his boots, when the door again squeaked open. Esther, with consummate ease, was carrying in a huge, steaming, black iron kettle with a two-gallon capacity. His instincts told him he should offer assistance, but he knew she could handle the thing far better alone. 'Claude! What on earth have yer been doin'?' she screeched. 'I thought yer'd be all stripped off by now.' She thudded the kettle down on top of the box and began to unbutton her blouse. 'Yer not going ter go all shy on me, are yer? After all, yer know the old sayin', don't yer? You wash my back an' I'll wash yours.'

'I th-think the word is scratch not w-wash,' he corrected helpfully.

Esther tiptoed up and planted the lightest of kisses upon his cheek. 'Sorry, me old Claude, but yer wrong there. For four weeks in this place, y'do nothin' *but* bleedin' scratch. Take it from me, no matter who does it for yer, scratchin' is really bleedin' boring. It's *washin'* that's the fun! C'mon, stand up an' we'll help each other.'

'W-Well shouldn't we put the w-water in the bowl f-first?' he asked. 'Otherwise, if we weren't careful, w-we could have a n-nasty accident.'

He had hardly spoken the words when he was leaping back as she poured out the steaming water in a swirling cascade that raced around the inside of the bowl and over the edge like the rogue wave of a mini typhoon.

Esther clapped her hand quickly to her mouth in mock horror. 'My good Gawd!' she muttered. 'Nearly done yer a right mischief there, didn't I? Anyway,' she added, wriggling out of her blouse, 'no real harm done, let's get washing before we really do have a mishap.'

Wonky's reactions were veering consistently between that of a bewildered virgin and a randy rake. Whilst anything was

113

better than running foul of the obnoxious Sid and his thugs, he wasn't really sure how far he could reach for the fruit without pulling the whole damn Wilkinson tree down on his head. Still, he couldn't fudge it for ever; a decision had to be made sometime. Throwing caution to the Kentish wind, he reached across and unfastened the remaining buttons of Esther's blouse and tugged it off her plump white shoulders. Though this move took up most of his attention, he was vaguely aware that she had made some movement towards the dresser and had pushed over one of the snapshots. Giving it little thought, he noticed the bra strap that had originally been dislodged when she had attempted her quick change was still hanging seductively off her plump left breast. He had just evened up the balance by tugging down the right strap when the door creaked open behind him.

'Oh, so this is what you're up to when you're s'posed ter be cleaning the hut, eh? There I am, lookin' after your kid and half-a-dozen brothers and sisters, to say nothin' of pickin' bleedin' hops till me bleedin' fingers fall off, an' all the time you're here planning ter have it away with good old bleedin' Wonky!'

'I wasn't "planning" anythin' of the kind,' protested Esther.

'Oh, no? Not bloody much yer weren't! How about that?' She pointed to the photograph that now lay on the dresser. 'If you hadn't *planned* anything, what's me photo doin' face down then? I know you, Essie Wilkinson; it was pricking yer conscience weren't it? And I'll bet that wasn't the only bit of yer yer were hoping would be pricked.'

'You're only jealous, Evie,' protested Esther to her sister.

'*Jealous! Jealous!*' screeched Evelyn. 'Of course I'm bleedin' jealous! Wouldn't you be, you inconsiderate bleedin' cow? I've been sitting on the side of that bleedin' hop-bin just thinkin' how long it was since I had a bit of the other and what do I find when I come back? Dear old Wonky happily playin' with me sister's knockers!'

'P-Perhaps I c-can explain,' offered Wonky. 'Y'see, it's n-not like it s-seems at all. I'm a bit s-sweaty and E-Essie o-offered . . .'

'Oh, yer don't have ter tell me what Essie offered. I can *see* what Essie offered.'

'B-But we were only w-washing!' he protested. 'We were g-going to w-wash each other's b-backs, that's all.'

'Fine!' announced Evelyn, tugging up her hop-stained jersey. 'If yer'd like ter collect the mattress an' come in an' shut the door, yer can wash mine as well.'

Wonky was suddenly seized by a terrifying thought. Before he could make any further decision he had to know the answer to one vital question that was almost paralysing him with fear. 'Wh-where's your m-mother?'

'Me muvver?' asked the puzzled Evelyn. 'Still down the hopfield with all the bleedin' kids, I expect. Why? Yer don't plan ter wash *her* back as well, do yer?'

'And sh-she'll be s-staying th-there?' he persisted. 'For s-some little t-time, I m-mean.'

'Mum? Of course she'll be stayin' there. I've just told yer, she's got all the kids. But I don't understand all this sudden concern about our mum? We're big girls. We can take care of ourselves.'

'I know,' agreed Wonky, nervously making for the door. 'B-But your mum's a "big girl" too, in fact a *v-very* b-big girl! I know 'cos I've s-seen her and I'm n-not washing *her* b-bloody b-back, I c-can tell you!'

Both girls screeched with laughter as, tugging his shirt around him, Wonky slipped nervously from the hut.

Pieshop had now recovered a little of his enthusiasm and trotted dutifully up to his master and made a half-hearted attempt at a tail-wag. Wonky dropped down a hand and gave the dog a token head scratch. Squatting down on a huge log, he began to assess his situation. There was no doubt the two sisters were not going to ease up. In fact they had probably reached the stage where it was now a question of honour between them who would be the first to lay him. Providing he could shut out their voices, he had no great aversion to being laid by either; but two together he found more than daunting.

From within the closed hut came the sound of the sisters' voices in tones that were about as seductive as they could manage. They repeatedly called, 'Claude, in here, Claude.' Wonky had a vague recollection of once reading a book about sailors who were lured onto rocks by the melodic voices of mermaids. Well, no one could think the Wilkinson sisters were melodic nor did they resemble mermaids, though when he had last seen Essie she was similarly attired.

'In here, Claude,' they persisted. 'The water's warm an' it's washtime.'

'It's all right f-for you, P-Pieshop,' he muttered, ruefully picking up the enormous mattress. 'You don't h-have th-those problems. Y-You can s-scatter your s-seeds where you l-like, do a runner and f-forget it.' The dog laid his head on his master's thigh and stared up in abject sympathy.

'Claude, darlin',' persisted one voice, 'Muvver an' the kids'll be ages yet. Why'nt yer come in?'

'P-Pieshop, I'm trapped,' Wonky confessed, rising to his feet. 'I've got to m-make the b-best of a b-bad job. If I'm l-laid first by Essie I'll upset Evie; if I'm l-laid by Evie, Essie'll k-kill me. I m-may not get a better t-time to make it an honourable d-draw. See y-you later, b-boy; th-think kindly of m-me.' The door gave its customary creak as he let himself into the hut and tipped the mattress onto the bed base. As an afterthought he turned and bolted the door behind him.

'First time that door's been bolted since the hut was built,' said Essie in thoughtful tones. 'Wonder if he's got wicked thoughts in mind, Evie?'

'I bleedin' hope so!' exclaimed her sister. 'My arse is perished standin' here like this.'

Any doubts Wonky may have harboured were instantly dispelled by the sight of the two sisters – they were as naked as marble statues and about the same temperature and size.

'I'm afraid we've had ter mislead yer a bit, Claude. We're not washin' till later, it's too bleedin' cold. Besides, we don't mind yer bein' a bit sweaty, and we like ter smell a good strong man nearby, don't we, Essie?'

Essie was not replying; she had other matters on her mind as she tugged the buttons on his shirt.

If, in later years, anyone had asked exactly what happened in the next half-hour, Wonky would never have been able to recount it. The whole world seemed to be full of moans, groans and soft pink female flesh. There was so much of it, it took out the daylight and smothered him in the bed. It surrounded him, warmed him and almost obliterated him. It anchored his thighs, spread across his chest and rolled around his face. It was in his hands, filled his mouth and engulfed his ears. At one stage, in a bewildering attempt to decipher a particularly confusing position, he was convinced he had fleetingly seen six nipples. Deciding that six was preferable to three, he dismissed it from his mind as an irrelevance. Throughout the whole session the straw mattress had rustled alarmingly. He had been vaguely aware of it but nothing more. But now, with passion spent, he realised the noise had been something of a warning, the warning being that stiff straw can slide through a well-worn sheet like a hot spike through cold porridge and, with a couple of buxom females bearing down on one's anatomy, the sensation is akin to a forward roll on a bed of nails. Any hoped-for pleasant afterglow was rudely interrupted by a sudden oath from Wonky.

'Bloody hell, girls!' he yelled. 'I've been skinned!'

'Claude!' exclaimed Evelyn. 'Your stutter – it's gone! Yer've been mutterin' all through our little romp and you've not stuttered once!'

'No, I never do when I'm emotional, but never mind about that. What does my back look like?' He twisted round and displayed his broad back to them.

'Well, at the moment,' said Esther, prodding it with a

stubby and none too clean fingernail, 'it looks like a half-hundredweight of chopped liver.'

'We're goin' to have ter clean it up,' said Evelyn as she frowned and pursed her lips in a sympathetic gesture. 'Get the salt, Essie.'

Minutes later, as Wonky bent over a chairback, the girls had washed and dried his wounds and were sprinkling a generous covering of salt from his neck to his buttocks. Wonky's first impression had been of an attack by a dozen blowlamps, but slowly the sheer rawness of the feeling subsided into nothing more than mild agony.

'Just think, Claude,' said Evelyn, washing her hands in the bowl. 'Weren't yer lucky lyin' on yer back! Just think what would've happened if yer were face down! That woulda wiped the smile off of yer carrot an' no mistake!'

Painful though his back was, Wonky certainly saw the wisdom of that observation. 'Phew!' he panted as he fought for breath. 'If this is what usually happens after a bunk-up at this place, how come there're so many kids about?'

'Well, first of all,' explained Evelyn, 'most blokes ain't so considerate as you are. Yer see it's always the girl at the bottom and *them* on top. Then, as they only visit here at weekends, they think everythin' will be healed up just fine for them by next Saturday night. Typical bleedin' men, see? Secondly – well, it *was* a bit of an unusual carry-on. I mean, no one usually does it in threes. An' thirdly, if yer lucky enough ter get half a chance ter plan fer it, yer can usually do it on a couple of sacks of apples. It's a bit nobbly that way, I grant yer, an' it can also bruise yer arse a bit but it ain't half as painful as that straw poking up yer arris!'

There was suddenly a rattling of the door and the sound of a dog barking plus the impression that half the kids in Kent were about to invade the hut.

'Oy, you kids, behave!' The unmistakable sound of Lill Wilkinson boomed into the room and echoed over the partitions and along the whole length of the row of huts.

'Open this door at once, d'yer hear me? What the bleedin' hell's goin' on in there?'

Diving into her skirt and tugging her stained jersey quickly over her head, Evelyn slid back the bolt and the door creaked back to let the bright sunlight stream into the hut.

'What've you two been up to?' demanded the suspicious elder Wilkinson. 'An' who's that in there wiv . . . Oh, it's Mr Lines! Mr Lines, sir, ain't they lovely girls, Mr Lines? Ain't they? I told yer they were, didn't I? All been havin' a nice wash, 'ave we? Oh, that's nice, that's real hygienic that is, Mr Lines. Not like some of 'em down 'ere. No names no pack drill, y'understand, but some of 'em don't see a bar of soap from the time they arrive ter the time they go back. Dunno 'ow they can live like it; bleedin' animals, some of 'em.' She folded her arms across her vast bosom and nodded her head in a particularly satisfied manner. 'Not somethin' they can throw at us though, is it, Mr Lines?' Walking over to the bowl, she dipped her hands in the water. 'Oh, it's still a bit warm. Shame ter waste it,' she said pulling at her grimy overall. 'Shut the door. I fink I'll 'ave a bit of a rinse meself.' The trio of screeching laughter followed Wonky as, for the second time in an hour, he fled the hut. 'Never mind, Claude,' called Esther. 'Perhaps when yer back's better . . .?'

8

Dripping wet, Billie Bardell emerged from her bath and slipped into a fluffy white towelling robe. Crossing the floor, she moved to complete her toilette at the wash basin by the window. Her customary scan of the garden at such times was frustrated by the steam that had begun to run in rivulets down the glass pane. Gathering her robe cuff into her hand, she wiped clear an increasingly large moist circle. Her movements eased to a stop as her attention was attracted by a young man and a young woman who were almost hidden from sight in the large greenhouse at the far corner of the lawn. Without once removing them from her vision, she stretched out her right foot and, with no little difficulty, hooked it around the leg of a nearby stool. Half dragging, half bumping, she finally manoeuvred it into a position where she could sit comfortably without disturbing her gaze. The movements of the young woman appeared to indicate a certain agitation with her male partner. One moment she would be so close that they appeared to be touching, the next there was a clear distance between them. Yet throughout this ritual, the young man hardly moved. Leaning back against a dozen or so sacks of peat, he half sat with arms folded and his feet spread casually apart. Eventually the girl raised high her right arm and appeared to waggle a warning finger at her impassive companion. With effortless speed, the young man suddenly reached out with his own right hand and, clamping her wrist, dragged her quickly to him and between his parted legs. Even from that distance, there was no doubting the intensity of either his hold or his passion. For a brief moment the girl wriggled wildly and for just that length of time, Billie could not be certain if it was from excitement or protestation. Her curiosity was soon satisfied as the girl's arms finally slid smoothly up and around the young man's neck as she appeared almost to bury herself into him. His hands then slipped gradually down her back and, through the silky black dress, began to caress and pull the firm rounded buttocks even tighter into him. The kiss, when it came, was intensely passionate, arousing not a little excitement in the observer.

After a couple of minutes, during which time neither participant had come up for air, Billie turned her head quickly and, over her shoulder, called through the open bathroom door.

'Alice! Here a moment.' The maid, who had been in the process of changing the bed, was still holding a clean pillowcase as she hastened anxiously into the room.

'Your Julia is one strange girl, y'know,' announced Billie shaking her head. 'If I was her age, I'd kill for that young man. It was only a minute ago that she appeared to be giving him a right roasting but he never took a blind bit of notice – and now look what's happened! He's almost eating her.'

'Oh, I'm sorry, Miss Bardell. But she's back on this political thing again and she's fair sendin' me nuts about it. That's what they mainly row about.'

'She's not still on about politics, surely?' asked the incredulous Billie.

'She is, I'm afraid. She reckons she's never really forgiven him for driving that tram in the general strike.'

'Bloody hell, that was four years ago! I must say your daughter certainly has a peculiar way of not forgiving someone. After what I saw a few minutes ago, I shouldn't think he cares if she never forgives him. Anyway, how old is he now? About twenty-two?'

'Somewhere around that, I'd guess,' agreed Alice.

'Well in the 1926 strike he could have only been about

eighteen years old at the very most and she could have only been what – sixteen? She can't still be angry surely?'

'Oh, can't she?' responded Alice despairingly. 'I'm afraid you don't know my Julia. Give her half a chance, miss, and she'll go on for hours.'

'So what has he got to say about it? I should think he must get quite annoyed.'

'Quite the reverse and that's really what makes her so angry; he doesn't get annoyed at all. Frankly, he don't give a jot. He just laughs at her and that makes her worse. Then, when she's really fed up about something, he starts to fuss her and that confuses her even more. I think the problem is, deep down, she's really nuts over him but refuses to admit it even to herself because she feels they are two such totally different people. For example, he reckons he didn't drive the tram to break a strike but because it was "fun". Apparently, he lied about his age and told the authorities he was twenty years old. I'm sure they didn't believe him but, if the truth be known, they probably would have accepted anyone too big for a pram.'

'Just think,' said Billie wistfully, 'being only eighteen and driving a tram! Must be one of the most exciting things in the world! In fact, I wouldn't mind having a go at one myself, even now, at my age.'

'That's as maybe,' said the maid, 'but it can't go on like this. I'll have a word with her, shall I?'

'For goodness sake, don't stop her, Alice. Look, even though she doesn't know it, your Julia is madly in love. Still, perhaps you do have a point. After all, I am paying the pair of them. As my gardener, he should be looking after my spuds and sprouts and not playing with your daughter's bum. And how about her? What was she supposed to be doing today?'

'Well, she *was* supposed to be preparing the salad for lunch. That's why she's in the greenhouse in the first place. I sent her over there for some tomatoes and a cucumber.'

'Well, I'm not sure about the tomatoes, but from what I've

just seen, I think she's got more than a sporting chance of a cucumber.'

'I'll go and get her, shall I, miss?'

Billie rose from her stool and began to dry the base of her scalp. 'No, leave her where she is for a while. Let her enjoy her freedom while she can. Once she gets an old man who knocks her about and a few screaming kids tugging at her apronstrings, she'll nostalgically tell herself that having her bum rubbed in the greenhouse was part of the good old times. Speaking of having your bum rubbed, how's *your* bloke keeping and when are you going to show him off to me? I understand your Julia's not that keen on him?'

'That, Miss Bardell, is the understatement of the year. Since she discovered he knocked me about, she refuses to even meet him. She said if she ever did, she'd knife him. So I think it's wiser to keep them apart.'

'Hasn't she ever seen him, then?'

'No, even without meeting him she hates his guts and makes no secret of it either. It does make life difficult for me though. I have to keep making up reasons for her absence.'

'Why? It's not your fault if she resents him. Are you saying because of that he takes it out on you?'

The maid was silent for a moment as she dropped her gaze and fiddled with the pillowcase until it slipped from her hand. 'Occasionally,' she murmured, 'but only when he's in a bad mood, mind.'

'You know, Alice,' mused Billie, 'all my life I've known women, good intelligent women most of 'em, who've been knocked silly by blokes who profess to love them. It's something I'll never understand. Personally, I wouldn't stand for it for a minute. I swear I'd knife the first bastard who tried it on me. But are you telling me it's also happened to you?'

The maid shrugged. 'It's in the nature of things for a working woman though, ain't it, Miss Bardell? Men are like that. It's just something you have to live with.'

'"Have to live with" be buggered!' Billie exploded. 'No,

you *don't* have to live with it, not for a second, you don't. Look,' she snapped, seizing the maid's arm angrily, 'I should think I've known more men than most women ever will and the majority of them have been devious, unreliable bastards. But I can deal with all that because I expect it. On the other hand, should I be lucky enough to find one that's not like that, then I'll consider it a real bonus and something else to enjoy. But, other than having my bum spanked, violence is definitely out. Once you let it start it just feeds off itself and eventually takes over the whole relationship.' She took hold of the maid's other arm. 'I'll have a word with him, if you like, because I don't want anyone upsetting my Alice. After all, men are ten-a-penny but a good maid is a bloody treasure.'

Alice gave a weak smile and pressed her head momentarily onto Billie's shoulder. 'You've been really good to me, Miss Bardell, but it's something I'll need to sort out for myself – but then I think you know that, don't you?'

Billie gave her the quickest of squeezes before releasing her. 'O'course I do,' she whispered, 'but just keep me up your sleeve as a sort of secret weapon, eh?'

Alice gave a quick nod and picked up the clean pillowcase. 'You bet, miss, and thank you again.'

'Well, now we've got that little task sorted out, I'll get dressed and go and find out why my two young employees are playing mums and dads in the greenhouse instead of earning their keep.'

'Oh, I'll do that, shall I, Miss Bardell?'

'No, you won't. It's about time I asserted my authority with that young couple, especially if I'm going to get any lunch today. Oh, and by the way,' she called as Alice made to return to the bedroom, 'no tiptoeing away and warning them. Let them make their own excuses to me for a change.'

Some ten minutes later, loudly singing the chorus of an old music-hall song, Billie strode round the lawn and noisily entered the greenhouse via the gravel path. In spite of this ample warning, the skirt that was whisked from the top of the peat sacks and the gasps and scuffles that came from the rear of the pile indicated that her entry had still been too premature. Meticulously dusting a small stool, she sat herself down facing the peat. 'Come out, come out, wherever you are,' she trilled, 'cos if I don't get lunch, I'm tellin' yer ma.'

Duncan was the first to appear. 'Well, well!' exclaimed Billie with no little sarcasm. 'We have been a busy little bee this mornin', ain't we? Not even had time to tuck in our shirt or button our flies. Tut-tut. At this rate perhaps you deserve a rise? What's that you say? Oh, you've just had a rise? Well that's more than can be said for my sprouts and spuds, and here was I thinking you were employed as a gardener! I suppose you're going to tell me you've been propagating a tender seedling?'

Before he could reply, a second figure emerged from the rear of the sacks. The young gardener took the opportunity to glance quickly down at his apparel. There was not an inch of shirt or a button out of place. He was immediately unsure whether to point out this fact or whether to let the matter quietly rest. Which was exactly the effect his employer had sought. His partner, on the other hand, was far more flustered and, though the young man may not have had an inch of shirt or a button out of place, she hardly had one in.

'I understand from your mother,' said Billie, 'you're supposed to be making a salad. I assume by the state of you, you're in the process of dressing it, are you?'

'With respect, miss . . .' began the girl in a defiant tone.

'Oh, it's that old chestnut, is it?' said Billie sharply. '"With respect" is it? Well, I tell you it's "with respect" my arse! Anytime anyone prefaces something "with respect", it means they're hoping to get away with something that's either bad-mannered or extremely insolent. Well, don't try either on me, young woman. I've heard it all before. I'll swap your "respect" for a bit of "dedication", primarily because it won't cost me so much.' Billie rose from her seat. 'Well, now we all know where we stand, I'll bid you adieu and let you get on with the tasks you've both been paid to do.'

'I don't think that's fair,' persisted the girl. 'You've not heard our side of the story. You've simply jumped to a conclusion and . . .'

The young gardener pulled her tightly to him for the second time that morning but this time covered her mouth with a hand instead of his lips. 'Take no notice of her, Miss Bardell,' he grinned. 'She's not daft all the time, only occasionally. Unfortunately this is one of her bad days.'

'Duncan Forbes!' the girl spluttered through his fingers, 'don't you dare speak of me like that!'

'Oh, and what way would you like me to speak of you then? Especially when you talk such a load of gibberish.'

Julia pulled angrily away and stood with hands on hips defiantly glowering at him. Billie Bardell, now determined to stay silent and watch developments, could not but admire both the girl's beauty and her fiery resolve. 'It is *not* a load of gibberish! In fact it's a typical employer's attitude. I'm not criticising Miss Bardell because she's usually a very fair-minded person. It's just that employers always assume the worst about their workers and that's exactly what she has done on this occasion.'

The gardener gave a long mocking sigh, then he picked up the girl as if she were a child and hoisted her, struggling and kicking, over his shoulder and towards the door. Just before he made his exit he turned to Billie. 'I won't be long, miss. I'm just putting her in the naughty corner. Then I'll get back to your spuds and sprouts.' Slapping the girl's bottom firmly he added, 'And as for you, little lady, I shall have to stop you going to that kindergarten if this is how you're going to behave when you come home.'

Billie quickly decided it was a diplomatic time to return to the sanctuary of the house. On the way, she saw that Alice, from the bedroom window, had also been following events with some interest.

'What was that all about, miss?' the maid asked eagerly

before Billie had finished climbing the stairs.

Doing the best she could with her version of events, Billie decided to change the subject to Duncan. 'When I first came to this house,' she recalled, 'I remember him being here as a child. Yet as he was talking out there, I realised I know so little about him.'

'Well, miss, he came from the foundlings home at Cricklewood. I think it was Sir Cedric's plan to educate him for higher things. For the first few years he lived with Basil the old gardener and his wife but when she died and Basil retired, the boy took on the garden himself. It was quite a risk for everyone. Duncan was very young and Sir Cedric had to take a chance because the boy had no official qualifications. But old Basil had taught him well and Sir Cedric also had him educated in the evenings and at weekends. The pity was, with Sir Cedric dying so suddenly like, the lad's career never got a proper start. If you ask me, miss, I never could see him remaining a gardener for ever, especially once the master died.'

'There's nothing wrong with being a gardener, Alice,' reproved Billie, 'particularly when they look as good as that lad does. I can't help thinking that whatever he turns his hand to, he's going to be a success, particularly if there's a female around who might conceivably have a say in his future.'

'By that I take it you're ruling out my Julia, miss?'

'Unless she changes her ways I certainly am! If I had to guess, I see both your Julia and that young man being a pair of grade-one heart-breakers and those sort of people never marry each other, or if they do, it's a disaster.'

'I think you're probably right there, miss.'

'You sound a bit mournful over that little observation, Alice. Why so?'

The maid shrugged. 'Oh, I dunno, I s'pose all mums would like to have a little say in who their daughter marries. It usually comes down to a type they wished they had married themselves, if truth be known.'

'So you have a little fancy for our Duncan, do you? Well, join the queue. If I was Boudicca, I'd feed him steaks and keep him chained up in my bedroom. Tell you what, seeing as you're my maid, I'd even let you borrow him on occasions.'

'What occasions?'

'Michaelmas and Shrove Tuesdays – and I'll tell you something else as a bonus. Besides being gorgeous, he's not the type who'll knock you about.'

Alice, now totally embarrassed, gave a nervous chuckle. 'No, but my daughter would.'

Further flights of fancy were cut short by the distant ring of the telephone.

'I'll get it, Alice. Meanwhile, see if you can ginger up your Julia about my lunch. After all, I don't want her standing in that naughty corner – wherever that is – for the rest of the day.' The maid nodded and hastened from the room.

'Hullo, Boudicca speaking,' began Billie frivolously, but after a few seconds of dialogue, she found herself desperately searching for the support of a chair.

'But for God's sake, Queenie, why? . . . So when did you find out? . . . My God! . . . Oh, the poor kid! . . . Look, Queenie, we can't talk satisfactorily about this on the telephone. I'll come over to you this evening, eh? . . . Will Jim be there? . . . Good, it'll be nice to see him and he's always a tower of strength at such times. Okay, see you around six o'clock. 'Bye, love.'

'Is everything all right, miss?' asked Alice anxiously reentering the hall.

'No, Alice,' replied Billie rising wearily from the chair. 'Everything is not all right. In fact it's anything but all right. I think you can forget lunch, and you can call me a taxi for five o'clock this evening.'

'Forgive me, but may I ask why, miss? Because within seconds you suddenly look terrible and whatever the news, I think you should eat something. You'll achieve nothing by starving.'

'I'm afraid I may have to get used to starving, Alice, because things are no longer what they seem. As it could affect you, I think in fairness you should know everything, so put the kettle on, sit down, pin back your ears and listen.' When Alice came back, Billie began.

'When old Cedric and I married, it was, to be honest, never a love match but more of a business deal. It was hardly a secret and it suited both of us. We drew up a written agreement and by it I was supposed to have an annuity for the rest of my days, whether he was alive or not and also I was allowed a maid and a gardener.'

'*Two* maids, surely, miss. You forgot Julia.'

'Julia's extra, I pay for her out of my annuity. Anyway, I've always been a daft cow as regards money and this occasion was no exception. You see, his four grown-up children were not at all in favour of the arrangement. Well, I can understand that, especially when they'd see me spending the money they thought they were due to inherit. But old Cedric was worth several fortunes and had already catered for them with each of them being millionaires in their own right. When I die, or, perish the thought, remarry, the estate reverts to them. So basically, they've been sticking pins in my image and praying fervently for my quick demise. I think they've now given up that idea, but a much better piece of luck has fallen into their laps and it's entirely through my own negligence. After the agreement between Cedric and me was drawn up and signed, I thought I was fireproof and so I lost interest. Big mistake! I know now I should have gone to the solicitors with him and signed the bloody thing there and then. Well I didn't, and what's worse, the agreement has now disappeared and they all know it.'

'So you've got notice to quit?' asked Alice.

'Not exactly, though with my lifestyle it's probably just a question of time. What they did was to send for me and present me with an ultimatum. As long as I lived here like some reclusive humpty-backed dowager, they would tolerate me. But should I fetch a whiff of scandal to the name of Hathaway, I was out on me ear double-quick.' Billie gave an ironic little laugh. 'That's a joke, that is, "Scandal to the Hathaways" – that's where they made their bloody fortune in the first place! There was a big case in the 1870s where they robbed thousands of small investors of their savings and yet they still got away with it.'

'But they are letting you stay here. That's really good of them, isn't it?'

'They are letting me stay here because they have fallen out with each other on how the money is to be split. When the estate reverts back to them, they will probably tear each other's throats out. As long as I'm in residence here, they've got breathing space. Meantime, the house and grounds are being well kept and increasing in value every year. It's like a bank for them really. The thing that upsets them most is that someone other than themselves is spending good Hathaway money.'

'But you've survived so far without trouble, Miss Bardell. What makes you think that you're so vulnerable now?'

'Because it's in my nature. Throughout my entire life, I've had disasters and crises but because I've been in charge of my own destiny, I've always coped. Well, now I'm not in charge, the Four Shysters of the Apocalypse are now dictating my life and there's not a thing I can do about it.'

'Oh, but you're being too pessimistic surely? I bet that between the two of us we can keep you on the straight and narrow, you see if we can't.'

'I'm afraid we've left it a bit late, girl. My head is already above the parapet and I think a bullet is winging my way.'

'I don't understand you. Why, miss, why?'

Billie was silent as she reached for the teapot and poured out two cups. 'D'you remember when my family were here a few days ago?' she resumed.

131

'Of course, miss.'

'D'you also remember the tale of the woman in the taxi?'

'Well, I was in and out of the kitchen at the time, but between Julia, myself and three London evening papers, we certainly got the gist of it, yes.'

'Well, Queenie was convinced the mystery woman was her daughter-in-law, young Grace. Apparently she's been out and about at strange hours and has a serious cut that is in keeping with an injury that could have been sustained by the woman in the taxi.'

'Did you say *cut*, miss?'

Billie nodded. 'That's exactly what I said.'

'But *where* was the cut?'

'The *cut*, my dear Alice, was on her right wrist and in a very similar place to mine that you have been so expertly dressing for this last week or so, the main difference being that she did hers deliberately, whereas I would have even given up my sexy gardener to have avoided mine. In other words, I was the woman in the taxi. You see, this sodding cut is ticking away on my wrist like a bloody time bomb and the only fuse it needs is for some clever dick to become suspicious.'

'Oh, but miss, it's healing up beautifully.'

'That still doesn't take care of the scar though, does it? I'll carry that particular guilt badge for the rest of my life.'

'How about Mr and Mrs Forsythe? Do they know?'

'No, as I said, Queenie's prime suspect was her own daughter-in-law. Even her son David who dealt with the accident has no idea who it was. By the time he arrived at the scene, the cab, with the exception of the driver, was empty.'

'If I can ask you a personal question, Miss Bardell, why did you run?'

'Strangely enough, it wasn't to protect my annuity if that's what you suspect. It was purely to protect my man. He's a budding politician and it would have slaughtered his career, to say nothing of his marriage, to be found in a taxi with an older woman and a dead driver at four in the morning in the Old Kent Road. It wasn't until later that I realised that I also had a good reason for being elsewhere at the time.'

'So what does he, your man as you call him, have to say about it now?'

'He says nothing. What more is there to say? Our relationship is water under the bridge anyway. We were good for each other and we used each other. But that was all there was to it. He would frequently tell me that he loved me and I probably told him the same thing, but deep down neither of us believed it; it simply made us feel good at the time.'

'And he's gone totally out of your life?'

'Totally out of my life.'

'The poor driver – what about him?'

Billie shook her head. 'I tell you, Alice, even if you'd never seen a dead body in your life, you'd have known instantly that that poor bloke was as dead as it's possible to be. Within seconds we both knew there was nothing to be gained by anyone to sit sobbing on the kerbside until the police arrived. Mark you,' she smiled ruefully, 'it would have put my bloke's principles to a real test if there had been, wouldn't it?'

'Yours too if the Hathaways were likely to hear of it.'

'That's true enough, I suppose, but what's done is done and there's nothing I can do about it now. The only thing to concentrate on now is poor Grace. Queenie says she attempted to commit suicide. My troubles seem fairly small beer beside that poor kid's lot. D'you know, I can't think of anything worse than loving your child, like she does, yet still wanting to end your own life. Queenie says that's what actually saved her at the time. She had cut one wrist and was about to cut the other when the child called out to her.'

'So how does her husband figure in all this?'

'As most husbands do, insensitively. You see, the maddening thing about David is that he's really quite a nice lad but, like his father, he's cussedly obstinate. At the moment, him and Grace don't have two ha'pennies to rub together, yet he consistently turns down all offers of help from Queenie and Jim.'

'But that's his pride surely.'

'Oh yes, that's his pride all right. In fact, he's full of pride. Piss, pride and principles if you really want to know. But then pride and principles are so easy for a man to uphold when some poor unfortunate cow is paying for them.'

'But even he must have realised something was wrong when she tried suicide, surely to God?'

'Not at all. Sometimes folks believe what they want to believe and nothing more. She simply told him some cock-and-bull story about cutting her wrist on a flowerpot and he just accepted it. That's what makes me so furious about the Hathaways. They jealously guard their millions, yet for the want of a few quid, kids like Grace feel they have more misery than they can cope with and try to end it all with a razor across the wrist.'

'I well know *that* feeling, I can tell you,' responded Alice wholeheartedly, as she gathered up the empty cups.

'Alice, on second thoughts, could you get me that taxi a couple of hours earlier than I asked? I'll call in at the shops on the way to Queenie's and buy young Grace something terribly extravagant out of the Hathaways' money. I'll enjoy that.'

Whether Julia did emerge that day from the naughty corner, Billie Bardell could not be sure, but having been persuaded to eat by Alice, her lunch, including tomato and cucumber, was served in ample time for her to change and prepare for the three o'clock taxi. She had not long to wait before the cab crunched its way over the gravel drive to stop at the front door. Pausing to give Alice a few orders concerning her return, she nodded to the driver who was about to pull away when the faint ring of a distant telephone could be clearly heard through the open front door.

'Wait, driver!' ordered Billie sharply, reaching for the door handle. 'I'll just answer the phone.'

'Stay there, miss,' called Alice, trotting back into the house, 'I'll get it.'

In view of all the potential disasters that were hanging around her head, Billie showed an understandable impatience as she tapped unrhythmically on the still open door. A few minutes later, the maid returned and gave a cheerful wave.

'It's okay, Miss Bardell,' she called loudly, 'it's a wrong number. G'bye, see you later this evening.'

As the gardener lifted his head from the rosebed and acknowledged the passing taxi, Alice was already sprinting back to the telephone. The hearing piece swung down from the hall table and every few seconds an impatient voice crackled out a sharp ''Ullo! 'Ullo!' With a last glance through the window at the disappearing cab, Alice picked up the mouthpiece.

'I thought I told you never to telephone me!' she hissed angrily. 'A minute earlier and Miss Bardell would have answered . . . Well if I must, I suppose so . . . I don't know about Julia, but Miss Bardell will probably be out until around ten o'clock . . . that's all very well but I still hurt from last time . . . yes, I know, but that doesn't make my pain less does it? . . . I'm sorry too . . . Okay, about seven then? . . . No, the back door. Bye.' She hung up the speaker and was suddenly smitten by a great surge of guilt. She knew she would never knowingly hurt her mistress but she also had a terrible premonition about this man. Oh, if only she didn't need him so.

9

It was an hour before dawn when Sid Grechen poured out the tea and laid out his plan to his two accomplices.

'I couldn't make up me mind whether ter wait fer a few days, but I ain't gonna feel better until I tear that stuttering git Lines's 'ead orf. 'E's definitely got it comin' to 'im. So I've bin lyin' awake givin' it some serious fort an' this is wot I've come up wiv. We'll go round there early this mornin', an' swift 'im away to my yard. I can take me time wiv him there an' really enjoy meself. Besides, after what 'e did ter me there, it'd be rather poetic if I got me revenge in the same place, don't yer reckon?'

As Sid was paying for the services of the two thugs, unanimous agreement was not unexpected and within the hour they were on their way to Blackfriars.

''E's got ter be in,' snarled Sid as they crashed on the door knocker for the fifth time. 'Where else can 'e be at this time o' morning?'

'P'haps he's out Dorising?' offered the older of the two henchmen.

'Nah!' said Sid dismissively. 'I know 'im too well fer that. No self-respectin' tart would 'ave anythin' ter do wiv a stutterin' barsted like 'im. I bet 'e ain't pulled a bird fer nigh on twenty years. Give it one more bang an' we'll 'ave ter fink of somewhere else.'

They had just completed the sixth hammering when a complaining voice arose from the flat opposite. 'Oy! Give it a rest! We're tryin' to get some kip in 'ere.'

Sid nodded to his two colleagues and the older man shifted his attention to this second door but this time with a more civilised knock.

'*Now* what is it?' came the irritable response.

'I wonder if me an' my fella hofficers might 'ave a word wiv yer, sir?' asked Sid in what he hoped passed for a cultured tone.

'Hofficers?' echoed the impressed voice. 'Er – yes, just a minute.' The bolts slid back and the door opened to reveal a scrawny white-haired old man with a frail bent witch-like woman peering curiously over his shoulder. 'Yus?'

'Hi'm sorry ter trouble yer but we're tryin' ter trace a Mr Claude Lines in connectshun wiv a rather urgent matter. 'E don't happen ter be in 'is flat. Yer couldn't 'elp us by hany chance could yer, sir?'

The old chap's eyes narrowed suspiciously. 'Why, what's he s'posed to have done?'

'Lord bless yer, sir, nuffink, nuffink at all. We're 'ere purely ter prertect 'im. 'E's in some danger an' we want ter warn 'im fer 'is own safety. It's a very serious an' urgent business,' added Sid confidentially.

'W-e-ll,' said the man, thoughtfully rubbing his chin. 'He's a bit of a mystery that one. He comes and goes such a lot, y'see, sometimes very early.'

'He could be down the hopfields,' cut in the witch. 'He said he'd like to go.'

''opfields?' queried Sidney. 'What would 'e be doin' down there then?'

'Pickin' hops?' she suggested helpfully. 'Although you don't usually get single men goin' hop-pickin' and he don't look much like a hopper. So p'haps he's only gone for a visit.'

'But I still don't understand why yer fink 'e's gorn 'opping,' persisted Sid.

'Well, he didn't actually *say* he was going hoppin' but yesterday he was telling me about Wateringbury and what a nice place it was and how he'd just been down there. He reckoned he'd like to go back sometime. I told him that we used to go hop-picking at Teston which is only about a mile or so further on. It's just that if he wasn't going to the hopfields, I can't imagine why he'd want to go there at this time of the year, that's all.'

'I see,' said Sid thoughtfully. 'Fanks, fanks a lot, sir. You've been most 'elpful.'

'Will there be a reward?' asked the old chap hopefully, but the three strangers were already out of hearing.

'Quick!' snapped Sid as they hastened to the car. 'I know where the barsted'll be. London Bridge stashun, I'll bet.'

The youngest heavy studied his watch. 'He'll be long gone by now surely?'

'Not necessarily. 'E's got no car, no 'orse an' 'e can't nick me lorries any more. So, unless 'e's flyin', 'e's gotta go by train. We could just be lucky – trains don't run too often at night. The first fing we've gotta find out, is what train goes ter – where'd she say, Water-bury?'

'Water-bury, guv?' queried the puzzled porter at London Bridge station. 'That'd be Wateringbury. You'll want the Paddock Wood train but it won't be running for an hour yet.'

''Ave there been any 'oppin' trains in the last few 'ours?' asked Sid.

'Some, but none to Paddock Wood since midnight, if that's what you're asking.'

'I bet he ain't even *gone* hoppin',' observed the more talkative thug.

'O'course 'e 'as!' snarled Sid. 'Where else would 'e go? 'E's got no relations an' 'op-pickin' would suit 'im just fine. 'E could lie low there for weeks an' no one'd be any the wiser.' Sid rubbed his face thoughtfully. 'Right, I'll tell yer what we're gonna do. There'll be no more of this poncin' about just wishin' somefing will turn up. We're gonna be systematic. We'll go back ter my place an' 'ave a little kip. Then after breakfast we're goin' dahn ter Water-bury, or wherever it is, an' we're gonna find the barsted an' skim strips orf 'im very slowly. Good idea?'

'Good idea, guv,' came the second unanimous verdict of the morning.

Though having no desire to be a captive stallion, Wonky had to admit there could be definite advantages to the job. Firstly there was the food. He found it amazing what culinary delights could be achieved in a huge old hopping-pot suspended above a crackling fire and a battered old biscuit tin buried beneath it. It wasn't just the quality, it was also the quantity. Lillian Wilkinson's tribe could normally put away enough food for a platoon of infantry but when the Kentish fresh air was also taken into account, it was equivalent to five thousand Israelites. Take the meat, for example. Judging by the amount he found in his stew, he thought Lill had solved the rabbit problem overnight. Using a crust of bread with great precision, he wiped up every vestige of gravy from his white enamel plate and leaned back with a great sigh of contentment.

'That was w-wonderful, Mrs W-Wilkinson, just w-wonderful,' he stretched contentedly.

'Oh there's more ter come, Mr Lines, sir. The kids found some cooking apples this afternoon so I've done us all a pudden.'

'What!' exclaimed the ecstatic Wonky. 'Not an *a-apple* pudding surely, Mrs W-Wilkinson? Not after that wonderful rabbit s-stew we've just had? I didn't know there was that much p-pleasure left in the w-world.'

'Well, if Essie sorts out the cupboard, you can have black treacle as well.'

'Mrs W-Wilkinson, tomorrow you have my p-permission to bury me on this h-hill because, by then, I will have known true p-perfection. Rabbit s-stew, apple-p-pudding and b-black treacle! M-Masterly! I can't imagine h-how you d-do it. You must be a g-genius.'

'Bless yer, Mr Lines, it's nuffink.' She dropped her gaze

and shuffled her feet in embarrassment. 'We can cook anyfin' 'ere that can be baked, boiled or fried.'

'Well, all I c-can say, Mrs W-Wilkinson, I just w-wish you'd been the c-cook when I was in the a-army, because if it wasn't c-corned beef it was s-soddin' porridge.'

The air around the fire hung damp with dew and the early dark had closed impenetrably around them. Yet the blackness only served to contrast the eager shining faces that reflected the flames. Meanwhile the faggots crackled and their sparks swirled up before vanishing into the night sky like tiny meteorites.

'Is hop-picking like th-this all th-the time?' asked Wonky blithely.

'Not really,' said Esther. 'This is Saturday night an' Saturday nights are always a bit special.'

'Wh-why?'

'Well, we don't 'ave to get up early for starters but there's more to it than that,' she waved her arms airily up and down the row of blazing fires. 'Most of the adults and older kids will go to the "Hoppers' Bar" behind the Pickled Trout at Teston an' those that don't will look after everyone else's kids as well as the sick an' the lame.'

'How d-do they get th-there – to Teston, I m-mean?'

'Walk o'course, how else d'you expect? We all go together and we come back together. You can hear everyone singin' from here to Dover Harbour. Locals don't like it, I can tell you. Still, there's not much they do like about us, is there, Evie?'

'That's a fact,' agreed Evelyn. 'They're always moanin'. They want us to pick their bleedin' hops but they don't actually want us here to do it. They complained to the local copper five times last year. Hope they do it again this year!'

'Wh-Why d'you want th-them to complain?'

She thrust the palms of her hands down between her legs and rubbed them hard together. 'Oooh he was good, that one! He gave me five private night tours of the 'opfields. I was pulling hops outa me underclothes fer days afterwards.'

'Oh, I remember that!' exclaimed Esther. 'Mum was ever so proud, weren't she?'

'Y-Yes, I bet sh-she was,' muttered Wonky almost to himself but then increased his tone to add, 'but wh-why d'you all go in a c-convoy if it m-makes so m-much trouble? Wouldn't it be more discreet to go in s-small groups?'

'We do it because it's so bleedin' dark we'd never find our way back. It's not like bein' in London, y'know. 'Oppin' nights are pitch black. If we keep singin' and stick together, we nearly all return. Least, that's the theory, though there's always one drunken bleeder who falls in the Medway river.'

'Pudden up!' announced Lillian. ''Ave you got that black treacle, Essie?'

'On its way, Ma!'

If Wonky was delighted with his stew, he was ecstatic about his pudding. So much so, he made a mistake that few ever make at hop-picking. He offered to wash up. It was such a surprise that Lillian Wilkinson did not even make a token refusal and the elder children, to whom the task usually fell, stared open-mouthed in astonishment.

'Don't get too carried away, kids,' advised Lillian. 'Nuala and Teresa will still need ter get the water.'

'Aw, Mum,' protested Nuala. 'If Mr Lines is washin' up, Mr Lines oughta get the water, 's only fair, ain't it?'

Lillian turned and gave Wonky a polite forced smile as she swung her hand out behind her to give what she hoped was a concealed wallop to the left ear of her outspoken child. 'Do as yer told, there's a dear,' she said through tightly clenched teeth. One of Lill's wallops was usually all that was required for any Wilkinson to see the error of their ways, so harmony was quickly restored.

It was doubtful if Wonky would have been quite so quick to applaud the use of black treacle if he had had any experience of removing it from enamel plates.

'Grass and ashes,' suggested Esther, 'usually works.'

Whether the remedy did actually work would obviously not be discovered until the next daylight meal, though the plates certainly looked passable enough in the evening firelight. Wonky was just polishing the last one, when he noticed the Wilkinsons had been reinforced by several more families from adjoining huts with further figures emerging from the dark at increasing intervals.

'Nearly ready, Mr Lines?' called Lillian from the open hut door. 'We're all orf soon! There's a wee drop a water left in the bowl if yer'd care fer a quick rinse?'

Squinting, he peered into the yellow glow inside the hut. Lillian seemed to occupy most of the space as she stood pushing a long hatpin into a dark straw bonnet. Just beyond her and on the edge of the bed, Esther and Evelyn appeared to be putting the finishing touches to their appearances. Wonky suddenly found himself quite impressed – in the poor light they could almost pass for ladies.

'C-Coming,' he responded.

At first glance, he guessed his was probably the sixth face to have plunged into the grey water in the bowl, though his main concern was to find a dry patch on the communal towel. He was still searching when Lillian entered carrying an assortment of men's Wellington boots.

'I've borrowed these from the other 'uts, Mr Lines; yer'll need 'em if yer walkin' ter Teston. Wot size d'yer take?'

'T-tens, Mrs W-Wilkinson.'

'S'what I guessed. Yer should get a decent pair outa this lot then.'

The second pair he tried fitted perfectly. 'These'll do f-fine, Mrs Wilkinson.'

'Oh, good gracious, Mr Lines, 'ow about that! First time fit eh? I reckon yer'll 'ave ter marry me now!' She had barely spoken the words before she dissolved into a gale of screeching laughter. 'S all right, son,' she whispered. 'I won't keep yer to it, frightened the life outa yer though, didn't I?'

Eventually, some thirty Wellington-booted adults, most

with their shoes tied round their necks, plus six older children, two torches and one oil lamp assembled in the glow of the fire. At the first notes from an ill-played harmonica, the whole group set off under a pitch-black sky along the river path towards Teston.

It could be safely said that within ten minutes Wonky had failed his first test miserably – he had utterly failed to remember the second line of any song sung. This in spite of being outrageously prompted by the two sisters who spent the whole journey clinging tightly onto his arms. In fact they had almost reached the pub before someone had the wit to introduce the song 'Who were you with last night?' and, as Evelyn acidly pointed out, 'Every bleeder in the world knows the second line of that!'

The saloon bar lights looked particularly inviting as the group emerged from the dark and into the softly lit approaches to the pub forecourt. Wonky suddenly felt the girls tug at his arm as he made eagerly towards the pub door.

'No, this way,' corrected Esther as they guided him in a different direction.

'But I th-thought we were going to the p-pub . . .'

'Not there, we're not,' snapped Evelyn. 'They'd sling us out before we'd got in. Carn't yer read the notice?' She nodded towards an illuminated board which read in bold black capital letters 'NO HOPPERS OR GYPSIES ALLOWED'.

'D'you m-mean they w-won't allow us in th-there! But why? We're not G-Germans!'

'It's all right, we've gotta better arrangement. We go ter our own special bar. They don't want us in the posh part of the pub so they give us a shed round the back. It's just fer us and it's called "Hoppers' Bar". Beer's cheaper too.'

Wonky stopped dead. 'But that's outrageous! I got almost t-taken apart in F-France! Are th-they now t-telling me I can't d-drink in th-their sodding p-pubs? I'm definitely not standing for th-that!'

'O'course you are!' insisted Evelyn. 'Don't be so stupid. Anyway, most of us actually prefer it; we consider it belongs to us. If we can't go in their pub, they certainly can't come in ours. We don't want any of those toffee-nosed bleeders hangin' around when we're havin' a good time, now do we?'

'Well all right,' he said grudgingly. 'B-But there's no other l-little surprises like th-that are th-there? Because if s-so, tell me now and get it over w-with.'

The girls did not reply at first but exchanged apprehensive glances.

'W-Well?' he demanded. 'I'm waiting. What is it n-now?'

'It's yer drinkin' glass,' explained Esther. 'Yer'll need ter keep a tight hold on it 'cos they do have a tendency ter go missin'. Yer see, there's a tanner deposit on 'em and there's always one shifty bleeder who'll nick 'em if yer not careful.'

'*What!* S-sixpence deposit on a p-pint of beer! Th-that's more than th-the beer itself!' Wonky bawled.

'Oh, come on, it's not as bad as the shoes,' protested Esther. 'Yer do at least get yer money back at the end of the night.'

'Oh, so now we've got p-problems with sh-shoes, have we? We don't h-have to pay to w-wear th-them by any chance?'

'No, but when yer change into yer shoes, yer do have ter be careful where yer leave yer Wellington boots. What we usually do is ter shove 'em all in a barrel and the kids take it in turns to sit on the lid. Then, at the end of the evenin', we give each kid a penny. Mark you,' she added, 'if yer've had too much ter drink it's a bit of a performance findin' the right boots.'

'S-So wh-what happens if we don't put them in the b-barrel?'

'Well, two years ago we put 'em in a box in the doorway and we lost the whole bleedin' lot. It was the gypsies, they reckoned. Anyway, whoever it was, could have equipped a herring fleet. The walk back took us bleedin' hours!'

'So let me get this s-straight. I've g-got to drink me b-beer in a shed, p-pay a tanner for me g-glass and hope me boots aren't n-nicked? Is th-that really all? I mean *really* all? Or do we have a s-six-month qu-quarantine as w-well? T-Tell me now b-because I'd hate to th-think there's another little t-treat in store s-somewhere.'

'Well, of course,' whispered Evelyn with a discreet nudge to his ribs, 'if it's a little *treat* yer lookin' for yer should have said! You an' me could always slip out back for a while. I'll even promise ter be gentle with yer this time.'

Before he could reply, Wonky found himself pushed into the Hoppers' Bar where an enormous woman at an upright piano had started to pound out a battle version of 'Tiptoe Through the Tulips'. She did it with such force that it rattled the windows and four full pint-glasses crashed down from the top of the piano.

'Not the best start in the world,' muttered Evelyn, sweeping up the fragments with her foot. 'That's four pints and two bob's worth of deposits lyin' in smithereens on the floor an' no one's had a drink yet! Got the makin's of an interestin' bleedin' evenin', I'd say.'

Wonky was surprised just how quickly the shed filled with hoppers; they had come from all over the district. Within minutes, as the temperature rose, windows were opened and the voices could be heard singing clear down to the Medway. The festivities had been in full swing for ninety minutes or more, when Wonky realised that the longer the evening wore on, the more attractive the Wilkinson sisters were becoming. His earlier reservations had gradually faded as the party warmed up. It was probably the fact that Evelyn seemed to become particularly attached to a tall bearded weekend visitor from hut forty-eight that finally prodded him into taking a renewed, and greatly appreciated, interest in Esther.

The pair of them had barely left the shed via the back door when an aggressive-looking trio entered the front. Sid Grechen's original plan had been to ask around generally for any knowledge of Wonky's whereabouts, but the sheer volume of hoppers in the shed caused him to show a greater discretion. He knew that tough as his two companions were, as a trio they would have had no chance against even a minority of those in the shed. Climbing onto a chair by the piano, he searched swiftly over the mass of sweating heads. Even this action began to arouse no little suspicion.

'Na!' he growled to his escorts. 'The barsted ain't 'ere. We'll check the Railway Pub at Wateringbury an' if 'e ain't there, we'll bed-an'-breakfast overnight and try all the 'opping 'uts first fing in the mornin'.'

''Scuse me, mate,' said a quiet little voice alongside him. Sid glanced down to see a quaint little moustachioed man of some sixty years sporting a battered bowler hat and a short clay pipe.

'Yerse?' he inquired suspiciously. 'Whadda *you* want?'

'Are you three blokes all hop-pickers?' the old man asked.

'Do we look as if we're soddin' 'op-pickers?' replied Sid tersely.

'No, yer don't,' said the little man. 'An' that's me very point. Yer see I'm asking yer to withdraw yer presence from 'ere forthwith like.'

'Y'er askin' *what*?' asked Sid seemingly unable to believe his ears but before he could respond further, his sleeve was tugged by the younger of the two thugs. Following his friend's gaze, Sid lifted his head to see a groundswell of bodies gathering all around.

'No offence, y'understand,' said the little man politely, 'but we've already had four glasses broken an' we can't really afford any more. Now, seeing as you can drink next door without payin' a deposit, I suggest that's exactly whatcha do. If yer think about it, I'm sure yer'll see it's fair.'

'Oh, I'm sure we will,' hissed Sid through clenched teeth. 'C'mon you two; 'e ain't 'ere anyway.'

The Hoppers' Bar may not have been overilluminated, but the contrast with the blackness outside was staggering as

Wonky and Esther groped blindly around in the dark.

'Sorry, g-girl,' he apologised, 'but this is b-bloody dangerous. I can't s-see a thing and the wind's g-got up as well. We'll have t-to go back inside.'

'O'course we won't,' Esther said dismissively. 'It's just a question of adaptin'. There's the stables around here somewhere an' it's got a fixed wooden ladder at the side that leads up to the hayloft. Keep hold of me skirt hem an' I'll find it soon enough.'

Though the giggling pair tripped several times, no fall was serious and Wonky's grip was soon transferred from skirt hem to hips. Gradually the night lost its total blackness as the shape of the stables became faintly silhouetted against the southern sky.

'There's the steps!' exclaimed Esther eagerly. 'Just in front of us. I knew they were here somewhere.' On reaching the foot of the ladder, she turned impulsively and threw her plump bare arms around his neck. 'It must have been the heat in the bar,' she said breathlessly, 'but bloody hell, I feel randy!'

Up to that moment, Wonky had not been a hundred per cent sure exactly how he felt, but the first touch of her body pushing against him cleared every doubt. 'I still can't see very much though,' he complained, but his stutter had vanished.

'That's easy – feel,' she suggested.

As she led the way up the vertical ladder, he was so close behind her that the hem of her skirt constantly brushed his forehead. On reaching the entrance to the hayloft, she stopped climbing to reach up with one arm to swing open the door. It was too great an opportunity to miss. Clinging to the ladder with his right hand, Wonky ran the other up her smooth left thigh.

'Bloody hell, yer daft sod!' she screeched. Clutching tightly to the door, her top half swung out into space whilst her feet remained precariously on the ladder. 'Yer'll kill the soddin' pair of us!'

Only then aware of the danger, Wonky hooked his right arm firmly round a rung and moved his left arm further up the front of her body in order to take her weight. Having reached her navel via the inside of her knickers, he spread his fingers wide across her belly and inched her safely back tight against him. With both hands now firmly back on the ladder she looked down and shook her head.

'Bloody hell, Claude! I felt like a swallow bein' fucked on the wing!'

Before he could respond, Evelyn's unmistakable tones came from deep inside the hayloft. 'If you daft bleeders don't climb in here and close that door, he still might have ter do just that! That draught's whistling round my clouts like a sailship in a force nine!'

'Hey!' exclaimed Wonky, as he later removed the last of Esther's clothing, 'I've just thought. How come you two know so much about this hayloft that you can find it in the pitch black? It's nowhere near your hopping huts at Wateringbury.'

'We told yer, didn't we?' sighed Esther, lying back in total surrender. 'Don't yer remember? That copper gave us a blindin' tour of the hopfields last year.'

'But this is not even near the hopfields,' persisted Wonky. 'It's a hayloft.'

'I know that, silly,' she murmured wistfully, 'but it was dark and we got lost.'

The distant cries of 'TIME GENTLEMEN PLEASE' floated on the late-night air and reached the quartet as they lay recovering in the hayloft.

'I've been thinking, Essie,' said Wonky at last as he thoughtfully gazed up to where he hoped the ceiling would be. 'If we couldn't see to get up here, how on earth do we get down?'

'Easy,' she replied struggling into her frock, 'we jump.'

'Jump?' he echoed. 'Jump where? We'll break our necks. There were all manner of farm bits and pieces lying around down there. I know, I fell over most of them.'

'Yer don't jump down *outside*, yer fool. Yer jump down inside. The ground floor's full of hay bales; it's good fun really.'

As to whether it was 'good fun', Wonky was sceptical, but there was no denying it was effective. Within minutes they had vacated the premises and they were following Esther back in single file towards the Hoppers' Bar. Evelyn's bearded companion had little to say but his reticence caused Wonky no distress because the day's exertions had caught up with him and he felt thoroughly tired. As they joined the rest of their group already assembled outside the bar, the search was on for stragglers. Esther shrugged. 'Depends who they are and whether anyone wants 'em back.'

He took his arm from her shoulder and stared at her in genuine surprise. 'D'you mean some p-people actually get d-deliberately left h-here?'

'Of course,' she replied, seizing back his arm and replacing it across her shoulders. 'Y'see, many hoppers have uninvited weekend visitors who they didn't expect and didn't want in the first place. So, if they get drunk and get lost on the way back . . .' she shrugged again, '. . . they either turn up perished and sober next mornin' at breakfast or the local police eventually fish 'em out of the river. Whichever it is, they never bother us again.'

'So h-how do I fit into that cat-category?'

She laughed. 'You? You've got no fears there, sweetie. My mum wouldn't let yer fall in the river. She'd drown both me an' Evie before she'd let that happen. My old mum's got great son-in-law plans fer you. She thinks yer a gent.'

All vestiges of sleep suddenly vanished from Wonky's mind and so did his stutter.

'Son-in-law?' he blurted. 'When did I ever say anything about . . .'

'Oh, it's all right, don't worry yerself!' she interrupted. 'I said it was me *mother*, not me or me sister. Still, yer'd better not 'ave put either of us in the pudden club this weekend or she really won't think yer a gent. She never has forgiven those two sailors for what they done ter me an' Evie and they could be anywhere in the world. But don't forget – you only live at Blackfriars. She can be round ter your place in five minutes flat – with an axe!' She tiptoed up to him and, with an exaggerated peer, pressed her face almost to his and chuckled, 'Let's have a look at yer. Hmmmn, just as I thought! You've gone white.'

With most stragglers accounted for and the group in good voice, they slowly moved off west towards the huts at Wateringbury. Most of the songs were sung in chorus but the occasional one was sung solo, either as a party piece or because no one else knew the words. One such old music hall song presented an apt epitaph to a rather strange day. From somewhere near the front, a raucous male voice gave forth with 'Put-a-Little-Treacle-On-Me-Pudden-Mary-Anne' and Wonky turned to Esther with a particularly suspicious look.

'Believe me, lover,' she pleaded, 'I had nothin' to do with it – honest.'

As they finally neared the huts, there was musical confusion as the songs of the approaching contingent fused with the songs of those who had stayed behind and had a little party of their own. The singing finally petered out to a chorus of 'G'nights' and 'See yers' as the whole assembly splintered down into small groups which in turn peeled off to their own huts.

Wonky had known from the moment he had arrived, there would be a problem about sleeping arrangements but he had assumed he would be allowed to curl up quietly in a corner. Or even, if the fire was stoked enough, to lie outside with a blanket. But on mentioning this to Lillian, she bristled and pointed out in no uncertain terms that for a guest not to be sheltered for the night would mean loss of face for her and pneumonia for him.

'B-But w-where then?' he pleaded.

'Yer can top-an'-tail wiv us o'course! Yer can sleep at the bottom with the youngest kids, while Essie, Evie an' me can sleep at the top with the eldest. S'easy, everyone does it that way. There is one fing though,' she added, thrusting a torch into his hand. 'I suggest yer make the latest trip possible up ter the carsi – that way yer might not need get up in the night. Always 'elps does that.'

'Don't forget Danny, Mum,' reminded Evelyn.

'Oh, yer,' said Lillian. 'Avoid Danny's front, 'cos sometimes 'e cuts it fine before he wakes up ter use his potty. Other'n that, yer'll sleep like a baby.'

Whatever Wonky may have thought of Lillian's briefing, her last remark was certainly true. Neither rustling straw, toes under his nose, a raw back or the threat from a dozy Daniel's bladder delayed his slip into oblivion for more than a few seconds. He was, in fact, asleep before the three females had even undressed for bed.

It was a good seven hours before he even stirred. After spending the first few moments assessing his whereabouts, he was conscious that the children were already awake and there was a certain amount of activity in the hut. His eyelids felt too heavy to open, but he persevered and was soon aware that Esther had obviously just returned from the lavatory.

'Claude, quick, wake up,' she ordered, shaking him violently. 'Come on! Come on!'

He rolled over towards her and let out a pained cry as his raw back rubbed the rustling mattress. 'Whassamarrer?'

'There are three cutthroats peerin' into every 'ut. They could *just* be coppers. They're obviously lookin' fer someone. It's not you by chance?'

The sleep fell away and he was fully awake in an instant. 'Wh-what do th-they look l-like?'

Her description of Sid Grechen was perfect in every detail including the facial abrasions that Wonky himself had inflicted.

'It's almost certainly me,' he agreed as again his stutter vanished. He looked frantically around the hut but there was little cover for anyone his size. 'How far away are they?'

'About four huts; they'll be here any second.'

'Just a minute, just a minute,' cut in Lillian. 'I ain't got all these kids for ornaments, yer know. You Evie, you take yer top orf an' 'ave a wash at the bowl. The rest of yer pick up all the puppies, coats an' toys and dump 'em all over the bed. You ruffle those blankets and pillers an' spread yerself, Essie, an' you, Mr Lines, you get in the middle of 'em and we'll sling everythin' over yer.'

'But . . .' began Wonky.

'Don't "but" me, son, there ain't time. Just do as yer bloody told.'

Treating it as some big game, even the youngest of the children entered into the spirit of the thing and within a minute or so, there was a loud double-knock on the door which was thrown open simultaneously. Sid Grechen was the first into the hut. Evelyn promptly wheeled around from the bowl with a towel to her left arm pit but ensuring that no other part of her torso was covered. All three of the intruders promptly stopped in their tracks and stared at the girl. Letting out the tiniest of screams, Evelyn transferred the towel to her chest, carefully ensuring that each breast was adequately exposed.

'Oh, Mother!' she exclaimed, in a voice that she desperately hoped passed for a frightened virgin.

Lill Wilkinson, ably assisted by a barking dog and daughter Esther, proceeded to pour torrents of scorn, plus shoes, Wellington boots and Daniel's part-filled potty on 'filthy perverts who come in 'ere and frighten a poor little gel outta her wits.'

'Okay! Okay!' pleaded the cowering Sid. 'I'm sorry, I'm sorry, it's a big mistake, it's the wrong 'ut.' The three of them almost fell out of the door as Lillian slammed it shut behind them.

'. . . *AND* I'M HAVIN' THE BLEEDIN' LAW ON YER FILFY BARSTEDS, WHOEVER Y'ARE!'

'Did you see the knockers on her!' exclaimed the younger thug in wide-eyed amazement. 'What a pair! It looked like a dead heat in a zeppelin race!'

'Shut up!' hissed Sid. 'I ain't payin' yer ter be a tit inspector. If we don't search the rest of the 'uts soon, the word'll git around and that barsted will 'ave flown again.'

'Yeh, but did yer 'ear wot the ol' lady called her?' persisted the younger one. 'She reckons she was a "poor little gel"! Well, *poor* she might be, but *little* she ain't!'

As the trio made off along the row of huts, Lill Wilkinson ceased her peeping through the chinks in the hut door. 'S'all right, they're movin' orf along the row. Lie still in that bed until they've gorn, Mr Lines, an' you, Evie, put somethin' on or yer'll catch yer deaf o'cold messin' about in that cold water.'

'Don't worry yerself, Mum,' replied Evelyn reaching out for her jersey, 'there's no water in the bowl.'

Wonky, unable to resist a last peep before the jersey was pulled down into place, lifted his head from beneath a mound of teddy bears, jigsaws, building blocks and puppies. 'Thanks, Evie,' he said as he watched her reach up to slip the jersey over her head, 'and I can well understand why they were distracted.'

'S'all right, Claude, anytime, though I can't say I'm enamoured with the company y'keep.'

'Well, Mr Lines, like I always say,' sang out Lillian, 'ain't they a pair of lovely gels?'

Wonky nodded his head approvingly. 'Well, they're certainly a lovely pair all right, Mrs Wilkinson. No one would give you an argument about that. Besides, they do wonders for me stutter.'

10

Alice Giles was rummaging deep into her wardrobe when her daughter Julia burst into their bedroom. 'I'll be home late tonight, Mum!' panted the girl excitedly. 'I'm going to the Phoenix theatre to see Noël Coward and Gertie Lawrence in *Private Lives*. They say it's ever so good!'

'Eh!' exclaimed Alice. 'Now don't tell me, let me guess. I know, you've finally nailed a millionaire. I'm right aren't I?'

'Close!' the girl laughed. 'Duncan's won three pounds in his football club's sweep so he's taking me to the dress circle and *not* the gallery! What d'you think of that?'

'But I thought you didn't like Duncan. You two are always fighting.'

'Oh, of course we are, and I still don't have to like him just because we're going to the theatre. This is more what you'd call a form of punishment for him.'

'Punishment?'

'Yes, of course! You see, on our train ride there, I'll keep telling him why his politics stink. You never know, one day I may even get through to him.'

'But the last time I saw you two together, you were screaming, kicking and threatening to kill him. Now you tell me you're going to the theatre with him?'

'Oh, that's nothing,' Julia said dismissively. 'First I made him apologise and now I'm getting him to spend his money. So really I've won the argument, d'you see?'

'Oh, yes, dear, I see perfectly clearly,' replied Alice without conviction. 'So when are you leaving?'

'We're leaving as soon as you vacate this bedroom and let me get ready. Because, wait for it, he's also treating me to a meal at Lyon's Corner House before we go to the theatre. Isn't that exciting?'

'W-e-l-l, yes, but doesn't that rather compromise your political principles, you know, having some poor little scivvy of a waitress dashing around at your beck and call?'

A frown suddenly crossed the girl's face. 'Oh, I never thought of . . .'

Alice burst out laughing. 'It's all right, love, I was only teasing. You go and enjoy yourself. Miss Bardell and me both think you've got a right good lad there.' She leaned forward and kissed the top of her daughter's head. 'Just don't push him too far.'

Within thirty minutes, Julia had bathed, changed and left for her mother a now totally chaotic bedroom. Together with her three-pound benefactor, she then headed happily out of the gate and down the lane towards Hampstead station. As the couple passed through the gate, the young gardener had instinctively slid a protecting arm quite casually over the girl's shoulder. Alice had watched the gesture with envy. There was no doubt that her own expected visitor who was soon scheduled to creep through her back door would bear little resemblance to the amiable easy-going youth who had just faded from sight down the lane. Sometimes she wondered why she was so obsessed with the necessity of having a relationship with a man. It wasn't as if any of them had brought her happiness. In fact quite the reverse. Most of them had been a disaster and the majority of the misfortunes of her hard life could have been unquestionably placed at the door of an ill-assorted selection of men. Yet in spite of these regrets and recriminations, still she searched. With a quick glance at the clock she resumed the exploration of her wardrobe.

It was the white silk dress that suddenly rekindled her earlier premonition. She had bought it after seeing Billie

Bardell in such an outfit three years earlier and had thought how stunning the woman had looked. The fact that the old music-hall star had poise and a figure she herself could never hope to emulate had simply never entered her head. Or rather it hadn't until the moment she had first seen her reflection in the mirror. Since that gloomy afternoon, the frock had not once seen the light of day. Well now it was going to. After all, if it had been rather ill-fitting before, the weight she had lost in the last few months ensured it was now or never. In any case, the chances were she would not be wearing it for long. Experience dictated her visitor's first requirement would be sex, though she never really knew why. She knew she was not even very good at it and usually only went through the motions with fake sighs and cries. Once it was over she would always wonder what possible pleasure he could have derived from it. Yet strangely it was one of the few things about her that he rarely criticised. Perhaps it was a sham for him too, or perhaps he even pretended she was someone else? If that was the case it was certainly not something that bothered her. She was gathering up her hair into a bun when she heard the loud tapping at the kitchen door. Although she had been expecting it, she still gave a little start of uncertainty. Who knows, perhaps this time would be different? It was at least a hope she always clung to. Hastening across the room, she paused at the mirror by the open door to turn and check her appearance one last time. Then, with a little sigh, she crossed her fingers and hurried down into the kitchen.

'Alice, me luv! Well I must say 'ow nice yer look. Fair gives me old eyes a treat it does, that's fer sure.'

Any greeting she may have prepared in return was lost at her first sight of the newcomer. 'My God! What's happened?' His face had sustained abrasions that, though slight in appearance, were many in number. Limping through the door he raised a bandaged left hand in acknowledgement.

'It's nuffin' really,' he said with patently false bravado.

'Just 'ad a little up-an'-downer wiv some geezer who jumped me when I weren't lookin', that's all. I've bin lookin' fer 'im ever since and 'is neighbours told me 'e's gorn 'op-pickin' at Wateringbury. We went dahn there but we couldn't find the barsted.' He limped to a chair and, flopping down into it, added, 'Cor! An' look at you, Alice, don't yer look a proper treat! If I wasn't in so much agony wiv me pain an' that, I'd be havin' you 'ere in this kitchen, over the table, on the floor, standin' up an' in every position known ter man, an' that's a fact!'

'But, but, but . . .' she began in a total state of fluster. 'Who did this to you and why? Have you told the police and . . .'

'Nah, you know me an' the coppers, don't yer? Me an' them don't git on, do we? I don't like 'aving anyfing ter do wiv 'em unless I 'ave to. Don't worry, I'm gonna settle this geezer me own way.'

'My God, Sid Grechen, you'll be the death of me! First you ring me here and Miss Bardell almost answers and then you turn up in this state! Anyway, you haven't told me what the emergency was that caused you to telephone so dramatically.'

'Well, it's a bit ticklish like,' he began. 'But I'm sure we'll be able ter sort sumfing out. Yer see, I'm a bit short of the readies right nah. This geezer wot jumped me, well 'e used ter work fer me and I found out 'e's 'ad 'is fingers in my till as yer might say, an' fer some bloody time as well. Wot I really need, and it's a bit urgent like, is a couple of hundred. Y'see, I've got dodgy people leanin' on me an' because this barsted's bin takin' me fer a ride fer so long, I'm a bit short. I just wonder if yer could see yer way clear to help?'

'Sid, you said a couple of hundred. A couple of hundred what?'

'Why, quid of course,' he snapped. 'What'd yer fink I was on abhat, winkles?'

'But I've never had that sort of money in my life! I get forty shillings a week plus full board and a clothes allowance. And that, I might tell you, is really good for a domestic servant, particularly the way things are at the moment. In addition, Miss Bardell pays an allowance for my Julia and that's a whole lot more than she need do. If that lady was to leave this place, me and my Julia would be in the workhouse, I tell you.'

'Why'd yer say that? Is she likely to leave 'ere then?'

'Well, that's strictly a confidential matter so I can't divulge it. Let's just say that no one is safe round here at the moment and leave it at that.'

'Yeh, but when yer 'ave a quick butcher's at this place, it reeks of cash. A blind man could tell she must 'ave a few bob stashed away somewhere. Couldn't yer speak up fer me? Who knows, she might be just the wench fer a quick short-term loan?'

'Sid, how can I get it into your head? *NO*, definitely *NO!*'

His eyes narrowed and the makings of a snarl began in his throat before he thought better of it. 'Yer, yer right, gel. After all, yer know yer own business best. If yer fink she ain't got it, then she ain't got it, an' that's good enough fer me. Tell yer what, I ain't come here ter upset yer. So, seein' as we've got the place ter ourselves, why don't we 'ave a little social evenin'?'

Sid Grechen gave an exaggerated shrug. 'Well, lookin' the way I do, I carn't very well take yer out, nah can I? I mean, wherever we went, people would be sayin' what's that good-lookin' bird doin' wiv such a battered old geezer? So it's a case of yer bein' all dressed up an' nowhere ter go really. So what I fort is –' he rummaged in an old Gladstone bag '– you an' me ain't 'ad a little drink fer a long time, so, if we make ourselves comfortable, we could pass a pleasant evenin' afore your folk return. What d'yer say?'

Alice's first reaction was to refuse, but his words made sense. It was true she was not terribly keen on alcohol, because her face would always flush and it usually made her lisp. But then a nice 'social evening' would certainly make a pleasant change. In any case, what was there to lose? Sid was right, she was already dressed up and there was certainly nowhere else to go. In addition to that, the house was empty, well, at least for the next few hours. As Miss Bardell would probably say, 'Damn it, give it a whirl.'

'Okay, Sid,' she agreed. 'I'm not expecting anyone back before ten o'clock at the earliest and I've certainly been a bit down lately. Who knows, perhaps all I need is just to sit down with a drink and unwind? I'll get some glasses and have a look round in the larder. I'm sure we've got some cold meat, bread and pickles we can use.' She found the idea of the unexpected treat cheering her out of all proportion and her face broke gradually into a happy smile. 'Tell you what, Sidney Grechen, you've got me quite looking forward to this now. Open the bottle and make yourself comfortable in one of those fireside chairs and I'll get the food and utensils.'

The first two hours passed by quickly, although Alice's face became steadily warmer. She told herself it was sitting close to the fire that caused the reddening, which was a convenient way of forgetting her facial flush was always due to her alcoholic intake. It took a rogue pickle that popped from a sandwich and into her drink to cause her first reservation.

'Good heaventh, Thid,' she blurted, 'I think I'm a bit tipthy. I don't think I should have any more drink, d'you?'

'Nonsense!' he chirruped, reaching for another bottle. 'You said yer wanted ter unwind, didn't yer? So what's a better way of unwinding than chatting ter a good friend in a comfortable chair wiv a nice drink in yer 'and.'

'Well, my face is very hot and . . .'

'Who gives a damn, eh? There's only me 'ere an' I don't care, so why should you? Yer face don't 'urt, does it?' She shook her head. 'Very well then.' He leaned across to her and announced confidentially, 'I'll tell yer what. If you don't look in the mirror, I'll pretend yer sunburnt. 'Ow about that, eh?'

'Thounds pretty good to me, Thidney boyo,' she giggled,

holding out her glass for a refill. 'Though I don't know what my Julia would make of it.'

'Tell me, Alice,' he began as he poured the Scotch into her glass. 'Why is it that whenever yer speak of the young gel, you always refer to her as "my Julia"? Whyn't yer give the gel 'er proper title – "*our* Julia"? Are you ashamed of me or sumpthin'?'

'No, Thid, it'th not that at all. But be fair, you may be her father but you did run off when you found out I wath pregnant, didn't you? I mean, I didn't thee the skies over you between Chrithmath 1910 and May thith year. You've hardly been a caring dad for the lath twenty years, have you?'

'But if you ain't ashamed of me, 'ow come you ain't told anyone about our relationship, an' what's all this old bollocks yer tell people about 'er proper dad bein' killed in the war?'

Alice knew she had absorbed far too much drink to be involved in such an intense discussion, but the debate was already out of her control. So, after a series of deep breaths, she began to punctuate her speech only as deliberately as an inebriate can. 'When you ran out on me, Thid – I was pennileth – and no one wanths a girl with a bathtard child – therefore – I pretended the father wath killed in the war. 'Ow the hell wath I to know you'd find me out – and come back in my life again?' She gave an ironic little snort. 'Even worth – how wath I to know I'd be daft enough – to have you back – ethpethially after the way you treated me and my baby, Thid Grechen.'

'Okay, gel,' he soothed. 'I grant yer I've not always done the best fer the both of yer but all that's gonna change from now, you see if it don't.' He glanced quickly around the room and leaned forward confidentially and whispered in her ear. 'I've got plans fer us, yer see, big plans. But I've got ter get a few quid first. I need it ter set up the business. So what I'm suggestin' is . . .'

'Oh, yes, an' that's another thing!' she said, prodding him in the chest with a finger, 'This bloody bithneth you're alwayth on about – In all the yearth I've known you, Thid Grechen – I haven't had the fainteth bloody idea what it ith that you do for a living – For all I know you could be a thodding ponth. In fact,' she said, turning her back on him, 'you probably are.'

'Nah, come on,' he snarled. 'Listen ter me, will yer? We ain't got much more time left. So pull yerself together an' listen, yer fuckin' daft cow.'

She turned and faced him once more. 'Aha!' she exclaimed. 'Your true colours at lath, eh?'

Moving quickly across to her, he knelt and placed both hands pleadingly on her knees. 'I'm sorry, gel, I'm sorry. I'm just a bit upset, that's all. Come on, let's not spoil the evenin'. Let's have one last drink an' be friends agin, what say yer?'

'It wathn't me who was thpoiling it in the firth place, I'm sure,' she pointed out haughtily.

'Yer, yer quite right, gel,' he agreed as he poured out yet another glassful. 'It was me an' I apologise. Nah, will yer listen ter what I've got ter say?'

'Of courth, Thidney,' she replied graciously.

'Good.' Rising to his feet he went quickly across the room to the window and, moving the curtain, glanced out into the dark. Apparently satisfied, he returned to Alice. 'No one knows this place like you do, Alice. Nah, what I want from yer is a list of the most valuable items in this 'ouse. So, we'll arrange fer yer ter leave a winder open an' then I'll return here and . . .'

'I can't pothibly do that, Thidney – and you know it – Mith Bardell hath been far too good to me – to even conthider it.'

'Yer not listenin' ter me, are yer, yer stupid bitch!' he snapped, seizing her arms tightly. 'Look, I don't propose ter take anyfin' of personal value to 'er. I'm just after fings that are insured by the company so she won't be the loser. I mean, if she's as skint as you say she is, she may even be glad of the readies.'

Alice's mind was now in a fog. What she was really needing was a comfortable pillow to lay her head until a respectable hour in the morning. Somehow, through an alcoholic haze, she had to explain to this man exactly why he should not be undertaking to burgle the kindest person she had known in her life. Swallowing the last of her drink, she concentrated on assembling her thoughts for one last valiant try.

'Now lithen to me, Thidney – You muthn't interrupt me, 'cos – I think I'm a bit tiddly – but I want you to lithen very carefully – all right?'

Almost in despair, he nodded to her whilst setting his mind on another course of action.

'You thee – Mith Bardell – ith in a whole new lot of trouble – that you don't even know about yet . . .'

As the tale unfolded, Sid listened in wonderment, hardly believing his good fortune. Here he was, searching in desperation for a regular source of revenue to tide him over until his luck changed and there was this drunken cow, almost forcing him to listen to what could be his very salvation! He prodded along her narration by the odd 'Good Gawd, what 'appened next?' and the occasional 'Oh, that's dreadful,' but in the main her tale flowed smooth and freely. Once he was satisfied he had the gist of it, he began to think how best to turn it to his advantage with the minimum of risk. Without the stimulant of his prodding, Alice had begun to drone on considerably and was now slurring her words so badly as to be unintelligible. It was already fairly obvious to him she would soon pass out. This would be no bad thing and it would give him more chance to think. She had barely begun to doze when he was struck with the perfect answer to everything. His trail could be covered and he need never return here. Yes, that was it! What time did she say they would be back? Ten o'clock at the earliest, wasn't it? He glanced at the clock and gave a relieved smile. Ninety minutes was more than enough time. He leaned closer to her ear.

'Alice,' he said softly, 'can yer 'ear me?'

The only response was a meaningless mutter, punctuated by deep breaths and a belly rumble. Propping her up with a cushion, he pulled out a grimy handkerchief and began to move quickly around the room wiping anything he may have touched. Once satisfied, he washed and dried his glass and placed it back tidily in the cupboard. He marvelled at his good fortune in that he had not yet entered any other room and, once satisfied that all was to his liking, he opened the door to the hall and tiptoed upstairs to reconnoitre. On reaching Alice's bedroom, he drew the curtains and began to scatter the bedclothing and tipped up most of the furniture. On his way back to the kitchen, he went quickly into most of the rooms and pulled out drawers, opened cupboards and gathered up anything of value that could fit easily into his Gladstone bag. Once back in the kitchen, he mentally rechecked his plan for flaws. There were none. Now satisfied, he moved to the fireside chair and, lifting up the slumbering Alice, carried her with ease up to her bedroom. As he laid her back on the bed she roused slightly and gave a little sigh.

'Oh, Thidney – please no sex – I thought I might – just have got away with it – thith time,' she moaned.

Shredding a sheet, he first gagged then spreadeagled her before tying her hands and feet to the brass frame of the bed. Once satisfied she was helpless, he ripped every stitch of clothing from her body. His plan had been to imply that a rapist-cum-burglar had struck. Assuming, because of her inebriation and his own lack of desire, he would be incapable of rape, he had mentally settled to inflict her with a few bruises and the odd abrasion. To his surprise, her nudity, or possibly her bondage, had excited him to a degree he had never experienced before. For a moment he faltered. If anyone were to return home early, even seconds could be vital, but the struggling and rapidly sobering body spread wide in front of him was too much of a temptation. Within seconds he had unfastened his clothing and thrown himself upon her. He was amazed at his own passion, yet, though his gaze devoured every curve of her body, he had no wish to look into her terror-struck eyes. Trying to avoid her stare though he might, it was just not possible. Yielding at last, he decided to confront her. Lifting his head from her breasts, he returned her wide-eyed stare.

'Stop struggling, yer silly cow!' he hissed, then added ominously, 's'all right, Alice, it's gonna be all over in a minute.'

It *was* all over within minutes, five of them to be precise. Both Sidney Grechen's libido and Alice Giles's life had ceased to function. His desire sated, he had picked up a pillow and pressed it down tightly onto her face. He had done this with an indifference that surprised even himself. Struggling to his feet, he adjusted his clothing with one hand, whilst slightly parting the curtains with the other. After an anxious glance at the drive and without giving another thought to the body grotesquely spread across the bed, he raced downstairs to the kitchen. Giving the room a final check, he suddenly saw a glint of metal beneath the fireside chair where Alice had sat. Stooping down he could hardly believe his luck. When he had first removed his handkerchief, his door keys must have been tangled in it. There they were neatly lying on the fireside rug under the chair. He could not afford any mistakes like that! He swiftly pocketed them and, using his handkerchief to turn the handle, let himself out. Closing the door behind him, he took off his shoe and, turning back, knocked out the glass panel into the kitchen and flitted away like a bat in the night.

As the young couple turned into the gravel drive, a distant church clock announced the eleventh hour. The evening had been so wildly successful that Julia had not mentioned politics once. The arm that had been draped so protectively over her shoulders on the way out and was now wrapped possessively around her waist on the way back, may well have had a passing influence on this omission. Anyway, she thought, there would be plenty of other occasions when she could renew her onslaught on his political naivety.

'There are no lights on. Perhaps everyone's in bed,' Duncan observed. 'We'll let ourselves in through the kitchen.'

'Then let's walk on the lawn,' Julia suggested, 'just in case the gravel wakes them up. Besides, we can take our shoes off and I love walking on dewy grass in bare feet, don't you? It's sort of well, you know, how can I put it?'

'Sexy?' he whispered, pulling her round and into him.

'Don't be daft, feet aren't sexy,' she protested, slipping out of his grasp and out of her shoes. 'Feet are *peculiar*; that's why they feel so good on cool damp grass.'

'Nonsense,' he argued, also kicking off his shoes and socks. 'It's a well-known fact that feet are very sexy.'

'Well, it's not well known to me and yours aren't for a start.' She pointed down at them. 'I mean, just look at them. They're all humpty-bumpty. They look more likes toads than toes, ugh!' She stared at them for a moment trying to make out their outline by the dim light of the stars. 'If ever I'm lucky enough to get married,' she announced thoughtfully, 'I shall refuse to sleep with my husband unless he sleeps with his feet outside the bedclothes. I shall simply refuse to have such dreadful things in my bed.'

'In that case,' Duncan said, seizing her hand and pulling it down towards his raised bare foot, 'I think you should make every effort to get to know my feet now, because I'm going to marry you some day and I have no intention of leaving my feet sticking out the end of the bed every night.'

'Well,' she said as she began to fondle his feet, 'I'll tell you this much . . .' Julia suddenly seized his ankle and tugged it hard, tipping him backwards onto the damp grass. 'The main reasons I wouldn't marry you are your lousy politics and your ugly feet.' With that, and with Duncan in playful pursuit, she scuttled off laughing towards the back of the house.

It wasn't until he caught her at the edge of the path at the rear of the house, that they realised their shoes were still back somewhere in the middle of the dark damp lawn.

'We'll need to get a torch from the kitchen,' Julia said. 'Otherwise they'll be there till morning and my mother won't be very pleased about that – they were hers!'

As they picked their way carefully towards the kitchen door, Duncan peered into the gloom. 'Hey, someone's broken the window! What're we going to do now? We've no shoes and we'll never find them in the dark.'

Julia's merriment vanished as she suddenly clung to him tightly. 'Duncan,' she said nervously, 'I don't like this, there's something wrong. If anyone was in the kitchen they would have heard us by now. But if no one is in the kitchen, then why is the light on?'

'Perhaps they forgot to switch it off?'

'Then why is the window broken? Neither my mum nor Miss Bardell would leave a window broken like that, especially at this time of night. Duncan! Something's happened, I know it has!'

'Wait here – no,' he countered, 'on second thoughts, if anything is wrong, you may be safer in the rhododendrons. Hide in there and I'll see what's happened. We're probably getting all worked up about nothing.'

'I don't care, I'm coming with you. My mother should be in there somewhere, so I'm certainly not hiding. Quick, let's take a look.'

For the second time that day, Duncan swept her up off her feet and carried her, but this time in very different circumstances. With the girl still in his arms, he kicked open the kitchen door and picked his way gingerly through the glass fragments before reaching the relative safety of the table. Setting Julia on the table edge, he scoured the room. Turning, he saw her sniffing an empty bottle. 'It's Scotch,' she said with a puzzled expression. 'Or at least it was.' She looked swiftly about her but could see only one glass. 'My mum would never drink Scotch, well certainly not on her own. There must be someone else in the house with her. Something dreadful has happened, I can feel it, Duncan. I'm sure I can.'

'You're worrying yourself unnecessarily,' he soothed. 'Perhaps Miss Bardell is home. Let's look.'

The girl raced ahead of him and just before they reached the open door of her shared bedroom, Julia paused, unsure. Before Duncan could reach her, she suddenly clamped both her hands to her mouth, hunched her shoulders and shuddered uncontrollably. Looking beyond her into the room, he suddenly saw the bed.

'My God!' he exclaimed, as she turned to him and buried her now ashen face deep into his chest. Her quaking sobs began to vibrate throughout his whole body.

At first, dumbstruck, he could not take in the full horror of the scene. As he slowly forced himself to absorb it, he knew he should remove the pillow from the woman's face. After all, there was always the possibility she might still be alive. Yet, even without experience of death, he instinctively knew he was staring at a corpse. At first he could not decipher the girl's words as she mumbled them deep into his chest. Gently easing her head away from him, he tilted back her chin with his hand, pausing only to smooth back some strands of stray hair. 'I couldn't hear what you said, darling,' he whispered.

'Take the pillow from her face,' Julia ordered in a cold, precise tone. Without waiting for a response, her voice suddenly leaped two octaves and she suddenly screamed and pounded at him. 'The pillow! THE BLOODY PILLOW. MOVE IT FOR GOD'S SAKE, MY MOTHER IS DYING!' With that she collapsed into a sobbing wreck.

After leading her to the chair by the door, Duncan moved apprehensively towards the bed. Even without an expert eye, he could see by the stained bottom sheet that the victim had clearly been raped. He also realised that rape was not all that had been inflicted on her. Reaching for the pillow, his stomach heaved at what might await him. Steeling himself, he peeled back the pillow and found it almost impossible to equate the twisted face of the corpse with the mature but previously lovely features of Alice Giles. Instinctively he untied the gag that cut so cruelly into the corners of her mouth before trying vainly to smooth out the twisted contours of her face. It was to no avail.

'Duncan, what are you trying to do?' asked the girl in an almost normal tone as she reached the bed.

'I'm trying to . . . I'm trying to . . .' he faltered. 'Julia, your mother was lovely . . . This, this . . .' he pointed down at the face, 'is not her. She never looked like this . . . I'm trying to make her . . . beauti . . .' He fell to his knees at the edge of the bed then leaned forward, sobbing onto the still warm shoulders of the poor dead maid.

169

11

Jim Forsythe, with only the occasional grunt, threaded the Austin through the late night West-End traffic while Billie Bardell sat quietly by his side in thoughtful contemplation. Her mood had not been entirely from choice, but Jim, with his dislike of driving, had not uttered a word since leaving Streatham. She had therefore been obliged to keep uncharacteristically silent. To begin with, she had found this particularly difficult – reticence was not something at which she excelled. But, as time passed, her speculations began to range far and wide with more self-analysis than she had attempted for a very long time. At no stage of her life had she been a pessimist but she was now beginning to think it would be heavenly to fall into a long deep sleep and emerge a year hence to find her worries had all been for nothing.

In spite of the uncertainties of her own tenure, it was the problem of Grace that bothered her most. It was almost eerie the way David and Grace's lives were beginning to mirror that of David's parents. They were even tenants in the same dreadful flat! David, though as stubborn and obstinate as his father in many ways, was probably not quite so unbending. Grace on the other hand, though sharing Queenie's earlier dread of poverty, lacked the maturity that the elder woman had always managed to show, even in her youth. Still, being a policeman, David was at least in a reasonably secure job and, providing he wasn't as headstrong as his father, he was likely to remain so. As they drove past the British Museum, Jim spoke his first words since Queenie had waved goodbye to the pair of them.

'Been offered a job near here,' he uttered briefly. 'Not sure whether to take it or not.'

'Jim!' exclaimed Billie. 'You talk! You *actually* talk! I was beginning to get quite worried. Here was I thinking I was losing my grip.'

'Your grip?' he echoed. 'I don't understand. It's me that wasn't talking, not you.'

'Well,' she replied disdainfully, 'I don't normally expect to be sitting so close to a man for so long and not get a word out of him. In fact, it wasn't so long ago I'd have been quite disappointed if I didn't have to fight him off.'

'Oh, it's nothing personal you understand,' explained Jim tensely. 'But I feel so ill at ease in these bloody cars that I couldn't show any interest in you if you were wearing just high-heeled shoes and mittens.'

'*Jim!*' she cried facetiously. 'You're a pervert! How wonderful! Just think, all these years and I've only just found you out! You must call round sometime. Anyway, to be more mundane, I didn't know you were looking for a new job. How long has this been on the cards?'

He turned his head to answer, but obviously thinking better of it, rolled the vehicle slowly into the kerbside and switched off the engine. 'Phew! That's better!' he muttered, mopping his brow with his sleeve. 'Well, it's been on the cards for some little time now for several reasons really. Firstly, I'm getting a bit old in the tooth for the hurly burly of coppering . . .'

'Hang on!' she interrupted. 'I thought they kept you in Scotland Yard now, you know, so you could plan all sorts of clever schemes that everyone else disregards totally or have I got that bit wrong?'

'Saucy bitch!' he grinned. 'Although you're probably more accurate than I'd care to admit. Yes, you're right, I am in Scotland Yard. Even so, that posting won't last for ever and I think there are a lot of changes coming about. Besides, at my age, I certainly don't want to be on the streets when they take place.'

'For instance?' she asked.

'Well, for number one, the cuts.'

'Cuts? What are they?'

'This government, although to be fair, they're not alone, is almost broke. Therefore what they are planning to do is slice at least ten per cent off every piece of expenditure. Expenditure, in this case, being wages, allowances, pensions and almost everything else you can think of. Now, if you take the poverty of young David, for example, and tell him he's soon going to be eight shillings and sixpence short on his weekly wage, whilst also remembering that Grace is not allowed to work, you may have some idea of what's afoot. You also have to bear in mind that there are several million others out there who are even worse off than he is. Already some sailors are making mutinous noises and the cuts haven't even started. I can see some terrible unrest on the streets if this plan goes ahead and the police are going to be at the sharp end.'

'By your tone, Jim Forsythe, I get the impression there is even more to this than you've mentioned.'

'Oh, there most certainly is. For a start, there is the situation concerning the commissioner. The Home Secretary is trying to ease out the present one – Viscount Byng of Vimy – so that Lord Trenchard can take over.'

'Is that so important – changing the commissioner? I thought it usually meant swopping one doddery old fart for another? Anyway, running your firm is always a job for the old-boy network. Everyone knows that surely?'

He smiled. 'Well with the exception of General MacReady, you may have been right, but with some of the ideas that Trenchard is already hinting at, he'll hit this force like an earthquake.'

'Sounds a good idea to me. It's about time some of you coppers realised we're living in the nineteen thirties. Queen

173

Victoria's long gone. Anyway, what's so terrible about a bit of modern thinking?'

'Well, men like me would never make the rank of superintendent for a start. In Trenchard's plans, my rank would consist entirely of degree entrants. His aim is to give the police force an officer class. If they arrive at Scotland Yard from university with the piece of paper declaring they're proficient in joined-up writing, they'd be welcomed with open arms and made inspectors. My sort, who'd worked their way up the ladder, would no longer exist.'

'Oh, come off it, Jim, I bet you're exaggerating. All you people do that when your job's threatened. It's only natural.'

He gave a long sigh and, switching on the engine, eased the car into gear. 'Am I? Well, I'm not waiting to find out. When Trenchard finally hits this job there'll be such a bloody exodus that my plan is to be one pace ahead of the crowd.'

The car gave three great jumping lurches before bouncing its way down Gower Street and for the next three-and-a-half miles the silence resumed its intensity, though Billie was roused from her meditations on at least two occasions by a growling oath from her companion, aimed usually at a taxi driver. Other than that, silence reigned until a sharp nudge to her right ribs was followed by the muttered request, 'Hampstead Lane, where now?'

Leaning forward, she peered through the windscreen. 'It's not far. Look, Jim, I've been thinking. Why don't you drop me off at the gate. It's quite late and even the faintest footsteps sound like a bloody army on my gravel drive. Alice doesn't sleep too well and I'd hate to wake her just after she's nodded off.'

'I certainly shan't leave you at the gate but I will leave the car outside and walk you down the grass verge, if that makes you happy?'

'I'll not argue with that, James. It's been a little while now since I've had a midnight walk with a good-looking man. In fact, the more I think of it, the better it sounds. Wouldn't fancy a starlight romp across the heath first, I s'pose. No? Oh well, always worth a try, wouldn't you say?'

He turned the car into the drive and switched off the lights and engine. 'Billie Bardell, you're absolutely incorrigible. I bet you torment the life out of that young gardener of yours. What's his name? Duncan something or other?'

'Forbes, Duncan Forbes,' she told him. 'But that just shows you how wrong you can be. As far as that young man is concerned, me and Alice are trying to be real old-fashioned romantics and match him up with young Julia. I think they're ideally matched except she's a bit of a daft cow and keeps trying to get him interested in politics.'

'I notice you still haven't denied tormenting him. Be honest now, Billie. You could no more ignore a good-looking lad like that than stop breathing, could you?'

She gave a quick wry smile as they alighted from the car. 'Okay, I'll grant that at first I was a bit naughty, but when I realised how suited the two of them were, my old romantic streak took over. Women like to feel they have been responsible for achieving a happy relationship, which is more than can be said for your lot.'

'That's true, I suppose,' he nodded. 'Men certainly would want no part of something like that. We'd probably be terrified we'd get the blame if the wheel came off. Though I notice you've gone a bit forgetful about your relationship with him.'

She linked arms with him as they strode over the grass. 'I was just being helpful, that's all. He cut down a tree and grazed his back badly. I took him upstairs to my bathroom and cleaned it up for him, that's all.'

'*Just* his back?'

She shrugged. 'His back and a few other bits, I suppose. Anyway, what's this got to do with – *Jim!*' she leaned forward and peered into the gloom. 'Isn't that an ambulance at my front door?'

'An ambulance? Yes, and a police car, I'd say.'

'And there are lights on all over the house!' She turned towards him with her mouth gaping wide. 'It's Alice, I bet it is! It's Alice!'

He took her hand and, for the second time that evening, a bewildered couple ran stumbling towards the house.

Breathlessly entering the open front door, they were making for the voices coming from the direction of the drawing room, when a loud 'OY YOU TWO!' from behind caused them to stop instantly.

'Just a minute! Where the 'ell d'you think you're agoin'?'

'Why, what's happened?' asked Billie anxiously. 'Come on, man, tell me quick!'

The police constable, who had been behind the door and slightly out of their vision, now moved forward to the centre of the hall. 'Never mind about what's 'appened! Don't yer be so bloody nosy, woman! What I want to know is, who the 'ell are yer an' what're yer doin' wanderin' about all over the place?'

Billie's eyes narrowed at the words. Then, placing her hands on her hips, she bent forward towards him. 'Listen to me, you uncouth lout,' she hissed. 'If you ever speak to me like that again in my house, I shall personally shove the hot kitchen poker up your arse and twist it frequently! Do I make myself clear, you loud-mouthed oaf?'

The venom in her reply rocked the constable to his foundations and he began to bluster. 'Er – I see, mam, er – you're the owner then of this 'ouse, are yer? Er – well,' he added, turning his attention to Jim. 'Wot about you then, guv', er – what's yer name an' what're yer doin' 'ere?'

'My name,' responded Jim, hiding his satisfaction with great difficulty, 'is Superintendent Forsythe from Scotland Yard and I have just escorted this lady back to her home. I will therefore say, Constable, that, judging by your aggressive attitude towards her, it was extremely fortunate for you that I am here because I have already seen what this lady can do with a hot poker and believe me, it fetches tears to the eyes.'

'Er – well, yer see, sir, I was only afraid the pair of yer might clump all over the house and bugger up the clues, sir.'

'Bugger up . . .' began Jim, his satisfaction fading fast. 'What clues, man? What do you mean? Just what has been going on here tonight?'

'I'm sorry, guv – er, sir, but I fort you knew, you bein' a superintendent an' all. It's murder, sir, an 'orrible murder 'as taken place 'ere. We're waitin' fer the CID to arrive, sir.'

'MURDER?' cried Billie. 'WHO'S BEEN MURDERED? HOW?'

'A Mrs—' the policeman glanced down at his notebook, 'a Mrs Alice Giles, mam. An' very nasty it was too, I'm sorry ter say.' He turned to Jim and added, 'Will you be takin' over the inquiry nah, sir?'

'No, no. I'm just a family friend. I'm sure your CID will cope. Where's the body?'

'Upstairs in a bedroom, sir.'

'And Julia, her daughter. Has she returned yet?' asked the distraught Billie.

'Yus, mam, she's in the parlour with a young man called—' he gave another glance down at his book, 'called Forbes, mam, and they're talkin' there ter two of me colleagues.'

'Take us to them, please,' ordered Jim, then added as an afterthought, 'it's all right, I'll take full responsibility for the interruption.'

Billie was already halfway to the drawing room before the request had been finished, and the next moment a red-eyed Julia fell sobbing into her arms. Meanwhile, new voices from the hall indicated that the CID had now arrived and within seconds they too had joined the group in the drawing room.

The questioning seemed endless, but finally, just before dawn, the two detectives finished their notes. Almost automatically, Billie poured her third brew of tea of the night.

'So what's the situation now?' she asked the senior of the two.

Detective Inspector Roger Evans was a Welshman and

could not have been mistaken for anything other than a former rugby player, not even in a half-mile of fog. His thick black hair topped off dark heavy jowls that rounded off a solid squat body. 'We've padlocked the bedroom, mam,' he told her, 'and I'll be leaving two uniform men here for a day or so until we've finished measuring and finger-printing. It would most certainly be helpful if your good self, Miss Giles and Mr Forbes could stay elsewhere for a couple of nights.'

'Of course,' she agreed. 'But what do you make of this dreadful thing so far?'

'Well, the indications are that originally a break-in took place. The poor lady could possibly have disturbed the suspect. It might well be that the rape was simply an afterthought. He could have possibly only intended to tie her to the bed to keep her quiet but then got carried away. In my experience, it is unlikely that he entered with the sole intention of rape. After all, until he actually entered, he may have been under the impression the house was empty. That's why I suspect his prime intention was theft. If I had to guess at this moment, I'd say the rape and murder were a sequel to the break-in, but there are still many more lines of inquiry to be pursued – one of them being, of course, the victim's mystery friend.'

'I don't know about this,' said Jim. 'What friend and what was the mystery?'

'Well, it appears that the deceased had a gentleman friend who would see her from time to time. Unfortunately, she also kept him very secret. So much so, that no one has laid eyes on him, not even her daughter.'

Before Jim could respond, Julia said icily, 'I wish you'd stop referring to my mother as the "deceased"! She was a person, a living caring woman. She wasn't a *deceased*! A deceased is some dead useless thing and my mum will never be that.'

'Of course, luv,' soothed Jim. 'But it's just a piece of legal phraseology. It's not meant to detract from your mum's memory.'

'But that's the whole point!' cried the girl. 'That's exactly what it does! Her name was Alice, Alice Giles and that'll be the name on the gravestone – not "deceased"!'

'I'm sorry, Miss Giles,' said the inspector in his soft Welsh accent. 'You're quite right, of course. From now on, except at the inquest, when I shan't have the option, I shall refer to her only as Alice Giles.'

The girl was silent for a moment before whispering a barely perceptible thank you.

'Look, Inspector,' said Jim, rising to his feet, 'if you've finished with us for the time being, I'll be making tracks for my home in Streatham before the morning rush hour starts. I telephoned my wife some hours ago and she's expecting us all for breakfast. We'll be easy enough for you to contact there.'

'So how long will they be staying with you, sir?' asked the Welshman.

'Until the precise minute you withdraw your two uniform policemen,' cut in Billie sharply. 'I can't possibly return with them clumping all over the place. Coppers always make me uneasy. Though if it'd help to put a rope around the scum's neck who killed my Alice, they could live here for the rest of my life.'

'*I* shall never come back here,' murmured Julia almost to herself.

'But you will, dear,' corrected Billie taking the girl's hands. 'You will. You'll see.'

Together with the subdued trio, the two detectives waited patiently at the front door while Jim walked to the gate to collect his car. As each of them placed their overnight luggage into the car boot, Billie suddenly requested that she might kiss a final goodbye to Alice.

'I'd sooner you didn't miss,' replied Evans solemnly. 'Apart from the fact there have already been too many people in that room for my choosing, Mrs Giles does not look very pleasant. However, if you would still like to see her, could I suggest you do that at the undertakers in a week or so? Those people can do wonders in these cases and, after all, it would be your final memory of her. If you think about it, I'm sure she would have preferred it that way, mam, don't you?'

Billie responded with a silent nod of agreement and Jim slipped a comforting arm around her shoulders. After a couple of brief handshakes, the sad quartet climbed aboard the Austin for the hour-long journey to Streatham. As they turned from the drive into the main Hampstead Lane, Evans stared after them thoughtfully before turning to his fellow detective.

'Well, Mac, what d'you think?'

'I first saw that woman on the stage when I was fourteen years old,' said his colleague nostalgically. 'That was twenty-two years ago and I remember every second. I was with my mate, Alfie Ironsides. He'd won a toy telescope at a fairground a few days earlier. We were leaning over the front row of the gallery and spent the entire matinée peeking straight down the front of her dress. We later lied to each other we could see her navel. I remember it well because I didn't sleep for a week. She was my first heavy lust and I swear she doesn't look a day older.'

Shaking his head, the Welshman stared briefly at the sky. 'That's *not* what I asked, you randy sod! I want to know what you think about that quartet?'

The detective sergeant mused thoughtfully for a few moments before replying. 'Well, I can tell you what my missus'd say if I turned up with Billie Bardell and told her she would need to sleep at our house for a few days, if that's any help?'

'And the others?'

'Well, if that superintendent's not sleeping with Billie Bardell, then he must be bloody queer. As for the two youngsters—' He shrugged. 'Seem two nice kids really, in fact, the girl is so gorgeous I could eat her. I would agree it was a chance burglary that went wrong but I'd certainly like to know a great deal more about Alice's mystery boyfriend, though.'

'Y-e-s,' nodded the detective inspector slowly. 'So would I, but unfortunately, because young Julia couldn't stand the sight of the bloke, she made a point of ignoring him. Basically all we know about him is that he's pig-ignorant and looks like a typical thick London thug. I personally know a good twenty villains – to say nothing of one detective-sergeant – who fall into that category, don't you?'

If Jim had not cared for his drive to Hampstead at one hour to midnight, it was as nothing to his journey home at one hour past dawn. It had been almost bearable until he had cleared the west end of London but once he had reached the Embankment he had to face his own personal nightmare. Trams were to Jim as dragons were to Saint George. He knew they had to be faced and he hoped to emerge victorious, but deep down he was full of nagging doubts. He thought the damn things could have been almost bearable if only they did not run on lines. He drove in constant terror of getting his wheels fixed on these lines and being unable to do anything but follow them. As a result, as soon as he reached tramcar territory, he spent so much time avoiding the lines that he had little opportunity to avoid much else. Duncan, who was not a good passenger at the best of times, had deluded himself that he might have been able to snatch a short sleep on the journey. Instead, once the first of the tramlines came into view, he spent the rest of the trip staring at the rails rigid with fear. Fortunately, the two women were so engrossed in comforting each other, they had little interest in anything else.

It was around six thirty that the car came to a final halt outside the Forsythe address and Queenie ran from the house to greet the quartet. Her first impression was one of dismay. Jim resembled a limp rag, Billie was still consoling a sobbing Julia and Duncan had the opened eyes of a terror-struck zombie.

'Come on, my dears,' she encouraged, 'I've warmed all the bedrooms, I've got a good fire going in the kitchen and I'll soon have a nice hot breakfast for you.' Of the four, it was Duncan who seemed to concern her most. 'Hey, young man,' she prompted, 'snap out of it. Give Julia a helping hand, there's a dear.'

Minutes later, as Queenie crouched by the kitchen fire, teapot in hand, she tilted the boiling kettle from above the flames, talking over her shoulder.

'Jim outlined most of what happened over the telephone, so I'll not ask any questions until you've all had a good sleep. I've already put hot-water bottles in your beds, so you can all toddle off just as soon as you've finished breakfast.'

'I think I'd better stay up, dear,' replied Jim. 'I'll need to tell my office that I'll be in late today. Anyway, someone's bound to ring me about the murder.'

'*I'll* ring your office,' she answered firmly. 'I doubt if you're indispensable and if anyone rings for you, or any of you for that matter, then they can just as easily ring back later.' She shook her head in despair. 'Look at you all, you look dreadful. You've been up all night and you'll be fit for nothing else until you've had a good breakfast and a good sleep. Now, I'll not hear another word. Jim, you can sleep in one spare bed so that Julia and Mum can use our bed and Duncan can sleep in the other spare. There you are, see. I can hold the fort quite easily, so there's nothing left to argue about.'

Julia, still white-faced, gave a brief weak smile and walked round the table and planted a light kiss on Queenie's cheek. 'I'm sorry, Mrs Forsythe, but I'm afraid I can't eat anything, though if I can just have a cup of tea, I'll certainly take up your offer of a bed.'

'Of course, dear. I'll fetch your tea upstairs. Give me a

second and I'll show you the way. Meanwhile, the rest of you help yourselves to breakfast.'

Once she had settled the girl in bed, Queenie spent some minutes fussing around the room. She drew the curtains, laid out towels and put away clothes before tiptoeing silently out, clicking the door to behind her. As she returned to the kitchen, Billie lowered the cup she was holding and nodded to her approvingly.

'You've done a good job there, daughter, I'm proud of you. We all have a great deal to discuss, but you're right, this isn't the time to do it. I'm really grateful to you and so's this dozy sod.' She jerked a thumb in the direction of Duncan. 'But he's too bloody whacked to tell you. Anyway, thanks again.'

Duncan, with a nod of weary apology, simply whispered, 'M'sorry,' before dropping his gaze once more to the floor.

Fifteen minutes later, Queenie had ushered all her charges to their allotted rooms and had returned to clear the breakfast dishes. Jim was already sleeping soundly in his bed as was Duncan in his. Billie meanwhile, was lying propped on her elbow gazing down at the barely awake, silently sobbing Julia. Smoothing the girl's hair back from her damp forehead, she suddenly thought how young and vulnerable she looked.

'It's not been much of a life for you, has it?' she said almost to herself. 'And I don't think it's going to get much better either, you poor cow.' She slipped an arm beneath the girl who then turned and buried herself deep into the warm security of Billie's ample naked body.

There, in the half-lit bedroom, the worldly woman and the bewildered girl lay quietly in each other's arms with only distant traffic and a ticking clock to disturb them. Billie slowly began to realise that, far from being exhausted, she was now further from sleep than at any other time of her life. What was more, she also knew why. Gently turning to the girl, she kissed her forehead lightly whilst easing away her own arm from beneath her. The movement, unhurried though it was, still caused the girl to open her eyes in some alarm.

'It's going to be all right, darling,' Billie soothed as she slid gently from the bed. Tiptoeing across the room, she took a robe from behind the door and stepped out onto the landing. As she opened the door opposite, the daylight from the landing escaped eagerly into the darkened room. It then raced across the floor and came to a final rest on the face of the sleeping Duncan. Kneeling down at the side of the bed she began slowly to shake him.

'C'mon, lad, c'mon!' she whispered with a quiet urgency. Eventually and after much blinking and squinting, Duncan's eyes reluctantly opened. He looked around the room in puzzlement before recognition dawned.

'Wassa time?' he asked thickly.

'It's all right, you've hours yet,' she whispered. 'But come with me, it's urgent.'

'Why, is it a fire?' he asked as he sat up and glanced quickly about him.

'Good God, no, boy. Look, just do as you're told will you, and don't make a noise!'

Dutifully, though semi-comatose, he followed Billie across the landing and into the darkened room opposite.

'We're changing beds, boy, because I think you two need each other more than I need either of you. But be kind to her or I'll have your guts for garters.' Assisting him between the sheets, she tucked in the blankets and walked to the door. Just before closing it she looked back at the couple. With arms around the girl, he was already asleep. More importantly, they looked as if they belonged. For the first time for hours a slight smile played round the corners of her mouth.

12

Queenie was quite surprised at how long her guests had slept. It was well after four in the afternoon and the only sound she had heard was the flush of the lavatory around midday. Judging by the sound of the footsteps, it was probably Jim who, even at civilised sleep times, would need to make that particular trip around three in the morning. She decided if she had heard nothing by five o'clock she would take them up tea. After all, if they were to sleep much longer it would hardly be worth them waking.

At fifteen minutes to the hour, she slid the old copper kettle from the rear of her kitchen range and onto the centre of the hob where it promptly began its customary cheerful dance. As she busied herself with tea caddy and cups, the rattling letterbox indicated the arrival of the evening paper. After filling the teapot, she approached the door and, by the thickness of the headlines, saw there was a newsworthy drama for the day. Whilst waiting for the tea to draw, she spread the newspaper over the kitchen table and saw that the headlines related to the extraordinary success of the German Fascist Party in the Reichstag elections.

'Damn politics,' she muttered to herself. 'Ours are bad enough without worrying about someone else's.' With a disapproving 'Tut' she skimmed quickly over the road accident statistics and turned the page. 'Oh, no!' she gasped as the two-inch headline caught her eye.

MUSIC HALL QUEEN AND SCOTLAND YARD DETECTIVE IN SEX SLAYING!

It stretched the full width of the page. Alice Giles was obviously not considered important enough in her own right, so the story was slanted towards Billie Bardell and Jim rather than the victim. In the obvious absence of a suitable photograph of poor Alice, they had made up for it by an array of photographs of Billie, many more than twenty years old and all taken from the archives and library.

The secondary story was little better. In this a photograph of Billie's house was shown and inserted into its foreground was a smiling and deeply cleavaged Billie. The accompanying headline ran – Merry Widow's Luxury Abode. The absence of a suitable photograph of Jim had mercifully reduced his role in the affair to that of supporting player. Of the two-thousand word story, less than a quarter related to the victim. The rest was of Billie's undisputed and frequently outrageous lifestyle and, after an obviously negative search of the cuttings library, a brief record of Jim's service record had had to suffice.

Queen shook her head in horror and, after rapidly folding the paper, she tucked it quickly under a cushion of a seldom-used chair. Stacking a tea-tray with crockery, utensils and biscuits, she angrily kicked open the hall door and headed for the staircase.

Her own bedroom was first to be reached and, balancing the tray with one hand, she eased open the door. The bright sun of the early morning had moved round the house and, with the curtains tightly drawn, the room was therefore darker than usual. Paying little attention to the slumbering figures in the eiderdowned bed, she swept a chair to the bedside with her foot and lowered the tray on it. Moving to the curtains, her intention had been to hurl them wide apart with a loud 'Wakey Wakey!' Before doing so, she turned her head towards the bed so that she could see the maximum effect of her actions.

Her first doubts arose when she saw the close proximity of the figures. They did not just share a bed, they shared a pillow. In fact, they almost shared a space. Relinquishing her firm grip of the curtains, she parted them just enough to allow sufficient light into the room. There were definitely two figures in the bed and one was clearly Duncan! But what was he doing here? Of course, Billie! She was obviously up to her old tricks again! Queenie was sickened with disbelief. There was her maid lying murdered and there was Billie, barely hours later, in bed with a boy less than half her age! That she should have even contemplated it at any time was bad enough but before the poor maid was hardly cold and in Queenie's own bed was the ultimate insult. She stamped the last two strides to the bed, and seizing the covers, hurled them back to the foot of the bed.

'Get up! Get up, you . . .' With an intake of breath she clapped both hands to her mouth. Far from being the wicked seduction of a young man by a mature wanton, it looked like a scene from Babes in the Wood. Both figures were certainly naked, but by just looking at them it was possible to surmise that all they had ever done that morning was to sleep consolingly in each other's arms. Still, whatever the circumstances, a naked couple in her bed was hardly something of which she would normally approve. Yet, just looking down at the entwined pair, she knew she could never reproach them. 'I-I'm sorry,' she faltered, hastily returning the covers. 'Your tea is there. No rush, take your time and come down when you're ready.' Without waiting for a response, she was almost out of the room before she realised she had left Jim and Billie's tea behind. Returning, and without once raising her eyes to the couple, she splashed out two cups of tea for them and gathered up the tray to scurry shamefacedly from the room.

Billie was already awake when Queenie almost fell into her room. 'What's been going on out there?' asked the older woman. 'And what's the time?'

'Is that your doing in there?' asked Queenie, nodding back over her shoulder. 'Those two kids in bed, I mean. If it's not, it's certainly got your handiwork written all over it.'

Billie gave a long stretch before replying. 'Oh, this is a comfortable bed and I did sleep well. Personally, I always think sleeping with someone is overrated, don't you? Oh, it has other advantages, I grant you, but for real luxury, give me my own bed every time.'

'Mum, please don't insult my intelligence by implying you put those two in bed together just so you could have a bed of your own. It won't wash.'

Billie glanced up at her daughter and then took her time to pour out her own tea before replying. 'Yes, you're right. Putting those two kids together *was* my handiwork.' She shrugged and stirred her cup slowly for a while. 'Oh I could give you all sorts of reasons why I did it. Such as, they-are-both-in-love-with-each-other-but-don't-know-it, or even more likely, they-won't-*admit*-it. But that would not be strictly true. Look, I tell you what. Why don't we just agree that I did it for the best and let it go at that, eh?'

'So what am I supposed to make of that for a reply, for God's sake?' demanded Queenie sharply. 'Before you went into that room this morning to sleep with young Julia, she was already fit to drop and I should think Duncan wasn't far from it either. Now I find you in *this* room and them so closely entwined in there that I couldn't see where he finished and she began!'

'Okay,' said Billie nodding. 'Exactly *how* did you find them, their position, I mean? Was he shafting her? Was she sitting across his face? Were they performing sexual acrobatics from the light fittings? Or were they perhaps innocently sleeping? Go on,' she insisted, 'you tell me what they were doing.'

'Well, not that it matters,' replied Queenie uneasily, 'but they were just fast asleep.' She allowed herself a momentary tight smile. 'I thought they looked like the Babes in the Wood.'

'So what's your complaint?'

Queenie felt her temper rapidly rising. 'What's my *complaint*?' she echoed. 'I'll tell you my bloody *complaint*! My complaint is that neither of them actually *are* the Babes in the Wood! She's a particularly sexually attractive girl and he's a Greek God. Not only that, you deliberately shoved two such people together at a very emotional time in their lives and now you conveniently consider all you have to do is say, "I did it for the best." Still, to be fair,' she added acidly, 'I must say there was an improvement. At least *you* weren't in bed between them.' She shook her head and, sitting on the edge of the bed, placed a hand on her mother's arm. 'Look, I don't want to be a preaching bitch, especially at a time like this, but Julia really is so young! What happens if she falls for a child? Is it to be the usual gut-exploding potions from the herbalists in Brixton Road or the curved hook from that butchering abortionist in Lambeth High Street? Or perhaps you'd prefer her to be like Rene Barclay? You remember Rene Barclay, surely? Half bottle of gin, a hot bath, a leap off the kitchen table and the next five years in Cane Hill asylum? Heaven knows the kid's had a bad enough time as it is. For God's sake, don't pile it on her even more. At least let her enjoy being a girl before you force her to become a woman.'

Billie slowly put down her cup and saucer and placed her hand on top of her daughter's hand. 'Queenie, I know you're right and I also know you are only acting from the best of motives. I accept that, but depending on how you see things . . .' shaking her head slowly, she gave a deep sigh '. . . some would say by taking such action as I did, I saved her from something even worse . . .' There was a long pause before she added, 'Still, who knows? Certainly not me.'

Queenie's earlier anger at what she considered her mother's irresponsibility gave way to bewilderment, but she had been her daughter long enough to know they would never be fully compatible. She cut short the exchange of confidentialities

189

by sliding her hand away and announced briskly, 'I'll have a cooked tea ready for you all in half-an-hour. I must call Jim now. See you soon.' Before she closed the door behind her, she glanced quickly round to see Billie looking towards the window with a pensive faraway stare. It was an expression she had never seen on her mother's face before and she found it worrying.

Entering Jim's room, she found him wide awake, sitting up idly watching the passing traffic through parted curtains.

'Afternoon, dear,' he greeted her, leaning forward and kissing her lightly on the forehead. 'I heard you outside on the landing some time ago. What's kept you?'

'Nothing really. Let's just say I'm old-fashioned.' She moved to the window and realigned the curtains. She loved him dearly, but if there was one thing about him that really grated, it was the careless way he threw open the curtains and then left them in whatever position they happened to rest. 'If you'd just like to stir yourself and beat the rush for the bathroom, I'll have a high tea ready in no time.' She had almost closed the door when he called her back.

'Queenie, am I being punished for not parting the curtains properly?'

'Don't be daft! What makes you say a thing like that?'

'Well, you're taking my tea away!'

She looked down and saw that after carefully balancing the tea-tray into the bedroom, she was now carefully balancing it out again. 'I tell you, Jim,' she muttered, 'I'm sure my mind's going! They say kids can be a problem but it's our bloody mothers who cause ninety per cent of the problems, not our kids!' She looked up and saw a half-smile on the face of her husband and added, 'And don't you *dare* smirk at me, Jim Forsythe, or I'll pour this tea all over you.'

Whether it was the smell of the toasted savouries that permeated the house, Queenie was not sure, but whatever it was caused a prompt attendance at 'high tea'. As the last of them took their seats, she told them Hampstead CID had telephoned to say that from 8 p.m. that evening, Billie was free to use her house again.

'That really *is* quick!' marvelled Jim. 'Billie must have put the wind up them with her outburst. Seems like there's something to be said for swearing at the CID after all. Perhaps I should have tried it years ago. By the way, Queenie, is there anything about poor Alice in the evening paper?'

'Er – no,' faltered Queenie. 'Leastways, I don't think so. It's not arrived yet.'

'Oh, I'm sorry,' murmured Jim, 'but I could have sworn I saw the lad coming up the front path when I was sitting up in bed a while ago.'

'Well, you're wrong,' she replied in a tone she hoped passed for casual. 'It looks like your eyesight is going as well as your memory.' Attempting desperately to change the topic, she turned her attention to Julia who had hardly spoken since she had entered the kitchen. 'You did say this morning, dear, that you could not face returning to Hampstead. Now you've slept on it, have you changed your mind?'

'No,' replied the girl firmly. 'I feel I have to start my life all over again. I must look for another job and accommodation.'

'But, child!' cried Queenie, 'your life's barely started! You may not think so now but you really will adjust. You must do! You're young but you're not unintelligent and you have your whole life before you.'

'And you, Duncan,' said Billie, 'what are your plans? Will you be returning to Hampstead with me?'

'Yes,' he nodded. 'I'll come back with you all right, but I'm afraid it won't be for long. I've known for some time that I need to move on and I think what's happened has given me the extra shove I needed.'

Billie thought she saw a momentary flash of alarm cross Julia's face, but the girl did not speak so she decided to force her hand. 'You've got to sleep somewhere, Julia. Why don't you just come and stay for a few days. Nothing permanent, of course, but just until the funeral and perhaps until you've had a chance to sort yourself out, eh?'

The girl did not even attempt a reply but all present could see that she was adamant.

'Well, if you don't want to stay at Hampstead, dear,' said Queenie, 'you're more than welcome to stay here for a few weeks. Isn't she, Jim? We've plenty of room and you can get to central London easy enough from here. Why don't you use this place, just as a base, you understand, until you're more sure?'

'That's very kind of you, Mrs Forsythe. If it's all right with Mr Forsythe, I would like that very much indeed. I promise I'll not wear out my welcome.'

'If I know anything about "Mr Forsythe",' said Queenie, 'he'll like nothing better than seeing a beautiful young lady over breakfast each morning.'

Jim suddenly glared at Queenie. 'Hold on a minute!' he cut in sharply. 'Don't I get a chance to speak for myself?'

'Okay,' agreed Queenie. 'Speak.'

Jim's face suddenly broke into a huge grin. 'I'd like nothing better than starting the day by seeing *two* beautiful young ladies over breakfast each morning.'

'Jim Forsythe!' Queenie exclaimed. 'It's taken me years to get a compliment like that out of you!' Turning to Julia, she added, 'And if this is the effect you're going to have in this household, young woman, *you* can stay permanently!'

Whilst this family chit-chat was taking place, Billie's attention was focused on Duncan. His disappointment in Julia's decision not to return to Hampstead was clear. His expression was almost a carbon copy of the one the girl herself had worn minutes earlier. That's the trouble with falling in love, she told herself. It's not only stupid, it's also bloody complicated.

They were beginning to finalise their collective plans when all conversation was interrupted by a persistent hammering on the door knocker. Jim had almost reached the door, when Queenie snapped.

'It's the local bloody hooligans, no doubt. Starting that old game again, are they? Just wait until . . .' Further comment was cut short by Jim's voice calling loudly from the hall.

'You're right there, old girl, it certainly is a hooligan. But don't worry, I've caught him. Come on, lad, in you come. What's your name, you hooligan? . . . What's that you say? . . . Benjamin Samuel Diamond? A villian's name, if ever I heard one! I bet you're the ringleader of them hooligans that your grandma's always on about, aren't you? . . . I thought as much! You're under arrest, you felon.' The gurgling voice of a child could be heard even though the words were not distinct enough to understand.

'It's Ben!' exclaimed Queenie, leaping to her feet. 'It's my Ben!' Queenie rushed to the door to be met by a smiling Jim with a laughing child draped over his shoulders.

'It's the hooligan element of your family to see you,' he announced. Spinning the small boy back over his shoulders, Jim raised the child's coat. 'Here y'are, Grandma. If you want to smack the little horror's bum, help yourself!'

Queenie wrenched her grandson from him and smothered the protesting child in kisses. A serious-looking David and Grace followed Jim into the room.

'We've heard the news,' said Grace looking directly at Julia. 'I'm so sorry for you, love,' she added softly as she sympathetically reached out to the girl.

As the two young women embraced, Duncan asked, 'But how did you hear so soon?'

'How did we *hear*?' echoed David. 'Why here, of course. You could hardly miss it!' From his pocket he took an evening newspaper and laid it out in all its stark obscenity.

Billie stared at it hard for several moments in unbelieving horror. 'But that's barely about my Alice at all! It's all about me! What's the matter with these people, for heaven's sake?' She picked up the paper and ran her eyes quickly from one pictured headline to another. 'They're like vultures feeding off a corpse . . . My God, how *do* they live with themselves?

What's that picture of me at the Palladium got to do with that poor woman lying smothered in her bed? Damn all their eyes! They're hardly any better than the bastard who killed her!'

Her words and manner had already alarmed the child and Queenie tucked the lad's face close to her own, as, for not the first time that afternoon, she stared angrily at her mother. However, there was no placating Billie until Jim seized hold of her and whispered a rapid warning in her ear.

'Of course, of course. I'm sorry,' she murmured, turning to her daughter. 'Please, Queenie, let me hold the little fellah. I beg you?' Without a word, Queenie handed over the child and, as usual, be they under six or over sixty, the male animal was drawn instantly to the magnetism of the old music-hall star.

'But what happened?' asked the bewildered David. 'And how come you all seem to be involved?'

Jim spent the next few minutes explaining the events of the past twenty-four hours to the newcomers whilst Billie cuddled the now adoring youngster.

Once the story had been related, everyone moved into the sitting room and sat round the large fire seeking solace in each other's company and conversation.

'And how are things with you, Davy?' asked Billie, still holding the now sleeping child.

David gave a quick but meaningful glance at Grace before answering. 'Well, to be perfectly honest,' he replied quietly, 'I thought we had a few problems. At least I *did*, until I saw that damn paper this afternoon. But how about you? You're not going back to that house until whoever did this is caught, surely?'

'Of course I am!' Billie replied indignantly. 'I'd be there now, but your clod-hopping colleagues were trampling about all over the place. It's my home, David,' she gave a little hollow laugh. 'Or at least it is for the moment and no murdering scum is going to drive me from it. In any case, young Duncan is coming to keep me company.'

'Just Duncan?' David asked, looking quizzically at Julia.

'That's right,' acknowledged the girl. 'Mrs Forsythe said I can stay here for a week or two.'

'But will you get work here?' he persisted. 'There's not much about these days.'

'Oh, there's plenty of work for girls,' she replied bitterly. 'Employers don't have to pay so much for female staff. The younger we are, the cheaper we come. I can get a job in almost any cinema as an usherette with very little trouble.'

'*Cinema! Usherette!*' exploded Billie in disgust. 'Why, these are the very people who killed off the music-hall! If it wasn't for them, I'd still be on the boards even now. For Gawd's sake, please don't tell me you're planning on being an usherette! Why that's sacrilege. I'll never sleep at nights!'

The girl gave a wry smile. 'It won't be for long, I hope. I do have other plans.'

'And they are?' asked Duncan pointedly.

'I'd sooner not say,' Julia replied softly. 'Then if they fail, no one will know and I shan't be so upset.' She leaned forward towards Billie. 'Would you mind if I held the boy for a while? I really do need a cuddle and if he wakes up I can always run through every nursery rhyme I can remember.'

'Well, you'll probably remember more than me, girl. I can only remember the rude versions. Here y'are, take him. He's becoming a weight anyway.'

The girl eased into a mothering position so effortlessly that Queenie was struck by an idea. Turning to her daughter-in-law, she whispered in her ear.

'It's certainly okay by me if it's okay by David,' came the ready answer. 'In fact, it could do us a big favour.'

At the mention of his name, David raised his eyes to his mother expectantly.

'Davy,' she said, choosing her words carefully, 'I'd hate to be thought of as an interfering old bat, but I've been thinking. Julia is going to stay here with us for at least a couple of weeks. Even if she does get a job, I doubt if it'll be for some time. If she would care to, could she not look after Benjamin this week? It'd give you and Grace a chance of some time together and it'll give her a sense of purpose. At least until she's had a chance to settle herself again, perhaps after the funeral?'

'Before you get too carried away with that idea,' interrupted Jim, 'don't forget it's a murder. Funerals are frequently not sanctioned for some time. It could easily be months. Especially if no one is arrested.'

'Oh, that doesn't matter to me, Mr Forsythe,' replied the girl eagerly. 'Please let me have Ben for a few days. I'll look after him, I swear I will.'

'I have no doubt about that, Julia,' smiled Grace, 'none whatever, and when he grows up he'll be furious when he discovers he went out with such a beautiful girl and can't remember it.' She looked hopefully at Jim before continuing. 'And if someone could run David and me home later, I'll sort out all the clothing Benjamin will need for a stay.'

As sombre as the gathering was, Queenie at least felt some progress was being made towards the readjustment of their lives. Distant though Alice Giles's death had been to her, she nevertheless had the feeling that none of them would be the same again because of it.

Contrary to his customary grim silence behind a steering-wheel, Jim drove his four passengers home in an unusually garrulous mood. He planned to drop David and Grace at Queen's Buildings, then, after collecting Ben's clothes and toys, move on to Hampstead with Billie and Duncan. He had the feeling today that his driving was becoming more competent as each day passed – a theory not universally shared by his passengers.

'So how much is your pay to be cut?' he asked David.

'Around nine shillings a week,' replied the young man curtly. 'They've got us by the balls and they know it. We can't go anywhere else and they can do just as they like and that's *exactly* what they're doing.'

'How will you manage?'

'Grace's friend, Sheila Bowen, works in Jenner's Brewery at the end of the street and she's managed to get Grace a little office-cleaning job between five·thirty and seven thirty each morning. The money is slave-labour rate, of course, but Sheila's a good friend and Grace is going to take Ben up to Sheila's flat each morning and collect him on the way back.'

'This Sheila,' said Billie. 'What time does she go to work?'

'She's a factory girl,' explained Grace. 'She doesn't start till eight o'clock and it's only three minutes from our building to the factory gates. It's certainly convenient. The only trouble is we never seem to be free of the smell of hops.'

'I thought wives of serving coppers weren't allowed to work?' queried Billie.

'They're not,' answered David, 'but if the hierarchy really stick to that policy, half of the lower ranks' families will starve.'

'Surely, as a senior officer you shouldn't have heard that last conversation?' Billie said to Jim.

'I'm afraid there's a great deal I choose not to hear nowadays,' responded Jim. 'In any case, it won't affect me much longer. I've decided to leave the force.'

'Since when?' asked Billie sharply. 'I always thought you loved the job? You don't have to go yet, do you? You're still relatively young.'

'No, I could serve for another seven years, but I want no part of the changes that are coming. When I first became a sergeant, one rueful old copper said something that stuck in my mind. He said if all supervisory ranks would only treat men as they would wish to be treated themselves, it would be a far more efficient force. I've always tried to make that my philosophy, but I'm afraid that's impossible now and . . .' He cut his words short and pulled into the kerbside. 'What's that over there? That commotion by the Elephant and Castle dance hall, I mean.'

'It's just the "Elephant" gang,' said David. 'Individually, they don't amount to anything. They're just a rag-bag of tuppeny ha'penny hoodlums, but when they're in a pack they can be dangerous.'

'But what do they do?' asked Duncan. 'Are they thieves, or what?'

'Well, in the main they usually fight other gangs. Some of them just belong to the gang to show off. Others will carry razors in their caps. I suppose you could say that mainly they're territorial. If anyone of their own type enters from another area, they'll think nothing of giving him a stripey and sending him back.'

'A stripey? What's that?' asked Billie.

'A razor slash down the cheek. If they really don't like their opponent, they'll do it with a cut throat razor but if they are only mildly upset, or perhaps in a tolerant mood, they'll do it with a safety blade inserted in a fold of their cap. A safety blade certainly does less damage but it's more difficult to spot, because until they take their cap off and start swinging, you don't know it's coming.'

'Do they do anything else?' Duncan asked.

'They try the protection racket from time to time, but that's usually with the more illegal side of trading – you know, street bookmakers, unlicensed traders, whores and that type of thing. Also, on very rare occasions, they may form up with another local gang, sometimes even one they traditionally hate, to attend a race course or dog track and then they really *can* be a pest.'

'Is this your patch?' asked Duncan.

'Certainly is,' agreed David. 'Salubrious, ain't it?'

Duncan stared in fascination at the small crowd. 'How I envy you!'

'Envy him?' exclaimed Billie. 'What on earth for?'

'Having that lot as an enemy, of course!' he replied elatedly.

'Fancy having something to fight as tangible as that. You know, something that you can actually see, hear and really get stuck into. Not like the shadowy scum that murdered poor Alice then sneaked out in the night like a jackal. I think you could get more satisfaction in one fight with them than in most other jobs in a lifetime.'

'Hang on a minute!' replied David swiftly. 'They're not white knights, you know. If you get them on their own, at least half of them are snivelling cowards but in a pack they can be far worse than jackals.'

'Can't you arrest them?' asked Billie.

'We do from time to time. If it's a quiet night and we've enough men available – assuming, of course, that we've a duty officer who's got enough guts – we'll take a van and sort 'em out. But basically, unless you catch them tooled up and ready to fight another gang, it's hardly worth it. Other than obstruction and insulting words or behaviour, there's not much you can nick 'em for. Mark you, once they actually *start* a gang fight, there's all the difference in the world.'

'Why?' persisted Duncan.

'Well, as opposed to demonstrations, drunks or even some football crowds, there is no such thing as a good guy amongst them. They are all equally at fault. You can therefore nick any one of them for causing an affray in total confidence that he is guilty as sin and will go down for it.'

'How does an affray differ from – what was it you said – insulting words and something or other?' asked Duncan.

David gave a chuckle. 'Well, if you nick 'em for insulting words or behaviour, it'll be somewhere between a ten- and forty-bob fine at the magistrates' court next morning. But if you nick them for an *affray*, it'll be a remand in custody for a couple of months, then up the steps at the London sessions for anything between eighteen months and seven years' penal servitude. Oh, I tell you, mate, they don't like an affray charge one little bit; they reckon it's cheating. That's why we don't use it too often; it sometimes serves a whole lot better as a threat.'

'Seen enough?' asked Jim as he eased the vehicle into gear. Before a reply could be made an empty beer bottle winged its way over from the crowd and smashed harmlessly against the base of a lamppost.

'That was meant for this car,' said David. 'They probably thought we're being too nosy. Anyone see who threw it?'

'Yes, that tall one at the end,' Duncan pointed. 'The one with the red scarf. He's just dived back into the crowd.'

'Well, I'm blessed!' exclaimed David winding down his window. 'So he's back on the manor, is he? That's Lofty Stanton. He's just done twelve months for assault on police. I bet he doesn't know I'm in here.' He put his head out of the window just about as far as he could and yelled at the top of his voice, 'Oy, Lofty! Lofty Stanton!'

A frowning head emerged suspiciously from the fringe of the group. David acknowledged it with a cheery wave. 'That's one I owe you, Lofty. But don't worry, it'll keep, old son.'

'Well, I'll tell you this,' observed Billie studying the rapid change in Stanton's expression, 'I've never met that gentleman before but I'd guess he's not a man who likes surprises.'

Jim, mainly with his paintwork in mind, now gave the crowd a wide berth as he drove the short distance to Queen's Buildings. Within a few minutes, Grace had run up and down the stairs with one large bag of clothing and another of toys. Goodbyes and kisses were exchanged as the remaining trio moved off towards Hampstead.

Once out of sight of the building, Jim turned to Billie. 'Well,' he asked, 'what d'you think?'

'I think the only good thing to emerge from these last two days is Julia's offer to look after their child. It may give David and Grace a chance to patch things up. They're a lovely couple but they've really got to work at their marriage. I don't think he knows quite how close he is to losing her. Shades of his old man there, I feel.'

'I agree,' nodded Jim. 'In the last two hours that Grace has been with us, she's barely spoken, and that pay cut is not going to help one little bit.'

To his surprise, Jim made good time and in less than half-an-hour his tyres were crunching on the loose gravel of Billie's driveway. A breeze had risen and was driving a collection of tufty clouds across the face of a starry night sky. 'D'you have your key?' he asked.

'Yes, we both have one,' answered Billie, peering at the house. 'The CID used Alice's key. You will come in for a moment before you leave, Jim, won't you?'

'Of course, I will, but are you sure this is really what you want? The offer to stay at our place still stands for the pair of you, you know?'

She gave a grateful smile and rested her hand on his arm. 'Yes, I do know that and it's extremely sweet of you but this is my home and I have a battle of my own to fight. I'm going to miss my Alice, I really am. For these last few years she's been my right arm and a dear, dear friend.' She gave a wry little laugh. 'There's not been too many of those in my life, I can tell you.'

As Billie opened the large front door, there was a chill in the air that Jim had never noticed before. He was not sure if it was his imagination or if it really was much colder. Almost in confirmation, Billie gave a little shiver and fingered the hall radiator.

'Should I light the boiler, Miss Bardell?' asked Duncan.

'Yes, please, and I think we'll also have fires in the drawing room and the bedrooms tonight. I've got to cheer this place up somehow; it's like a morgue.'

'Not the best choice of words I've heard,' said Jim.

'Oh, I don't know,' she responded. 'I'm sure if Alice does come back, she'll be the most friendly of ghosts. With her nature she couldn't be anything else.' Billie turned to him and took his arm once more. 'Jim, you look tired. I think you've done all you can for the time being. Duncan and I can sort ourselves out now. If we do need anything, I'll give you a ring – and thank you again.'

He nodded. 'Yes, I'm suddenly quite tired. Perhaps I'm not yet as competent in that bloody car as I thought I was. If you're sure you're all right . . .?'

''Course, we are! C'mon, off you go. I'm in enough hot water with Queenie as it is!'

With an embrace for the woman and a warm handshake for the young gardener, Jim walked out into the night. Two false starts, one loud backfire and three or four lurches later, he turned the car into Hampstead Lane and was gone.

Billie watched him finally disappear before she closed the large front door.

'I've lit the fire in the drawing room, Miss Bardell. I'll go downstairs and light the boiler now, shall I?' asked Duncan.

'Thanks, love,' she said with a wan smile. Wandering into the kitchen she found herself absent-mindedly scratching the scar on her forearm. Glancing down at it, she could not help thinking that all the recent misfortunes had stemmed from that one moment. Her thoughts were interrupted by the sound of Duncan shovelling the coal in the basement. He had only been at it for a few seconds when the telephone rang in the hall. Lifting the receiver, she expected it would be Queenie inquiring the time of her husband's return. The contrast to the expected tones could not have been greater.

'Right nah, lissen careful,' said the gravelly voice. 'You an' me are gonna 'ave ter 'ave a little business talk. Fer a little remuneration, I'm in a position ter do yer a very big favver indeed but on the ovver 'and, if yer don't, I'm gonna . . .'

'Who is this? What d'you want?' Billie demanded.

'Never mind abaht who I am. You just lissen to me careful like . . .' As the voice imparted its directions, Billie's face aged and drained of colour. Weakly, she reached for a chair.

13

On the drive home, Jim began to muse on how his life had changed in the previous few months. Just a year earlier he had been moving along at a sedate pace towards retirement. The General Strike had been over for four years and, though there had certainly been street disturbances, there had been no great upheaval. But now, with an ever-increasing slump and his family troubles, it seemed like every day begat its own fresh disaster. To his disgust, his drive home had been so smooth as to be boring. Not once did he stall, clout the kerb or even skid on the tramlines. Wasn't that always the case when no one was looking? He made it to the Elephant and Castle in excellent time and found himself strangely drawn to the area adjacent to the dance hall. He had had no need even to travel that route, but for the gang he had seen earlier, he had found a compelling fascination. He had grown up in the very same streets as these lads, with poverty worse than they had known, yet such gangs had been relatively unknown in his youth.

To his surprise, though the gang was still there and with newcomers arriving all the time, the young men were in a much more orderly form. They appeared to have congregated in the confined space of an open yard between the dance hall and a warehouse and were all facing in the same direction as if being addressed. Yes, of course, that was it! They *were* being addressed, but by whom? Whoever it was certainly held their attention. But not only were they attentive, standing so quietly in the damp misty night, they were almost submissive. As a senior police officer, he felt he should know the reason for this assembly, yet at his age he could hardly mingle unobtrusively in such a throng of young people.

Parking the car some distance from the dance hall, he strolled back to give himself time to think. He had almost reached the hall when the obvious answer struck him. Pulling his cap over as much grey hair as possible, he entered the foyer and slid a half-crown between the grill and the brass-topped till. 'One, please,' he grunted.

The smoke that curled from her cigarette caused the skinny redhead to close one watering eye. Without even looking up, she pushed back one shilling and sixpence and whirred up a ticket whilst continuing her conversation with someone just out of sight. Pocketing his change, Jim crossed the foyer to where a stooped elderly man with an enormous cap and a totally ludicrous mauve uniform saluted half-heartedly and tore his ticket. Meantime a band wailed 'Stardust' through the door. He pushed into the small, crowded auditorium to be greeted by a billowing wall of cigarette smoke. The lighting was dim but there was just enough to see the sign EXIT AND TOILET above a door away to the left. As urgent as he felt his mission to be, he knew he had to adjust to the gloom for a moment or he would be clattering into everything that stood between him and that exit.

''Ullo, sweetie,' said a gravelly voice from behind him. 'Lookin' for somethin' a bit special are we?'

His instinct told him there would be a shock in store when he turned round yet in spite of this premonition he was still appalled. To give credit, the hair was exceptionally neat. It was jet black with a thick fringe, cut dead straight an inch or so above the eyes and then fell neatly down the side of the face and over the ears like a shiny black helmet. The face was gaunt to the point of deformity and the teeth, or what there were of them, were rotten. She displayed a light sleeveless dress that needed poor light and tapering thin arms that needed a cloak. In addition, she swayed and reeked of gin. Her whole image was finally rounded off by a ludicrously long cigarette holder that held an inch-and-a-half-long stale butt.

'I can see by yer cut that yer used to better places than this, darlin'. Lookin' fer someone, are we?'

'Er – yes, matter of fact, my – er – daughter.'

The crone winked knowingly and slipped her right arm in his. 'I'll 'elp yer, me lovely. No, no,' she held up her left hand to cut short any protest. 'It's nothin' at all. I'd do it fer anyone. What's yer name, lovely? Mine's Felicity.'

'Duncan,' he said, snatching at the first name that came into his head.

'Duncan, eh?' she said approvingly. 'There's a lovely name. Scots are yer?'

'Er – yes.' For one stupid moment he was even tempted to try an accent before sanity prevailed.

'What's she look like, this daughter of yours?'

'Oh er – you know, just like they all do nowadays, I s'pose. She's wearing well, a sort of frock, I s'pose you'd call it and . . .'

The light was just about good enough for him to see the disbelief radiating from her bleary eyes. 'Look,' she said increasing her grip on his arm, 'yer don't wanna wander round this place lookin' fer young gels. What yer need is an experienced lady. Yer know what they say about the best wine don't'cha?' She gave him a violent nudge and cackled. 'It's always kept in older bottles, eh?'

Jim knew he was becoming accustomed to the light when he could finally see her full display of rotten teeth.

'Look,' he said, releasing his arm, 'I must go to the lavatory first. Tell me where you're sitting and I'll join you in a minute or two.'

She gave him yet another nudge and swayed alarmingly before whispering, 'Well, if yer sure yer wouldn't like me ter 'old yer dicky for yer, I'll be waitin' over there by that table near the bar. Shall I order some drinkies fer us, lover?'

'Er – yes, if you like,' he bleated. 'I'll not be long.'

As he moved away from her and made his way around the fringe of the dancers, it was all he could do not to break into a sprint. Once out of the auditorium and into the corridor, he could clearly see twin doors, the left was to the lavatory and the right was to the exit. With a sigh of relief he could not resist a feeling of smugness. If the rest of his calculations were as correct, all he had to do was partially open the exit door and, saxophones permitting, he should be able to hear every word of the meeting. Placing his hands on the bar release, he heard a speaker, though not distinct enough to catch the words. For the best effect he definitely needed to ease the door open a fraction. Though he gradually increased pressure, still the bar did not move. Looking down he soon saw why. A large fat padlock secured an inch-thick chain. It was an emergency door that was closed to emergencies. Before he could decide on any further action, his deliberations were cut short by the dreadful Felicity's voice from somewhere back down the corridor.

'Coo-ee, Duncan, darlin'. I've got our drinkees. Could yer pay the barman, lover?'

Panic-stricken, he looked around desperately and pushed open the lavatory door. The cubicle showed 'ENGAGED', but at least the sour-smelling urinal bowl was unoccupied. He looked above the bowl to where a frosted-glass window rested on two metal bars. If he could just open those bars an inch or so, the window would drop and he would be out. The problem was, he would need to stand on the urinal bowl to reach the window. But supposing whoever was in the cubicle made an exit? He would then find a police superintendent with a foot in a urinal, climbing a lavatory wall to force a window to escape a witch clutching two drinks he hadn't paid for whilst surrounded by a razor gang in a seedy dance hall. Just how would that sound at the discipline inquiry? 'I was just doing a bit of off-duty observation, sir.' The chances of that being believed were less than zero. A superintendent's pension was now looking extremely remote.

It was whilst he dithered that he heard the tearing of toilet paper. If he was going at all, then this had to be the moment. Placing one foot on the basin, he balanced precariously and, with surprising ease, forced apart the two rusty bars. The window crashed down splintering into a thousand tiny fragments and the welcome breeze that surged in served to remind him just how foul the air had become. The sound of the lavatory chain being pulled coincided with his head and shoulders emerging into the cool night air and, before the lavatory door was finally unbolted, he had dropped down onto a dust-covered pathway. His relief was doubled when he found himself in a small open coal store off the dance hall. Though an eight-foot fence still separated him from the gang, he at least had a breathing space. It was now quite dark but the light that shone from the broken window enabled him to see his way comfortably around the tiny store.

He was about to climb the fence, when he realised the orator was just on the other side. He could now hear him very clearly addressing the gang. Suddenly, everything fell into place. The man was an excellent speaker, of that there was no doubt. Although much more cultured than any of those listening, he still held them in the palm of his hand. His pauses, intonations and shouts all indicated someone who would not usually be heard delivering a thirty-minute oration in a south London yard. The man's words were totally inflammatory but he spoke of something they wanted to hear. He promised work and he promised power; all he sought in exchange was total allegiance to himself and to the doctrine of race purity. There was no doubt that Oswald Mosley had found himself a very receptive audience.

The voices that were now rising in volume from the dance-hall lavatory reminded Jim he was now between two fires. But in spite of this, he knew he could never again face the dreadful Felicity. Decision made, he scaled the fence and dropped down just a yard or two from the speaker. Two surprised bodyguards started quickly towards him but when they heard the commotion from the window, they assumed he was fleeing an unpaid bill and showed no further interest. To a chorus of surprisingly good-natured jeers, he made his way swiftly through the audience to the sanctuary of his motor car and home.

As Jim swung into the short driveway, Queenie had already taken up a stance at the window. She greeted him with a rather brusque kiss.

'Jim, where've you been? I nearly rang Billie, but I thought if you were genuinely delayed I might alarm her unnecessarily – and look at the state of you! You're smothered in coal dust and you look like – like – a vagrant!'

He nodded in agreement. 'Fair description, I'd say. Anyway, how's me grandson. Is that young lady looking after him properly?'

'She's upstairs putting him to bed. But you still haven't answered my question.'

'Well, I've narrowly escaped arrest for deception, almost been kidnapped by a gorgon and lucky not to have been razored by the Elephant gang. Other than that, it was a good trip. I tell you, my driving's definitely improving!'

'Jim Forsythe!' she interjected. 'It's not a bit of good your trying to tell me such outrageous lies, because . . .' She was interrupted by the shrill ring of the telephone.

'I'll get it,' he said quickly. 'It may save me answering too many questions.'

Queenie looked anxiously at his face as he took the call. Placing a hand momentarily over the speaker, he whispered, 'It's okay, it's Davy. He's been sent to a call box by your daughter-in-law to check you're not poisoning his son and heir.' He turned his attention back to the telephone. 'Actually, I'm pleased you rang, Davy, because something strange happened on the way back.' He then recounted his adventures in and around the dance hall. 'It seems like the leader of this new party, Oswald Mosley, a former cabinet minister, is trying to recruit some of the street gangs. If that's the case I find it a little worrying. The one thing these gangs lack is discipline. If he can offer them that, there's no telling what he might do. I'll have a word with Special Branch tomorrow; it's more their pigeon. I just thought as the local law your nick should be amongst the first to know . . . Yes, your mother assures me he's fine. Wouldn't you be if you were being looked after by that little lass? Well, she's putting him to bed right now . . . Uh huh, wouldn't we all! . . . Okay, thanks for ringing. 'Bye.'

'Jim,' said Queenie anxiously, 'that meeting you mentioned sounded so sinister.'

'It is, I suppose. This bloke Mosley has just stormed out of the government over unemployment and he reckons he's going to form his own political party. It's going to have a sort of semimilitary basis. I think he intends making the rounds of as many of these young gangs as possible, just to sound them out before he tries anything further.'

'But what does he intend to do that's not been done before?'

'Oh, I don't know. I've never really studied it but he is very anti-immigration, particularly Jewish immigration. If you ally that with an anticommunist stance, you really could have a street war on your hands. Anyway,' he said, fondly kissing her forehead, 'I shouldn't think it'll come to that. Why don't you tell me about my grandson. What are the plans you have for him this week?'

'Personally, I have no plans,' Queenie replied ruefully. 'Julia has them all. She seems to have every minute accounted for for the next few days at least. It looks like giving her Benjamin to look after was the best idea I've had since I married you. There's such a vast improvement in her! The last time she spoke, she was making arrangements to take him to the Lord Mayor's Show. Just think, three years old and he's going to see the Lord Mayor's Show! I've been around for over forty years and I've *never* seen it!'

'Why don't you go with them? You could make it a real family outing?' Jim said.

'It's interesting to hear you say that,' she replied thoughtfully, 'because Julia isn't actually *family*, is she? In fact, until recently we'd never even met her. Yet here we are trusting our only grandchild to her care – and I must stress – happy to do so! But listen, I should have asked you how my mother took to returning home. I think she was more upset about the death of poor Alice than anything else in her life. She's going to need that young gardener with her for some time yet, because that house is a very big place to be lonely.'

Further conversation was interrupted by a footfall on the stairs and they both glanced up to see Julia descending on tiptoe and rubbing her eyes.

'He's gone off like a good 'un, Mrs Forsythe,' she whispered. 'Trouble is, so did I.'

Jim gave a chuckle. 'I hear you're thinking of going to the Lord Mayor's Show tomorrow,' he said. 'Should be right up Benji's street. I see by the evening paper they have a few elephants from the circus on Clapham Common.'

'Have they?' she asked excitedly. 'That settles it then. I love elephants. Perhaps we'll buy some buns on the way and try to feed them.'

'I don't think that's on, Julia, love,' said Queenie warily. 'Elephants can be very dangerous.'

'Only joking, Mrs Forsythe. Honest.'

The three them shared a pot of tea and within minutes Julia was again closing her eyes as the stresses of the previous two days began to take their toll.

'I think we're all a bit washed out,' said Jim. 'Why don't we take the opportunity to have an early night and face the world afresh tomorrow?'

'I'll not argue with that,' agreed Queenie wearily as she put her arm around the slumped Julia. 'C'mon, love, up you go. You can sleep the clock round if you wish.'

The girl roused herself with a weak smile and gave an approving little nod.

Next morning, Jim Forsythe had already left for Scotland Yard before either Julia or the boy had woken. But within minutes of their awakening, Julia was inviting Queenie to accompany them to the Show.

'I was so hoping you'd ask that!' said Queenie excitedly. 'I can tell you now, I've already cut our sandwiches! Can't think for the life of me why I've never been before.' She bent down to the boy and swept him up off his feet. 'Benji Diamond,' she exclaimed, plonking an enormous kiss on his rosy cheek. 'You're not the only one who's going to feel three years old today!'

It was a little after eleven o'clock when the tram deposited the trio at the north side of Blackfriars Bridge. The surrounding roads had already been closed to daytime traffic and they joined the throng making their way on foot along the Thames Embankment. The early morning showers had cleared and it appeared set for a fine day. Benjamin was more taken by the boats on the river than by the street entertainers, all of whom were either singing or playing harmonicas and banjos.

'What's that, Auntie Julia?' he said, pointing towards a group of young men, who between them shouldered a large wood-planked platform. In the centre of this platform perched a red-painted, life-size model lion with fierce countenance and rampant tail. The bearers were also singing some rather bawdy songs and letting off the occasional firework.

'I've no idea, Ben,' she replied. 'But if your grandma doesn't know, we'll ask that policeman.'

Queenie's shrug of ignorance caused Julia to make the day of the enormously tall City policeman by repeating the child's inquiry to him. 'That's Reggie, that is, miss. Comes here every year does Reggie. He's the mascot of the students from King's College and he's always presented to the new Lord

Mayor, just here on the Embankment. It's a bit of old London tradition, you might say.'

'I thought people weren't allowed to let off fireworks in the street?' muttered Queenie huffily.

The constable shrugged philosophically. 'Nor they ain't, mam, but yer see them are medical students and as such, considered ter be gen'lemen. When gen'lemen does sumphin' like that, then that's construed as "high spirits". Now,' he said pointedly, 'if they *weren't* gen'lemen, but, let's say, factory lads, their feet wouldn't't'a touched the ground. They'd be swifted away by us coppers for being rogues or vagabonds, or such like.'

'Well, I still think they look more like rogues and vagabonds than gentlemen,' replied Queenie curtly.

'Perhaps you won't say that in a year or two when one of 'em takes out yer appendix, mam. Though lookin' at 'em now, I wouldn't let 'em bath me dog.'

The threesome soon found a place on the kerbside where they sat and ate their sandwiches whilst absorbing the sights and sounds of the large crowd.

It was some thirty minutes later that the same tall policeman strolled along the roadway telling sitting spectators they must stand as the procession was imminent. This caused a little irritated shuffling and it took some minutes for the crowd to resettle. Any exasperation was soon wiped away by the distant sounds of massed brassed bands. Heads craned forward as cheers increased and excitement built up.

The first of the bands was followed by several floats and carriages, then, in the distance, came the elephants. There were four of them and they ambled regally along the centre of the road in single file with decorated harness and a mounted mahout. Queenie, who was still concerned about the fireworks, was more than pleased when the tall policeman made his way through the crowd and spoke to the students. By this time the first of the elephants was just yards away, plodding along with eyelids so drooped it could have been sleep-walking.

Suddenly the semi-slumber of the first elephant was disturbed when a particularly loud firework exploded. At first it gave no great sign of distress. It simply cast a bored eye over the heads of the crowd in the general direction of the explosion. Unfortunately, its gaze suddenly rested on the large platform which was being bounced rapidly up and down to a chorus of chants from those beneath. 'Gen'lemen students' don't mean an awful lot to the average elephant, but a rampant lion, particularly one painted red, has a very different connotation. The creature stopped dead. Then, lifting its head, it curled up its trunk and trumpeted a great defiant roar. The mahout, though trying valiantly to distract its attention, proved completely ineffectual. Apart from alarming the crowd, the actions of the first elephant aroused great interest from its three trailing companions. Now, if one roaring rogue elephant is alarming, four can be terrifying. The crowd in front of the lion disintegrated like a sea wall made of feathers. There were screams and cries as people stumbled over each other to escape the furious animals.

As the crowd broke and ran, most of the students sensibly did likewise. Misguidedly, however, two or three decided to hide Reggie by dragging him away into the sanctuary of the trees in the Embankment Gardens. If any elephant had harboured secret doubts as to the authenticity of the lion, the fact that it was now seeking the safety of the trees was proof enough. Whilst three of them attacked the still rampant but immobile Reggie, the fourth decided to amuse itself by chasing the terrified students around a tree. Finally, after a minute or so, the lead elephant picked up the lion and, after tossing it casually in the air, stamped on it twice. Honour thus satisfied, it then allowed its mahout to lead it calmly back to rejoin the procession. Two of its fellow creatures then followed suit and even the one chasing the students soon became bored and rejoined its friends.

Although the whole event had barely exceeded three minutes, the aftermath looked like a battlefield clearing station.

Screaming children and crying mums were scattered over roads and gardens. Because of the hysteria, it was not at first easy to judge the severity of any injuries, particularly those of the children. The first to succeed in this was Julia, who, after assuring herself that Queenie and Benjamin were relatively unharmed, swiftly soothed even the most terror-struck child by her confidence and quiet demeanour. Soon ambulances began to arrive and, once the tears were wiped away and families reunited, the casualties were found to amount to no more than a dozen or so.

The remainder of the procession had lost its magic for Queenie, Julia and Benjamin and they dejectedly made their way back to Blackfriars Bridge. They were about to run for a tram when a taxi pulled into the side of the road slightly ahead of them. The door opened to reveal a slim, elegant, white-haired lady of some sixty years.

'I'm sorry to trouble you, my dears,' she said, 'but I felt I must compliment this young woman on her coolness back there.' She nodded towards the Embankment. 'Panic can be a terrifying thing and the fact that there was so little of it, has more to do with you, young woman, than any of the professionals in attendance. May I have your name? I would so like the Lord Mayor to write you a letter of thanks.'

'Er – er – well,' stammered Julia. 'I don't really know what to say. You see I'm not living at . . .'

'I couldn't agree with you more,' cut in Queenie, suddenly sensing an opportunity. 'As for her address, she's staying with me in Streatham until she is able to find herself a job. It's very difficult for a young girl nowadays.'

'A job, you say?' asked the woman. 'What sort of field interests you, my dear?'

'I'm afraid I don't know,' confessed Julia. 'You see, I have only been a maid and I certainly don't want to do that again.'

The woman reached out and placed an expensively gloved hand on Julia's arm. 'My dear, you are a born carer,' she said. 'The way you were instinctively able to soothe the fears of those young children, to say nothing of their mothers, is a gift with which few are blessed. You should at least try one of the caring professions.'

Julia felt the conversation was getting beyond her. To her best recollection, all she had done by the roadside was something that came naturally to her. It was certainly nothing to fuss over. Yet she sensed that Queenie had become quite excited about the whole incident.

'So what are you suggesting?' asked Queenie.

'Excuse me,' said the woman politely, 'but are you her mother?'

'No,' conceded Queenie, equally politely. 'Her mother has recently died but I'm as close to being her mother as anyone is ever likely to be if that's of help?'

'Look,' said the woman, 'I'm going to Dulwich and you're bound for Streatham, is that correct?'

'Correct,' echoed Queenie.

'Very well. Why don't you join me in the cab and after we've had a little talk, I'll drop you off at your home. How does that suit you?'

'If it saves us lurching about for five miles on top of a tram,' said Queenie, 'I'd say it's wonderful, though I'm not sure if our little lad here would agree. He loves trams.'

As soon as they were all seated in the taxi, the woman looked quickly from one to the other. 'I don't mean to be presumptuous, you understand, but could I just know exactly *who* is who of you three?'

Julia laughed, and with introductions finally over, the lady outlined her suggestions to the two women for the rest of the journey.

It was seven hours later when Jim climbed the four steps to the front door. Benjamin had been allowed to stay up to say goodnight. Much as Queenie and Julia loved the child, they could barely wait for him to go to bed in order to impart their news. Finally, at a few minutes to eight, Julia came downstairs to announce the boy was asleep.

'According to the evening paper,' Jim began, spreading it out over the table, 'there was almost a safari hunt on the Embankment today. I take it neither of you were involved?' he asked.

'You take it wrong, Jim Forsythe,' said Queenie smugly as she searched the news columns for an item she might vaguely recognise. 'Not only were we there but young Julia covered herself in glory – and that's from no less a source than Lady Clarissa Pethwick-Dorrington!'

'Who?' he demanded.

'Lady Clarissa Pethwick-Dorrington,' she repeated, 'the wife of the Lord Lieutenant of the County. He was in the Lord Mayor's Show and she is a real lady – fetched us home in a taxi!' she added proudly. 'She reckons that our Julia was a real natural in a crisis.'

'You haven't told him the important bit, though,' Julia pointed out.

'No, I was just coming to that. And she's also recommended her for a nursing course at the Miller Hospital in Greenwich.'

'You sure that's what you want, love?' Jim asked the girl quietly. 'It's a long hard slog you know?'

'Four years, to be exact, and I must confess I didn't know I wanted it so badly until she mentioned it,' said Julia honestly. 'But once she suggested it, I suddenly knew that a nurse was all I ever wanted to be.'

'Great, then!' he marvelled. 'Let's keep our fingers crossed for you.'

'So what's your news, Mr Forsythe?' asked the girl.

'Do you know anyone named Lines – Claude Clement Lines, usually known as "Wonky"?'

'No,' said the girl. 'I'm sure of it. Who could forget a name like that? Why?'

'Well, this is confidential, mind, but because of information received, everyone is looking for him and he's definitely gone to ground somewhere. The strange thing is, there's not a snout in London who knows his whereabouts.'

'So what's the vital information that caused this manhunt?' asked Queenie.

'And what's this Wonky man suspected of?' added Julia.

'Murdering your mother,' replied Jim quietly.

14

'This Wonky, or whatever his name is, who is he? What's the connection between him and my mother?' asked Julia.

Jim shrugged. 'I'm afraid I don't know too much about him. In fact, I've only heard about it indirectly but I did check that Wonky Lines is the chief suspect at the moment. Apparently he lives in a tenement somewhere in Blackfriars. I only mentioned his name in case it rang a bell with you.'

Julia shook her head slowly. 'My mum met very few people. She seemed so happy to be with Miss Bardell that she hardly socialised at all. But I understood from the detectives at the scene that she was murdered by a casual burglar?'

'That was their first theory, I grant you,' Jim admitted. 'But quite frankly, at the moment I don't think they have the faintest idea *who* murdered her. Hence they are checking on every conceivable suspect. But it's still early days; something will turn up soon, love. You'll see.'

'Yes, but they do appear to catch some murderers very quickly,' persisted the girl.

'It just seems that way,' Jim explained. 'You see, the vast majority of victims are usually killed by either a member of their family or someone close. But in a case like this, when it could have been committed by any thief in London, then it's a totally different situation and a whole lot of routine leg work has to be done.'

'So where does the name Wonky Lines come from?' cut in Queenie.

'It was on a small piece of paper found under a fireside

219

chair, together with a pencil stub and a small rubber eraser. Detective Inspector Evans said it looks like something such as a handkerchief or scarf was pulled from a pocket and these three items tumbled out with it. Whoever killed Alice appears to have wiped every door handle and surface he touched. This would indicate the suspect didn't originally intend to kill her or else he would have arrived with gloves on. So, if he wasn't intending to kill and he had no gloves, then there must have been another reason for his call. But what was it? A social call? Business call? Who knows?'

'Does he think the murderer wiped the surfaces with his own handkerchief?' asked Queenie.

'I think he's pretty sure about that,' agreed Jim. 'And if we assume all three items fell from his pocket together, then something obvious caused them to fall. Which fetches us back to the handkerchief again.'

'But who goes around with his own name and address on a piece of paper in his own pocket, for God's sake. Surely even the dimmest burglar knows where he lives?'

'That's certainly a point, but when the local police went to the address, they were told by neighbours that Lines seems to have fled.'

'Well, how about fingerprints? Surely there were some on the pencil stub?'

'There were, but nothing distinct enough to lift a decent print. Whoever it belonged to was a great pencil chewer and there was hardly a fraction of it that didn't have some deep indentation.'

'This Lines character,' said Queenie. 'What do they know about him?'

'Nothing at all. Criminal Record Office have no record of him and he's not known by the CID at his local station. This apart, he does keep very irregular hours and has little to do with his neighbours. But there is one strange thing. According to the neighbours, three plain-clothes officers called on him a few days before the murder. Yet no one at the local CID office has any knowledge of this.'

'Could these men have been from another station?' asked Queenie.

'Oh, yes, quite easily, but then they should have notified the local CID of their call either before they went or as soon after as possible.'

'Couldn't they be identified?'

'Sadly, no. It was in the early hours and the light was bad and the neighbours elderly. However, all CID offices in the metropolitan area are being circulated, so something should turn up. Meantime, they do have a couple of leads, the most hopeful one being that he may have fled to the Kentish hopfields with a dog.'

'I'm sorry,' murmured Julia, 'but this is all getting a bit beyond me. There are too many things I don't understand. Firstly, why should anyone who lives in Blackfriars go all the way to Hampstead to do a break-in? There must be thousands of large houses closer than that? Secondly, how did he know that everyone except my mum would be out that particular evening? And thirdly, if you agree no burglar would carry his own name and address on a piece of paper, then what burglar would forget his gloves and so have to go around cleaning up half the furniture in the house?'

Jim gave a rueful smile. 'Well, it is only just theories at this stage, but there is no doubt that this Wonky Whatsisname has got to be spoken to as soon as possible.'

'So wouldn't all these circumstances indicate that my mum was murdered by someone she knew, rather than a stranger?'

'But that still doesn't explain the broken glass in the kitchen door,' pointed out Queenie.

'That's an old ploy,' Jim said. 'Breaking a window, turning over a few chairs here and there, ripping out the telephone – it all helps to disguise the real fact that the murderer was let in because he or she was known to the victim or perhaps was a friend.'

'A friend! Of course!' exclaimed Julia. 'She did have a "friend" she kept very secret. I bet it's him. That would explain such a lot.'

'I take it you did mention this man to Detective Inspector Evans?'

'Of course, I did,' Julia said. 'But I didn't say that he would frequently knock her about though. You see, Mum was quite infuriating at times. It was as if she expected that it was part of a relationship to be thumped around. I don't think she'd ever known anything different.'

'You think this Wonky character could be your mother's mystery man?' asked Jim.

Julia gave the deepest of sighs. 'Oh, I don't know. Could be, I suppose. I'm now just so angry with myself for refusing to see him. I had several opportunities, but I wanted to make it quite clear to her that I was not having anything to do with any relationship that caused her hurt. If I hadn't been so bloody pious, I would at least know now what the bastard looks like.'

'Do you think it was serious?' asked Jim. 'This relationship, I mean?'

'If I had to guess, I'd have to say no,' she replied. 'At least not serious like you or I think of as serious. You see, as happy as my mother was with Miss Bardell, she always seemed to need a man somewhere in the background.'

'But why?' asked Queenie. 'It couldn't have been for security surely? There's no protection in being belted around.'

'No, and it wasn't for sex either, in case that's what you're thinking!' the girl snapped sharply. 'Mum wasn't like that!'

'No one is saying she was,' soothed Queenie. 'I was just trying to work out why a lovely woman like your mum would allow herself to be maltreated by a man who she isn't even married to.'

'Oh, I don't know!' replied the girl bitterly. 'If truth be told, I don't suppose she knew herself.'

'Look,' said Jim softly, 'I think we've gone about as far as we should with this conversation. I'll give Taff Evans a ring at the murder room and acquaint him with what you've just told us. He may have guessed some of it anyway, but it'll do no harm and in the meantime I think we should all try to help you get on with the rest of your life. What d'you say?'

The girl made no reply, but slowly nodded her head.

It was nine o'clock the following morning when Detective Inspector Evans entered the rather grandly named murder room. It was nothing more than the Aides room which had been tarted up with a map, blackboard and a few extra chairs and tables. The Aides room was a small extension to the CID general office where the trainee detectives were expected to carry out their paperwork. Though most of these novices would try valiantly to give the outward appearance of experienced hard-nosed detectives, within the force their official title was 'Temporary Detective' or 'Aide to CID', or unofficially, simply 'Aides'. This position usually ensured they fell between two conflicting stools, with older CID officers radiating mistrust and older uniform officers radiating contempt. The spartan amenities of the Aides office well reflected their standing.

'There's a message for you here, guv,' said one of the aides in what he hoped passed as an experienced detective's tone. Evans's icy glance told him his assumption was wrong and he quickly added 'er – sir.'

Evans brusquely took the note from the young man and read it through before asking, 'When did this come in?'

'Er – last night, sir, somewhere around ten thirty.'

Evans nodded a response, then asked, 'Any luck yet with the three CID officers who were supposed to have called on this geezer Lines?'

'No, sir.'

'And Lines himself. What about him? We must have something by now, surely?'

'Nothing's come in, sir,' replied the young aide, now

desperately hoping his detective inspector would soon ask a question he could answer positively.

'I find that most strange,' muttered Evans, almost thinking aloud.

'Sir?' queried the young man, now beginning to feel personally responsible for the dearth of useful information.

'This Lines character – what little we do know of him so far – indicates he's just the sort of bloke who would come regularly to the attention of police.' He shook his head before adding, 'But not only can we not find him but I now have three alleged detectives who've also disappeared. Very peculiar indeed.' He tapped a pencil on the table top for a few seconds before adding, 'I wonder?'

Voices outside in the corridor announced the arrival of other members of the squad. These consisted of two more aides plus three detective constables and Detective Sergeant Douglas McIntyre.

'Mac!' called Evans, as the door opened, 'I've just been told we've had no luck yet from our circular as to the identity of the three plain-clothes officers who called on Lines. What d'you make of that?'

'It could be that they haven't read the circular yet, but that's unlikely because even if they hadn't seen it someone in their office would. Alternatively they could have come in on an inquiry from one of the surrounding counties, say Kent or Essex. Other than that, all we're left with, is they were on the fiddle and they don't want anyone to know they were there at the time. Of course, there's always the possibility they weren't police officers at all but just pretending to be.' He scratched his head. 'But if that's the case, why?'

'And how does it tie up with murdering a poor middle-aged maid in Hampstead?' asked Evans.

'Seeing as we've got a blank so far from the metropolitan CID, guv, I think we need to circulate their description to the counties,' suggested McIntyre.

'I agree,' said Evans. 'And we'd better include this geezer

Lines while we're at it. One of his neighbours seemed to think he sometimes frequents the hopfields.'

'Him and sixty thousand others, guv,' said McIntyre wearily.

'Not entirely,' Evans said, running his finger down a statement. 'Says here that Lines owned a dog and may be somewhere near Wateringbury; that should narrow the field a fair bit.' Turning to the young aide he then added, 'Okay, son, get busy and circulate all four descriptions, plus dog, to all four counties with a particular request to Kent to check the hopfields at Wateringbury. By the way, what's your name?'

'Darling, sir, Sebastian Darling.'

Evans heard a stifled chuckle from the direction of his detective sergeant.

'Well, I'm certainly not calling you Darling, so you'll have to be Seb. Okay?'

'Seb will do fine, sir,' replied the young man, now convinced he had finally arrived.

He was almost out of the door when Evans's voice boomed, 'And where's your hat?'

The young aide instinctively raised his hand to his head. 'Hat, sir? I ain't got one. I've not had one since I outgrew it and me mum gave it to me brother when I was twelve.'

'Then you'd better get another one, hadn't you?' ordered Evans curtly. 'You'll never be a proper detective without a hat. And incidently it'd better be a real hat. You'll need a decent trilby and not one of those dosshouse caps.'

'Sir!' acknowledged the young man as he disappeared into the corridor still holding his head.

As the days shortened, the hops became fewer until it was obvious that Wednesday morning would just about see the last of them. It was a moment that Wonky had tried hard not to think about. He had enjoyed every moment of his stay but he wondered if the Wilkinsons had realised that, if he valued his life, he could hardly return to London to borrow another of Sid Grechen's lorries.

It was a particularly misty evening as he sat thoughtfully stroking Pieshop by the fireside across from Lillian Wilkinson. The younger members of her brood had been in bed since darkness fell, whilst Evelyn and Esther were having their daily strip wash in the hut. He had spent some time thinking how best to broach the subject of their return home when suddenly Lillian spoke.

'So what we gonna do abaht a lorry, Mr Lines?' she asked quietly. 'We've accumulated so much extra junk since we've been 'ere, we'd never even get it ter the railway stashun, never mind gettin' it on the bleedin' train.'

Wonky stared open-mouthed across the flames. 'Wh-What made you say th-that?' he asked bewilderedly. 'About th-the lorry, I mean. Here I was just th-thinking of the best way to f-fetch the subject up and you've done it f-for me!'

She shrugged philosophically. 'Me mum always said I was a witch. P'raps it's true. In any case, yer don't 'ave ter be a genius to know we're goin' 'ome in a couple of days, do yer? It's Monday now, so fer Gawd's sake don't waste too much time thinkin' abaht it. All I wanna know is 'ow we gonna get there?'

Wonky scratched his head thoughtfully. 'If I had enough m-money, I s-suppose I might be able to hire a truck in M-Maidstone. But th-they'd want cash d-down and I haven't g-got enough.'

'What d'yer mean 'aven't got enough, o'course, we've got enough, or at least we will 'ave by Wednesday morning. We'll all be paid by then. My family might not be everyone's cuppa tea, Mr Lines, but they're bleedin' good pickers. We must 'ave close on twenty quid due us.'

Wonky broke up a particularly large log on the fire before replying. 'I s-suppose I could go to M-Maidstone on the bus tomorrow and put down a d-deposit. Th-Then once we've been p-paid, I could go back the next day and c-collect it.'

'But won't that mean yer'd 'ave ter return the lorry all the way back ter Maidstone?'

'Th-That's not a p-problem,' he replied. 'It's only about an hour from L-London.'

Further plans were cut short by the voice of Esther calling from the hut door.

'Claude, darlin', we've finished washin'. Your turn now, lover.'

Giving Pieshop a dutiful pat, he rose slowly to his feet and stretched his arms up into the autumn darkness. 'Ah w-well, b-boy,' he murmured to the dog, 'I'd b-better make the most of th-this. A quick r-rinse at our k-kitchen sink won't e-ever s-seem th-the same again.'

It was early next morning that the Wilkinsons made their way to the last hopfield and Wonky set off in the opposite direction for the Maidstone bus. About an hour later, he alighted and a postman directed him to a small cluttered yard three streets behind Maidstone railway station. The yard consisted of three open garage sheds on one side and the chassis of five open-back trucks plus a variety of wheels, tyres, gearboxes and oildrums scattered over the rest of it.

In the sheds there appeared to be a large quantity of spares. These were scattered everywhere without any apparent system. A tiny wooden hut with the name SPENSER'S HAULAGE stood in a dim corner of one of these sheds and was illuminated by two oil lamps, one of which smoked so badly it appeared about to explode.

'Anyone about?' called Wonky.

'Here!' replied a female voice from the direction of the hut. The door of this hut was raised some three feet above floor level and a greasy railway sleeper lay just beneath the door, presumably serving as a step.

'What can I do for you, mate?'

The voice appeared to come from behind the door and, as Wonky peered round it, he was surprised to see a grimy woman of some thirty-five years. She was attired in blue overalls at least two sizes too large for her, Wellington boots, a turbaned headscarf, a pair of large dangling earrings, a cigarette and with an inordinately greasy face.

'Th-the postman said you h-hire out l-lorries,' Wonky said with waning enthusiasm. 'Th-that right?'

'That's right enough, cocker,' she agreed. 'I've actually got two but they're both out at the moment,' she glanced up at a clock, 'though they shouldn't be long.' She nodded to the corner of the hut where a black kettle was steaming away on a small oil stove. 'If you'd like to make the pair of us a cup of tea, they'd probably be back before you've had a chance to drink it.'

Although intending to carry out her wishes, he felt he could do nothing until he had adjusted the smoking lamp. Without a word, he raised the glass and trimmed the wick and, after a couple of other minor adjustments, relit it to throw out a bright new yellow light.

'Well, aren't you the clever dick!' the woman said. 'Here, you're not a genie, are you?'

'N-No,' he said, lifting the lid from the teapot. 'If I w-was, I'd'a conjured up a l-lorry for meself.'

'Yeh, s'pose you would. So, if you're not a genie, what are you and why d'you want to borrow my lorry – and for how long?'

'Just for a d-day. I w-want to run s-some hop-pickers b-back to s-south London.'

'Oh, I ain't so sure about that,' she said, shaking her head. 'I've had trouble with your lot before. You're bloody bad news, you are. On at least two occasions I've had to go up to London to collect the sodding thing myself.' She waved her arms around. 'As you can no doubt see, I don't have time to bugger about going up there. I hate the bloody place at the best of times without scouring around shitty streets looking for me own truck.'

'Th-This y-yard belongs to you then?'

'Haven't I already made that clear?' she shook her head despairingly. 'Well, you're not the brightest bloke in the world, are you?'

With anger rising, Wonky returned the pot to the top of the stove and turned slowly to the woman. 'L-Look, I've just c-come in here to hire a t-truck. I've mended your l-lamp, made y-your tea and l-listened to your insults. Now I don't want a ch-character r-reference, I want a truck. So d-do I get one or d-don't I?'

For the first time, the woman smiled and, sliding back her chair, rose swiftly to her feet. Wonky's first impression was of height, she must have been six feet if she was an inch. His second impression was of her general bearing; considering her size, it was particularly feminine though any shape she may have had was entirely lost in the numerous folds of her overalls.

'Yes, sorry about that, mate, but things are a bit hectic here at the moment.' Sniffing, she cuffed her nose on her oily sleeve which caused a wide black streak from her nose to her cheekbone. 'Well, actually that's a lie, things are a bit hectic here *all* the bloody time.' She leaned back and appeared to size him up and down for a moment. 'You don't know about lorries by any chance, do you? I mean, really *know* about them?'

'Y-Yes, o'course I d-do,' he replied. 'Th-that's my game. I w-was employed by a f-fellow until a sh-short time ago and he used to l-let me run the y-yard myself.'

'That so. Don't want a job by any chance, do you? Three quid a week and overtime?' She nodded out to the yard. 'In fact plenty of bleeding overtime!'

'W-Whoa!' exclaimed Wonky, raising his hands. 'I c-came in here to h-hire a truck, y-you then s-start off having a r-right go at m-me, now you w-want to give me a job! Wh-what's goin' on h-here?' He broke off to gesture at the state of the yard. 'I can obviously s-see you could d-do with s-some help but th-there's plenty of p-people out of work. Why don't you t-try some of th-them instead of a c-complete s-stranger?'

'Because I think you'd suit and I get the impression you know what you're doing. Anyway, I've tried "some of them", as you put it, and "some of them" ain't very good. Hence the state I'm in. Look, anyone who knows anything at all about motors can see what's wrong here in a flash. You saw it straight away, didn't you? How about a week's trial? If you don't like me or I don't like you, finito! What do you say?'

For a full minute Wonky did not say anything. Finally he murmured, 'You don't know how t-tempting th-this is to me right n-now. I c-certainly can't do anything for you at the m-moment, but if I can have a day or two to th-think it over, perhaps when I return the l-lorry, I'll tell you th-then?'

Before she could answer there was an enormous rattle as an old Fordson truck bounced through the gate with a similar truck in tow. 'Well, there they are,' she announced. 'Which would you like?'

'The one that actually goes, if it's all the same to you,' he said.

'They both go, stupid,' she said tersely. 'It's just that the one being towed ran out of petrol and I sent the other one out to tow it in.'

'H-How much to hire for a full d-day, say eight in the m-morning till eight at n-night?'

'To you – hmmnn – fifty bob, and I'll sling in the petrol. Fair?'

'F-Fair,' he agreed. 'Except I don't w-want it until Wednesday and I can't pay you until I p-pick it up. Fair?'

She cuffed her nose again which extended the mark another inch. 'Not really, but it'll do.'

Wonky took his leave of the woman, and as the sun began to rise above the mist, he decided to spend a couple of hours sightseeing in Maidstone. However, hunger cut short his plan as he suddenly remembered the copious amounts of food that Lill Wilkinson would soon be sharing out for her brood at the hopfield. So within an hour of first arriving in Maidstone, as there was no bus, he was seating himself on the train for his return.

It was as the train panted past the old stone bridge at

Teston that, for the first time, Wonky really understood Lillian's romance with the hopfields. The Medway river shimmered in the sun with only the faintest trace of mist still clinging amongst the thicker reeds of its banks. The old steam train busily puffed out its own clouds that at first revelled joyously in their release but soon ran out of enthusiasm and fell wearily down on the river. There, after resting momentarily on the surface, they faded gradually from sight. As he handed his ticket to the collector, he suddenly realised how far away were those smoky verminous Blackfriars streets. It was certainly going to be an enormous temptation not to take the job at Spenser's Garage.

On leaving the station, he decided not to call in at the hopping hut but to go straight to the field where his hunger pangs soon told him he had made the right decision. Lillian had laid out a large, if somewhat dubiously white cloth over a heap of vines and was passing around enormous chunks of cheese and burnt crusty bread. Thought it was still quite early for lunch, the baker's van had just called at the fields and the smell of fresh-baked bread had been too much of a temptation for everyone working there. Breakfast seemed years away as even the most discriminating tore, with hop-stained fingers, into midge- and wasp-covered sandwiches.

'Why, it's Mr Lines!' Lillian greeted him as she dealt out a few wallops to the more impatient of her throng. 'Well, 'ave we got ourselves a lorry, Mr Lines?'

'We h-have, indeed, Mrs W-Wilkinson, we h-have indeed, mam!'

'Then 'ave a cheese-an'-pickle sandwich, Mr Lines. I reckon yer deserve it!'

Wonky was halfway through his sandwich and had reached the satisfying stage where he believed that cheese and burnt crusty bread was God's own food, when his appetite disappeared in a flash.

'Yer only missed those two coppers by minutes, Mr Lines,' mumbled Lillian through a doorstep sandwich. 'But yer quite safe. We told 'em we didn't know yer an' 'ad never seen yer.'

'Wh-What!' he exclaimed. 'Wh-What coppers? And wh-why were they looking f-for me?'

'We did ask, but they wouldn't say. A right pair of shifty buggers, if yer ask me.'

He thought hard for a moment, then said, 'L-Look, Mrs W-Wilkinson, are you sure they were p-police? I know they *said* they were, but there's a b-bloke l-looking for me and it's j-just the sort of stroke he'd p-pull.'

'Well, a funny thing yer should say that, Mr Lines, 'cos I kept noticin' 'ow one of 'em never took 'is eyes away from my Esther's knockers. Mind yer, the saucy cow kept winkin' at 'im but it's not 'ow a policeman would behave, is it, Mr Lines?'

'D-Did th-they say if they'd be b-back?'

'Well, the one oglin' Esther said they'd definitely be back, but the other one said they've gotta search the whole of the Wateringbury 'opfields first.'

'S-So when d'you th-think is the earliest we can l-leave h-here?'

'Well, we won't get paid till Wednesday mornin', so say about two o'clock? That's unless yer want ter go down ter the Railway pub ter celebrate?'

'If you don't m-mind,' said Wonky, 'I'd s-sooner celebrate wh-when we get h-home.'

'Mr Lines, I can see yer real worried abaht those two scabby coppers. Well, don't be. If they turn up agin, we'll chuck the barsteds in the river.'

Up until that time there had not been a moment at the hopfields when Wonky had not wanted to stop the clock, but now Wednesday could not come quickly enough. It was an indication of the urgency he attached to leaving Wateringbury that he left the hut before breakfast early on Wednesday morning. To save time, he even travelled to Maidstone by train, in spite of the fact it was tuppence dearer than the bus.

However, his sacrifice counted for nothing when he found the yard had yet to open.

He had lurked near the gate for some twenty minutes before the roar of a motorcycle finally drew his attention. It rattled up to the gates and a tall, leather-coated, goggled-helmeted figure dismounted. As soon as he saw the rider's movements, he knew exactly who she was. Or rather, he would have done if he had taken the trouble to discover her name.

'Blimey, mate, you're early,' she said, putting a key in the huge padlock. 'Did you shit the bed or were you frightened the price might go up?'

'Er n-no,' he bleated. 'L-Look, if I can't manage to return this l-lorry tonight, can I return it first th-thing in th-the morning?'

'Sure,' she agreed. 'It'll cost you extra though. One and ninepence if you decide to work for me and ten bob if you don't. Fair?'

'F-Fair,' he sighed. 'Oh, and b-by the w-way. Wh-what's your n-name?'

'Spenser, Olive Spenser. Will you remember it or shall I write it down?' she asked tartly.

He made no reply, but followed her into what passed for her office. The coat she was wearing was as massive and as stained as the overalls she had worn two days earlier. He was more than surprised, therefore, when she tugged off her helmet to reveal a mass of tumbling red hair and a clean face. He was just beginning to admire both features when she shrugged off the old battle coat to show a trim figure clad in brown jodhpurs and a green jersey. The thought of working for this woman suddenly took on a whole new dimension for him.

'C-Can I ask you a q-question?' he said.

She shrugged. 'You can ask anything you like. It doesn't mean to say you'll get an answer. Still, fire away, you may be lucky.'

'It's v-very unusual to s-see a woman r-running her own t-trucking b-business. Wh-what made you try it?'

'No choice. It was my husband's. He survived four years of war and was killed in this yard by a truck on the very day of his return. It was sell it or work it. I chose the latter. Anything else?'

He shook his head. 'N-no,' he replied.

'Well, I'm pleased about that. If you'd care to give me the balance, you can be on your way and I can get on with earning my living.' She took the cash and a minimum of details from him. She then scrawled out a brief note on a sheet of headed paper and tossed him a set of keys. 'That's it. Look after it and I'll see you back here tomorrow morning about this time.' She rose quickly from the desk and was halfway into her old overalls before he had stepped down into the yard.

An hour later, with the weather still holding, Wonky drove the truck up the damp track towards the row of huts. There were a couple of other vehicles and a horse and cart there, but the main body of pickers were already trailing with their bundles down the hill to Wateringbury station.

With every last item finally stored, Esther and Evelyn flashed an acre of plump thigh at Wonky as he assisted them over the tailboard. Lillian, meanwhile, took her last look around before climbing solemnly into the driver's cabin.

'Okay, Mrs W-Wilkinson?' he said. 'Th-then we're off!'

The drive home could not have been smoother and Wonky was particularly impressed with the running of the lorry. Because of the evening rush hour, Wonky had left the Old Kent Road some mile-and-a-half from home and was meandering his way through the maze of lanes and alleys that crisscrossed the back streets of Walworth. It was as he approached Rodney Road police station that he had his first occasion to stop. The familiar figure of Reuben Drake sitting on his cycle with one foot on the kerb announced to Wonky he was almost home.

It may have been a different lorry but small details like that never fooled the eagle eye of the burly copper. He did not even make the gesture of dismounting from his cycle but simply half lifted an arm. 'Wonky, m'lad!' he boomed. 'Yer looking very well, me old fruit. Where've yer been? Ain't seen yer about fer weeks. How's that old cutthroat yer work for, still avoidin' me, is he?'

Wonky promptly fell into his customary dithering mess with Drake and bleated some weak tale about Grechen moving away to the west country. However, for a change, fortune for once favoured him. Though he did not know it, the constable was five minutes away from his meal break and, after an assurance that Wonky was no longer working for Grechen, he was allowed to continue.

It was an hour later when the Wilkinsons had finally unloaded the lorry and Wonky had politely turned down a meal with them in order to return to his own home. By this time, Reuben Drake had eaten a pair of best Yarmouth bloaters and was standing feet astride in the lavatory in order to empty his bladder before the second stint of his late-turn duty. As Detective Inspector Cardwell took up the adjoining bowl, Drake did not trouble even to acknowledge the senior man's presence. This indifference was by no means unusual. Very few old uniform policemen would even speak to a CID officer unless it was absolutely necessary. To his surprise, the detective inspector actually addressed him.

'You've been at this nick for some years now, er – Drake, isn't it?'

Without lifting his glance from his fly-buttons, Reuben grunted, 'Twenty-one of 'em. And it *is* Drake.' The omission of the word 'sir' was deliberately apparent.

'As much as that eh?' marvelled the detective in a patronising tone. 'Don't happen to have run across a geezer named Lines during those years, I s'pose?'

Drake made no reply at first but, after securing the last button, walked across to the wash basin and for the first time in his entire service, actually washed his hands after urinating. As he reached for the roller towel, he finally spoke.

'Wonky, alias Claude Lines. Yeh, I know 'im an' see him from time to time. Why, what's he been up to?'

The detective's eyes narrowed. 'You mean you don't know? Are you actually saying you weren't aware this man is wanted urgently by the CID all over London or even what he's wanted for? If that's what you're saying, I just can't believe it!'

'Yer can believe what yer like,' shrugged Reuben. 'That's privilege of rank but it don't make it true.'

'This man is at least a suspect for murder, burglary and for good measure, probably rape. He's also gone smartly to ground and, not only that, but you're bloody insolent, Drake!'

'Then, with *respect*, sir!' snapped Reuben, 'I must tell yer that's total bollocks. Wonky Lines may not be adverse to a little fiddlin' but 'e wouldn't hurt a fly, so I'm not concernin' meself with that shit. What I'm more concerned about is that your department seems to 'ave been tearing around like a ten-legged rabbit looking for him, whilst us – the uniformed branch – didn't even know! I consider that far more important, and d'yer know why?'

Cardwell's first instinct was to throttle the old copper but he had a feeling he was about to learn something, so he simply shook his head.

'Well, it's exactly what's wrong with this fuckin' job! It's a classic case of you-up-there-and-us-down-here, ain't it? I bet your lot 'ave been slingin' fuckin' memos about all over the place. Ter each other, ter the county CIDs, ter Scotland Yard, an' for all I know ter the Peckham branch of the fuckin' Primrose League. But I bet there's one fuckin' branch yer've totally ignored. Yeh, that's right, it's *US*! It's us poor bastards out on the streets. D'you know, guv'nor, there's 'ardly a PC at this nick who *doesn't* know where Wonky Lines could 'ave been seen these last few weeks? If you'd asked any of 'em, or even taken the trouble to look in the accident record book, you'd have found out weeks ago that he was the driver in a fatal accident. I've spoken to 'im barely an hour ago – 'e was almost outside the nick! 'E ain't the fuckin' Scarlet Pimpernel, yer know. 'E's just dear old fuckin' Wonky. If yer'd like to stick yer 'ead in the snooker room at teatime and tell the first uniform copper yer see that Wonky Lines is wanted, they'll swift 'im back in the charge room within the hour. So in future, just simply *tell us*, guv'nor! It might come as a surprise but we are in the same fuckin' job!' Then, with hands still wet, Reuben Drake stormed out into the station yard.

For the first time in his life, Detective Inspector Cyril Cardwell was not so much speechless as dumbfounded. The fact that he should have reported Drake for just about every insolent discipline case it was possible to think of, had not even entered his head. It was the fact that the insufferable sod was right. That was what really hurt. Scores of detectives had been chasing shadows whilst every copper at this very nick had always known the suspect's whereabouts!

Wonky Lines had blithely stopped at Old Lewes for a pie-and-mash on the way home and, after resuming his journey, he turned out of Webber Street into Blackfriars Road. At last, almost home! The car that was outside his address caused him to halt a few yards back. As he watched, he saw two men leave the vehicle and go into his entrance. My God, had Sid traced him already? He ducked down below the windscreen and waited until their eventual reappearance. Rejoining their colleague in the car, the trio held a deep conversation before driving briskly away. Wonky lit a cigarette and thoughtfully stroked Pieshop's neck.

'Y'know wh-what, m-mate?' he murmured. 'I th-think we'll spend a c-couple of weeks at S-Spenser's Haulage, sort of c-convalescence as you might s-say. I'm sure the air'll be healthier. Don't you agree?'

Pieshop sniffed a weary acknowledgement and closed his eyes.

15

Jim Forsythe's announcement that the police had the name of a suspect for her mother's murder had not helped Julia to recover from the loss one bit. Not only that, three weeks had elapsed since the disclosure and the meeting with Lady Clarissa Pethwick-Dorrington and she had not heard a word from the Miller Hospital. She had now reached the stage when she no longer expected to. It seemed simply one more twist to the knife. At times she was so numb that she felt she had entered a void with no exit.

Kind as Jim and Queenie were, she knew if she did not leave them soon, her life would drift aimlessly and her mother would never seem at rest. There were also periods when she physically ached for Duncan, yet the very last thing she wanted was to be the victim of another of his thoughtless deeds. Nothing would be worse, she felt, than to be let down by him when she was so low. At times even suicide crossed her mind. It was not a particularly serious thought but she did find it recurring with increasing regularity. She was beginning to wonder if she was to be one of those people who were better at managing other people's lives than their own. Probably the saving grace for her at such moments was young Benji. Though he had a child's mattress in the corner of her room, she had taken to putting him in her own bed and sleeping with him each night. There was something really comforting about those long night hours with his little body tucked snugly into hers. The child was fortunately a good sleeper and was not disturbed by her tight little cuddles or her pre-dawn sobs. Yet in spite of this, or perhaps because of it, she was aware the day was fast approaching when he must return to his parents. It was a moment she thought of with ever-increasing dread. She knew if she had not made a fresh start before that time, then her life really would be over.

It was after one particularly restless Friday night that she discovered Queenie had propped a typewritten buff envelope against the breakfast teapot. They both knew where it had come from, but Julia could not bring herself to open it.

'Oh, go on,' encouraged Queenie. 'It's not as if it's an exam result or anything like that. They are probably just inviting you for a chat.'

'But supposing it's not? Supposing they are saying that they are full up, or they've never even heard of Lady Pethwick-Dorrington? What then?'

Queenie did not answer but crossed to the table and, having picked up the envelope, turned it over. The flap had not been sealed properly and had come adrift, presumably in transit.

'I wouldn't normally admit this,' she confessed, 'but when I saw it in that condition, my curiosity wouldn't allow me not to peek. I've been as pent up as you have these last few weeks. Open it, girl, for God's sake. It's *not* bad news, it really isn't. I can tell you that much!'

Julia seized the envelope and tore at it frantically. The accuracy of Queenie's forecast was confirmed as the first words caught her eye, '. . . and we look forward to your calling in for a chat on Tuesday 23rd . . .'

'Oh, Mrs Forsythe! You crook!' she cried, devouring the rest of it. 'You knew all the time!'

'Just as well Jim isn't here,' responded Queenie, putting her fingers to her lips. 'I think it's a five-year stretch for tampering with the Mails.'

The girl smiled, closed her eyes tightly and rocked herself back and forth. 'You have no idea what this means to me,' she finally whispered. 'It's a lifeline, a real, real lifeline.'

'Look, love,' replied Queenie, her mood changing, 'you mustn't build this up too much. It is just for a *chat*, you know. I couldn't bear to think of you having another disappointment. Especially . . .' her voice faded away.

'Especially?' echoed Julia, opening her hands in helplessness. 'Especially what? Tell me, Mrs Forsythe. Please, please tell me! Oh, no! It's Benji, isn't it? I'm right, aren't I? He's going home, isn't he? Oh, my God! When?'

'Today, I'm afraid,' murmured Queenie. 'David has his first Saturday off for six months and they are calling for the boy this afternoon.' She shrugged. 'They seem to have resolved their differences. I just hope it works out for them. I didn't tell you before because I was praying you'd receive this letter first. I was cutting it so fine that I've not slept for two nights.'

Julia put down the letter and stared at Benjamin as if in a trance. Suddenly everything seemed to erupt and she reached out quickly and seized the child to her. With tears streaming down her cheeks, she buried his face deep in her bosom whilst kissing his head passionately. The suddenness of her movement alarmed the boy and his Marmite soldier tumbled to the floor. At the first hint of his fright, Julia's distress quickly evaporated. Composing herself, she lifted him onto her lap and fondly ruffled his hair.

'Oh, we knew it was coming sooner or later, didn't we, Ben?' she sighed bravely. 'I guess I just kept putting it out of my mind by trying not to think about it.' She gave a dry little laugh. 'Quite selfish really. David and Grace have their lives to lead and you're part of it.' She finally lifted her gaze from the child. 'But I tell you this, Mrs Forsythe. I am not even worried about this "chat" at the hospital or even about my exam. I'm going to sail through everything these people put in front of me because I'm sure now that this is my destiny. It's got to be, because there is nothing else for me.'

Though Queenie had quite lost her appetite, it was a

problem not shared by either Benjamin or Julia. In fact, the girl looked happier than at any time since her mother's demise. As Queenie stared at them chatting away to each other, she thought how much the boy would miss her. She was now as much a part of his life as he of hers.

'Right, come on, you two, eat up and get out of my kitchen. I've got lots to do today and I don't want you two wasters under my feet.'

'Mrs Forsythe,' said Julia calmly, 'instead of David collecting Benji this afternoon, could I take him home this morning? It would seem more complete somehow.'

'I don't see why not. I could drive you there. I could do with the practice and we've certainly accumulated some junk since he's been here.'

'No, please,' cut in Julia. 'It's very kind of you, but if you don't mind, it's something I want to do for myself.' She gave a rueful smile. 'Sort of self-cure, you might call it.'

The preparations for leaving plus Benjamin's natural excitement caused Julia to overlook the possibility that his parents might not be at home. In fact, the thought never entered her head until she turned the corner of Collinson Street. There, and for the first time, she saw the massive grey-brick, six-storey Victorian tenement stretching away across three streets, with two and a half thousand tenants caged in twelve hundred rooms. It may have been fifty years since it had been a prison but, other than the name, little appeared to have changed. Even the grandiose title of Queen's Buildings was not too far removed from Queen's Prison.

Its first impact stunned her with concern. Though there must have been some sixty children playing happily in the street, she still had difficulty in believing people really lived there. Why was she deliberately returning a child that she loved into such a slum? Though her steps faltered for a moment, a small call from across the street caused her to change her mind. There were several youngsters, none of whom appeared over six years of age, all playing a street game that seemed to revolve round a chalk-drawn pattern on the pavement.

'Wot'o, Benji,' called a short girl in a long frock. 'Are yer playin'?'

The boy tugged her hand like a dog on a lead. 'No, Benji,' she said gently. 'Let's see Mummy and Daddy first, eh?'

The child may not have actually disputed her suggestion but his eyes indicated clearly where his preferences lay. However, after entering the entrance and starting to count the steps to the flat, his attention was sufficiently distracted to becoming quite excited at the prospect of seeing his parents. Whilst still two flights below the fourth floor, the customary odour of cats gave way to the more pungent smell of disinfectant plus the sounds of someone scrubbing and singing.

As the pair turned to climb the last flight, a kneeling young woman glanced over her shoulder to see who was about to walk on her freshly whitened door space. 'I can't give you anything but love, bab—' Grace Diamond suddenly broke off her song with the cry of 'BENJI! What are you doing here? We weren't supposed to see you until this afternoon!' Leaning forward, she pushed her head round the open door and yelled, 'Davy, it's Benji!' Springing to her feet, she tugged her sacking apron from her waist and with arms spread wide almost fell down the freshly scrubbed steps. Sweeping up the child in a great arc, she swung him as much as it was possible in such a narrow space. Clutching him tightly to her, she looked over his shoulder at the smiling Julia.

'I can't thank you enough for what you've done,' she said to the girl. 'I'll never forget it. I'm sure you've saved my sanity.' In a garbled dialogue of laughter and tears, she attempted to embrace the girl with her son still in her arms.

'Be careful,' came David's warning from the open door. 'Those steps are still wet. If you really want to give that lass a cuddle, I'll do it for you. Just a friendly family gesture, you understand.'

The euphoria was suddenly broken by a request from the youngest member of the quartet. 'Can I go and play hopscotch with Rosie, Mum?' he pleaded. Then, as an afterthought that might just sway the verdict, added, 'She did ask me.'

'But you've not been back two minutes, darling,' began a disappointed Grace. 'Why don't you wait until . . .'

'Isn't that what being home is all about?' interjected David quietly. 'Playing hopscotch with Rosie?'

Lowering the boy, Grace nodded. 'Of course, it is,' she agreed. 'Now I come to think of it, that's exactly what it is about!' She gave the child a friendly pat on his backside. 'But stay in the street and don't go away, there's a good lad.'

A look of anxiety immediately crossed Julia's face. 'Er—' she faltered. Both David and Grace looked at her expectantly. 'Well, don't misunderstand me, but, well, isn't he a little, you know, *young* to be out on his own?'

David smiled. 'Not in Queen's Buildings, he's not. Look around you. If you were his age, where would you sooner be? Up here with us or down there with them?'

'Down there with them, I suppose,' she said grudgingly. 'But the street is so far away and it's practically out of sight.'

'You think so?' asked David. 'Then look at this.' He led her into the flat, then into the second of the two rooms that obviously served as family bedroom and parlour. Sliding up the sash windows, he invited her to look out. Doing so, Julia was surprised at just what she could see.

'Don't just look at the kids,' said David. 'But lean forward and put your head out as far as you can. Then look down at the sides of this building and tell me what you see.'

She gave him a puzzled glance, but did as requested. 'Heads!' she exclaimed. 'Dozens and dozens of them. They look like they're all waiting to be guillotined.'

He laughed. 'Well, there are a few for whom that might not be a bad idea, but mostly half of them are looking out for their kids and the other half are just nosy buggers. But with three hundred windows facing onto this street, there's not a stranger or a secret that goes unnoticed. Grace and I both played there when we were kids – and that was during a war. Anyway, as a kid, you're far better off in the street. There are no vermin, you see, or if there are, you can outrun them.'

Julia gave an involuntary shudder and looked quickly about her.

'It's all right, just joking,' David laughed. 'They don't come out until dark.'

By this time, Benjamin had reached ground level and David waited until he saw the boy was totally accepted into the group before closing the window. 'Now, young lady, would you like to tell us what you're doing here? We weren't expecting to see our son until this afternoon. Why so soon?'

Julia recounted her reasons but she soon sensed that David's regular nods meant he was just being polite and did not fully understand her motives. Grace, however, leaned across and squeezed her hand.

'You poor kid,' she said softly. 'We were so caught up in our own troubles that we never even noticed anyone else's. We owe you such a lot.'

Further conversation was interrupted by a tinkling of bells and a long chorus of children's voices calling loudly from the street.

Grace nodded towards the mantelpiece clock. 'Quarter to twelve,' she said. 'Regular as clockwork, isn't he?'

'Who is?' asked David.

'Oh, of course, I forgot. You wouldn't know, would you? At this time on a Saturday you're usually either at work or else you're asleep. It's the roundabout man. You'll have your son calling up any minute now for a ha'penny.'

'A ha'penny? What's he get for that?'

'A ride on a little roundabout. The man has it on the back of a cart and when he turns the handle, the roundabout goes around. At least that's the plan but so many kids want to turn the handle for him that he doesn't even have to do that. All he does is put a nosebag on his pony and collect the money. There, listen, what did I tell you?'

'What is it?' asked David. 'All I can hear is a street full of kids calling out for ha'pennies.'

'That's right and your son is amongst them. Hear him?'

They all went to the window and sure enough, standing on the opposite pavement with a hand cupped to his mouth, was Benjamin Diamond, yelling so loud his face was blood red.

'Sodding little cadger,' grumbled David, searching his pocket for change. 'He's only been home for ten minutes and he's after money already. Don't want him back by any chance, do you, Julia?'

'No fear,' smiled the girl. 'Not now that I know his true nature. I was hoping to be a kept woman. Instead it looks like he was just after my money.'

'Well, you'll certainly need plenty of loose change if you spend time here on a Saturday afternoon,' said Grace ruefully. 'On a nice day they line up to perform.'

'Who does?' asked Julia.

'Street entertainers,' replied Grace. 'There are dancers, singers, fire-eaters, stilt-walkers and a bloke with a performing dog. They do their act for ten minutes and, if you like them, then you chuck whatever you think they're worth into the street – and that could be tuppence or a stale bun.'

'Are they any good?' asked the curious girl.

'Most are,' replied Grace. 'Otherwise, they don't get paid!'

After David had tossed the coin from the window, the trio sat down for a cup of tea and Julia finished recounting her plans.

Though David had not paid full attention to her tale, he certainly perked up when Wonky Lines's name was mentioned.

'You couldn't begin to know the trouble old Wonky has caused in our nick,' he said. 'Because of him, Reuben Drake has stirred up a right bloody hornet's nest. I know Reub can sometimes be a wicked old sod but he was dead right on this one.'

'This man, Wonky, I believe you call him?' said Julia. 'D'you know him well?'

'Not well,' admitted David, 'but if you're about to ask me if I think he was capable of killing your mother, then, no, he wasn't.'

'So if it wasn't him, who was it?' she persisted.

'I honestly don't know, but because of this lack of communication, a tremendous amount of time has been wasted. They've roped in a good dozen suspects this week and that's from our manor alone.'

A tinkling bell announced the departure of the street roundabout and caused Julia to look at her watch.

'I'd better go before your variety acts begin,' she said, reaching for her coat. 'Otherwise, I'll stay here all afternoon.'

'And that's something you're welcome to do whenever you please,' said Grace.

'I'll call up Benji so he can say goodbye to you properly,' said David moving towards the window. 'I know he'd like . . .'

'No!' she cut in sharply. 'Please don't. I'd hate to interrupt his play. I'll just speak to him as I go by.'

'As you wish,' shrugged David. 'But I still think it's something he ought to do.'

Julia was about to take her leave when an overpowering smell suddenly invaded the staircase. It soon reached her eyes and throat and she spluttered into a sharp fit of coughing.

'My God, what's that!' she panted. 'It took my breath away.'

'Are you all right now?' asked David, trying to conceal a smile.

'Y-yes, I think so,' she replied gingerly, 'but it felt like I was sticking my head in a hot tar barrel. What on earth is it? Is there a factory nearby?'

'Oh, there's a few factories, love,' he conceded, 'but none

247

that smell quite like that. How's your head? Is it clear?' he asked mysteriously.

'My head?' she asked, instinctively raising her hand to her forehead. 'Yes, it's fine. Why shouldn't it be?'

Both David and Grace finally burst out laughing.

'It's old Maggie Baldwin in the basement,' David explained. 'She's probably pouring out her paregoric delights.'

'What on earth are they?' asked Julia, still dabbing her eyes. 'Paint removers?'

'You may sneer,' said Grace. 'But there are hundreds of folk who swear by them. But not us!' she added hastily. 'You see the basements here have all been condemned as being unfit for human habitation. So they are let out as storerooms and one-man businesses. Down there she makes Ma Baldwin's Olde-Tyme Paregoric Delights. They are small marble-type sweets and she melts a concoction of them in a mould from time to time then lets them cool.'

'But what on earth does she put in them? It's taken the lining off my lungs!'

'God only knows,' admitted David. 'Sump oil and ether by the smell of it.'

'But it's a wonder she doesn't wipe out half the population of the borough!' persisted the girl. 'If no one is allowed to live in these basements on health grounds, how can she possibly be allowed to cook in the damn place?'

'Well, according to the sanitary inspector, cooking is okay. Old Mac makes his toffee apples next door and cooks his toffee in a pot that hasn't seen a wash for ten years to my certain knowledge. I mean, look at it logically, girl. There ain't a germ in creation would survive that bloody stink, so why worry?'

'Are there any others?'

'Well, there's Mister Gandhi the Indian toffee maker. He works two blocks away and then there's Doctor Dawes, further down the street.'

'Gandhi? That's not his real name, surely?'

248

'No, it's not,' agreed David. 'But his name is so difficult that he uses Gandhi because most folk can manage it.'

'So how does Indian toffee differ from English toffee?' asked Julia.

'Well, it's pink and tastes like sugared horse dung,' said Grace.

'And she's not joking,' David assured her. 'They say life expectancy in New Delhi is thirty years. If that's right, then someone should look at their toffee.'

'And Doctor Dawes – what does he cook?'

'Oh Doctor Dawes doesn't cook anything. Doctor Dawes makes ointment, except he's not really a doctor. He's one of those quacks that work the markets. His speciality is boils and pimples. He makes tubs of his ointment out of gelatine, olive oil and soft soap. Now that really *does* stink! No one here would buy an ounce of the stuff, but it does very well in the street markets.' The breeze that blew through the glassless window on each landing, had now cleared all trace of the Olde-Tyme Paregorics so Julia decided to take her farewell whilst the opportunity presented itself. The goodbyes were warm and affectionate and, minutes later, Julia had descended to the entrance. After a nervous glance down the steps to the basement, she waved across the street to Benjamin. He frowned for a moment as if trying to remember her. Then, having done so, gave her the briefest of smiles before resuming his game with his friends.

'And for three weeks I slept with the sod,' she murmured. 'Typical bloody male!'

It was early evening before Jim Forsythe returned home, and whilst Queenie was preparing their evening meal, he scuttled in quickly to check the day's football results. 'Cowdenbeath 2 Hamilton Academicals 3,' said the flat voice from the radio. 'Arbroath 2–'

'That always sounds like a contradiction in terms to me,' called Queenie from the kitchen. 'Hamilton *Academicals*, I mean. After all, when did you last know an academic even remotely interested in football?'

'Bloody hell, woman!' Jim exploded, slamming down his pencil. 'What is it about you that you always want to prattle on when I'm taking down the football results? For all I know I may have won a fortune on the pools this week and now I've missed half the Scottish second division! I might need a good win to supplement my pension.'

A saucepan lid clattered to the floor as Queenie entered quickly from the kitchen. 'You've never even mentioned your pension before, Jim. What's fetched this up?'

He sighed and folded his paper. 'To put it simply, I've resigned,' he said. 'The new commissioner arrived last week and he's spent the last few days going through the headquarters staff with a small toothcomb. He implies I've been overpromoted. He said he didn't think anyone without a formal education should be ranked higher than sergeant.'

'But that's stupid! The fact that you reached the rank of superintendent *without* such an education should stand you in better stead than someone who has had his path smoothed for him.'

'*You* think that and I think that. Unfortunately, we don't make the regulations. Trenchard does.'

'But he can't demote you without good reason, surely?'

'No, that's right, he can't,' agreed Jim. 'But what he can do, in fact, has done, is make my position so untenable that I'll have no other option but to resign.'

'But isn't that giving way to him?'

'I grant you that, but I won't be the only one leaving. So I'm taking up my new job offer while it's still there. There's going to be such a scramble for a civilian post now, because not only has Trenchard arrived, but the eight per cent pay cuts start next week.'

'But if we pull in our horns we can still get by,' said Queenie. 'After all, lots of folk get by on much less than we do. My David, for example.'

'*Our* David,' he corrected. 'Yes, of course, I realise that, but the fact remains I used to love this job and now I don't. It's as simple as that.'

She bent over and kissed the top of his thinning hair. 'Then that's all that was needed to be said. I didn't need the grand lecture on morale and economics, you dope. So when do you leave one job and start the other?'

'Well, they want to interview me on Tuesday week at two o'clock. All being well, I should be working for them in about a month. Ironically though, Trenchard has instructed all headquarters staff to accompany him to a lecture at Queen's Hall on that Tuesday morning. He wants to speak to as many of the lower ranks as possible. He says he wants to outline his plans for the future of the police, but it's my guess he just wants to show off to the serfs. He's good at that.'

'So,' said Queenie, 'the twenty-third is going to be a turbulent day for everyone! What with Julia going for an interview at nine o'clock, you at two o'clock and the commissioner reading the riot act sometime in between, this could be a very solemn house by teatime. Do you think I should get myself a job as a taxi driver in case neither of you make it?'

'Not with your sense of direction, sweetheart.'

Julia had taken little part in the banter and Jim, noticing she was unusually quiet, said as much. 'Something on your mind, m'dear?' he asked.

'I keep thinking of those dreadful buildings,' she said, 'and how sad that people have to live in them.'

'It's usually only people who *don't* live in them that feel so bad about people who do,' he countered. 'How long did you spend there this morning?'

'Oh, I dunno, a couple of hours, maybe.'

'And did you see many unhappy people – adults or kids?'

'No, I didn't. In fact, I'd have to say the youngsters seemed particularly happy.'

'I know,' said Jim. 'You see Queen's Buildings is one of

those places where you only realise how bad it is when you leave. Every time we return to see David and Grace, my stomach turns over. It appears the same thing happened to you today.'

'I think it was seeing Benji looking so relaxed that did it to me,' she murmured. 'After living in this house for three weeks, I just assumed he would be so disappointed to be returning. In fact, he clearly loved it, the little sod!'

Further conversation was interrupted by the telephone. Julia, being the nearest, replied with the number. She then repeated three hullos before the dialling tone clicked off. Turning to Queenie, she shrugged. 'Must be a wrong number. They never even answered.'

'That's strange,' replied Queenie thoughtfully. 'I had two similar calls yesterday. One wrong number I can understand, but three makes me uneasy.'

'Oh, someone has a similar number, I expect,' said Jim dismissively. 'Nothing to worry about. Happens all the time. What should be really concerning us, is Julia's interview. Seeing as she has little medical background, I think we could at least try to prepare her by firing the occasional pertinent question at her. What d'you think?'

Queenie looked dubious. 'Can't say I know any pertinent questions to fire at anyone,' she replied. 'Particularly medical ones.'

'You don't have to be a physician to ask medicinal questions, you know,' said Jim with some irritation. 'We just have to ask what skills does she think she can fetch to nursing. That type of nonsense.'

'But, Jim!' Queenie protested. 'She can't deceive a nursing selection panel. Don't be so stupid.'

'Course she can!' he replied. 'Good God, woman, if selection panels aren't about deceit, what are they about? I should know. I've presided over enough of them!'

'But I can't really say I have any skills,' said the girl honestly.

'Nonsense!' cried Queenie. 'Anyone who saw you at the Lord Mayor's Show would know that wasn't true.'

The girl gave a little smile. 'So I tell them I'm an expert with elephants, do I? I don't think that'd get me far, do you?'

'Oh, come on,' said Jim. 'You're not even trying! Look, so you don't know anything about the treatment of diseases? Well, with no medical background, that's totally understandable. No one will expect you to. But how about prevention? You could easily put forward plenty of ideas about that. You know the sort of thing – dental care, personal hygiene, living conditions, stuff like that.'

'You mean slum basements being used to make confectionery and medicines?'

'There you are, you see, you've got it already! Concentrate on that.'

'But what do I *really* know about it?' asked the bewildered girl. 'Other than a good plumber would probably be better than a good doctor. That's about the limit of my knowledge.'

'Great!' cried Jim. 'So that's what you'll tell them at the interview. That's first-class stuff, you see! Pile it on; they'll absolutely love it!'

The next two weeks dragged by in the Forsythe household and there was an unreal atmosphere about the place as all three of them appeared to be just going through the motions. But at last came the crucial day. As Jim and Julia left early, Queenie wondered how best to spend her day. She knew she needed to be occupied, but with what? Anything needing concentration was out, so it had to be something she could do automatically and yet would take all day. She would clean; yes that's it, she would clean! She would light the big copper boiler in the kitchen and sort out every drawer, cupboard and corner for every item that could boil or soak.

Meanwhile, over a thousand police officers had packed into the Queen's Hall in mixed anticipation of what they were about to hear. By ten o'clock, everyone was in their allocated places except Trenchard himself. As Jim sat at the end of the top table, he glanced at his watch. Five past ten! Julia would probably be well into her interview by now. It might even be over. He hoped she had remembered the piece about plumbers and doctors; he had a feeling it could go down well.

'You think the old goat's changed his mind?' whispered a bearded superintendent.

'Not in a million years,' hissed Jim in reply. 'He'll just be working on a regal entrance. He couldn't just *walk* into a place to save his life. He always has to enter – and enter *grandly*!'

'SILENCE! ALL STAND!' boomed a fat sergeant from the side of the stage.

The commissioner strode in from the wings, reeking in self-importance, but before he reached his chair, he stopped dead and glared around him. A dapper uniformed man of some sixty years, his clipped moustache seemed to have a life of its own as it suddenly twitched and bristled.

'This hall is stuffy!' he boomed loudly. 'Everyone leave immediately and open every door and window and keep them open. I want no one back here until the air is fit to breathe!' With that he spun on his heels and stormed out.

'God, you were right!' whispered the superintendent rising to his feet. 'I've never seen anything like it. He makes Captain Bligh look like a tin of peas. He even makes an entrance when he's leaving!'

It was some forty-five minutes before Trenchard made his second appearance. He did not waste a second as he immediately stressed his intended policy to those sitting before him.

'You can sum it up easily!' he told them. 'My practice is to be firm but fair.' He stared around him for a moment then announced, 'To emphasise this, I invite questions from the floor. Sensible questions, that is. I don't want my time wasted on trivia . . . Yes, you there, second row, what is it?'

'I have no academic background, sir,' admitted a tall young sergeant, 'but I am studying for promotion. I've heard that you plan an officer class for the force. How will that affect men like me?' A murmur of support ran around the vast hall.

'The question is out of order. NEXT! Yes, you, you there, third from the left. What's your question?'

'When men wish to report sick, sir,' said a pale-looking constable, 'you've stipulated they need a certificate from the police surgeon. This usually means waiting for several hours to see him. Couldn't this be done by our own doctor?'

'A trivial question and out of order at a gathering like this. NEXT!'

'I would like some information about the pay cuts, sir, and . . .'

'That question is completely out of order. NEXT!'

And so it went on with question after question arbitrarily dismissed. Soon after midday His Lordship tired of the charade and, gathering his papers, indicated the audience was at an end by marching out of the hall.

Jim gave a sigh of relief as his fears of missing his afternoon interview faded. The muttering of 'What a waste of bloody time!' emanated from more than one voice at the top table.

It was at about that moment Queenie decided to check all Jim's suits for pocket handkerchiefs. A small collection of quite disgusting items were frequently unearthed on such occasions and today was no exception. As she tugged a piece of unwholesome-looking linen from one jacket, the top of a white envelope was clearly revealed. Even clearer were the typewritten words 'For Attention Of Supt. Forsythe. PERSONAL'. She did not hesitate for a moment and quickly slipped the contents from the envelope.

'Dearest Jim,' the note began, 'I have telephoned you several times at home, but I have been unable to speak to you. I am therefore writing this to you at Scotland Yard. I *must* see you, Jim. Please don't let me down. Tuesday the

23rd about 3 would be best because I will be alone the whole day and we can have several hours to ourselves. Ring me as soon as you can to confirm or I'll go crazy. Love, B.'

She had to read it twice before she believed it, but before she had finished for the second time, the strength drained from her. The 23rd was today, yet Jim had not mentioned going out for the evening or, for that matter, even being late home. In fact, only that very morning, he had said how much he was looking forward to swopping interview experiences with Julia. It had to be some kind of mistake. There was undoubtedly an innocent explanation for the whole thing.

Suddenly the sound of the front door closing caught her attention.

'Mrs Forsythe! It's me, Julia!' Queenie knew by the girl's tone that the interview had been a success and in spite of her shock she was instantly delighted.

'Put the kettle on, love, and tell me all about it,' she called. 'Every word, mind.'

It appeared that Jim's advice had indeed been valuable and the topics of drains and slums were an aspect rarely mentioned in nursing interviews. Though Julia was hardly an expert on such matters, she had certainly been one step ahead of the panel and it had stood her in good stead. 'I've already got a starting date,' the girl panted excitedly. 'Three weeks from next Monday. Oh, Mrs Forsythe, I can hardly wait. Won't it be just perfect if Mr Forsythe has also passed his board?' She glanced up at the clock. 'What time are you expecting him in?'

'In about an hour-and-a-half,' replied Queenie. 'Tell you what. Let's make a real evening of it. I'll get out the candles and a bottle of wine and we'll really celebrate. What d'you say?'

'Can we dress up?' asked Julia.

'If you wish,' laughed Queenie. 'We'll get all ready so it's a surprise when Jim comes in. I'll go and have a bath, and you can have one while I'm putting the finishing touches to the dinner. Okay?'

'Fine,' agreed the girl. 'I'll prepare the veg and arrange the table.'

It was ten minutes later that Julia tapped and entered the bathroom. 'Oh, Mrs Forsythe, it's such a shame, isn't it?' she said.

'What is, love?'

'Mr Forsythe not being able to get away from work this evening. He's just telephoned. He's passed his interview but something urgent has come up and he doesn't expect to be home until midnight or even later. It's always the same, isn't it? Just when you think you're going to be happy, a wheel falls off.'

Queenie held up a full sponge of water and lay back in the bath and trickled it very slowly down her face. 'I just hope it *is* only a wheel, love, and not the whole damn engine.'

16

Within minutes of leaving the Queen's Hall, five PCs from the Rodney Road contingent had adjourned to the local pub. It was universally agreed that Lord Trenchard's lecture had not impressed either by content or delivery.

'Complete waste of bloody time,' complained Reuben Drake, reaching for his beer. 'An' it cost me money.'

'How did it cost you money, old chap?' asked Poshie Porter, already halfway through his first pint. 'I thought we all went in our duty time?'

'I cost me money because I 'ad a little private job arranged at the horse auctions at the Elephant and Castle.'

'What do you actually do there, me old fruit?' asked Poshie. 'Because, if you don't mind me saying so, you are not everyone's idea of an auctioneer.'

'I don't *auction*, yer bloody fool! What I does is watch the crowd an' chuck out anyone smokin' a clay pipe,' came the surprising reply.

'What is so heinous about a clay pipe?' asked the puzzled Poshie. 'A fire risk?'

Reuben shrugged. 'Fire risk? No more'n any other pipe, I imagine.'

'Then why throw them out?' persisted Poshie.

'Looks bad,' explained Reuben solemnly. 'Management reckons it looks like the place 'as no class. Not only that, it pulls down the tone of the area.'

'How can you possibly pull down the tone of an area like the Elephant and Castle?'

A sharp tug on his sleeve made Poshie realise the dangerous path he was treading in provoking Reuben Drake. He was therefore relieved when David took over the conversation.

'Nevertheless, Reub, you certainly take a chance working unofficially at the auctions, especially with that sycophantic sod Marsh creeping about,' said David, draining his glass. 'He'd like nothing better than to hit you with a discipline charge, particularly now a pig like Trenchard is running the ship.'

'Slimy blokes like Marsh don't worry me, son. I've always made a point of learning as much about them as possible. Marsh wouldn't dare risk shovin' me on a charge, especially as he's still waitin' a promotion board. Yer see, not only does 'e know that I know he's a gutless groveller, but I think 'e's also worried I might cut 'is throat!' He roared with laughter at his own words. 'The Marshes o' this world ain't never bothered me, son, nor will they. Now a good straight bloke like Station Sergeant Barclay would be a very different kettle of fish. I gotta lot o'time fer Bill Barclay. Yer do realise that all coppers like 'im are gonna be the first to suffer under Trenchard's regime, don't yer? It's taken 'im sixteen years ter reach the rank of station sergeant an' now 'e's told he won't be goin' further. 'Owd' yer reckon 'e's goin' ter feel when 'e sees the first boy wonder sittin' at the front desk?'

The debate was suddenly interrupted by a voice that David found vaguely familiar yet could not place.

'Davy Diamond, isn't it?' said the voice. 'We only met once, but I do remember you quite clearly. Would you or your friends care for a drink?'

David might have been unsure of the voice but the invitation was one every copper would hear underwater in a force nine gale. Five empty glasses were slid as one towards the benevolent young newcomer.

'That's very kind of you, er—' began David.

'Duncan,' said the young man.

'Oh, yes, of course – Duncan!' said David. '*Duncan Forbes,* if I remember correctly. And how is Miss Bardell these days? We've seen so little of her lately and, ah yes, that's right, five pints of bitter, thank you. Come on I'll introduce you to this lot.'

Once the introductions were made and the five pints received, Duncan raised his own glass. 'To you all,' he toasted. 'But you're a long way from Rodney Road nick?'

A hubbub of explanations rang out during which the reputation of the new commissioner was slanderously taken apart.

'Oh dear,' said Duncan. 'That's unfortunate to say the least, though it does explain why I've spent part of the day on a wild-goose chase.'

The puzzled looks this reply generated caused him to enlarge on this.

'You see, one of the reasons I'm in town today, is to make inquiries about joining the police. In fact, I've been making the rounds of the various services – you know, army, navy and air force, and for that matter, anything else I can think of. But when I got to Scotland Yard, they told me no one was available and to come back tomorrow.'

'Hang on fer a minute,' said Reuben Drake, turning to David. 'Is this the bloke yer were tellin' us about? The one who works fer that sexy wench, Billie Bardell?'

'That's him right enough,' nodded David.

Reuben turned his attention back to the young man. 'Yer mean ter say yer thinkin' about chuckin' up workin' for her, ter come an' join this bloody job? What's a matter wiv' yer son. Barmy?'

Duncan gave a little chuckle. 'Oh, I don't argue that working for her has its compensations,' he replied. 'First of all she's a marvellous employer and secondly, well, she *is* Billie Bardell, I suppose. But, after all, I have to move on sometime and now is as good a time as any because . . .'

'My arse, it is!' snapped Reuben. 'With a eight-and-sixpence-a-week pay cut and Vald the Impaler as commissioner? I'd say it was the worst fuckin' time since Robert Peel died!' He leaned across confidentially and muttered, 'Look, son, seein' as yer've been good enough ter buy us all a pint, I'll put yer straight on a little matter. Join the navy, join the army, even join them pansies in the air force if yer must, but fer Gawd's sake stay outa this lot, cause it'll break yer soddin' 'eart, an' that's a fact.'

Duncan shook his head. 'My mind's made up, I'm afraid.'

'But why are you leaving Billie Bardell?' asked David. 'You said you "have to move sometime". But why? What's wrong with staying where you are? I bet you get more money working for her than you will with any of the services. You do enjoy working for her, I take it?'

Before Duncan could reply, Reuben interrupted wistfully. 'Tigers couldn't tear me from a wench like that.' He turned to Poshie Porter and moaned plaintively. ''Ave yer seen the body on that woman, lad? She's like Venus herself.'

'No,' said Poshie, 'I must confess I haven't and it would appear one of the great losses of my life, but with respect, Reuben, you are a little nearer her age than this young man. Doubtless he has younger fish to fry?'

'Well, as a matter of fact,' said Duncan, 'if you haven't seen Miss Bardell lately you might be unpleasantly surprised, even shocked. Something has happened to her. I don't know what it is but she's certainly changed these last few weeks.'

'Changed?' echoed David. 'In what respect?'

'Well, for a start, she doesn't chase me around any more, but I know it's more serious than that. Somehow she's different. She's quiet, and, I hate to say it, she's aged. People who knew her long before I did would all say she hadn't changed in donkey's years. Well, now she has.'

'Is that why yer leavin' her?' asked Reuben curtly. ''Cause she ain't chasin' yer around any more?'

'Of course not!' snapped Duncan. 'She knew I was only going to stay while she settled in after the murder, then I was going to be on my way. I told her that.'

'You think it's the murder that has changed her then?' asked David.

Duncan shrugged. 'Well, it certainly hasn't helped. It's a big house and though I've been sleeping in the next room she's still nervous. Yet I don't think that's the real reason. There is definitely something else. I've asked her several times, but whatever it is, she's not saying. Well, not to me anyway.' He dropped his gaze and, staring idly into his beer, swirled it slowly around the glass.

There was silence from the six men that seemed all the more poignant in the general hubbub from the rest of the bar. David thought it was time to change the subject.

'And how's that young lady of yours?' he asked. 'She looked radiant when she returned my son a couple of weeks ago. Any plans for her?'

For a moment Duncan looked puzzled. 'Young lady? Oh, you mean Julia?' he said. 'Oh, I'm afraid Julia's just a little too intense for me. She always seems to want to fight someone else's battles. Don't misunderstand me, though. I do like her, in fact, I like her a great deal. I particularly like her company and I miss her enormously when she's not around. But she's always got some deep scheme or other that she thinks I should be a part of and I don't always see it that way.' He paused, gave a sad little sigh and took a long draught from his glass. 'Do you know, once when we had the house to ourselves, we went to bed and made love all afternoon. It was bloody marvellous! But two minutes later she started to prattle on about some bloody cause or other and I dozed off. I woke up a quarter-hour later, and d'you know what? She was still going on about it! She was so carried away she hadn't even noticed I'd been asleep!'

'Then it's possible that the same incident has caused both women to change,' murmured David. 'Because I feel she's grown up a great deal in the last few weeks. Oh, I agree she's probably better with other people's problems than her own but she is certainly different. Did you know she's applied for nursing college?'

'Great!' exclaimed Duncan. 'She'll be brilliant at it.'

'Why so sure?'

'Because she has a lovely get-better face and not only that – I've had sexual fantasies about nurses since I was two!'

'Why, yer randy little bastard!' exclaimed Reuben. 'Don't fancy tellin' us about 'em, I s'pose?'

The young man smiled, then drained his glass and rose to his feet. 'Sorry, mate, top security,' he replied. 'Anyway, I've still got a few more job inquiries to make and all this talk about Julia has made me nostalgic. I think I'll give her a call. I'll see you sometime, lads; look after yourselves.' He shook hands all round and eased his way out through the crowd.

''E's a likable bastard,' said Reuben Drake grudgingly. ''E's the sort that usually does well in life, in spite of themselves.'

'Coming from you, Reuben, old chap, that's very philosophical,' said Poshie. 'I *am* impressed.'

'I always become impressive when anyone buys me a beer, Poshie,' replied Reuben. 'Yer oughta try me some day.'

Though Julia Giles had never faded totally from Duncan's mind, his disclosure to the group contained a large element of truth. He was more fond of the girl than he chose to admit, even to himself, but that did not alter the fact that he could find her infuriating. She was the only girl amongst his female friends whose future concerned him. He could never see her as a comfortable plump mum who could take six kids and a husband comfortably in her stride. She was more like Joan of Arc than an Earth Mother, although he would never dream of telling her so. He also knew he was not without fault in their relationship because it was always a compulsive challenge to annoy her intensely. Having done that, he would then ingratiate himself to such an extent that she would surrender to him totally. He was not particularly proud of this and felt that if she would just occasionally settle for a quiet cuddle after their love-making, it would at least placate his conscience. Instead of which, she would gradually work herself into such a frenzy about social injustice that he felt he should hide all sharp instruments.

As he strode across Trafalgar Square, he paused on a traffic island whilst the point-duty policeman allowed a stream of horses and carts to roll by. At that exact moment, with his brain disengaged, he chose the army as a career. When he thought about it later he did not even know why. Of course, there was a current mutiny over pay in the navy at Invergordon and, even though these cuts would not last for ever, a mutiny was hardly conducive to recruitment. As for the air force, well, he had certainly been tempted but only if he could fly. The thought of being an overalled grease monkey clambering over the dirty bits whilst others claimed the sky had no appeal for him at all. Then there was the police. Well Reuben Drake had demolished most of his illusions about that. In popularity stakes, Reuben placed Trenchard behind Jack the Ripper. So it would appear that the army won by a process of elimination rather than by careful selection. Whatever the reason, his stroll down Whitehall led him directly to the recruiting office of the Life Guards, the King's Shilling, a whole new career and a reduction in pay.

It was late afternoon before a now committed Duncan had left the recruiting office. After a leisurely stroll down to the Embankment, he entered a call box and dialled a number. Queenie Forsythe was less than a yard from her ringing telephone but stared at it as if unsure what to do.

'Are you all right, Mrs Forsythe?' called Julia from the door of the dining room. 'Would you like me to answer?'

'N-no, Julia, love, I'm fine. I'll answer it.' Apprehensively she raised the receiver and whispered her number. 'Who? . . . Oh, Duncan! It's lovely to hear you! . . . Where? . . . The Embankment? What are you doing there? . . . You never have! You must be mad! . . . Yes, she's close by. Just a minute, I'll put her on. Goodbye, the best of luck and I hope it works out for you. Here she is.' Placing her hand over the receiver, she thrust it towards Julia and whispered, 'It's your bloke; he's just joined the army!'

Julia looked quite perplexed. 'What bloke? I don't know anyone that daft!'

'It's DUNCAN!' hissed Queenie. 'Duncan Forbes. Hurry up, he's in a call box and there's a queue.'

Julia took the receiver with a marked lack of enthusiasm. 'What d'you want? . . . Well you're too late. Mrs Forsythe and I are eating in tonight . . . No! I don't even care if you've joined the heavenly angels. I'm not coming out with you, Duncan, and that's final! . . . No, I tell you, not even *after* dinner . . . You want to know why? Good, I'll tell you. For the last few years you've twisted me around your little finger and I've decided you're not going to do it any more. Since I've been free of you, I realise I don't have to put up with it, so go and take advantage of some other poor girl . . . Pardon? . . . Well, I'm sorry, but I *don't* believe you. So you're saying that after the way you tormented me these last few years, I'm supposed to believe you suddenly had a change of heart? . . . Duncan, I don't care if they are sending you to Mars. The further the better in my book! Stay away and goodbye!' She slammed the telephone down so hard that she missed the cradle and the whole apparatus crashed to the floor.

'Phew!' marvelled Queenie. 'That's certainly telling him. Pity you didn't mean it. That would have made it even more convincing.'

'Well, he makes me so angry!' snapped Julia. 'He's made no attempt to get in touch with me since I've been here and now, because he looks like being sent to God knows where, he suddenly feels a need for female company – *my* damned company! Anyway,' she added belatedly, 'I meant every word I said, truly I did.'

'Yes,' said Queenie, oozing disbelief. 'About as truly as I'm riding this bike.'

Julia gave a rueful smile. 'I do try with him you know, Mrs Forsythe. In most respects he's a great fellow. It's just that he – well, he has this maddening knack of infuriating me. I can go from a high to a low in seconds. Anyway, if I'm going on a three-year course and he's joining the army, we're hardly going to be Romeo and Juliet, are we?'

'At least he won't be able to infuriate you, dear,' smiled Queenie. 'Anyway, come on, once those potatoes are done, you and I have a large dinner to eat.'

Judging by its progress in rush-hour traffic, Duncan's tram was making surprisingly good headway. All being well, it should reach Streatham in another fifteen minutes. But after that – what then? After her diatribe on the telephone, this next meeting with her was not something he relished. He practised a suitable opening gambit because he felt the first few seconds would be vital. If he could only surmount them he was home and dry because, given time, he could usually talk her into anything.

The women had two laden dinner plates before them when there was a double thud on the door knocker. Queenie gave a start and felt instantly queasy.

'Take no notice,' said Julia quietly. 'Ignore the bastard.'

'But we don't know who it is?' protested the older woman. 'It might be Jim.'

'Oh, I know who it is right enough,' said Julia. 'It's Duncan Forbes, ten-to-one!'

'But how do you know that?' persisted Queenie.

'Because he's predictable. You'll see.'

'Then why don't you let him in?'

'What! And pander to his conceit? I should say not! No, let the bugger stay outside.'

'I'm sorry,' said the flustered Queenie, 'but my curiosity won't let me do that.' Sliding back her chair she almost scuttled to the front door.

Julia gave a smile of self-satisfaction as the distant voice opened with, 'Oh, Mrs Forsythe! How wonderful you look! I did not expect such a treat so soon, but . . .'

'Duncan! Come in, come in. Julia's been – well sort of expecting you, one might say.' She chuckled. 'As she will doubtless tell you herself.'

As he entered the dining room, the young girl cast him an indifferent glance. 'If you want anything to eat, you'll find the vegetables and pease pudding in the bottom of the oven in the kitchen, but you'll have to slice your own bacon. There is plenty.'

Although confused, this did not prevent Duncan from raiding the oven, and he emerged a few minutes later with a sizable amount of boiled bacon, several potatoes and carrots and two great dollops of pease pudding. Sitting himself down at the table, he asked, 'Er – how did you know I was coming?'

'Because you're so bloody predictable,' Julia replied calmly.

'But you couldn't possibly have known,' he protested. 'I didn't know myself until I saw the telephone box half-an-hour ago and it would have taken a good two hours to prepare this meal.'

'Duncan Forbes,' she said acidly, 'until today, you've not bothered to contact me once since I've been here. Correct?'

'Well, I – er – won't say that exactly. You see . . .'

'Correct?' she repeated.

'Correct,' he acknowledged.

'And I'll tell you why you've bothered to phone me today, shall I?'

He made no reply, but gave an almost imperceptible nod.

'Someone, or something, reminded you that I still exist and you thought, "Bloody hell, I'd forgotten all about that dozy cow and I'm going in the army! I know, I'll give her a ring. After all, there's always the possibility I might score." I'm right, aren't I?'

With his head bent forward to meet a forkful of best bacon, he gave her a quick wink and, as his face broke into a grin, he nodded in agreement.

In spite of her worries, Queenie could not resist a quick

smile of her own which she failed dismally to conceal.

'Don't laugh at him, Mrs Forsythe,' protested Julia. 'It'll only encourage him and he certainly doesn't need *that*!'

'Julia, love,' said Queenie. 'I don't think I've ever known anyone like you two. If he's off to the army and you're off to nursing, wouldn't this be an ideal moment to bury the hatchet – not in each other, though,' she added hastily.

Duncan nodded a frantic agreement and, once he had swallowed half of the contents of his mouth, he spluttered, 'Y'know, she's right, kid! Why don't we . . .'

'And please don't call me *kid*! I'm almost twenty-one. I'm a big grown-up girl and I was taught not to talk with my mouth full!'

Giving two large swallows and quickly wiping his lips, Duncan then raised his hands in token surrender before placing them together in a gesture of prayer.

Queenie knew that Julia was looking to her for support, but she also knew she dare not look up in case she caught the young man's gaze again. For some seconds, she deliberately stared out of the window until she felt composed enough to return her attention to the couple. She was assessing what to say when a smile broke slowly across the girl's face.

'You are a bastard, you know, Duncan, and if I pass out as a nurse, you'd better not seek medical help from my hospital. Not unless you have a high resistance to arsenic.'

'It's *when* you pass out as a nurse, my sweet, not *if*! So have no false modesty, I shall recommend every poor wounded soldier in the entire British Army to submit to your tender loving care. There, you see, I'm not one to harbour a grudge.'

As there suddenly appeared to be a degree of amity between the couple, Queenie decided it could be an appropriate time to change the subject. 'What does my mother think about your leaving her employment, Duncan?'

He shrugged. 'I don't think she's ecstatic about it, but she knew I was only there to tide her over. But while we're on the subject, I am a little worried about her. She's not been her old self lately. I have asked her about it a couple of times, but she always insists she's fine.'

'You've made me feel quite guilty,' said Queenie. 'I haven't spoken to her for weeks. She's fiercely independent and doesn't like me to keep ringing to inquire about her welfare. I suppose I should have been more insistent. I'll ring her directly after dinner. So, tell us about your regiment. Where and when d'you have to report?'

'Well, it's the Life Guards and the date's not finally decided yet. I shall need a medical and a quick check to prove I'm not a foreign agent but that should be completed within the next couple of weeks. After that and all being well, I'm off to the regiment's HQ at the Horse Guards and then basic training at Windsor.'

'Are you having any second thoughts?' asked Queenie. 'About the army, I mean. At least, if you joined the police you could resign. Can't do that in the army, though, Duncan, can you?'

'True,' he agreed. 'In fact if I'd had a response when I called at Scotland Yard, I may well have joined the police, but after seeing the Rodney Road mob so disenchanted after their meeting today, I'd be mad to do so.'

'This Rodney Road mob,' said Julia. 'Was Davy Diamond amongst them?'

'Matter-of-fact he was,' agreed Duncan. 'He was the only one I actually knew.'

'That's when you were reminded of me!' exclaimed Julia triumphantly. 'David told you I looked after young Benjamin until the Saturday before last, didn't he! I knew you'd never have remembered me on your own!'

'Children! Children!' began Queenie, 'I thought we'd agreed on a truce? Anyway, if you'll excuse me, I'm going to telephone my mother. Shan't be long.'

As the sound of the dialling could be heard coming from the hall, Duncan offered a peace plan to Julia. 'Providing I'm not called up first,' he said, 'how about me escorting you to

your nurses' quarters on enrolment day? Even you'll admit
I'll have nothing to gain from that?'

The offer put Julia in something of a dilemma. In truth,
the very last thing she wanted was a complete break with this
maddening young man. On the other hand, she felt it was
time he realised that whenever he whistled she would not
come running.

'I'll think about it,' she answered huffily.

Duncan looked up in surprise as Queenie returned to the
room. 'That was quick,' he said. 'Aren't you two speaking?'

'There was no one at home,' replied Queenie. 'She's out
gallivanting, I suppose.'

'I doubt that,' said Duncan. 'She said she didn't feel too
great when I left home this morning and she was going to
have a quiet day. Give another ring in a few minutes. She was
probably in the bathroom.'

'Perhaps I should get the car out and drive over there?'
said Queenie anxiously.

'No, no,' said Duncan, 'she wasn't that bad. Just a little
out of sorts, I'd say. Besides, it would take you ages to drive
there at this time of the evening.'

Queenie gave a worried sigh. 'You're right, I suppose,' she
said, 'but I could kick myself for not phoning earlier. It was
thoughtless of me.'

'Nonsense,' cried Duncan. 'Look, tell you what. As I've
cadged a dinner off you, how about me taking you both to
the cinema at Brixton? There's a really funny Marx Brothers
film. I've seen it once, but I'd love to see it again. It'd cheer
you up no end, honest.'

'That's sweet of you, but you don't want me along playing
gooseberry. You two go and enjoy yourselves. I really couldn't
settle to anything until I speak to my mother. Go on, off with
the pair of you. I won't hear another word about it.'

Duncan knelt before Julia and raised his eyebrows. 'Well?'
he asked. 'How about it? I trust you note the pose?'

'Suits you,' said the girl. 'Stay there and I'll get my coat.'

Queenie watched from the window as the young couple skipped down the steps and onto the front path. The girl looked happier than she had for weeks. Yet, though she was fond of them both, she could not get them out of the house quick enough in order to telephone Billie again. She had a feeling Duncan was right. Her mother was in. She decided, come what may, she was going to let the damn bell ring until she *did* answer.

It must have been a good five minutes before a familiar voice whispered, 'Yes?' but the voice did not belong to her mother. It belonged to her husband, Jim Forsythe. Closing her eyes, she made no reply, but lowered the telephone onto its cradle. It can't be right, surely? Yet what did the note say, 'I will be alone the whole day. Ring me or I'll go crazy. Love B'? Racing to the bathroom, she was violently sick.

17

Billie Bardell sat at the table with knife and fork poised. She watched with total attention as Jim Forsythe slowly replaced the telephone.

'Well?' she asked.

He shook his head. 'No one, no one at all. I thought I could hear some very distant traffic, but I couldn't even swear to that. Whoever rang did not want to speak to me, that's sure.'

'Then it must have been him,' she whispered. 'He would have been expecting me, because Duncan very rarely answers the telephone. Instead he got you. That's why he rang off. How about if he rings back,' she asked. 'What then? If he gets your voice a couple of times he's bound to smell a rat.'

'Unfortunately, my dear,' said Jim wistfully, 'there's no rat to smell at the moment. I only wish there were.'

'Come back to the table, Jim. At least eat your herrings while they're hot.'

'Billie,' he said quietly, 'you can't give up everything to these scum. You have to fight them. Let me have a word with the local CID. It's best, really it is.'

'You're not talking about those idiots who made such a pig's ear of my Alice's murder, surely? Let *them* investigate? Huh! I should say not! I'd sooner pay the bastard than have those useless oafs traipsing over this house again.'

'If you feel like that, then why did you ask me here in the first place? I'm still a police officer, you know?'

'Oh, don't be so stuffy, Jim, for God's sake! I just wanted

to explain to you why – should I ever get the chance – I will kill him. Should I be blessed with enough luck to do just that, I know I can rely on you to tell my side of the story.'

'Billie, I can't do it, you know I can't. If I was to agree to that, it would seem I was a party to all that had passed between you and the blackmailer. If it came out that I had colluded, at the very least I would get the sack.'

'But I thought you said you've put in your retirement notice?'

'So I have! But I've still a month to serve. Not that that would make much difference. If I was to involve myself in anything like that, even once I'm out of the job, I'd still lose my pension.'

'But all I need from you is your expertise in tracing this blackmailer. You can leave the rest to me. As long as I get him, I'm past caring. Help me, Jim, please.'

He leaned across the table and took her hands in his. 'Look, Billie,' he said quietly, 'stop digging. You're in a deep enough hole as it is. There is only one way to do this and it's the official way. Blackmailers rarely succeed because it doesn't matter how clever they think they are, they still have to pick up the cash.'

'You helped Queenie right enough before you married her. Didn't you?' she said bitterly. 'You covered up for her all right and I'm not even asking you to take part in my plan, just point me in the right direction, that's all.'

'Billie that's not fair and you know it!' he snapped. 'I'd do almost anything for you but this is just too great a risk. Not just for me but for you as well. Besides, I don't think you've really thought this out.'

'Not thought it out!' she exclaimed. 'I've hardly thought about anything else since he first contacted me. I feel I know everything there is to know about this man except what he looks like.'

'Precisely, and that's my point! In effect, you know *nothing* about this man. You're so understandably consumed with hatred for him that all you know is the sound of his voice. So what are you going to do? Walk around listening to everyone in London and then cut the throat of the first one who sounds like a blackmailer? Oh, come on, sweetie, that's not going to work and deep down you know it isn't, don't you?'

'So what do I do then?'

'Let's try to think for a while. Has he asked for any money yet?'

'Not an exact figure, no, but he's made it perfectly clear it's coming very soon.'

'How many times has he rung?'

'I don't know for sure. Probably about a half-dozen, I'd say.'

'Is there a pattern to his calls? I mean mornings, evenings, or is it any time?'

'Any time.'

'The voice? Is there an accent? Is it light, deep, or have anything unusual about it?'

'Well, it's a London accent and very very coarse. Yet, the strange thing is, I don't think he's putting it on. It's almost as if he doesn't care. I tell you this, though. I would know the bastard the first time I heard him.'

'Has he made any indication yet of where he'll want you to deliver the money?'

'No, though he did say he's looking for a suitable place, like someone looking for a house, I suppose.'

'You say your husband's will that allows you to stay at this house with an allowance was never properly signed?' She nodded. 'And that your dead husband's family know this?' Again a nod. 'And, as I understand it, they've reluctantly let you stay but you've got to walk a very tight moral line?'

'Yes, but the voting was close. Two of them are particularly keen to dispossess me but the other two are so jealous of the first two that they are marginally on my side. The problem is, they could change their views any time. It's basically a question of family envy rather than my welfare.'

'Yet someone else knows that it was you in that taxi when the driver was killed last September?' He rubbed his chin thoughtfully. 'Look, let us go over everyone who could possibly know and see exactly what they have to gain from that knowledge. Right?'

'Well, there was the fellow who was with me at the time.' She shrugged. 'But that relationship is water under the bridge and, as a bright young politician, he has far more to lose than me. Besides, he's recently been appointed an undersecretary, or something like that, in the Foreign Office and they've shoved him up the Zambezi, or is it the Amazon? I never did learn my bloody rivers. Anyway, I know it wasn't the Thames. That only leaves my maid Alice, and she's dead! And don't forget how the poor thing died! Amongst other things she was raped. She was hardly likely to say, "Oh, yes, seeing as how you've raped me, I've got something else I'd like to tell you before you finish me off with that pillow . . ."' She shook her head vigorously and pounded the table. 'That's what's so maddening, Jim. My Alice was the soul of discretion, so how the hell could anyone else have known?'

'If you are totally convinced that only these two people knew, then we must assume that one of them *did* tell. If that's the case, then I'm afraid I would go for your maid.'

'Typical bloody man!' she muttered. 'So how do you arrive at that conclusion?'

'You said yourself that the fellow with you had much to lose. On the other hand, your Alice had little to lose.'

'You think not? Then how about her job?' said Billie sharply. 'She would always say how happy she was here. She would never risk that just to divulge some tittle tattle.'

'Perhaps she didn't just *tell* someone. Perhaps it was forced out of her?' He rose to his feet and walked round the table. 'Look, Billie, the investigation of Alice's murder was nothing to do with me but because of my connections with you, I obviously took a great interest. The postmortem showed that Alice had been drinking and . . .'

'But Alice didn't drink! All the time she was working with me I'd not known her to touch a drop!'

'Nevertheless, there was a considerable quantity of alcohol in her system. If you say you'd never known her to touch alcohol, that could also mean that she wasn't used to it or chose to keep it secret. If you ally that to the fact that she was knocked about and raped before she died, who's to say how she would have reacted?'

'Oh, my God!' she cried, shaking her head as if trying to dismiss the words from her mind. 'How could anyone do such a thing to such a kind and beautiful person? Whoever it was, I pray I outlive them and can be there when they die, preferably an inch at a time.' She raised her head and looked at Jim's expression. 'What is it?' she asked. 'What have you suddenly thought of?'

'Only that your blackmailer is probably her killer,' he murmured quietly. 'Either that or the killer has told a third party about his conversation with Alice. But I must say that's extremely unlikely.' He glanced up at the clock. 'Look, I must contact Roger Evans and have a chat with him about all this.'

'But you won't tell him about the blackmail, will you?'

'Don't be silly. I *must* do. This will possibly be the best breakthrough he's had since the case began!'

'But I told you all this in strict confidence, Jim. You can't possibly do this to me now, surely?'

'I have no choice, Billie,' he pleaded. 'You want to see Alice's murderer caught, don't you?'

'More than you'll ever know, but I can't see how destroying my life is going to help poor Alice.'

'But if we catch him, he won't be able to destroy you.'

'And if you *don't* catch him. What then?'

'Billie, I know how you feel, really I do, but in the long run this is for the best.'

'No, Jim, you *don't* know how I feel! You've absolutely no *idea* how I feel and your idea of what is *best*, is what's best for the police force, not what's best for the victim. I tell you this, Jim Forsythe. If you mention any of this conversation to that fool, Evans, I shall simply refuse to cooperate and I'll say that everything that has passed between us has been a figment of your imagination.'

'Oh, c'mon, Billie,' he pleaded. 'No one's going to believe that and you know it.'

'Very well, then, I shall simply say that I have now forgotten it. Senility has taken over.'

He smiled gently at her. 'No one who sees you, my dear, is going to believe that senility rubbish for a start. You're much too glamorous and attractive for that.'

'I might have bought that line a month ago, Jim Forsythe, but not now. I see myself every morning in the mirror and I know this thing is taking a toll of me. Thanks for the brave try but I would have preferred your loyalty.'

He gave a particularly deep sigh. 'Okay, you win. I think this is totally wrong and I certainly wouldn't do this for anyone else, but I'll hold my tongue. I tell you what though, the twenty-odd days before I retire are going to pass like an eternity.'

'Thanks, Jim. I knew I could trust you. That's why I called you in the first place. I'm sorry I was so dramatic about it but I had to see you soon. Having failed with the telephone, I decided to write.'

'I haven't fully understood why you had to make such a mystery about me seeing you, though?'

'The main reason was Queenie. If she knew there was a blackmailer lurking about, she'd turn over the whole of London. She's a good honest girl is Queenie and you'll find none more loyal. But subtle she ain't.' Alarm suddenly clouded her face. 'By the way, I take it she knows nothing of this meeting?'

'Nothing at all,' he assured her. 'If she did, she would have been here like a shot. I did ring to say I'd be late, but Julia answered, so I left a message and didn't even have to speak to

Queenie. Your secret is safe for the moment at least.'

'Come and sit by the fireside before you go, Jim, and have one for the road. Hey, that's a point. Where's your car?'

'Didn't come by car. I came straight from my interview by bus. Though if you could call me a taxi to go home I'd be obliged.' Lying back, he stretched out from the settee and crossed his feet on the pattern in the carpet. Billie poured out a Scotch for him and a gin for herself and eased herself down alongside.

'So, blackmail aside, Billie, what have you got planned for the future?' Jim asked.

She shook her head, 'I really don't know, Jim, but I've certainly got to get some help. Young Duncan is leaving soon. He reckons he wants to join something or other. It's bad enough as it is, but it's going to be particularly lonely when he goes. I really miss him when he's not here. Besides, this place is much too big for one person.'

'What d'you mean, he wants to join something or other? Do you mean the police?'

She shrugged. 'Who knows? Police, Boys' Brigade, Flat Earth Society, might even be the bloody Ovaltinies, for all I know. Truth is, he doesn't know himself. I don't blame him, though. If I was a good-looking lad like him I'd be off somewhere too. He's got his own life to lead and he's about at the right stage to try it.'

'How about young Julia? At one time I thought the two of them might, well . . .' his voice faded, '. . . have a go at it.'

'Oh, I think they had a go at it all right,' she agreed. 'There were times when I'm sure he did little else. But the trouble is, temperamentally they're streets apart. She wants to fight the world and he wants to sleep with it. In fact, he usually does – the female side that is!' she added hastily.

'Yes,' said Jim, giving her a suspicious look, 'I can imagine.'

'Anyway, the only certain thing is that he will be leaving soon.'

'Then what?' he asked. 'Perhaps it could be an ideal time

for you to reassess your life. Who knows, the four Hathaways may be only too pleased to move you into a smaller place, perhaps a flat, somewhere a bit more central. Think of all that money they'd be saving.'

'They are saving as it is,' she stated. 'Every year this house increases its value. It's better than a money box to them. Besides, if they were to find out my true financial state, they'd all strike like jackals. They're an unforgiving lot, the Hathaways, I tell you.'

Jim looked slowly round the room. 'It seems an eternity since I called here and saw a houseful of people on Benji's birthday, but now . . .' He gave a token wave.

'I know exactly what you mean, Jim,' she said sadly. 'I have this gut-churning feeling that things are changing, but for the first time in my life, I realise I can't influence them.'

'Nonsense,' he said reassuringly. Reaching out, he placed a hand lightly on her arm and kissed the side of her temple. 'You've lost none of your old magic, believe me, sweetie.'

She gave a little laugh and for a moment he saw a flash of her former sensuous beauty. 'Jim, boy, I'm afraid your gesture gave the lie to your words. I was never a woman for brave little kisses on the side of the head and by no stretch of the imagination was I ever a "sweetie"!'

He slipped his hand away from her and gave a deep chuckle. 'You're certainly right there. Perhaps I should have called you "me buxom beauty!"?'

She leaned forward and gave him a full kiss on the lips. 'Well, if you *must* tell me lies, I'd sooner be a buxom beauty than a sweetie. Anyway,' she glanced up at the clock, 'I don't know how late your pass is made out but d'you want me to ring for a taxi?'

'Yes, but before I go, can I make a last attempt to persuade you to change your mind and speak to the local CID?'

'No thanks, Jim,' she declined as she rose to her feet. 'I know you're going to think I'm crazy but, although I don't believe in astrology or any of that mumbo-jumbo, I'm absolutely convinced that whoever killed my Alice is mine and one day I'm going to square the account for her, I just know it. You'll see.'

He drained his glass whilst she spoke into the telephone. She then covered the mouthpiece with her hand and whispered to him, 'It's a local hire car and I'm afraid the driver is not familiar with south London. Wants to know if you'll give directions there *and* back?'

'Bloody hell, it's only Streatham!' he said, shaking a disbelieving head. 'Ask if I get a discount if he gets lost.'

'Shame on you, James,' she reproved. 'Didn't you know that Hampstead folk are much too grand to mention the word discount. It's considered much too common.'

The taxi arrived within a few minutes and announced its presence by a double blast on the horn. Billie accompanied Jim to the hall door and without another word being exchanged, embraced him and buried her head deep into his chest.

'Sure you'll be all right?' he whispered as he softly fingered her hair.

'I'll be fine, don't worry,' she assured him. 'Just keep in touch, eh?'

He nodded, then turned away towards the taxi and, although she watched until the vehicle faded into the darkness, he never once looked back.

The journey was uneventful and by a series of curt directions, the taxi soon slowed to a halt by Jim's address. He was about to say, 'Thanks driver, this'll do fine,' when he saw Julia and a familiar figure approaching his house arm-in-arm. Duncan! what on earth was he doing here? Though he was not aware of the reason for the young man's presence, he did not want it to be common knowledge that he had just travelled from Hampstead by taxi, especially as the sensible thing would be for Duncan to return the same way.

'Er – carry on to the next corner, please, driver,' he suddenly ordered, 'and drop me by that post box.'

To his annoyance, the driver not only stopped short but immediately beneath an all-too-bright street light. Rapidly searching his wallet, Jim paid off the man with as much haste as possible. 'It's all right, keep the change,' he blurted anxiously, fearing one or other of the lovers should look back. He had already left the taxi some yards behind him when he was summoned back by a shout from the cabbie. His first thought was that he had short-changed the man.

'The lidy said yer'd tell me the way back ter the West End, guv'nor. Piccadilly'll do. Sorry abaht that, but sarf London's always been a bloody mystery ter me.'

'Er, oh, yes!' faltered Jim with a nervous glance at the couple. Concealing his head in the driver's cabin, he rattled off the briefest of directions.

'Nah, I'm sorry guv,' apologised the cabbie, 'I still ain't got it. Couldn't write it dahn on the corner of me newspaper, could yer?'

Jim made no effort to conceal his irritation and quickly scrawled a half-dozen street names and turnings in the margin of the evening paper.

'Okay, guv, I reckon I can manage nah. G'night ter yer.' With a cheery wave, the driver gave a cursory glance over his shoulder and swung round onto the opposite side of the road and headed off north towards Brixton.

Tugging down the brim of his hat, Jim peered beneath it and was relieved to see the couple still engrossed in each other. By the time they had reached the front door of his house, he was barely a yard behind them.

'Mr Forsythe!' exclaimed Julia, turning round at Jim's footsteps. 'Where'd you spring from?'

'If you hadn't been so engrossed in this young man,' he replied, 'you would have seen me. I've been walking behind you for some little way.' The distant street light just about illuminated a sudden and fetching blush from the young woman. Before either of them could knock, the door swung open to reveal an expressionless Queenie.

'What is this? Magic, Mr Forsythe?' asked Duncan. 'You appear out of nowhere and now Mrs Forsythe opens the door before we've even knocked! Between the pair of you, you're like a couple of genies.'

'I was drawing the bedroom curtains,' explained Queenie, 'and I saw you all walking down the street. I decided you two in front were either a four-legged fat man or two slim people pretending to be in love.'

Though Julia's blush deepened, Duncan smiled and said cheerily, 'Oh you're just a sweet old romantic, Mrs Forsythe. Between you and me, it was only a pretence on my part so I could see you again.'

'Enough of this blarney,' said Queenie. 'Come on in. Between the three of you, you must have lots of tales to tell.'

'Oh, yes indeed!' exclaimed Jim. 'I nearly forgot. How'd you make out at the interview, Julia?'

'Well, it wasn't without its heart-stopping moments,' she confessed, 'but in the end, I have to say your theories worked like a charm, Mr Forsythe. The panel seemed particularly impressed when I said a good plumber can often be better than a good doctor. I didn't have the courage to say I stole most of my ideas from you, though.'

'Don't worry, girl,' he assured her. 'That's not stealing. It's proper name is plagiarism. Though if you're shrewd, you'll call it research. Interviewers are always impressed with good research.'

'And you, Mr Forsythe? I understand you were successful with the detective agency, so how'd *your* interview go?'

'Yes, Jim,' said Queenie pointedly. 'How did it go? Must have been easier than you feared if you were able to get away in time for yet another meeting this evening. What with Lord Trenchard this morning and your job interview this afternoon, it's been quite a day for you one way and another, hasn't it?'

Before he could reply, Julia cut in excitedly. 'And don't forget Duncan, Mrs Forsythe. He joined the army!'

Seizing the opportunity for at least a short reprieve, Jim

played the surprising news for all its worth. 'The *army*?' he asked incredulously. 'What brought that on? It's a bit of a leap from being Billie Bardell's gardener, isn't it?'

'Yes, isn't it just,' agreed Queenie acidly. 'Makes you wonder what she's going to do for a replacement – for a *gardener*, I mean of course.'

'Yes, but he's not just joined the *army*, Mr Forsythe,' said Julia proudly. 'He's joined the Guards. Haven't you, Duncan?'

'The Guards?' asked Jim with now genuine interest. 'What Guards? And why?'

'The Life Guards,' said Duncan. 'I think I joined them for the simple reason that they were there. I'd just met David and a bunch from Rodney Road nick and they had talked me out of joining the police force. I just came out of the pub and wandered into Trafalgar Square. I turned one corner and found myself outside the recruiting office. It seemed like fate. I suppose I was lucky it wasn't the Foreign Legion. I'm bloody sure I would have joined.'

'Turn round,' said Jim. 'Let me see the back of your head. Hmm,' he said as he studied it closely. 'It's not there yet. I suppose they'll do it to you as soon as you report to the barracks.'

'What's not there?' asked the anxious Julia. 'And what will they do?'

'The scar,' explained Jim. 'You know all about the Guardsman's scar, don't you? I thought everyone knew.'

'Well, I for one don't,' Julia said worriedly. 'What is it?'

'Well, it is said that if you examine the back of a Guardsman's head, you'll find the scar where they took his brains out. I was just looking for it, that's all.'

'Mr Forsythe,' said the girl with a tight smile, 'I think that's very cruel.'

'You're dead right, m'dear,' admitted Jim. 'Especially with no anaesthetic.' Ruffling the back of Duncan's head, he laughed. 'No, seriously though, I hope it all works out for you, Duncan, and, if your choice really was between the police and the Guards, I'm convinced you've made the correct one. When do you report?'

Duncan repeated the same story he had recounted earlier whilst Queenie remained patiently poised to resume her questioning of Jim. Finally, a conversational lull gave her the chance.

'You didn't finish telling us about your evening meeting, Jim,' she persisted. 'Where was it?'

'Oh, it was at Scotland Yard. The commissioner wanted to know how we thought his morning lecture had been received.'

'Well, that's a surprise, I must say! I would have thought that the fact people *had* to listen would be all that mattered to him. So exactly where did you have this meeting?'

'Er – in his office. It ran a bit late, so I took a cab home.'

'Yes,' she agreed, 'I saw you from the window. At one time I thought I might have to run down to you with some extra cash.'

'Oh, no, it was just that the driver didn't know Streatham very well and he needed directions to get back to town.'

'D'you mean to say that a taxi driver needed directions from here to the West End? Why? Was it his first day on the job?'

'Of course not,' replied Jim. 'It was just that he lived in north London and he rarely ventured south of the river. Understandable, I'd say.'

'Yes, but if he lived in north London, it's a pity you didn't recognise these two lovers before you let the cab go. Duncan might have used it.'

'No, not me, Mrs Forsythe,' said Duncan, sensing the growing atmosphere. 'I'm a tram and bus bloke myself. I'm sure Mr Forsythe was aware of that.'

'Oh, I'm sure he was Duncan,' snapped Queenie acidly. 'I'm quite sure he was.'

By now, Jim realised if his story was to have any credence it was time to pick up the gauntlet. 'Queenie!' he said curtly, 'something wrong? You seem a bit touchy this evening. Anything I can do?'

'No, no,' she said. 'Nothing to worry about, just a woman's thing you know.' She looked quickly from one to the other. 'Now, who would like tea?'

Though Jim was not remotely convinced by her reply, he was relieved to be given a chance to drop the subject. He had barely slipped out of his coat when Queenie added, 'As it's so late, perhaps you'd like to stay the night, Duncan? I daresay we can squeeze you in somewhere.'

Jim suddenly remembered Billie's words, 'I really miss him when he's not here,' and almost repeated them. But he was saved by Duncan's quick reply. 'No thanks, Mrs Forsythe, Miss Bardell will be expecting me. It's very kind of you, I'm sure, but if you don't mind, I'll dispense with tea and be off.'

By now, Julia had also sensed the change of mood. 'I'll walk you to the tram stop, Duncan,' she murmured. 'It's not far from here.'

With farewells made, the door closed on the young couple and Jim was frantically trying to decide if this was the best opportunity for his surprise. Taking a chance, he felt in his pocket and took out a small package.

'Here you are, luv,' he said with forced bonhomie. 'I got someone to make a successful bid for me at the property auction last week, but I've been waiting for the chain to be fixed. I liked it the moment I clapped eyes on it. Suit you a treat, I reckon.'

Queenie was certainly taken aback by this new development. Rows and fights between herself and Jim were so rare that there was no trusted formula to fall back on. Almost to her own annoyance, she bleated a polite 'Thank you' and sought the comfort of an armchair whilst unravelling the wrapping paper.

Pretending unconcern, Jim looked away and showed a sudden and not too convincing interest in yesterday's newspaper.

'Why, Jim, it's beautiful!' she cried as she gently lifted the delicate pendant from its box. Moving to the mantelpiece mirror, she held it against herself. 'Is this the one you spoke of some months ago?'

'Is, indeed,' he replied. 'As soon as I saw it, I knew it would suit you perfectly. It's not *just* your colouring; it could have been made for you.'

She curled the chain back into her hand and leaned forward to kiss him in gratitude. Though she was still angry about his lies, it was not in her to ignore such a gesture.

Having held it to her neck in a variety of poses, she was about to return it to its box when Julia's footsteps could be heard. The girl looked flushed and though her lipstick was smeared, she radiated happiness in waves.

'What d'you think of Jim's retirement present to me, luv,' asked Queenie. 'A real beauty, isn't it?'

'May I?' smiled the girl reaching out for it. Standing in front of the mirror, she too went through the same variety of poses. Suddenly her expression changed and a mystified expression that Queenie missed came over her face. Fortunately it vanished as quickly as it appeared.

'Oh, it's no use, I can't wait,' said Queenie excitedly. 'I'm going upstairs to see what it looks like against my new cream two-piece suit. Shan't be a minute, so prepare yourself, folks, for a grand entry.' She trotted swiftly up the staircase and once out of earshot Jim turned quickly to Julia.

'What's the matter, girl. Why did you look like that?'

'I've seen it before. I'm sure of it.'

'Seen what before?'

'The pendant, of course!'

'Where, for God's sake?'

'Miss Bardell lent it to me to attend my Aunt Flo's wedding.'

'Miss Bardell?' echoed Jim incredulously. 'Lent it to you?'

'That's right,' replied the girl. 'I'd know it anywhere. She loved it, but it went missing a few months ago.'

'Are you positive?'

'Of course, I'm positive! If you look very closely, you'll see a wee hinge and if you prise it open you'll see a tiny photograph of a uniformed policeman.'

'A policeman? Well, who the hell . . .'

Jim stopped short as a white-faced Queenie came slowly down the staircase. In her left palm was the now open pendant. She held it out and he saw quite distinctly the small photograph. It was of *his* dead best friend and Queenie's first husband.

18

The moment Jim Forsythe's taxi turned south from the gates of her house, Billie Bardell had felt totally empty. Wandering back to her drawing room fireside, she flopped down in the armchair and stared wearily at the two empty glasses. After a while she fell into a short sleep and, on waking, gave a sigh and leaned forward to pour herself a refill. Minutes later, with drink untouched, her stare moved to the dying embers of the fire whilst her thoughts ran randomly over her life. It had been one hell of a time, of that there was no doubt. But for some little while, she had felt that fate was about to examine the books. Yet it was not the 'examining' that worried her, it was the 'balancing' that could be the big problem. Still, whatever was in store, she was pretty sure she would emerge on the credit side. In some respects, because she had always subscribed to a win-some-lose-some theory, she was quite philosophical. She considered if she lost every round from now till the end of time, she would still be in the black. Without consciously trying, she had always been something of a fatalist and had accepted the peaks and troughs as part of everyday life. Personal regrets rarely figured in her thoughts because she felt they balanced themselves out in the end.

But of the misfortunes of others, particularly those close to her, she was not so sure. This was particularly so of Alice Giles. In that woman she had found a gentleness she had never known before. Yet, even to herself, she could not fully explain why, of all the tragedies she had experienced, the death of her maid had been her greatest. If she was ever to know just one more peak in her own life, she prayed it would be the death of Alice's killer. Whether it was the departure of Jim or the expectation of Duncan's arrival that had caused her to fail to chain the front door, was really academic. Whichever it was, it was greatly appreciated by the masked and gloved intruder presently entering the house. Once inside, he did not make the same mistake but hooked the chain securely in place.

After taking a sip from her glass and idly wondering if Duncan would return that night, the telephone at the side of her chair gave a solitary ring. She had a fleeting thought that a single ring was unusual before dismissing it from her mind. She knew the voice before the second syllable was uttered and her stomach heaved.

''Ullo, me ole darlin'. Missed me, 'ave yer?'

'Like the pox,' she snapped. 'I was hoping you were dead, slowly of course.'

'Yerse, yer always wuz fond of a little joke, weren't yer.' There was a slight pause before the voice resumed. 'Bit too fond fer yer own good really. Well, nah I fink it's time yer 'eard my little joke, 'cos I'm quite a comedian, yer know.'

'You're a snake's turd if that's the same thing,' she hissed.

The anger crackled from the receiver. 'That clever little remark'll cost yer a bit more, me lovely. Anyway, I'll explain all this when I see yer in a minute.'

'See me?' she said sharply. 'D'you mean you're calling here?'

'Callin'?' he mocked. 'Huh! I'm already 'ere, so be ready, my flower.'

Her thoughts raced. How close was he? As soon as he rang off perhaps she could telephone the police? With any luck they could be here before he arrived?

She could also back it two ways by smuggling a good-size kitchen knife in her clothing. On the other hand, whether it was the gin or the sheer emotional experience of the evening, she knew she was not equipped to tackle him alone – at least not tonight.

'You can't call now,' she whispered. 'I have someone here. We'll have to make it another time.'

'Don't give me that bollocks,' he hissed. 'I saw 'im leave ages ago – in a cab it was. I've bin 'angin' around an' waitin' ter make sure 'e didn't come back. I s'pose the randy bastard's shacked up with the ole slut's daughter, ain't 'e? That's somefing else ter be paid for as well.'

'Saw him leave?' she thought frantically. Then whoever he was, he must have been hidden in the grounds for more than an hour, because the front of the house was not visible from the road. She gave a shudder at the mere thought. Yet, though he had obviously seen Jim leave, he had not been close enough to recognise who it was. He obviously thought it was Duncan. Perhaps she should agree to his visit. With any luck Duncan might return? But then supposing Duncan didn't return? What then? She would be alone in the house with, in all probability, the killer and abuser of poor Alice.

'No, you must believe me,' she blurted. 'I am not alone. Make it another time, any time you wish, but my friend may wake and find you here, then anything might happen.'

The sound of a brief chuckle could be heard down the line. 'I'm gonna put this phone dahn, darlin', then I'll be wiv yer afore yer knows what time it is. Nah, don't do anyfing silly, like telephoning the local law f'rinstance, will yer? Guide's honour? Promise?'

The sound of the telephone being replaced was the only response to her pleading.

'No, listen to me, you must listen to me, whoever you are. I swear to you he's here. Honestly he is!' Realising whoever had been speaking to her had gone, she fumblingly replaced the receiver before lifting it again and quickly dialling.

'Who's a naughty gel then?' growled a voice from the hallway door. ''Ere I am, simply come ter 'ave a friendly little chat wiv' yer and what do I git? Fibs! Bloody great fibs! Tut

tut!' The intruder made the distance between them in seconds and, pushing her heavily to the floor, replaced the handset.

Though shaken and certainly frightened, Billie turned round in an attempt to see her tormentor. She was instantly disappointed to see his head was securely hooded. She placed him as a man of a little under six feet with what she guessed was a rounded pudgy face. The inch or so she could see of his hair at the back of his neck appeared greasy and black. His age was difficult to place, with his body movements being those of a man in his early forties but his coarse, gravelly voice could easily have been seventy or even older. The one thing that was crystal clear, however, was the menace that seemed to ooze from every pore of his body. In fact, his build was irrelevant. Even if he had been seventy years of age and five-feet nothing, he would still be a frightening and evil creature. Billie could fight her corner better than most, yet this man made her blood run cold.

'Git up and sit on the settee. If yer button yer lip and do as yer told, yer might not upset me. I upset easily yer see.' He sat down at one end of the settee whilst she took up a position as far away as possible at the other end. 'Nah, Miss High-an'-Mighty Bardell, we're here ter discuss rates. I'm a fair-minded man, but I do believe in the goin' rate fer the job in these matters.'

'I haven't the faintest idea what you're talking about.'

He leaned forward slowly and rested his clasped hands on his knees. For a moment he said nothing and, although she could not see his face behind the hood, she did see his eyes – and instantly wished she hadn't. 'Y-e-r-s-e-,' he said deliberately. 'I fort yer might say that.' He turned slowly to his left then brought the back of his gloved right hand in a mighty swing straight to the centre of her right cheek. She sprawled back in stinging pain and covered her face with her hands. When she finally eased them away, she saw that the whole room was now revolving.

'First debatin' point ter me, wouldn't yer say?' Moving his

position, he edged closer towards her. 'Nah p'raps we can 'ave a sensible discussion. What would yer say the goin' weekly rate was fer the average workin' man?' He stared at her for a couple of minutes but all her attention was on trying to manipulate her stinging jaw. 'No luck?' he sighed. 'Oh well, I'll tell yer then, shall I? Give or take a few pennies, it's abaht three pounds, fifteen an' sixpence a week. That's only if 'e's in regular employment, o'course. Tell yer what. Let's be generous. We'll allow 'im four shillings an' sixpence a week bonus, shall we? Just so we can round it up ter a neat four quid. So now that's four pound a week fer fifty-two weeks. That's, let me see, two hundred an' eight pound a year. Am I right?' He gave her a moment's glance, but she made no reply. 'Yeh, I fort you'd agree.'

As the room settled, she slowly focused on him and asked icily, 'Just what is it I'm supposed to have agreed to?'

'Wages!' he announced. 'Everyone's entitled ter wages, ain't they? After all, that's what old Lloyd George promised every one of us, didn't 'e?'

'I doubt if he promised them to a shit like you, though,' she said defiantly.

'Ten pound fine fer contempt o'court,' he snapped.

'But I don't know what you're talking about!' she cried. 'You're speaking in riddles.'

'Right, then pay atten'shun 'cos I won't be repeatin' it.' He eased up even closer to her and placed his right arm heavily on her shoulders. 'I just 'appens ter know that yer are a very lucky gel ter be still livin' in this grand place. If your ole man's family ever got ter know abaht yer little misfortune in the taxi, yer'd be out on yer fanny an' no mistake. Nah,' he sniffed, 'I'm not a greedy man. Fact is, yer'll find me quite generous. I've got many strings ter me bow, but wot I really needs is wot all them moneyed toffs calls a sound financial base. Geddit?' Without waiting for a reply he carried on. 'Yer see, if yer pays me four quid a week wages, which is two 'undred an' eight quid a year, plus the ten quid fine yer just incurred, that leaves me free ter pursue me other activities. This way the arrangement suits the pair of us, don't it? I've got me base an' fer a small price yer've got yer peace o'mind, see?'

'So you're blackmailing me. That right?'

'Nasty word, blackmail,' he murmured quietly. 'Not one I care for very much.'

'No?' she queried. 'Then how about rape, assault, murder? Care for those a little better?'

He shook his head and whispered, 'Nah, but I certainly find 'em more excitin'.' With that, he seized her face in his hand and twisted it up towards him. He did not so much kiss her lips as batter them with his own. They pressed so hard on hers, that the wool from his hood caught in her teeth as her lips were forced apart by the sheer pressure. When he finished, she wrenched away from him and spat straight into his face.

He growled back at her. 'Nah, nah, business a'fore pleasure, me lovely,' cuffing her spittle from his woollen cheek. 'I fink we should discuss means of payment, don't you?' She stared back at him and glowered with hate. 'I don't fink it'll be sensible fer me ter collect me wages every week, so I'll do it once a year, in advance o' course. So yer owes me two hundred and eighteen quid. Once yer pays it, I'm out of yer way for another year.'

'So how long does this go on for?'

'It goes on fer as long as you go on fer, me sweet.'

'Or you!' she said pointedly. 'Because your days must certainly be numbered.'

He gave a loud, forced laugh. 'I can't see yer stickin' a blade between me shoulders just yet, ducky. After all, I might be just the man yer been lookin' fer all yer life.'

'If you think that,' she said, reaching slowly up to his hood, 'why don't you let me see what I might be getting? For all I know, beneath that lot you might well be the Hampstead Horror.'

'I ain't that dim,' he growled as he pushed away her

searching fingers. 'But there are ovver ways o'seein' wot yer gettin'. F'rinstance,' he leaned forward and began to tug up the hem of her dress. 'Anyway, fer a woman like you, I doubt if it's me face that'd interest yer. Wot I'm gonna show yer don't need no mask.'

'*Wait!*' she exclaimed. 'Before you start anything, you've not told me how I'm to pay you.'

'All in good time, me ole darlin', all in good time. I shall give yer a few days ter git the cash together first. Yer see I'm really quite considerate. Then p'raps I'll ring yer an' tell yer where ter leave it.'

As he said these words, she suddenly heard the one sound she had been praying to hear since Jim left. It was the familiar distant crunch of shoes on gravel. It could only be moments before his untuned ears also heard it but until then she had an advantage.

'If you want to get two hundred and eighteen quid off me next week,' she said, 'the last thing you want to do is to tear this dress. It cost me a bloody fortune in Swan and Edgar's. Wait a second, I'll take it off.'

She realised he was instantly confused. His animal instincts needed him to be in command, to rip the dress from her body in ribbons if need be. On the other hand, she still had a voluptuous figure and the idea of watching her undress slowly, perhaps even to his orders, was equally attractive to his perversions.

'All right,' he grunted, 'but while yer at it, do it slow-like an' listen ter wot I tell yer ter do. Understand?'

With a well-practised theatrical smile, she slid smoothly from the settee. Standing legs apart before him, she stretched upright then slowly ran her hands down herself and traced every curve of her body. Stooping before him, she crossed her arms and took a hold of the hem of her dress. If he hadn't been so intrigued with his own fantasies, he must surely have heard the scrunch of gravel by this time. She also knew that any second now the doorbell would ring. With a great flourish, she swept up the dress by its hem and tugged it over her head. He barely had time to see what had been revealed as she threw the dress playfully over his face mask. Before he could remove it, she had seized the gin bottle and crashed it down over his head where it splintered to a mass of fragments. At the same time, she hacked at his shins with the pointed toes of her high-heeled shoes. As a background to this commotion, a loud double knocking added to the cacophony as Duncan Forbes pounded to get indoors and out of the sudden rain shower.

Billie snatched the dress from the partially stunned figure and began to claw at the hood but Sid Grechen was a tough individual and had already begun to recover his thoughts. Blindly pushing her to one side, he adjusted his eye slits and stood for a split second taking in the change in the situation. He realised time was short but he also realised that whoever was outside could not get inside, at least until the door was opened. If nothing else, it gave him a few precious seconds. He could only hear one person and that was at the front door, so perhaps he could escape as he had before, via the kitchen. Yes, that was it! Pausing only to give Billie a stinging punch on the ribs and snarl, 'Yer ain't seen the last of yer, yer fuckin' bitch!' he was gone.

'MISS BARDELL! MISS BARDELL,' came the voice through the letterbox. 'ARE YOU OKAY?'

Miss Bardell was anything *but* okay as she gritted her teeth and raised herself by the arm of a chair. Her attempt at an answer caused her to think her whole ribcage had disintegrated. To an accompaniment of Duncan's shouts, she eased her way towards the hall door before, after what seemed like hours, she slid back the chain and fell into his arms.

'What is it! What's happened to you?' Holding her firmly, he looked in horror at her rapidly swelling face. She winced as his left arm touched the spot where Grechen had punched her.

Looking up at him, she gave a tiny smile. 'Typical Bardell luck,' she whispered breathlessly. 'Half-naked in the arms of a gorgeous young man – and too bloody knackered – to enjoy it!'

Duncan carried her gently back into the sitting room and, leaving her on the settee, draped her dress over her as cover. 'What is it? What is it?' he insisted. 'Who's done this to you?' In the absence of an answer, he looked frantically over his shoulder. 'The kitchen!' he exclaimed. 'It must be the kitchen!'

'No, Duncan, no!' Billie begged. 'Let him go – please.'

Ignoring her pleadings, he hissed, 'I'll kill the bastard,' and ran from the room.

Sure enough the kitchen door was ajar and moving slightly in the breeze. Running out into the garden, the garden of which he knew every inch, Duncan was well aware of the futility of searching it in the dark. In its shrubs, sheds and greenhouses, a dozen men could hide comfortably. Cursing the absence of a torch, he groped blindly and uselessly into corners and recesses. After some minutes, he suddenly remembered Billie's vulnerability. He had rushed out into the garden leaving open both front and kitchen doors. Cursing his stupidity, he spun on his toes and raced back towards the kitchen. As he did so, he saw a light come on in the first-floor bathroom. At least someone had to be *there*! He cleared the dozen stairs three at a time and was relieved to see, through the open door, Billie Bardell sitting in front of the mirror examining her injured face. In the few minutes since he had left her, the swelling had increased in size and she had dragged herself up the staircase.

'Close the door there's a dear,' she mumbled with difficulty.

'Okay, but just a minute,' he said breathlessly. 'I've been tearing about all over the place, leaving every bloody door open behind me. Now I know where you are, I'll check the house and go down and shut everything properly. Won't be long.'

In spite of her pain, she shook her head in amused

admiration. The sound of his thumping footsteps echoing from all corners of the house indicated not only his location but also his enthusiasm. True to his word, he was not gone long. Minutes later he burst breathlessly into the bathroom.

'Okay, Miss Bardell,' he panted. 'The house is now clear and locked up. Shall I call the police?'

'No, Duncan,' she murmured through tightening lips. 'Pull that other stool up alongside me and listen to what I have to say, please?'

'But the police, Miss Bardell! We must ring them. The bastard is getting further away by the minute!'

'Duncan,' she repeated, again pointing to the stool, 'will you sit here, please?'

Without further protest, he slid the stool alongside her and addressed her reflection in the mirror. 'Miss Bardell,' he said quietly, 'I really feel you should go to hospital. Your face is swollen and God knows what your ribs are like!'

'I'm going to try very hard *not* to go to hospital, Duncan, but I'm not stupid. If I *have* broken something, then I've no choice.' She gave a painful shrug. 'But in the meantime, bear with me, eh?'

'Anything you say, Miss Bardell, but are you going to tell me what happened?'

'I owe you that, Duncan, that I most certainly do!' Billie leaned forward over the wash basin and, turning her head to the left, she began to sponge her right cheek with cold water. She then began to recount the tale of Sid Grechen's blackmail attempt. Though she told the young gardener almost everything, she omitted to say she believed Grechen was also responsible for Alice's murder.

Duncan listened intently, but if she thought that her story would satisfy him, she was badly mistaken. Almost before she had finished, Duncan asked softly, 'This hooded bloke, I take it he was the one who killed Julia's mum?'

Dabbing her face dry, Billie draped her bare shoulders with the towel and turned towards him. Reaching out with still wet hands, she took his fingers into her grasp.

'Duncan, you must believe me when I tell you if I thought for one minute that telling the police of the blackmail would catch Alice's killer, then I would do it like a shot. But it won't. Not only will it achieve nothing, it will destroy me in the process. Even that wouldn't matter if my Alice was avenged, but that won't happen either.'

'So you intend to go on paying this leech for ever? Because you will, you know, that scum will never let go.'

'Don't think I haven't thought of that a thousand times. But you see—' She sighed as she sought the words to explain. 'The amount he has requested is really quite clever. To be honest, I *can* afford it but only *just*. If he came back for a few pounds more, the balloon would burst and the decision would be out of my hands. As long as the figure doesn't increase, I can just about manage. I may be deluding myself, but hatred of this man will see me through, I know it will.'

Duncan put his hands to his head. 'I don't believe I'm hearing this! Do you know what I've done this morning? I've joined the bloody Life Guards! That means I shall be leaving here soon. You can't possibly stay in this place on your own now! This bastard murdered Alice and has now returned and attacked you. He seems to know his way around this place as well as we do. Bloody hell, you're as vulnerable as a kitten!'

In spite of her pain, Billie thought she could not let such a simile pass uncontested. Propping her hands on her hips, she let the towel slip from her shoulders and with her white satin slip hugging her body like a second skin, she faced him square on. 'Duncan Forbes, I ask you! Do I *look* like a bloody kitten?'

He gave a grin. It was the grin that had eased him out of numerous scrapes and into many beds. It was the grin of a likable rogue; it was also the grin of a true friend. 'No, you don't,' he concurred. 'Bad choice, I agree. But you must remember even tigers are vulnerable. Tough as they are, people still hunt them and whilst you may not be a kitten, you're also no tiger.'

'Listen to me,' she ordered, slipping the straps of her slip from her shoulders, 'my ribs still hurt from that wallop and while I'm arguing with you, I'm not getting them treated, so if you think you might be embarrassed, push off. If not, make yourself useful.'

'How?'

Draping the towel back over her shoulders, she wriggled the slip down to her waist. 'Have a good prod about will you? I don't think he broke anything, but he may well have cracked a rib.'

'How am I going to know that?' he complained.

'Bloody hell, lad!' she exploded. 'What sort of a bloody Life Guard are you going to be if you can't comfort a poor distressed female who's had a bang in the ribs!'

Duncan lifted her arm and ran his fingers gingerly down her side.

'Oh, God!' she exclaimed as he brushed the damaged rib. 'That's the bugger. What one is it?'

He began once more at the top and counted six down. He then proceeded to push and prod the puffy flesh around it. 'That hurt?' he found himself repeating every few seconds. Finally the area was localised between the sixth and seventh rib. 'Okay, so what d'you want done?' he asked.

She nodded to a wall cupboard, 'There's some cotton wool in there. Just swab it with cold water, I suppose.' She cast the towel to a nearby rail and bent forward over the basin whilst he dabbed and patted the afflicted area.

'Well, come on?' he encouraged. 'Just because you're semi-nude doesn't mean you've wriggled out of the questions. You still haven't told me how you're going to cope when you're here alone?'

'He won't be back,' she assured him confidently. 'I'm sure of it.'

'Why so convinced?' he asked. 'To me he sounds just the

sort who'll keep bouncing back like a rubber ball.'

'Because he's no reason to come back now,' she replied. 'He's got all he needs. He's explained only too clearly how much he wants and when he wants it, so why should he take another chance and come back here?'

'Because he's bloody mad!' said Duncan. 'That's why!'

She straightened up and, turning towards him, again reached for the towel and began to pat herself dry. He marvelled, as many before him had, at her ability to be two separate people. When he had first arrived at the house, he had shared the briefest of relationships with her, but with the appearance of Julia, these had changed to the platonic. Yet experience had taught him, that in spite of her maturity, she could still be an exciting woman. As she sat towelling her naked torso, she calmly chatted as if they were discussing spring planting.

'Oh, by the way, Duncan,' she said finally as she lifted her arm to expose her now darkened rib, 'splash on some of that arnica will you? It's good for bruising.' Then obviously satisfied with his efforts, Billie wriggled an ample bosom down into the tailored cups of the slip. Easing the straps over her shoulders, she breathed a sigh of relief. 'Pass me that frock, there's a sweetie.' As he handed it to her, she smiled a thanks and began to circle an elbow. 'Phew!' she puffed, 'thank Gawd for that, feels better already. Fancy a gin?'

He nodded wearily and rose to his feet. 'Oh, that's a pity,' she said sorrowfully, ''cause I whacked that bastard's head with it. It'll have to be Scotch, I'm afraid. D'you mind?'

'Do me fine,' he replied.

'Good!' she said. 'Help me downstairs, shove some coal on the fire and tell me how you became a brave soldier.'

At that precise moment, Jim Forsythe would have given anything to have been a brave soldier. Young Julia Giles, sitting by the fire as a spectator, was learning more about the Forsythe family in thirty minutes than she had about English social history in her entire school career.

At first, Jim had begun with a faltering excuse, but once he realised that Queenie had known all along of his evening assignation, he confessed the truth.

'But what I can't understand,' she seethed, 'is why both my husbands had and have such an obsession with this damned woman! Even if I accept there was nothing physical between you and her, the fact that you deliberately kept the whole thing from me is unforgivable. I won't rest until I see this—' she shook her head in frustration before hissing '—this whore!' Pounding her fists on his chest, she continued, 'Because that's what she is, you know, a half-a-crown, end-of-the-line, pissy-drawed, Waterloo Road WHORE!'

As soon as he had seen Queenie with Sam's mini photograph in her hand, Jim knew he would have to fight a defensive battle. The fact that Queenie had also been simmering during the time he had blatantly lied about the evening meeting had not helped. Nevertheless, there was a way to handle Queenie that her first husband, Sam, had never discovered. In their arguments, Sam would trade blow for blow with her right from the start and it would soon become a clash of Titans. But Jim had long discovered the reverse worked better. He would willingly concede the early ground and by this apparent humility, she would overstretch her case, often by a single point. He then found that by counterattacking on this one point, he could exclude almost everything else she had alleged. But at this stage in their current fight, he was not even sure of his best approach, so he let her tirade continue whilst his own thoughts raced ahead. It was Queenie herself who gave him the clue when he heard her say, 'I wouldn't mind, but my own *mother*, by God!' Of course, her own *mother*, that was it!

'Queenie,' he said quietly, 'why don't you just step back a little and think what you're saying?'

'Such as?' she demanded with staring eyes.

'Such as your mother could never be regarded as an

ordinary person. She is what she is and she couldn't possibly be anything else. Now let's take this photograph that you're making all the fuss about. If you study it closely, you'll see it's a copy of one taken from the newspaper when Sam was shot in Tottenham. Am I right?'

She nodded suspiciously.

'If you cast your mind back, you'll remember that Sam slept with her before you had any claim on him. You must know that; you were her maid at the time. So, if you knew it then, you must know it now. If your mother copied a photograph that was taken from a newspaper even before you married, there's nothing that Sam nor anyone else could have done to prevent it. Lots of people carry pictures of other people in lockets, but it doesn't mean they're sleeping with them. If I carried a picture of Queen Mary, does it mean that King George could shoot me for treason?'

'It's not the same,' she protested.

'Of course it's the same,' he said dismissively. 'Even she wouldn't dispute her fascination with Sam, would she? But it was *you* Sam chose, wasn't it? Billie Bardell was one of the brightest stars of the stage in those days, yet it was *you* he married. You can't dismiss all that factual evidence because of one tiny picture in a locket, can you? Well, can you?'

She was silent for a moment before muttering, 'S'pose not – but that doesn't let *you* off the hook though, does it? You deliberately lied to me and spent the evening with her. Then, to compound it, you returned here as calm as you like and had the audacity to give us that bullshit about Trenchard! I'm pleased Julia's sitting here to see for herself just how deceitful you are, James Forsythe.'

'Whoa! Just a minute, just a minute! Don't forget we're talking about your mother who also happens to be a unique woman! She's had a murder, a rape and robbery in her house and now some evil bastard's putting the squeeze on her. Yet, in spite of this, she's still a vibrant and courageous woman. She's never going to be the type who sits at home knitting and no one who knows her would expect her to be. Your mother is a total *experience* and if she was *my* mother, I might well despair at times but usually I'd be so proud my shirt would bust!'

'But that doesn't alter the fact that you . . .'

'Yes, it does, Queenie, it alters *everything*! Listen, in twenty years' time, wouldn't you be thrilled to pieces if your daughter-in-law took the risks to show support to you and your wishes that I took today to support your mum and hers? Or would you prefer her to shake her head and give you some drivelling excuse that she couldn't do anything unless she consulted David? I tell you this with all the conviction I can muster. If you were in her position, you would have done exactly the same. She knew she needed help but she didn't want to alarm anyone else unnecessarily and no matter what other conclusions you may jump to, you can't condemn that sort of courage.'

Queenie stared quizzically at her husband as if puzzling out some difficult crossword. 'If you've tried to make me ashamed of my outburst, James Forsythe, then you haven't succeeded one bit. Then, on the other hand . . .' She gave a great sighing shrug and slipped her arms around him. 'Oh, I do so hope there's nothing in heredity!'

'You've no desire to be like your mum then?' he asked guilelessly.

'Don't push your luck, mate,' she retorted. 'But I'll tell you this. There's no way I shall be wearing that pendant no matter how much you paid for it. Okay?'

'Okay,' he agreed. 'So what do I do with it?'

'Well, as I guess it was far too expensive to do what I really think you should do with it, I suggest you give it to this young lady sitting here, who's quietly listened to us wash all our dirty linen in the last few minutes. Let's say it's a little present for her new career, eh?'

'What d'you think, Julia?' he asked. 'Would you like it?'

'Mr Forsythe!' she exclaimed before turning to Queenie.

'And Mrs Forsythe! I think it's beautiful! I promise you both I shall really treasure it.'

Queenie smiled. 'You don't have to. For you it's just a pendant, for me it was a bloody millstone.' Stifling a yawn, she glanced at the clock. 'I think I'm getting too old for many more days like this. Remind me to ring my mum in the morning. Who's for bed?'

'I should think we all are,' said Jim. 'You go on up and I'll just lock up.'

Queenie left Julia by the fireside happily examining her newly acquired pendant. Meanwhile Jim disappeared towards the front door and the windows. Minutes later he returned to see the girl sitting with the fully opened locket in her lap. She had eased out the picture and concealed behind it, hitherto undiscovered, was a lock of hair. She handed it to Jim who recognised it instantly as belonging to Sam. He glanced nervously round before dropping it down into the dying embers of the fire. Within seconds the tiny flames danced, the hairs sizzled briefly then vanished in a wisp of smoke.

'Phew,' he whispered with a relieved wink at Julia, 'I couldn't go through all that again, even if he *was* my best mate. Goodnight, Julia, and thanks, thanks a lot.'

19

Within a month, Julia, Duncan and Jim, had all left their old occupations and taken the first tentative steps into their new. Of the three, Jim's was the smoothest with his work allowing him home most nights. He found, though he missed the close camaraderie of the police, most of the work was similar. His induction was therefore relatively easy, both for him and for Queenie. But if he was honest, he would have confessed to wishing himself in a more glamorous role. Much of his new work consisted of administration and supervision. Secure though it was, the serving of summonses and the delivery of writs did not have the same excitement as bursting through the door of a Chinatown opium den or Park Lane brothel.

Julia's was certainly the most overwhelming change, with lectures, demonstrations and classes following each other in a confusing whirl. She also found the after-hours studying so exhausting that she could not see beyond the end of each week. Life seemed to be a blurred round of cold classrooms and antiseptic corridors. Her living quarters were at the nurses' home which was less than ten minutes' walk from the hospital. Sometimes, particularly after a taxing day, she felt that the walk back to her quarters was like a short parole in the midst of a life sentence. Perhaps she would not have found it quite so challenging if she had been more academic. Though by nature bright, she had not studied since leaving school at fourteen and found class work very difficult, particularly in the early weeks. Her strength lay in her practical ability, but that was going to take time to evolve. Yet, in spite of this, from the moment she had climbed the steps to the hospital entrance, she had known this was to be her calling.

Probably the best of her early experiences had been the companionship of her fellow student nurses. One blessing was that all the trainees were of the same age and, though only eight in number, friendships had already developed that were to last a lifetime. By the fourth week, characters were also emerging. The shortest and plumpest of these, Betsy Buntingdon, a fireman's sweetheart, proved also the most adventuresome. In spite of her buxom build, to say nothing of matron's all-seeing eye, Betsy could shin a drainpipe with a dexterity Tarzan would have envied. Julia was more aware of this than most because the drainpipe in question was immediately outside her bedroom window and it was from her sill that Betsy would depart and return on her nocturnal adventures.

Of the three new ventures, Duncan's was easily the most traumatic. The shock of Guards' discipline on such an amiable and complacent individual could well have been disastrous. As it was, Duncan did what Duncan always did in such situations – just about enough to get by. No matter how the tempo of his training lifted, he always seemed to find another gear and, after a faltering start, he would coast serenely through.

A Guards' recruit needed to serve a month before being allowed out of training camp and then for only a half-day. Frantic letters had passed between him and Julia, but the difficulty of two people parted by half the width of London to meet at a mutually convenient spot for four hours on a Saturday afternoon, seemed to present the logistical problems of a colonial war. Finally, at the cost of half his wages in postage stamps, they were due to meet at Queenie's house at one o'clock on Saturday afternoon. To Duncan's mind the location was not ideal, but because of the impossibility of arriving together, it seemed a fair compromise.

Finance, of course, was always going to be a difficulty. If

the pay cuts had hit fully trained servicemen hard, then recruits were little more than paupers. The one cause for hope was Bertie Littlejohn, a fellow recruit from Battersea. Bertie was particularly sought after by Duncan because he believed the former's possession of a 250 cc Triumph solo motorcycle could provide all the answers to the transportation problem. One small snag was its condition. Even Bertie considered it a little sick. Less sensitive recruits considered it dead.

'It *should* git us back ter London,' said Bert optimistically. 'After all, there ain't no hills. If we rest it somewhere around Hounslow, I reckon we'll make it easy.'

Though Duncan was not encouraged by this statement, the two shillings-and-fourpence fare saved was not an economy to be taken lightly. To avoid too many questions at the company guardroom, the two recruits arranged to meet a short distance from the depot.

Duncan had not long to wait before a cloud of smoke and a sound like dustbins being dragged over rocks drew his attention to a heavily clad rider and a smoky machine. The sight of Bert's attire caused some concern to his intended passenger. With leather helmet, enormous gloves, iron-framed goggles, ankle-length rubber coat and high lace-up boots, Bert looked more equipped for a long journey to Peru than a short trip to Battersea.

'Hop on,' he sang cheerfully. At least Duncan *thought* that was what he said. Throughout the journey, Bert hardly ceased talking, but with Duncan catching roughly one word in five, it did not make for intelligent conversation.

To be fair, the machine behaved impeccably until they reached Hounslow. Whether the bike feared it was not going to have its customary rest or it simply took a dislike to the Staines Road, Duncan had no means of knowing. But suddenly a sound like worlds colliding and a vibration that almost shook them from their seats, caused the engine to cut and, as the wheels locked, the thing skidded to a silent stop.

Bert calmly raised his goggles and turned casually round to his terrified passenger. 'Slight problem, Dunk', old son,' he sniffed. 'Chain's broke.'

'So what happens now?' asked Duncan, amazed to be alive.

Bert nodded to the ground all around them. 'Well, if yer could pick up some of the pieces it'd be a help,' he said.

'Er – I hate to ask this, Bert,' said Duncan swinging his leg from the machine. 'But how long is this likely to take? I should be meeting my girl in an hour.'

Bert gave another great sniff and after a moment's thought replied, 'Hard ter say. Depends what you pick off the ground and what I've got in spares.'

'Have a guess,' pleaded Duncan.

Bert screwed up his nose in thought. 'Somewhere between a half-hour and two days.'

'*Two days!*' cried Duncan. 'We're supposed to be back to barracks at six thirty!'

'Oh, that's all right,' said Bert placidly. 'If it ain't fixed in time I'll leave it here. No one's going to nick it, are they? Tell yer what. You turn right over there into Bell Road an' that'll take yer down ter Hounslow station. If yer lucky yer'll be in Waterloo in fifteen minutes.'

'Thanks, Bert,' said Duncan gratefully. 'Sure you don't mind?'

'Mind?' replied Bert. 'O'course I don't *mind*. I'm sitting here instead of being at home, me chain's in pieces and me bike's knackered. If I can't mend it, I've got to go back to barracks in a coat you could hide the Household Cavalry in. No, I don't mind at all. I will, though, if yer don't pick up those bits of chain.'

Duncan scuttled quickly around and minutes later deposited a half-dozen assorted lengths of grease-covered chain into Bert's cluttered toolbox. Having earned his dismissal, he bade goodbye to his friend and raced down to Hounslow station.

Bert had certainly been right about the trains. Having caught the 12.15 Staines to Waterloo by his fingertips, Duncan arrived breathlessly at the tram terminus outside Waterloo station just a half-hour after deserting poor Bert.

Of course this misfortune had made an unexpected hole in his budget. After reaching Brixton, Duncan needed to change trams and, after counting his coins, had contemplated walking the last two miles to save the fare. His recruit allowance of twelve shillings a week had already been badly eroded, firstly by stamps and now by the unforeseen train fare.

He was just striding out briskly when he saw a familiar figure staring out of a passing tram window. If it had only been a month since he had last seen her, how *could* she look twice as lovely? Spotting a gap in the traffic, he raced into the road and managed to grasp the rail of the tram as it gathered momentum up Brixton Hill. The conductor, assuming the newcomer had more than a sporting chance of breaking his neck, did what conductors will always do in such situations, he trotted swiftly upstairs to collect fares.

Far from breaking his neck, Duncan landed without even breaking his stride and in three or four steps had lowered himself into the empty seat immediately behind Julia. For a moment he sat and savoured the cut of her hair, lobes of her ears and shape of her neck, like a small boy gazing at his favourite sweets. Eventually, he bent forward and, as his face brushed her hair, he smelt the first fresh aroma of her toilette. His first instinct was to kiss her neck, but mischievously he changed his mind and instead whispered slowly in her left ear, 'Giss'a feel till Friday!'

He was quick but he wasn't quick enough. Her right palm swung round and landed full force on his cheek, the impact sending his cap spinning to the floor.

'Don't you dare show me up in public, Duncan Forbes!' she hissed. 'And if you think I'm having anything to do with anyone with such greasy hands and idiotic haircut, you're wrong.'

'How'd you know it was me?' he asked, as he searched for his cap and ruefully rubbed his cheek.

'Because you're the only one I know who is coarse and stupid enough to say such a thing. Besides,' she said with the merest hint of a smile, 'I saw your reflection in the window.'

There were only a scattering of passengers on the lower deck and if their attention had been drawn by the walloping of a Guardsman's ear, they were left open-mouthed as the assailant then threw her arms around the victim's neck and almost devoured him. Without even parting to take breath, Duncan moved from the seat behind, into the gangway and finally into the seat next to Julia before coming up for air. As they both fell back gasping she squeezed his arm and buried her head deep in his rough khaki uniform.

'I've missed you, you sod!' she murmured. After a wordless period, she finally lifted her head and at that precise moment he opened his mouth to speak.

'Fares, please!' came the curt command from the conductor immediately behind him.

A few minutes later, the tram stopped to change crew at the Telford Avenue garage and, though both driver and conductor alighted, no replacement immediately appeared. Just to sit quietly when time was so precious seemed anathema to both, so clutching hands, they jumped from the tram to skip lightly down the pavement towards Streatham.

The pair had made no great plans for that afternoon in view of the uncertainty of their respective arrivals. But it was a pleasant enough day and they hoped Queenie and Jim would allow them to sit quietly in some sheltered corner of their garden – the weather was certainly warm enough. As they turned into the short driveway to the house, Duncan's optimism plummeted as he saw that every door and window of the house was closed and a small white fluttering note was pinned to the side of the porch.

His anxious glance at Julia told him she already shared his concern. Before he finished climbing the steps he had already read the first line. '*Dear Duncan and Julia, we're sorry but,*' it began. Having read thus far he felt no desire to read on. He closed his eyes to prepare himself for the inevitable disappointment of the subsequent lines, when a spanking big kiss on the side of his cheek told him Julia was way ahead of him.

'That Jim Forsythe is one great old romantic,' she exclaimed joyously. 'Oh, I love him!'

'Eh?' responded Duncan, who suddenly read the quickest three lines of his life. '*We forgot it was Q's birthday,*' it continued, '*so if you're away by 5p.m. you won't even have to tell what you've been doing! Key's at 'Ella's' No. 27 opposite. Tea & bickies in kitchen, love. J & Q.*'

Without a second's delay, Duncan sprinted his way through the heavy Saturday traffic to number 27. There at the side of the house, a smiling pudding of a woman was taking down a line of washing.

'Er, Ella?' began Duncan, not too sure how to phrase the request.

Thrusting her hands into a deep overall pocket, she pulled out a set of keys. 'These what you want?'

'Well, yes but, don't you want any identification from us because . . .'

She threw the keys in a loop towards him. 'Don't worry son, that haircut's proof enough. Drop them in my letterbox as you leave, 'cos I'll be out.'

Moments later, with the front door of Queenie's house already closed behind them, Duncan and Julia stood facing each other with happy grins.

'You know what's so particularly good about this afternoon, Julia?' Duncan said as he took her firmly into his arms. She shook her head. 'Time,' he mumbled, in the middle of a kiss.

She leaned back from his lips with a puzzled expression. 'Why time?' she asked.

'Because we know exactly how long we've got,' he said, resuming the kiss. 'That's a luxury we've never known before.

We have exactly two hours and—' he glanced at the clock, 'fifty minutes all to ourselves. I think this is what it must be like if you're a millionaire, don't you?'

'Uh huh,' she whispered. 'Tell you what, darling. Let's go to my bedroom, draw the curtains, ignore the traffic and, until four thirty this afternoon, pretend that there's only us two in the whole world. It's ours, we can say what we like, do what we like and you're not allowed to argue with me. How about that?'

'Argue with you?' he echoed. 'It's always *you* that argues with *me*, surely?'

She quickly placed a finger to his lips and whispered, 'Shush, you've just lost two minutes! It's only two hours and forty-eight now!'

'You're right! Of course, you are!' he agreed enthusiastically. 'D'you know I think that's the best idea I've heard in my life. What're we waiting for?' Hand in hand, the pair ran to the staircase and within seconds had, by closing a door, mentally stepped off the planet for two hours and forty-eight minutes.

Three miles away in his kitchen, David Diamond was chasing the last stubborn hair from his chin with a cutthroat razor.

'Are you anywhere near ready yet?' called Grace from the bedroom. 'You take longer to get ready than Cleopatra.'

'Cleopatra did not have to shave in cold water,' he retorted, 'especially when the other occupant of the house has nicked all the hot.'

'Then you should have boiled another kettle.'

'But you keep telling me we haven't time.'

From the depths of a dress that was halfway over her head, she agreed. 'Quite right too! If we're to get that present to your mum for her birthday, we only have this afternoon to deliver it.'

'I still don't see why we couldn't have posted it, especially as it's the last day of the football season. I could have taken my son to The Den this afternoon to see Millwall for his first proper match.'

'But it's your mother's *birthday*, Davy! When they get older, mums are funny about these sorts of things. They like to see their sons *and* their grandsons *on* their birthdays. I warn you now, I shall be exactly the same when I'm her age, so prepare yourself. Button me up, will you?'

'Oh, if only I could, if only I could!' he mocked. 'The world would be a much quieter place!' Reaching up, he began to secure the three buttons at the back of her dress. 'Hey, don't you think it's a lot more fun undoing buttons than doing them up?' he asked, dropping one hand down to caress her tight buttocks, 'especially as it's one of my rare Saturdays off?'

She turned slowly round and, with her nose touching his, whispered very slowly and deliberately, 'Will-you-get-yourself-dressed-*please*?'

'There you are, you see,' he said facetiously. 'Just a few years married and romance is out of the window already. Tut-tut!'

She placed her hands on her hips and stared straight at him. 'Oh, so it's *romance* now is it?' she asked. 'I didn't hear much about romance a moment ago when you were suggesting buggering off to football all afternoon!' Reaching forward, she seized his ears and gave them a little tug. 'I'm-going-to-get-you-to-your-mother's-today-if-it-kills-me!'

Raising his hands in final surrender, he pulled on his clothes and called his son up from the street.

It is possible that if Duncan Forbes had been aware of what was afoot, his approach to making love to Julia Giles might have been a touch speedier. After all, as delightful as it might be, it does take rather a long time to kiss every inch of a woman, particularly when the woman cheats and insists several places were either missed entirely or insufficiently treated. There were at least four parts of Julia's anatomy that brushed Duncan's nose three times to his certain knowledge. Nevertheless, it was still a pleasurable action which may well have lost a little of its magic if he had known that three intending visitors were presently alighting at a nearby tram stop.

'I don't even know what the present is,' grumbled David, 'yet it's supposed to be from me!'

'The reason you don't *know,* my love,' explained his wife sweetly, 'is, if I left you to buy it, you'd not only buy her *nothing* but you'd get it a day late!'

'Mummy's bought Grandma a photograph,' explained Benjamin.

'Photograph?' echoed David, turning towards Grace. 'What of?'

'Your son, of course! She said she didn't have an up-to-date picture, so I took Benji to a studio and had a couple taken. Her copy is all nicely framed and packaged and only cost four and six.'

'Since when is four and six, *only*?' he asked. 'For your information, four and six is exactly half of my pay cut!'

'I hate to pile on the agony, Davy,' said Grace, pointing to the house, 'but if doors and windows are anything to go by, your mother's not at home. I can't see the car and the place looks shut up.'

'You mean to say, after dragging me all the way here, denying me my football, to say nothing of my conjugal rights, you hadn't even told her we were coming?' he asked incredulously.

'Of course I didn't arrange it with her, you twit. It was a surprise.'

'Well, it's certainly that all right,' he grizzled. 'The surprise is going to come when she finds out we've been here and she wasn't in.'

'Tell you what,' offered Grace. 'If she really isn't in and if it stops your moaning, you and Benji will just have time to make that three o'clock kick-off.'

'How about you? And what are we going to do with the photograph?'

'Well, you've got your mother's spare keys, haven't you? We can leave the present in the house and I can get the tram and do some shopping. I can catch you both after the match at home. Fair?'

'Can think of nothing fairer,' he chortled. 'C'mon, Benji, lad, let's see if Grandma's in. If not, we're off to The Den.'

The three of them were just about to go in at the gate, when David saw Wally Kershaw from number 27 opening his front gate. Wally was a good neighbour to Queenie and another Millwall supporter of many years standing.

'What ho, Walter,' he called. 'Not driving to The Den, by any chance?'

'I am that, Davy,' agreed Walter. 'I never miss the last game of the season.' Wally nodded a cheery greeting to Grace, then promptly annoyed her by ruffling Benji's carefully combed hair. 'But your mum and dad are out, Davy. They went out at midday. They spoke to Ella about it. I don't know exactly what they said except they wouldn't be back till around five o'clock. It's Queenie's birthday or something and yer dad's givin' her a treat, I distinctly remember 'em sayin' it.'

'Perhaps Ella knows where they are?' suggested Grace politely.

'I'm sure she does, my dear,' agreed Walter, 'but she went shopping in Brixton a half-hour ago. Anything I can do?'

'Well, if you could give us a minute, Wally, could we cadge a lift to Millwall? Because if no one's in, that's where me and Benji are bound.'

'Certainly,' agreed Walter. 'Nice to have your company. I'll wait.'

'Well, come on then, Grace!' said David eagerly. 'Let's get that door open and we'll leave it on the kitchen table or somewhere equally obvious. Thanks, Wally!'

The idea of a quick dash in with a present left on the table may have appealed greatly to David – he had the door open in an instant – but Grace did not share his enthusiasm.

'I still feel disappointed that we've come all this way and haven't seen your mum, though, Davy,' she said, as she laid the package in the centre of the table. 'Benji will be so disappointed. He would have loved to have seen her open it. Kids always do.'

'Can't be helped,' David said. 'After all, he is going to Millwall in a *car*! That should cheer him up. Can we go now?'

'I was thinking,' said Grace brightly, 'how about if we stand the picture on her bedside table? She probably won't notice it until she goes to bed and it'll be a lovely surprise for her?'

David gave a sigh of impatience. 'All right, but can we please be quick about it? Otherwise old Wally'll bugger off without us!'

Grace soon slipped off the wrapping and proudly held the picture in the filtering spring sunshine. 'It really is a lovely . . .'

'Grace!' he exploded in irritation. 'How much longer are you going to look at that bloody picture? Yes, it's a lovely photograph! Yes, he's a lovely lad! Yes, it's a lovely frame! He's lovely, you're lovely, I'm lovely, the whole bloody world's lovely if you like, but Wally Kershaw is waiting outside to drive me and our son to The Den. If he goes without us, then we'll have to get a tram and miss half the game.'

'Temper! Temper!' she whispered. 'It won't take a minute. You wait here. I'll be back before you know it.' She turned to the child. 'Come on, Benji, let's put the photo in Grandma's bedroom.'

The child ran on ahead and eventually past Queenie's bedroom. 'No, Benji,' called Grace. 'This one's Grandma's room.'

The boy pointed to the only closed door on the landing. 'This was my room, Mummy, when I used to stay with Auntie Julia.' To prove his geographical knowledge of the house, the lad turned the handle and opened the door. The sight that greeted him was more biological than geographical, particularly the two smooth thighs down a broad muscular back. The child stared for a moment then tilted his head in puzzlement.

He wasn't the only one.

Moments later, a red-faced Grace almost tumbled down the stairs into the hall, dragging her son behind her. 'Full marks, girl!' said David approvingly. 'You really were quick!'

'Daddy,' cried Benjamin excitedly pointing back up the stairs, 'Auntie Julia's up there an' I don't think she's very well.'

'Auntie Julia?' he echoed, looking to Grace for guidance. 'What's the child talking about? If she's here why didn't she answer the door?'

'Auntie Julia is here all right,' said Grace. 'But Auntie Julia did not answer the door because you did not *knock* at the door, did you?' Her face broke into the most fleeting of smiles as she added, 'And even if you had, I doubt if Auntie Julia would have answered – and nor, for that matter, would *Uncle* Duncan.'

'Julia? Duncan? I still don't understand. I thought Benji said she's not well?'

Grace gave a short laugh. 'Oh, she's well, right enough. In fact other than a little exposure, I doubt if she's ever been better.'

Whether it was the anxiety for his car ride to the football that had dulled his senses, David never knew, but as the penny dropped, he clapped his hands to his head. 'Oh my giddy . . .' he began, staring open-mouthed at Grace. 'What? You mean, they're at it? Up there?'

'Uh huh,' she nodded.

He suddenly burst into laughter. 'I bet they were really impressed with Benji's picture weren't they? Did they say how lovely it was and thank you for showing it to them?' Turning to his son, he swept him up in his arms. 'Well, lad,' he said, as he gave him a great plonking kiss, 'I suspect you've just lost a favourite aunt. Come on, I'll take you down The Den to see Millwall. That'll compensate.' And the three of them tiptoed quietly out of the house and closed the door gently behind them.

Other than a quick reflection of a puzzled little face in the dressing-table mirror, Duncan Forbes had seen almost nothing of the interruption. But the opening of the door plus all the other sounds in the house had more than quenched his ardour. Even if they hadn't, his would have been a solitary sexual exercise because Julia had slid speedily from the bed with both sheet and eiderdown wrapped tightly around her. Peeping through the curtains she finally announced, 'It was young Benji and his mum and dad. What on earth were they doing here?'

'Well, as the precise time they opened that door is permanently engraved in my mind,' said Duncan pointedly, 'that's a particularly easy question to answer. They were staring straight up my bum.'

'DUNCAN FORBES!' she cried, 'that's a disgusting thing to say!'

'Is it?' he asked. 'Do you know what I've been doing for this last month? No? Then I'll tell you. I've run like an athlete, climbed like a monkey and been scared witless on a motorbike. I've been parched and I've been wet. I've been cold and I've been hot. I've been up before dawn and tired all day. People have shouted at me, swore at me, underpaid me and, in general, given me a bloody miserable time. The one light at the end of the tunnel was knowing I was going to see you. Then, when we arrive here and I find we can also make love, I thought I was as happy as anyone with just three-and-fourpence to his name could be. BUT, just as I think I'm entering heaven, I see a leprechaun in a dressing-table mirror and it nearly gives me a sodding hernia. So, Julia Giles, if I *am* disgusting, I've more than earned the right to be.'

'Oh, you poor lamb,' she laughed as she ran back across the room and hauling back the sheet and eiderdown, enveloped them both.

'Y'know,' Duncan whispered, 'I'm bloody cursed with you. Whenever we seem to be set fair, there's always a disaster. Perhaps I should marry you.' He rubbed his chin thoughtfully. 'I'm sure you'd be a lot less trouble then.'

'See!' she cried, sitting bolt upright. 'There you go again! You can never be serious or give me a compliment without either a little dig or a little joke.'

Sensing his afternoon of passion was now receding fast, Duncan reached up to repair the damage, but Julia, with pride ruffled, was having none of it.

'I'm going to the bathroom,' she announced a split second before she slammed the door. 'If you want tea, make it yourself.'

Duncan gave an enormous yawn and stretched himself to the far corners of the bed. Then rising, he slowly dressed and, as he walked past the closed bathroom door, he tapped lightly upon it.

'Yes?' snapped Julia.

'You'll laugh about this in a year or two, Julia, honest you will,' he assured her. 'Meanwhile, would you like a ginger biscuit?' He assumed it was nothing heavier than a bar of soap that thudded against the door.

20

Olive Spenser walked across the yard balancing a tray containing two chipped mugs of steaming tea and a plate of dripping toast of doorstep proportions. Placing the tray carefully on one of the huge wheels that lay beside the old truck, she crouched and peered beneath its bodywork. 'Grub up, Wonky,' she announced. 'Don't let it get cold.'

Wonky Lines emerged from beneath the truck by rolling himself out on the wheeled cradle. Rubbing his greasy hands down his even greasier overalls, he smiled up at his benefactor. 'I c-can do with th-this and no m-mistake,' he said heartily. 'I'm bloody s-starving!'

Pulling up two more lorry wheels as makeshift chairs, the pair sat to enjoy their feast.

'I hate to tell you this, Wonky,' said Olive, 'but we're getting very close to decision day.'

'Wh-what decision?'

'Oh, come on, you *know* what decision! The decision as to whether you're going to stay here, of course!' she snapped. 'I know you've done your best to avoid making it, but I must know by Saturday. Old Ebie Parkinson from Parkinson's Buses has offered me an excellent maintainance contract for his fleet of charabancs. It's a very good deal, but I can't make the commitment if you're not staying.'

Wonky did not reply at first but continued to stir his tea long after every grain of sugar must have dissolved. 'I knew th-this'd come sooner or l-later,' he said finally. 'I know I'm a p-pain, Olive, but, you see, it's a very difficult choice.'

'I must say you've been a tremendous asset, Wonky, and you've certainly seemed happy enough. After all, you've been here a month and I thought if you had any complaints you would have aired them by now. What is it that's bothering you most. Is it your sleeping arrangements?'

'S-strangely enough, I don't mind them,' he said turning to face the corner of the yard where a small section of old railway carriage stood on a dozen piles of bricks. 'I admit it's a b-bit of a b-bind running across the yard to the l-lavatory l-late at night, b-but I could live happily with th-that if I had to.'

'So what is it, then? Is it those gangsters who were looking for you. Have they made you nervous?'

'N-No, I should th-think I'm pretty s-safe here. I can't th-think how they would know of this place.' He paused as if searching for words. 'You s-see, other than my army s-service, I've never been out of London for any length of t-time. I would have th-thought I'm too old to be h-homesick, yet I keep having this hankering to r-return to the smoke. I suppose at h-heart I'm not really a country l-lad and I feel I m-might be missing out on s-something.'

'Well, you're hardly at the other end of the earth, are you? Catch a train here and you're at London Bridge in an hour!' In the absence of a response, she continued, 'Oh, well, I can't make your decision for you, though I obviously don't want you to go. But I must have a definite answer from you by Saturday – or would you rather give it now?'

'I'd r-rather give it Saturday, if you don't mind,' he replied apologetically. 'About a m-minute to m-midnight okay?' he asked hopefully.

'No, I'd like it at least an hour before *midday*, and that's more than late enough!' she snapped as she rose to her feet. 'And if you want any more tea, you can get it yourself. I've work to do.'

Wonky watched her go with feelings of guilt and sorrow. Guilt, because he knew her business had improved greatly in the time he had been there and, in spite of the agreed trial period, she had already come to depend on him. Sorrow, because of his stupid and compulsive desire to return to London. Whilst he knew he could not live in a railway carriage for ever, he also knew he could obtain a more permanent address if he only put his mind to it. However, if he did that, he would also have to admit an increasing fondness for the woman. Though nothing had passed between them and, if it was left to Wonky, probably nothing ever would, this did not reduce his admiration for her. It may well have been this affection that was causing his uncertainty. The idea of being indefinitely smitten by some unrequited love had no appeal for him at all. After all, if it was purely a physical relationship he sought, the Wilkinson girls were more than ready. No, there was something about his feelings for Olive Spenser that were different and it was this that triggered his uncertainty.

If he had but known, his procrastination was needless because at that exact moment, Detective Inspector Roger Evans was studying a snippet of information passed to Scotland Yard by one of Kent's more alert young detectives – namely the whereabouts of the desperately sought Claude Clement Lines.

'So, Mac, where the hell is this place?' asked Evans.

'Er, let me see,' began the detective sergeant scanning the report. 'Barely a stone's throw from Maidstone railway station, apparently, guv.'

'How does he know the suspect is there?'

'He'd heard that Lines may have been in the Wateringbury area and he spoke to a farm worker who was closing up the huts at the end of the season. Apparently the man remembered seeing a lorry. This lorry seems to have changed owners a couple of times, but on the date in question, it seemed it belonged to a Spenser's Garage in Maidstone. He had a quick glance around and he reckons a bloke who fits Lines's description works there regularly.'

'How soon can we be there?'

The sergeant screwed up his face in thought, 'Say, an hour to cadge a car from somewhere or other, an hour-an'-a-quarter for the journey, half-hour to find the place . . .' He shrugged. 'Oh, about three hours, I'd say.'

'Would it be quicker by train?'

'Oh, yes, with the yard so close to the station, it certainly would. But judging by the state of the deceased, Lines could well be violent and we can control him better in a car than we ever could on a train. I'd say a car's favourite.'

'Okay, give Rodney Road nick a ring and grab someone there who can identify him. There's no point in nicking the wrong bloke. We've waited long enough, another few minutes isn't going to make much difference.'

'I've taken a chance and already done that, guv. Seems that half the nick knows him and I got the first PC that the duty officer could lay his hand on. He'll be waiting for us in the station yard. His name's—' he glanced once more at his notes, 'David Diamond. He helped to report an accident that Lines was involved in last September.'

'This Lines geezer. D'you reckon he'll be armed?'

'Wouldn't do any harm to be prepared, guv. If he's hiding in a garage, there's bound to be plenty of tools lying around.'

'I was thinking the same thing. Tell you what. Make sure this David Diamond is not in uniform. Perhaps we could drive straight into this garage as if we've got a problem with the car. If Diamond can put the finger on him right away, it might save us a lot of grief later.'

'There is just one problem, guv.'

'Just one?' replied Evans acidly. 'Well, there's a novelty! Go on, what is it?'

'It's the question of the car. As we're out of the metropolitan area, we can't use the station's patrol car. Unfortunately, the area CID car is on a heavy observation for bandits on Hampstead Heath and we don't have another.'

'Oh, this is bloody ridiculous! This is 1931 not 1831. I

thought this was supposed to be the age of the motor vehicle?'

'Er—' began the sergeant tentatively, 'there is one vehicle which isn't in use at the moment. Although it'd be better if the approach for its use came from you.'

'And that is?'

'The chief superintendent's car. His sergeant tells me the old man's got meetings for most of today, so I can't see he's likely to need it, can you?'

'Hmmn-no,' agreed Evans thoughtfully. 'Though you know what a cantankerous old bugger he can be?' He tapped his fingers on the desk for a moment before exclaiming, 'Damnation! We're in the same bloody job, aren't we? I'll ask him. After all, it is a murder investigation.'

'Well, if it's not, it maybe *will* be when you tell him you want his car,' chuckled the sergeant.

It was a full thirty minutes before Evans returned tight-lipped and flushed to the CID office.

'Well, we've finally got it, Mac,' he said. 'But what a bloody palaver. You wouldn't credit the fuss the old prat made. He insists we use his civilian driver for the trip and not travel more than twenty-five miles an hour. He's also gone over the car with a small toothcomb and listed even the minutest of scratches. Whatever you do, Mac, when you're in the car, don't drop cigarette ash, slam the doors or even breathe, otherwise the old fart'll have apoplexy.'

It was an hour to the minute before the black Riley saloon rolled out of Hampstead yard with its two passengers and driver.

'I take it you know where you're going?' asked Evans of the civilian driver.

'Er— Rodney Road nick, apparently, but I don't know where it is.'

Evans shook his head in disbelief. 'I bet you're a north Londoner, aren't you?'

The driver looked at him in surprise. 'Yeh, how'd you know that?'

'Easy,' continued Evans, 'if there's one thing I've learned since I came down from Wales, it's that no one who lives in south London knows anything about north London and people who live in north London are amazed south London even exists!'

'Well, it's the river yer see, guv,' explained the driver. 'That's what does it.'

'Why? Do we have to swim it then?' asked Evans irritably. 'Good Heavens, man, there are ten bridges in central London! How long have you been a driver?'

'Since the war, guv.'

'And since you've been driving, how many times have you been to south London?'

'Er— about ten, I'd say.'

'Ten! Bloody hell, that's less than once a year! It's not a plague city, y'know. People don't walk round in big hoods ringing bells.'

'Yer, I know, guv, but once I'm over the water I don't feel comfortable any more.' He suddenly brightened as a mitigating thought struck him. 'My old dad never did cross the river, not once he didn't. Not in his whole life and he lived to be eighty-one,' he said proudly.

'Direct him there, Mac, for God's sake, will you, or I'll swear I'll have a breakdown. Wake me just before we get there.' With that, he tilted his hat over his eyes and slid back in his seat, muttering to himself, 'Eighty-one and never crossed the sodding river. Ye Gods!'

David Diamond sat on the stone steps in the police yard at Rodney Road and wondered if he might just have time to pop to the market for some light refreshments before the Hampstead CID arrived. Inspector Marsh had been his customary unhelpful self when he had told him he was to accompany the officers to Maidstone. He had revealed neither time nor duration of the trip. His only disclosure was that David was to wait at the steps for a detective inspector who would arrive sometime that morning. Experience had taught David that, on all such mysterious assignments, basic welfare considerations, such as eating, drinking and lavatories, were not a force priority. He rightly guessed the detective had started duty at nine o'clock whereas he had been on duty since daybreak and was famished. After the first fruitless hour, he knew he could easily have been to the market a dozen times, yet there he was, none the wiser and twice as hungry. Deciding to risk it, he jumped down the steps and was out of the yard and heading post-haste for Edwards the Butchers. Though not considered dignified for a police constable to sprint in uniform, especially for pease pudding and faggots, David's leaping stride did ensure him a speedy return to the station steps. Unfortunately not speedy enough as the shiny black car that now stood in the centre of the yard clearly indicated. Meanwhile, a flustered Inspector Marsh appeared to be receiving an almighty ear-bending from a trilby-hatted, overcoated figure who had bad-tempered detective inspector written all over him.

'There he is now!' exclaimed the relieved Marsh. 'Where've you been, Diamond? Detective Inspector Evans has . . .'

'Never mind about that now,' snapped Evans, turning to David. 'You Diamond?'

David gave a nod of acknowledgement. 'Sir,' he replied curtly.

'You know a Claude Lines?'

Again a crisp acknowledgement.

'Then get a civvy overcoat over that uniform and get in the car. We've wasted enough bloody time as it is. What's that you've got in that paper?'

'Faggots, saveloys and pease pudding, sir.'

'Did he say faggots, saveloys and pease pudding?' called the detective sergeant from the open window of the Riley. 'That's my favourite! Where'd you get it from, mate? Is it close by?'

'Mac!' snapped Evans, 'I hate to remind you but you're

hardly allowed to be *breathing* in that car, never mind eating that muck. We also have a murder, rape and assault outstanding since September! How about we solve it?'

'Sorry, guv,' pleaded the sergeant, 'but I've not had faggots, saveloys and pease pudding for years. Hope he's not sitting next to me while he eats it.'

'He certainly is!' growled Evans. 'I'm not having him sitting next to me. I hate the bloody stuff.' He shook a despairing head, 'God, but you Londoners eat some shit! Okay, driver, move on!'

Ten minutes later, as the car threaded its way through the chaotic Lewisham traffic, David rolled the empty greasy paper into a ball and stuffed it under the front seat. Meanwhile, the detective sergeant chewed on the last of the saveloy that David had quietly smuggled to him. The driver, who had spent nearly as much time watching his two hungry passengers as he had watching the road, breathed a sigh of relief.

'Right,' said Evans, turning to David. 'If it's not too much trouble, I'd like you to pay attention to what I've got to say.' For the next few minutes he explained how Wonky Lines had been finally traced to a Maidstone garage and how it was hoped to carry out his arrest with the minimum of fuss.

'Can I say something, sir?' asked David.

'Is it that you want to tell me that you don't think Claude Lines is capable of murder and rape? If so, forget it. I've heard that enough times already.'

'I'm afraid that's exactly it, sir. Perhaps I should shut up?'

'Perhaps you should,' agreed Evans, and all four of them lapsed into silence.

The A20 was as busy as usual, but they made good time and soon entered the outskirts of Maidstone. Glancing down at some written notes, the sergeant gave a few curt directions to the driver and soon tapped his shoulder as an indication to stop.

'There it is, guv,' he announced. 'Hundred yards on the left.'

'Okay,' said Evans. 'This is it. Let's make sure we all know what we're doing, eh? Take us in slowly, driver. Make it look as if we've got some mechanical problem. And you, Diamond, directly you see Lines, point him out and we'll rush him, we hope before he knows what's happening.'

'What if he's not there?' asked David.

'Don't even think about that,' said the sergeant. 'After the trouble we've had, I refuse even to consider the possibility!'

'Any more questions?' asked Evans sharply. 'Because I'd prefer it if everyone knew what they're doing.'

'How about Lines's dog?' asked David.

'Dog?' queried MacDonald nervously. 'What dog? I didn't know he had a dog. Is it fierce? Dogs don't like me.'

'Did he say *dog*,' cried the driver. 'Oh, I couldn't allow a dog in here! S'posing it shits? The chief superintendent would crucify me! Sorry, but definitely no dogs. If there's a dog, then you'd better get a train because you won't be coming in this car, that's for sure!'

'Look!' snapped Evans angrily. 'I'm not jeopardising this whole operation because of some bloody hound! If there *is* a dog, then kick it up the arse or something, because I haven't spent the last few months looking for this bloke just to be stuffed because of a damned dog!' He glared all around him. 'Now, can we please get on!'

Olive Spenser had just driven the front of an old Foden lorry up onto two steel ramps. Securing the handbrake, she was glancing round the cluttered yard for a pair of wooden chocks to put under the rear wheels, when her attention was caught by the Riley saloon. Her first reaction was one of admiration for its mint condition. Evans's theory that she would assume they were potential customers was destroyed the instant she saw the four occupants. Though Wonky had been quite confident about his new cover, she had never been totally relaxed. Four men in a slowly moving car, creeping quietly into her yard spelt only one thing – gangsters!

Her cry of 'RUN, WONKY, RUN!' made him edge his

head out warily from beneath his lorry. He needed no second telling. Pushing his cradle to the opposite side of the lorry which was adjacent to the lowest wall of the yard, he had rolled out before the three police officers had cleared their doors. Leaping on the bonnets of a couple of old Fords, he was immediately within reach of the top of the wall. It was a fact not wasted on Evans.

'Outside!' he yelled to the driver. 'Cut him off, quick, man!' Not expecting to be part of the drama, the sudden command flustered the driver. Nevertheless, he had completed a fair part of a three-point turn before Olive Spenser decided a little diversion might assist the escape of her best mechanic. Quickly releasing the handbrake on the old Foden, she watched with satisfaction as it rolled straight down the twin ramps and neatly into the front of the immaculate Riley.

Wonky was in process of making his leap to the wall when he heard the crash. In spite of the imagined danger he found himself in, his curiosity won. At the vital moment as he jumped, he turned his head towards the sound. This caused him to miss the top of the wall and tumble down between the two old cars. To his complete amazement, the first person to reach him wore a policeman's uniform under an unbuttoned topcoat.

'H-Here!' said Wonky squinting up. 'I know y-you, d-don't I? You helped out at my accident, didn't you?'

'S'right,' agreed David, gently easing him to his feet. 'And it looks like I'm doing the same at another one. D'you make a habit of this?'

'N-n-no,' stammered Wonky. 'I'm s-sorry I th-thought you were a gang of h-heavies who've b-been after me for s-some time.'

'Are you in one piece?' asked the concerned David. 'You did come down with a bit of a wallop.'

Wonky quickly shook himself and smiled. 'It's mainly me p-pride that's d-dented.'

'This him?' demanded Evans. 'This the geezer we've been looking everywhere for?'

'It's him, right enough,' agreed David. 'Apparently thought we were gangsters.' He then moved his head to see around the lorry that was obstructing his view. 'What was that crash, d'you know, sir?'

'*I* know,' said Detective Sergeant MacDonald, edging his way between the lorry and a breakdown truck. 'And I wish I didn't.'

The colour faded from Evans's face. 'That crash,' he began. 'It wasn't – tell me it wasn't – it wasn't our Riley, was it? Say no, for God's sake, Mac, please, say no!'

'Afraid it was, guv. That tall bird, y'know the one in the overalls? Well, she's made a few modifications to the front of our Riley with a ten-ton truck.'

Evans sat on the front bumper of one of the Fords and, removing his trilby, despairingly buried his head in his hands. Finally he mumbled through his slightly parted fingers.

'Lines, I'm not only going to make sure you hang, but I'm going to swing on your fucking feet as they do it!'

Wonky bewilderedly turned to David. 'Wh-what's he t-talking about, do y-you know?'

'I think so,' sighed David. 'But don't worry, I think he's wrong.'

MacDonald handcuffed himself to Wonky and led him back to the Riley which was in the sorriest of states.

'You dopey cow!' cried Evans to Olive. 'I'm going to nick you for attempting to assist a felon to escape police custody; criminal damage; treason; vandalism; espionage and anything else that comes to mind. With any luck, you can both hang together!'

'Wasn't my fault,' she protested. 'I didn't ask you to come into my yard. You should have stopped outside first and asked permission. What you did was trespass. If your car hadn't been there, that truck would still be undamaged. Instead you've put a dent in the rear of it.'

'*I've* put a dent in the rear of it!' Evans almost screamed and pointed to the Riley. 'Then what would you say *you've* done to *that* – wax-polished it?'

'All I've done,' she said calmly, 'is run a truck a few yards backwards on my own property. It's something I do a dozen times each day. If you choose to park your car behind it on my property without my permission, I can't see as it's anyone's fault but yours. And as for assisting a felon to escape, that's rubbish! Escape from who – you? If you come barging in here without as much as a by your leave, how am I supposed to know who you are? The only bloke with a uniform on is him, and he's got a bloody overcoat over the top of it! I reckon I've got a claim against you and your lot!'

Whether it was the anger of her approach that finally got through to Evans or whether it was his own professionalism that finally emerged was not certain, but he did not need the hissed whisper, 'She's got a point there,' from MacDonald to realise she did indeed have a point there. He quickly consoled himself with the fact that the operation had not been a total disaster, after all. They had caught Claude Lines.

'Then there's my Claude,' she continued. 'Look what you've done to him! He's covered in bruises, frightened out of his life and he's handcuffed. Why?'

'He's handcuffed,' said Evans huffily, 'because he's wanted for questioning for rape and murder.'

'Rape and . . .' she began before shaking her head in disbelief. 'That's even more ridiculous than "assisting a felon to escape". What's come over you, mate. Are you barmy? Besides, where d'you think you're taking him?'

Evans suddenly realised that was indeed a fair question. Where *were* they taking him? It did not look like their car would be going anywhere under its own steam and as for their driver, he was still crying. It was time for serious decision-making. 'That breakdown truck of yours. Operational is it?'

'Of course, that's why it's here.'

'If you give us a front-lift back to town, I'll drop charges against you. A deal?'

'Not bloody likely!' she raged. 'You just reckoned you were going to hang him!'

'Figure of speech,' replied Evans. 'He's simply being questioned, that's all.'

'Anyway, whereabouts in town?'

'Hampstead.'

'*Hampstead*! Are you mad? That's the other side of London! It'd take us ages.'

'It's a good offer, I tell you. Just think, if you were charged and we tied your offence into his, you could be backwards and forwards to London each time he was remanded. It could take months. Who'd run your business then?'

'But you said he was only going in for questioning?'

'That's right, so he is. But if he did it, what then?'

'Can I s-say something?' interjected Wonky.

'Go ahead,' said Evans.

'I would like to g-go to L-London with you as soon as p-possible. I haven't th-the faintest idea wh-what you were t-talking about when you s-spoke of rape and m-murder but I feel I sh-should at least get it s-sorted out.' He turned to Olive. 'C'mon, luv, g-give them a front-lift, eh?'

'For you, sweetheart, yes.'

'G-Good,' responded Wonky, turning towards the detective inspector. 'Can Pieshop j-join us?'

'What's Pieshop?' queried Evans.

'It's not a "wh-what", it's a d-dog,' explained Wonky in a hurt tone. 'It's over there in the office.'

'I've already told yer there'll be no dogs in my car!' cried the driver.

'I'll second that,' said MacDonald eagerly.

'But you've hardly got a car now, mate,' pointed out David.

'Okay! Okay!' said Evans. 'It can ride in the front of the breakdown van. Now can we please *go*!'

One great blessing about a front-lift that came readily to David's mind, was the necessity of dispensing with a driver in the towed vehicle. This was a stroke of good fortune considering the emotional state of the chief superintendent's driver whose condition had deteriorated steadily with each passing mile. Finally, two unnerving hours later, both vehicles slowly negotiated the narrow entrance of Hampstead police station yard.

'Okay,' said MacDonald unfastening the handcuffs, 'so who's going to break the news to old Grizzly Guts that his car's had a whack?'

'I don't think you need bother, Sarge,' said David. 'Is that him looking out of that first floor window?'

'Aw, God, yes,' muttered Evans. 'Er— look, I think I'd better take the prisoner to the interview room. Perhaps you'll explain to him about the damage, Mac, eh?'

'Now why did I guess that?' asked MacDonald softly.

'I take it you don't want me any more, do you, sir?' asked David. 'If not, I can get a part-way lift in the breakdown van.'

'I'm afraid I *do* want you, Diamond,' replied Evans. 'You're my only means of identification at the moment. You'd better join us for the interview, because, as matters stand, you're here for at least an hour or so.'

'Well, that's just as well,' cut in Olive, 'because I'm not leaving this place until I know what's happening to my Wonky,' she said emphatically.

It probably did not need the forty-five-minute interview by Evans to realise that Wonky Lines was *not* the man who was going to give an additional boost to his investigative career. Nevertheless, the time was not wasted, as Sidney Grechen began to figure more and more in Wonky's story.

'But why did you do a runner?' persisted Evans.

'B-Because Grechen knows m-my address and even t-traced me to the h-hopfields.'

'Yes, that's another point,' said Evans. 'Where's your proper address? Are you still living at the garage in Maidstone or are you returning to Blackfriars? You're not out of the woods yet, you know. At the very least, you're a vital witness. Before I can release you, you'll need a permanent address.'

'For the time b-being you'd b-better show me at M-Maidstone then,' said Wonky wearily. 'I'd like to r-return to L-London, but I'll need to find another p-place. D-Don't know any, I s-s'pose?'

'No,' said Evans, equally wearily. 'But stick around. When the chief superintendent sees his car, I might be taking lodgers.'

An hour later, as Evans watched the breakdown van containing Wonky, David, Olive and Pieshop roll slowly out of the yard, he knew the day had not been the most successful of his career. It was true he at last had the identity of a good suspect, but it was also clear he had been chasing a stuttering wild goose for the last few months. As he reached for a clean sheet of paper, the door suddenly burst open and a burly, boiled-faced chief superintendent glowered down at him.

'My car,' boomed the newcomer, 'is a write-off! Before I do the same to you, can you explain what this was doing under my seat?' He thrust forward a ball of screwed-up newspaper.

Evans stared at the exhibit in puzzlement. 'Er— no idea, sir, none at all.'

'Well, I'll enlighten you, shall I? You see, I don't even permit anyone even to *smoke* in my car. Which, if you remember, I explained at some length when you first requested its use. But according to my driver, the one who's now suffering first-degree shock, by the way, before you actually got around to wrecking my vehicle, you had a debauched feast of saveloys, faggots and pease pudding and this is its wrapping! Smell it. It stinks! Ye gods, man, you're a damned vandal! All I can say is, Lord Trenchard hasn't arrived in this job a moment too soon. Just don't go making any long-term plans.' With that, he left the room, slamming the door so violently that the windows trembled.

Detective Inspector Evans watched him go then put a fist to his own head and shot out his brains with an imaginary gun.

21

'Where can I drop you off, Mr Diamond?' asked Olive as she sat behind the wheel in the cramped cabin.

'Anywhere in the centre of town'll do fine,' said David. 'But London Bridge'll suit even better, if it's not too much trouble.'

'No trouble at all, and London Bridge it is,' she replied, 'because if it hadn't been for you, me and Wonky would still be at Hampstead.'

David nodded a gesture of thanks before turning to Wonky. 'You asked Evans if he knew anywhere in London where you could get accommodation. D'you mean it?'

Wonky raised his head in surprise. 'Of c-course! Why? D'you know s-somewhere?'

'Matter of fact, I do. It's not much of a place, mark you. Many say it's a slum, but it's a central fifth-floor flat with two tidy rooms, and the rent's cheap.'

'S-Sounds ideal,' said Wonky excitedly. 'Where is it?'

'It's the flat above mine,' David explained. 'The old widower who lived there died last week and I'm going to his funeral tomorrow. It's in a bit of a mess but I'll have a word for you at the estate office. They don't know he's dead yet, so they won't have let it. I'll get my wife to tell them tomorrow when she pays the rent. Can I contact you at the garage?'

'Yes, th-that'll be f-fine, Mr Diamond, th-thanks a lot. I'll keep my f-fingers crossed until I h-hear from you.'

Though David was not fully aware of any deep relationship between Wonky and Olive, he sensed her disappointment at his suggestion. Tentatively he turned to inquire if he had made the wrong move.

'Er— but how will you manage? I mean, if you're working in Maidstone, it'll be a hell of a drag each day from Queen's Buildings, won't it?'

'I've been th-thinking about th-that,' replied Wonky. 'I like w-working at M-Maidstone and I th-thought I might still continue to do s-so. That way I c-could come back to L-London each w-weekend. Th-there's only me and P-Pieshop so, it w-would be easy, wouldn't it?' He turned to Olive. 'Would th-that be all right?'

The indifference of her reply, 'It's your life, please yourself,' did not match the look of relief that crossed her face.

'Well, you haven't got the flat yet,' pointed out David, 'so this could all be premature but I'll do what I can. Okay?'

Thirty minutes later, as the truck crossed London Bridge, David said goodbye and dropped off quickly at the corner of Tooley Street. Glancing at the clock at London Bridge station, he noted he was five hours late for dinner. Hoping that one of his colleagues had told Grace of his delay, he increased his pace. Ten minutes later he was breathlessly turning the key of his door.

'Yes, I know all about it and you're quite safe to enter,' called Grace, as she hung the washing outside on the balcony. 'Poshie Porter popped in to tell me you'd be delayed. I'm not sure he did you any favours though.'

'Why's that?' he asked, greeting her with a warm kiss.

'Well, I've not been able to do a thing,' she complained. 'You know what Poshie's like? If you give him as much as a cup of tea he sits down and you can't get rid of him. He only left a half-hour ago. If it hadn't been for Benji coming in for his bedtime, he'd still be here.'

'You know why that is, don't you?'

'No, why?'

Sliding his arms round her waist, he pulled her tightly to him and jiggled his hips against hers. 'Because he fancies you like buggery. He always has. I don't blame him, though, I do too.'

'Well, I think your phrasing could have been better but I think I get your drift. Anyway, if what you say is right, he has a funny way of showing it. He spent a good hour reading the newspaper.'

'Ah, yes!' exclaimed David. 'You *thought* he was reading the paper, but I bet he was peeping over the top and staring at your bum as you bent over that sink.'

'Don't be so silly.' She blushed. 'Anyway, you've been touring the hopfields, so how would you know?'

'Because my sweet,' he said, caressing her buttocks, 'it's something I do all the time. You really do have a delicious bottom you know.' He kissed her again before adding, 'Nevertheless, I must have a word with Poshie, the cheeky sod can find his own crumpet in the future. By the way, when you pay the rent tomorrow, will you tell Miss McKenzie that Alfie Spreggs has died and I know someone who'd very much like the flat?'

Quickly slipping her arms from his neck, she replied acidly, 'Oh, very romantic! One second I'm a *femme fatale* with a jealous husband, the next I'm the angel of death leasing out flats!'

'I knew no good would come of giving women the vote,' he sighed. 'They've become far too impertinent. Get me my dinner, woman, and be quick about it.'

She returned smiling to his arms and, after giving his left ear the lightest of kisses, whispered softly, 'Damn you, you pig, get it yourself.'

Miss McKenzie had been the estate officer for Queen's Buildings, for more than thirty years. Even so, she had never really come to terms with the contrast of its depressing prison-like appearance and her own pleasant garden flat in Kensington. Each morning, for a moment or so as she left the Elephant and Castle underground station, she needed to brace herself when the huge tenement first soared into view. But the mood quickly passed and she would soon readopt the mantle of judge, jury and executioner in all matters appertaining to the estate. Though now into her third generation of tenants, nowhere during her reign, had anyone ever called her by anything other than 'Miss McKenzie'. If she did have a Christian name, not one of the thousands of tenants who had passed through its portals had ever learnt it. Miss McKenzie was respected to the point of fear. Even the noisiest of children would fall into a reverent silence when the dramatic whisper, ''Ere comes Miss McKenzie!' flitted amongst them like news of the Black Death.

A short, stocky, asexual woman, she always dressed in brown tweeds, heavy brown brogues, thick lisle stockings and a large floppy hat, the brim of which would all but conceal the eternal cigarette holder with which she would frequently jab to emphasise her more stringent discussion points. Her voice belied her appearance. It was refined and gentle, but no one who was ever confronted by those steely grey eyes and determined jaw would ever have underestimated her determination and power. During her time, hundreds of neighbourly disputes had been settled by the magic words, 'Miss McKenzie said so.' If Miss McKenzie had indeed said so, then it was stone-carved without appeal. To request an interview with her was tantamount to an audience with Solomon. She would look up from her desk and fixing the interviewee with piercing, almost unblinking, eyes, she would ration her words and deliver a judgment that necessitated total acceptance.

Grace's plea for a tenancy for Wonky was greeted with the irritated response, 'Why wasn't I told of Spregg's death?'

The jokey reply, 'Sorry Miss McKenzie, I didn't kill him. Honestly,' was treated dismissively by the interrogator.

'This man Lines – friend of your husband? Or is he a felon?'

Deciding to forget Wonky had been sought by half of

London's CID for rape and murder, Grace crossed her fingers and said he was a friend.

'Very well. Get the gentleman to make an appointment and I'll consider his application. Thank you, good day.'

At three minutes' duration, Grace's audience was classified as one of the longest and it was with high optimism that she told David of her success on his return from the funeral.

Three weeks later, Wonky moved into number ninety-three. It could have been even earlier, but it had taken two men a full day to dispose of the junk that Alf Spregg had accumulated after his wife's death. In turn, Wonky had cut down savagely on his own possessions. The idea of carrying anything up a hundred-and-ten steps that was not going to be vital to his wellbeing, appalled him. The result was, he left more of his possessions in the Blackfriars Road than he took with him to Queen's Buildings. His plan to spend weekdays in Maidstone had one big advantage. It enabled him to fumigate thoroughly both rooms for bed bugs before taking up full occupancy of the flat. It did, however, make for turbulent weekends, not least for the three Diamonds, as the sound of him cleaning and decorating percolated down late into the night.

Finally, after several tiring weekends, Wonky, in company with Pieshop, arrived at David's door late one Saturday. Clutching a large box of chocolates and a small bottle of sherry, he announced the flat was almost ready for occupation. He presented the sweets to Grace and the sherry to David in gratitude for their tolerance. At the same time, this did not inhibit him from requesting one final favour. This was to pass the key to a plumber who was due to call at his flat the following Wednesday. After inviting Wonky to tea, Grace's curiosity got the better of her and, much to David's embarrassment, she inquired about his romantic intentions concerning Olive Spenser. Contrary to David's fears, it was as if the old soldier had been aching to talk of his dilemma and words cascaded out. His feelings for Olive had certainly blossomed, but whilst Sid Grechen was roaming freely, he feared for her safety.

'Should only be a matter of time before he's nicked, though,' said David hopefully. 'After all, Grechen's description has been widely circulated as a suspect for rape and murder.'

'I-I know,' said Wonky ruefully. 'So was m-mine!'

With Wonky's fears still fresh in his mind, David cycled to work the following morning determined to discover the latest developments in the hunt for Grechen. What he found dismayed him. It seemed that Sid had totally disappeared. All known addresses had been thoroughly searched, not only Sid's but those of his associates, yet no trace of the old blackguard had been found.

'Typical bloody CID,' said Reuben Drake contemptuously. 'Couldn't find a bullock in a bathroom.'

'Still,' said Poshie Porter optimistically, 'I should think Wonky will be fairly safe, especially now he's living above your flat. After all, it wouldn't be easy for an assassin to make a quick getaway from the fifth floor, would it?'

'Cuts both ways,' pointed out David. 'It'd be just as difficult for the victim to escape.'

'Hmmn, tell you what, old boy,' said Poshie thoughtfully. 'How about this for a hypothesis. Dear old Sidney gets the wrong flat and kills you instead? Perchance that happens, how about bequeathing me your delightful wife?'

'Piss off, Poshie.'

'Just a thought, old bean, just a thought.'

The news of Sid Grechen's disappearance put David in something of a dilemma. He had no wish to alarm Wonky unnecessarily, but at the same time he felt he should at least acquaint him with the situation. It was late Sunday afternoon before David returned home from work and, whilst Grace put the finishing touches to their meal, he planned to seek out Wonky.

'You've just missed him,' she said. 'I heard him go down the stairs a few minutes before you came in. I think he was taking Pieshop for his walk. He could be some time, though. He always has a long river walk on Sunday evenings.'

David cursed quietly, then added, 'Well there's nothing we can do for the moment. I'll just listen for his return.'

The evening chill plus the cash collection by the assembling Salvation Army band had driven in most of the nosy parkers who spent Sundays leaning over cushioned windowsills whilst watching the comings and goings of the street. The same chill and the gathering dusk had also driven Wonky back early from the river. It was shortly after six o'clock that David heard the breathless grunting of Pieshop still several flights down. This was followed by the slow distant footsteps of Wonky Lines.

He was not alone in his interest. Having just emerged from a doorway of the brewery at the end of the street and now making haste towards the building's entrance, was a very sinister figure indeed. Sidney Grechen had long realised that Wonky Lines, apart from having had his hand in the till, could also be a very dangerous witness in court. He had also realised that if he was to discover the whereabouts of the said Wonky, he would need to do so himself, or at least at his own expense. Now, after three months of painstaking and expensive inquiries, he had succeeded. The only thing now needed was the exact door number. Once he had found that out, he could pay others to do the dirty work as he considered he had already taken at least one chance too many. Tiptoeing up the stone steps, he could clearly hear voices from some three flights up. To his amazement, he also heard mention of his own name.

'. . . there is definitely a warrant out for Sid Grechen, but you really must take care until he's caught. I'd say you're safe enough here but make sure you know who's at your door before you open it, no matter how convincing they sound. Got it?'

'Yes, th-thanks, Mr D-Diamond, th-thanks a lot for your t-trouble. I'm sure you're right and I'll take care. G'night.'

'G'night,' came the response as a door shut and a pair of solitary footsteps continued even higher.

The communal stone and brick staircases of Queen's Buildings, were dank and narrow but they had one big advantage for Grechen, they were poorly lit and it was only possible to see one flight at a time. All a pursuer needed to do was stay within earshot. As Sid reached the fourth floor, he heard the jangling of keys and a few muffled words to the dog. Then a lock turned and finally a door slammed. Sid rushed up the next two flights and, with an ear pressed to the closed door, heard Wonky's voice still chatting to the animal. Looking up at number 93, he knew, at least for the moment, his task was complete. With the hint of a twisted smile, he turned away and made a thoughtful descent of the stairs and stepped out to the gas-lit street where the Salvation Army were ending a spirited rendition of 'All Things Bright And Beautiful'.

'I realise stew is not much of a Sunday dinner, Davy,' said Grace apologetically ladling out some grey-looking mutton, 'but I promise we'll have an old-fashioned roast the first day your pay is reinstated.'

David was about to tell her of Poshie's request for a bequeathment, when there was a rattle at the letter box. This was followed by a similar rattle opposite and footsteps hastening up the staircase. A small pamphlet fluttered slowly to the floor. Retrieving it, he studied it for a moment then shook a worried head.

'What is it?' asked Grace. 'Not another bill, surely?'

'Worse than that, I'm afraid, luv,' he muttered. 'See for yourself.'

The pamphlet was headed THE NEW PARTY! It then announced a meeting that was to be held at the local baths a few days hence to discuss the party's proposals to rescue the country from the depths of its current slump.

'What's so terrible about that?' she asked. 'Sounds a great

idea. No one else seems to care.'

'I know,' he agreed, 'that's the danger. You know who this group is, don't you?'

She confessed she did not.

'It's the fascist mob that Jim told us about, remember, that night he got trapped in the dance hall? Well, it's them. They've recently formed themselves into a political party and they've been holding meetings all over the borough.'

'But they were just local louts,' she said. 'No one's going to take them seriously, surely?'

'Oh, yes, they are! And don't you delude yourself for a moment! In any case, as you've rightly said, no one else appears to care about the state of the country. You see, if you're an out-of-work family man without any prospect of work, what would you do? At the very least, you'd probably give this mob a try. But I tell you, if they ever take off, a copper's job will be ten times more difficult. Just have a look who's the local organiser. See, there in the bottom corner.'

'Roger Stanton. Who's he?'

'Alias "Lofty" Stanton. He's an aggravating lout who's recently done a stretch for assault on police. If *he*'s the organiser they are either very desperate or have plans to beat up the rest of the country.' Looking down at Benjamin, he ruffled the child's hair. 'I hope things get better before you grow up, son. Because the way this world's going, I'm not sure I'll want to be part of it.'

Grace stared at him for a moment as if a bell had been rung. Suddenly pushing open the bedroom door, she turned and seized each of their hands, dragging David and Benji across the room to the windowsill. 'Well, what're you waiting for. Open it,' she ordered her puzzled husband.

'We're not jumping, are we?'

'No, you idiot,' she laughed. Slipping her hand into her overall pocket, she drew out a sixpenny piece which she gave to the boy. 'Throw it, Benji, throw it to the band playing that nice hymn.'

Benjamin's aim was reasonable. It was close enough to the band to be seen but not close enough to injure an ear.

'What's provoked this unaccustomed generosity with our money?' asked David.

'Because I'm unsure about God,' she said quickly.

'You're unsure about God – so you give away sixpence?' he queried. 'Just as well you're not indecisive, it might have been a pound.'

'I'm *unsure* because I'm not certain if there *is* such a person as God,' she explained. 'There's really no way someone like me can prove it. So, if there really *is* a God, the nearest of his friends I'm likely to meet are the Salvation Army. I just thought I'd play it safe. Can't do any harm, can it?'

'I see,' said David with fake solemnity. 'So you've just booked a tanner's worth of heavenly support for your son, have you? If it works, let me know, because I've already got eight bob saved up in the Christmas Club. If I can only make it two quid, I reckon I might make superintendent, though at this precise moment, I'd settle for mutton stew.'

As was their usual practice at mealtimes, the couple spent some time talking about the day's events and David decided it was time to declare his fears over Wonky's safety. 'Don't forget,' he told her, 'if you see anything, anything at all, don't hesitate, just lock yourself in here and scream like mad out of the window. No felon is going to hang around five floors up if you do that.'

'Until this Grechen is arrested, it must be terrifying for poor Wonky,' she said sympathetically. 'I just hope he hasn't much longer to wait.'

'Just because he stutters,' said David, 'don't underestimate him. He's a tough bugger and I certainly wouldn't like to upset him. If it was a one-to-one I'd back Wonky every time but I doubt if Sid Grechen is a one-to-one person. He'll certainly have thugs behind him and that could be Wonky's biggest danger.'

The next day, Monday, David was on late-turn duty and,

though he would never admit it, he always enjoyed the freedom of the bed once Grace had left for her cleaning job. During the early night, they had made love with some considerable passion and he still felt a tranquil, if dozy, afterglow. Usually on such occasions, once Grace had left for work, he would revel in the luxury of spreading himself diagonally across the bed and pray that Benjamin would sleep an extra hour or two. His prayers were usually granted because the child also enjoyed undisturbed sleep instead of being carried to Sheila Bowen's flat whilst barely awake.

Grace's footsteps had hardly faded down the staircase when he heard Wonky's door close and his footsteps descending. This was followed by a stage whisper through the letter box.

'D-Davy, y-you awake?'

David felt so relaxed that he was tempted not to answer, but fearing the voice might disturb his son, he tiptoed quickly to open the door.

Seeing his sleepy state, Wonky apologised profusely. 'I h-heard Grace go to work and I th-thought you'd be up and about, s-sorry.'

David leaned wearily against the doorframe and with closed eyes and closed mouth grunted, 'So?'

'J-just wondered if y-you could give the k-key to my plumber when h-he c-calls on W-Wednesday. H-he'll pop it in your l-letter box when he's f-finished – if it's n-not too much t-trouble, that is,' he added hopefully.

'Fine,' said David, sliding slowly down the wall. 'That it?'

'Y-Yes,' blurted Wonky. 'Th-that's it. S-See you S-Saturday – S-Sorry!'

'So am I,' agreed David as he closed the door and staggered back to bed.

For some weeks, the weather had been typically springlike. One day would be like midsummer whilst the next was as turbulent as Cape Horn. Wednesday, 22nd April was one such wild and wet day. It was a soaking wet and bedraggled plumber who climbed wearily to the fourth floor of Queen's Buildings and knocked for a key at number ninety-one. David answered the door and was instantly dismayed at the man's plight.

'Here, give me that and sit yourself down by the fireside, mate,' he said, relieving the newcomer of his toolbag. 'I'll make you a cup of tea. You can't possibly start work in that state. Grace,' he called over his shoulder, 'find this poor man a towel, he's drenched.'

Grace replaced the flat iron on the glimmering gas ring whilst David moved the kettle to the centre of the hob. 'Shouldn't be long now, mate,' he soothed. 'You'd get bloody pneumonia if you started work like that.'

Vic Wainwright was extremely grateful for the Diamonds' concern. Though he had made a passable recovery from his childhood tuberculosis, a hundred-odd stairs and a thorough soaking could not be easily shaken off at the age of fifty-five. Grace hung up his old overcoat and David shook the rain from his cap and scarf.

'It's real charitable o'you folks,' smiled Vic gratefully, 'but yer mustn't spoil me too much or I might git the taste fer it. Anyway, I shouldn't be up there fer more'n a couple of hours. Once I've 'ad me tea, I'll be orf an' out of yer way.'

'Okay,' said Grace, 'but leave your wet clothes here by the fireside. You can collect them when you return the key. By the way,' she added, 'if you're working upstairs, you'll probably need a couple of pennies for the gas meter. Grey days make these flats very gloomy, you know.'

'Bless yer, mam,' said the old plumber, touching his brow. 'If yer don't mind me sayin', yer are as considerate as yer are pretty, an' I thanks yer fer it.'

True to his word, Vic did not dawdle, and within less than fifteen minutes, he could be heard upstairs walking across the bare floorboards. He quickly came to the conclusion that Mrs Diamond was indeed right – grey days in Queen's

Buildings were gloomy. Before he even undid his bag he took out his matches and put a light to the two gas mantles that protruded from the wall above the fireplace. He watched anxiously before deciding the flickering yellow glow gave him just enough light to work by. However, in spite of being five floors up, his were not the only eyes showing interest in the illumination. Sitting in the back of a car, with a pile of partly read newspapers, Sid Grechen suddenly sparked into life.

'There! Look, the light's just come on! It must'a bin 'im that went into the building a short time ago wrapped up in all those bloody clothes, crafty bugger! Okay, you three, yer know what ter do?'

'O'course, guv,' came the reply. 'We've got the bastard cornered this time; there's nowhere else for him to run.'

'One more point, though,' said Sid quickly. 'Seein' as I'll be waitin' at the front, you'll need ter use the back of the buildin' fer the job. Because that'll be where all the attention'll be drawn when we're scarpering away afterwards, see?'

'Sure, guv.'

'Okay. Collars up, hats down, orf yer go, an' good luck ter the three o'yer.'

Vic Wainwright had just turned off the water when there was an official-sounding rat-tat at the door. Spanner in hand, he opened it to find three rather large well-dressed gentlemen clad in smart black overcoats, brown trilby hats and brown leather gloves.

'Ah, glad to find you in, sir!' exclaimed the first of the men. 'We're from the council. We wonder if you could do us a little favour?'

'Er— well,' began Victor, 'I'd like ter, but yer see I'm not really the—'

'Oh, it won't take a minute of your time, sir, an' we'll be off. There's just something that we must draw to your attention under the bye-laws. You don't have to worry about it, sir, it's only a formality. You know what a red-tape lot us council types are, don't you, sir?' he laughed.

'But as I was sayin' ter yer just a minute ago . . .'

The second man already had the balcony door opened as the first and third men persuaded Vic through it. Vic had decided that if it would speed these three on their way, he would see whatever they wanted him to see and acquaint Wonky with it later.

'There, sir, look,' said the second man as he pointed to the balcony ceiling. 'See, up there! Dreadful, ain't it?'

Vic raised himself on tiptoe and squinted up at the spot in question. Even though the day was overcast, other than a few cobwebs, he could see nothing to bother anyone, let alone the town hall. 'Well I'm blessed if I can . . .'

Having appropriately blessed himself, Vic Wainwright was suddenly seized in three vicelike grips and propelled into space and the start of a seventy-foot drop onto concrete. His death cry, plus that of a scream from a woman who was gathering rainwater for her aspidistra, drew Grace's attention to her window.

'Davy,' she said matter-of-factly, 'looks like someone's fallen over in the yard. If I didn't know better I'd say it was the plumber from upstairs. But it can't— DAVID! IT *IS* HIM! IT'S THE PLUMBER AND HE'S FALLEN FROM THE BALCONY!' she shrieked.

'*What?*' cried David. 'He can't have, he's hardly been up there for . . .' He stared at her for a second before rushing to the front door. Racing up the two flights of stairs he was confronted by a closed door. Without even bothering to knock, he kicked at it until the locked splintered from its frame and both he and the door fell into the room. Racing to the window he saw a small crowd already gathering around the crushed body of the plumber. The incessant rain was already diluting the blood into one vast light crimson stain. From the position of the corpse, it was extremely unlikely he could have jumped out that far. So, if he did not jump, he would have had to have been thrown. Yet no single person could have possibly thrown him that distance. But if there were more, where were they? The flat was empty and no footsteps had been heard since the scream, so whoever they were could not possibly have come down. If they didn't come down, then they went up. Yes, that was it, they had gone up! Onto the damned roof!

Racing up two flights, David found the roof door wide open, but of the assassins, not a sign. They had obviously leaped the low walls between the roof of each block. In fact, as he approached the first of the walls, the trio had already left by an exit three blocks distant.

'Well?' demanded Sid Grechen, as they returned to the car. 'Could he fly?'

'No, guv, you totally misled us. He couldn't fly an inch. We were really disappointed.' So saying, the quartet burst into laughter as the car eased smoothly away towards Southwark Bridge.

22

With head tilted sideways, Billie Bardell stared at her drying hair in the bathroom mirror. Then throwing back her head she shook it vigorously before reaching for a brush. As she dragged the brush across her scalp she moved over to the window and was saddened at the sight of her garden. Infuriating though Duncan Forbes could frequently be, there was no doubt that for a young man, he was an excellent gardener. Though he had been gone for only a few weeks, the alternating wet and warm spring had already produced an abundance of weeds. The autumn-planted bulbs were all bravely showing, but a carpet of unwanted perennial weeds such as buttercup and twitch grass were already staking a territorial claim. If the garden was not to run totally out of control, it would need immediate attention, especially if it was to retain anything of its former beauty. She knew a gardener should not be too difficult to come by with three million unemployed and there certainly would be no shortage of applicants. Yet, without Duncan, it would not seem the same place, particularly if she was to look from the window each morning and not see his handsome form tormenting the susceptible Julia. There was no doubt that the whole soul of the house seemed to have vanished with the two youngsters.

Slipping off her towelling robe, Billie reached for her clothes. As she dressed, she heard her new maid busying herself in the bedroom. Young Elsie Parker was certainly a willing girl but she would never be an Alice. With her bewildered wide-eyed stare, tiny build and thin frizzled hair, she looked exactly what she was, a bewildered age-limit discharge from a less than charitable orphanage.

Billie was just about to pull a dress over her head when the telephone rang. Instinctively she gave a little start, just as she had every time since that day Sid Grechen had telephoned her from another room in the house. She heard Elsie recite the number followed by a short muffled conversation. Running footsteps were followed by the bathroom door being thrown open and the harassed maid blurted out, 'Please, marm, it's the police.'

'Police? What do they want?'

'He said he's Sergeant someone-or-other and he sent one of his men to speak to you about a half-hour ago. He wants to know if he's arrived yet. He said, if he ain't, will you send him back directly because his wife's just had a baby.'

'Whose wife has just had a baby?'

'The policeman who ain't here, marm,' said the girl helpfully.

Billie raised her eyes. 'Do they get nothing right at that bloody station?'

'Marm?' queried the girl.

'It's nothing, really, Elsie,' she sighed. 'Perhaps I'm getting a mite touchy, but it does get my goat when the only thing they choose to tell me concerning my Alice's murder is that one of their bloody coppers, who ain't here, is a dad.'

'So shall I tell them you'll send him back as soon as he arrives?' asked the anxious girl. 'After all, marm, it might not be anything to do with Mrs Giles's murder.'

'You're right,' agreed Billie wearily. 'They probably just want me to be godmother or pay for the pram. Tell him directly he arrives we'll kick his arse out. That should suit them.'

The maid, never sure if Billie was really serious, nodded dutifully and ran back to the telephone.

Ten minutes later, as Billie sat down to breakfast in the dining room, she asked Elsie if she happened to know anyone who could manage a garden. The girl said there was a young man who had been required to leave the orphanage at the same time as herself. She added that though she did not think he was a proper gardener, he certainly had worked in the orphanage vegetable garden. 'After all, if you could grow globe artichokes,' said the girl optimistically, 'pansies shouldn't present a problem.' Billie considered there could be some logic in this argument and suggested the maid should contact the gardener as soon as possible.

It was whilst the girl was attempting to do so that the door from the kitchen suddenly opened and Sidney Grechen strolled casually in. Calmly sitting himself down at the end of the table, he waved an admonishing finger at the stunned Billie.

'Tut-tut,' he said, 'after all the trouble yer've had, I fink it's real careless of yer ter leave yer kitchen door unlocked. I mean, I could'a been a dastardly chap instead of the bearer of good news, couldn't I?'

Billie rapidly calculated all the options open to her but there was no doubt, much as she hated this man, she knew he was no fool. With Elsie on the telephone, perhaps a loud scream might possibly alert whoever was on the other end of the line. But if it didn't, what then? He was barely an arm's length from her and she could be dead before Elsie came, let alone an unknown gardening orphan several miles away.

'I have to tell you, there's a policeman on his way here,' she said nervously. 'In fact I'm expecting him any minute.'

'Oh,' laughed Sidney loudly, 'yer don't mean the one who's missus is 'aving a baby, do yer? I don't fink 'e'll be comin'.'

'Was that you?' she asked, furious with herself for being so gullible.

'Yer, good, weren't it? Yer see I weren't sure if there'd be any coppers abaht. Yer new maid was quite helpful though. Tell me, what does she look like? As yer know, I'm quite partial ter maids. D'yer reckon I'd fancy 'er?'

'She's just a kid,' hissed Billie. 'Leave her alone, you scum!'

His apparent relaxed manner suddenly changed. Shooting out a hand, he grasped her by the neck of her dress and snarled. 'Right, listen carefully. You an' me 'ave a new contract. I've got ter git away fer a while, so I'm releasin' yer from our previous little agreement. I want a one-off payment fer as much as yer can lay yer 'ands on an' then yer won't ever see me again, that's a promise. I'll be outa yer life fer ever. That's fair, ain't it?'

'Oh no,' she said, shaking her head angrily. 'I'm not falling for that one, not again. You can do *what* you like *to* me, and you can tell *who* you like *about* me, but your gravy train has just been derailed and . . .'

The solitary 'ding' of the telephone told them that the maid had finished her call and they both looked up as she breathlessly entered the room.

'Oh, marm,' she began before stopping dead in her tracks when she saw Sid Grechen with his hands at Billie's throat.

He disdainfully looked the girl up and down as if considering a casual purchase. 'Nah,' he finally said to Billie, 'she's safe enuff. I wouldn't feed her to me cat.' He then turned his attention back to the girl. 'Right, now listen, sweet'eart, just do as yer told an' nuffink will 'appen ter either you or Miss Bardell, d'y'understand?'

The terrified girl nodded frantically. 'Yes, sir,' she blurted.

Resuming his conversation with Billie, he said, 'I want every bit o'cash yer got in the 'ouse. Not *cheques*, y'understand, cash! But don't fink yer gonna fuck me abaht, 'cos I want it this very minute!' He twisted the top of her dress so that it cut deep into the folds of her throat. 'Yer understand me, NOW!'

'But I haven't got any cash!' pleaded Billie. 'You must believe me!'

His eyes suddenly narrowed. 'Yerse, I've suddenly realised I'm doin' this arse-about-face, ain't I?' he snarled as he released Billie. 'Silly old me.' He slid his hand into his pocket and pulled out a short-bladed knife with which he casually dug out a piece of the table. He then pulled the screaming maid onto his lap and tugged her backward until she lay helplessly across him. ''Ow would yer like a piece outa her windpipe? Say abaht the same size as that piece o'table, eh?'

'You scum!' cried Billie.

'I ain't got time fer compliments, darlin',' snapped Sidney. 'Watch.' He twisted the girl's face away from him and with the tip of his blade, casually drew a sharp line down the whole left side of her cheek. Four separate trickles of blood steadily threaded their way down to her jaw and then to the top of her white collar. Billie watched in horror as four crimson stains linked into one.

'Leave her alone, you filth! Just tell me what it is you want,' screamed Billie.

'Yer know what I want! It's cash! Or at least its equivalent an' I want it now!'

Billie ran to her handbag and tipped out the entire contents onto the breakfast table. There were four gold guineas plus seven or eight banknotes.

'I've got another two hundred pounds upstairs in the safe,' she said. 'Now, let the kid go.'

'That's more like it!' he smiled. 'But if yer goin' ter visit the safe, I fink I'll come along. Yer never know, there might be the odd little keepsake yer'd like ter give yer old friend Sidney afore he leaves yer for ever.'

Fifteen minutes later and three hundred pounds richer, to say nothing of a couple of thousand pounds worth of jewellery and enough food for a month-long siege, Sid Grechen had tied both Billie Bardell and the bloodstained maid to two kitchen chairs and bid them goodbye.

'Ain't yer gonna cuss me blind afore I go?' he asked Billie. 'It won't be the same unless yer do. I shall quite miss it.'

'Die slowly, you maggot,' she hissed.

As the door slammed and Grechen's footsteps faded away

on the gravel, Billie looked anxiously across at the maid. What little colour the girl had ever possessed had long faded, and slumped back open-mouthed on the chair, she was slipping slowly into unconsciousness.

'Elsie, Elsie, Elsie,' cried Billie, kicking against the girl's feet. 'C'mon, wake up, Elsie!' But in spite of all her efforts, the maid's chin sank lower and lower to her thin little chest.

Billie looked around frantically, seeking something, anything, that might prevent the maid passing out completely. Suddenly the telephone in the hall gave a shrill ring. As Billie watched helplessly, the girl gave a lurch and her eyelids flickered momentarily. This reaction gave new energy to the old music-hall star and she began to bounce her chair in the direction of the door, praying whoever it was did not ring off before she reached it.

The door was fortunately ajar, and, after kicking it wide open, she had bounced alongside the telephone just as it stopped ringing. The silence it left in its wake was overpowering. Billie slumped in frustration and looked back at Elsie. As she did so, the telephone sprang once more into life. There was only one thing for it, she had to take a chance. Lifting her legs as high as the bindings would allow, she swung her limbs sideways against it and sent the telephone and its base, tumbling to the floor. A tiny distant voice kept repeating 'Hullo, hullo' as she screeched back 'WAIT! WAIT!' in reply.

Slowly tilting her chair, she tensed herself as it gathered momentum and she crashed to the floor alongside the telephone. With one final wriggle she managed to position her face within inches of the mouthpiece and yell, 'Who's speaking?'

The voice left her almost speechless with delight. 'Billie?' it said, 'are you all right? What on earth's happening there?'

'Oh, Jim! Jim!' she blurted, 'thank God it's you!' And within seconds she had spilled out most of the story.

'Listen carefully,' he said once she had finished. 'I'm going to ring off now and telephone both the police and the ambulance service. Don't risk hurting yourself any more than necessary. Help should be with you in a few minutes. I'm in my office and I'm going to get a taxi right away. With any luck I could be with you in a half-hour. Whatever you do, don't try to release the maid until you are free yourself, otherwise you could make the situation much worse. Have you got all that? . . . Good! I'm ringing off now. I'll see you soon.'

Sure enough, the ambulance arrived within six minutes which was marginally ahead of the police. By now, Elsie had passed out completely. Once the ambulance attendant had released Billie, she became aware that her right shoulder had taken the full force of her fall and any movement made above her waist was agonisingly painful. Declining hospital treatment until Jim arrived, she watched anxiously as the ambulance crew slid Elsie Parker gently into the ambulance. Any relief she might have felt at this was counter-balanced by the sight of the blood seeping continually through the pad on the side of the girl's face.

'Will she be all right?' Billie whispered to the elder of the two ambulance men.

He nodded. 'Oh, she'll be fine physically, although she'll have a hell of a scar,' he said. 'But she looks the type of kid who may have great difficulty coping mentally, particularly after such a wicked attack.' He spread his hands wide and gave an exaggerated shrug. 'But who knows? At this stage, we can only hope.'

The two young policemen who had arrived did not seem to annoy Billie. It was the arrival of the detective inspector and his sergeant who were to cause the outburst.

'If you and your clods hadn't spent so long chasing around in circles arresting the wrong man, this might never have happened!' she screamed. 'That poor kid's face will haunt me for the rest of my life.'

'How d'you know we were chasing the wrong man?' asked Evans in a tone of irritable suspicion.

'I told her,' came a voice from the door as Jim Forsythe strolled briskly into the room. 'When I heard that Grechen had failed in his attempt to kill Claude Lines, I telephoned Miss Bardell to be on her guard. Once he realised his mistake, I knew Grechen would need to lie low for a while and would need as much money as possible. Where else would he go for it but here?'

'No, I don't see it,' argued Evans. 'Why should he return here? If anything, I should think this would be amongst the last places he'd call. What d'you know about this case that I don't?'

Jim stared briefly at Billy. 'It's no good, luv,' he said quietly. 'You'll have to tell them everything now. There's absolutely nothing to be gained by keeping it a secret any more.'

Evans had not once taken his eyes from Jim since he had arrived. 'Just what is it that I should know, Ex-Superintendent Forsythe?' he repeated pointedly.

Jim sighed deeply before replying. 'Grechen's been regularly blackmailing her and . . .'

'And he came here to restock his treasury, eh? That what you're saying?'

'Afraid so.'

'Of course you know the seriousness of what you've done, and that I'll have to report it?'

Jim nodded.

'And, as an ex-senior officer, you realise the position you've placed yourself in?'

Jim again nodded a reply.

'No, it was my fault!' cried Billie. 'You must believe me! I took advantage of our friendship. He told me what might happen if it was ever to come out but I was too bloody selfish to listen.'

'So you're saying he was fully aware of the risk right from the beginning?' Shaking his head sadly, Evans added, 'If I was you, Miss Bardell, I'd shut my mouth because you're not just digging him into a hole, you're burying him.'

Ignoring the pain from her shoulder, she suddenly ran to the detective, and pounding his chest, yelled, 'Why is it you're so bloody efficient now but you were so bloody useless when that scum killed my Alice!'

'Because, Miss Bardell, *when* that scum killed your Alice,' he almost whispered, '*someone* did not tell me all the facts, did they, Miss Bardell?' He then turned to Jim. 'And how come you were able to telephone her to say she was likely to be visited by Grechen so soon after his failed attempt to kill Lines?'

'Because I had just heard about it that very minute,' replied Jim.

'From *where* did you hear it? You were ahead of us and you're now a civilian. How could you possibly have known so soon?'

'Mr Evans,' said Jim politely, 'I may be a civilian but I *am* a private detective. One assumes I was employed for my expertise. Please give me some credit, eh?'

Evans said nothing for some moments but tapped his pencil lightly on the table.

'Okay, there's enough shit flying about at the moment, no sense increasing the volume. You don't know anything else I should be aware of by any chance?'

Jim gave a weak smile. 'No, but if I do learn anything, rest assured you'll be the first to hear.'

'Okay,' said Evans. 'You two better listen hard because you've caused me enough precious time as it is. Our first priority is to nail Grechen.'

'How about the other three blokes who did the actual murder?' asked Jim.

Evans pointed an admonishing finger and shook his head almost in disbelief. 'You really did have some good information, didn't you, Ex-Superintendent. Pity you didn't retire a little earlier. You might have been able to solve the whole damn case by yourself.'

Jim raised his hands in apology. 'Sorry to interrupt. Please continue.'

'Like I say, Grechen is priority but what your excellent informant obviously has not told you, Mr Forsythe, is that one of the three geezers who killed the plumber has already been nicked and, after a bit of leaning on, he's blown the whistle on his two mates and indicated that Grechen is doing a runner to relatives somewhere in Connaught in Eire.'

'That's great!' exclaimed Jim. 'But how did you catch him so soon?'

'I hate to say it,' confessed Evans, 'but it was by chance. Tower Bridge CID were turning his place over for some stolen underclothing and dresses when he returned home. He got the wrong end of the stick totally and they quickly realised there was more to it than a few frills and frocks. Anyway, it's about time we had some luck on this job. Right, now listen,' he said, turning to Billie. 'Firstly I'm getting someone to run you to hospital with that shoulder, and secondly I want you both at the nick for a statement. I warn you now, you'd better bring your sandwiches because you've got a hell of a lot to tell!'

Having been dropped off at casualty by a patrol car, Billie and Jim soon found themselves in the waiting room. It was there that she was first able to ask Jim how he managed to obtain his information so soon.

'It was David,' he told her. 'He telephoned me from a call box. Unfortunately I was out, otherwise I might have been able to warn you earlier and saved that poor kid's face. He left a message for me with the office secretary.'

'That was risky, wasn't it?'

'Well, she's a reliable girl. Besides, he didn't leave his name.'

She took his hands in hers and stared him straight in the eyes. 'Jim, I want the real truth now. How serious is this business of me not reporting the blackmail?'

'For you?' he asked. 'Not too serious at all. Everyone

knows it's stupid to pay blackmailers because they always come back. If you remember I told you that at the time, but no one's going to hang you if you don't report it.'

'You're not answering my question, are you? Okay, I'll ask you *again*! How serious is it for *you*, Jim Forsythe? You I'm talking about, no one else.'

He sniffed and rubbed his chin a couple of times. 'It's *very* serious.'

'So, what will happen?'

'No idea. Perverting the course of justice by assisting a blackmailer is not something that's common amongst retired superintendents, well not as a general rule. It's more a question of what they *can* do to me rather than what they *will* do.'

'So, what *can* they do to you then?'

'They can charge me. If they do, it'll probably be an Old Bailey job.'

'Will they, though? Will it go that far? After all, it wasn't your fault.'

He gave a wry smile. 'Billie, my sweet, it *was* my fault. I knew exactly the risk I was taking, so I've only myself to blame. But if I had to guess . . .'

'C'mon, c'mon,' she urged.

'Well, it could be an absolute gift for the new commissioner. You know, a new broom and all that? I mean, what could be better than taking over the metropolitan police and ensuring a superintendent is shoved away for a five-year stretch as one of your first ritual sacrifices? Alternatively, he may consider such action would be detrimental to the force as a whole. Now I'm retired he would be unable to punish me by dismissal. That only leaves prison or my pension.'

'They can't touch that, surely? That's yours, you've paid in for it.'

'Don't you believe it! The Home Office can stop that whenever they like. All they'd need is the nod from Trenchard.'

'Oh, Jim!' she cried. 'What have I done to you?'

'Well, at the moment, you haven't done anything. So let's not get too mournful. In the meantime, we'll need to get your shoulder fixed and our statements made, plus one other very vital matter.'

'And that is?' she queried.

'Your daughter,' he said. 'Because I think I'll give her a detailed dossier on the whole damn show this time. I'm certainly not going through the aggravation I went through last time I kept a secret from her. I'm not sure which of you is the more impossible when you feel you've been slighted, but I'm married to her.'

He was interrupted by the arrival of a small young nurse who breezed rapidly into the waiting room clutching a white card.

'Miss Bardell, please!' she called, glancing up and down the dozen or so waiting patients. As her gaze settled finally on Billie, she added, 'This way, madam,' and strode purposefully out of the room. Rising to her feet, Billie nodded admiringly at the disappearing girl. Turning to Jim, she whispered, 'Well I'm more impressed by this lot in one minute than I was with your old firm in six months. Wish me luck.'

As Jim heard her high heels fade down the corridor, he was, for the first time since his conversation with Evans, alone with his thoughts. No one knew better than himself the gravity of his situation. It would have been a serious enough matter at any time but with the new Trenchard regime, his outlook was positively grim. Unfortunately, should action be taken against him, it would be a double jeopardy and he was not sure which he dreaded most. Firstly there would be the law and secondly there would be Queenie. It seemed everything he tried to do for both her and her family was destined to explode in his face.

Weighing up his prospects, he considered the positive side first. After all, he was currently in work. Unless Scotland Yard were to insist on a full pound of flesh, then his employment should be fairly safe. But if he were to lose his pension, then that would be a considerable loss of income. Which in turn led him again to Queenie. Apart from genuinely loving her, he had nothing but admiration for her spirit and her ability to have survived the appalling poverty of her early years. But it was this ability that was now his biggest doubt. After all, she had been much younger in those days and, if he were to be imprisoned and lose his job, what then? For almost a decade she had accepted, even taken for granted, the good life he had been able to provide. Could anyone, even Queenie, emerge from the ashes twice? He doubted it. Yet in spite of all these considerations, he knew the whole thing was now out of his control. During his service in the force, he must have heard a hundred prisoners whine, 'Oh, if only I hadn't done that . . .' Well, now it was his turn, but the fact remained he had done *exactly* 'that' and with no one to blame but himself, 'that' would now take its toll.

The prime cause of these deep ruminations was currently being examined by six young male students and a mature registrar in a curtained cubicle in casualty. For Billie Bardell, perched in front of an attentive male audience with most of her torso exposed, it was quite reminiscent of old times. The main difference was that the present audience could touch anything at will and she wasn't obliged to sing.

'Yes, you, Mr Robbins,' said the registrar, pointing to a rather haughty young student. 'What do you make of this patient's shoulder?'

Robbins, deciding there was nothing like a good prod to begin a diagnosis, gave it his very best. This immediately caused an oath from the patient that at least three of the students had never heard before.

'Congratulations, Robbins,' said the registrar icily. 'With only one prod, you found the seat of the pain, incensed the patient and learned a naval expression that's been extinct for nigh on forty years. Masterly! You wouldn't care to diagnose the injury by any chance?'

'I'm not having that daft bugger touching me again,'

announced Billie defiantly. 'He's bloody dangerous!'

'Did you hear that unsolicited judgment, Robbins? The patient reckons you're bloody dangerous. I must say it's an observation I find hard to dispute.'

'Er— I'm sorry, sir. I didn't think I prodded that hard. Perhaps the patient is a trifle oversensitive?'

This was too much for Billie. Spinning round to face the student, she snapped, 'You'll be an extremely fortunate young man, Mr Robbins, if, in the fullness of time, you meet a woman who's been prodded more times than I have. The difference being, my dear Mr Robbins, that most men of my acquaintance have *known* how to prod. Whereas you, you shit-faced young oaf, have all the delicacy of a house brick.'

'I think that summed up the situation rather well, Mr Robbins, don't you think?' asked the registrar. 'And I would only add this advice to the next student from this group who examines this patient. I first saw her at the Royal Command Performance at the Palace Theatre in 1912 – as a matter-of-fact I still have the programme. But, if anyone had been rash enough to upset her at that time, the rest of the nation would have considered he qualified for a spell – not to say a lifetime – in the Tower of London. So be warned, Miss Bardell is still a national asset.'

Billie's anger vanished in exactly the amount of time it had taken the registrar to sum up. Her delight was further increased by his eventual personal medical attention.

'I think we can safely say it's rather a nasty sprain, Miss Bardell,' he said finally. 'Seeing we can't very well strap cold compresses all over such a location, I would just recommend a good rest and you should be all right in a week or so. I'm not sure exactly how much medical knowledge my students will have absorbed today, but I can assure you, they now have greater knowledge of the quality of the music hall than any other students that have passed through this hospital.'

As Billie bade her farewell in the treatment room and

approached the waiting room, Jim was amazed at the difference in her appearance.

'Why, Billie, you look great! What on earth have they done to you! You've shed ten years!'

'Half-a-dozen young men surrounded me, stripped me half-naked and gave me a right poking,' she said casually. 'Does wonders for a mature woman.' Rubbing her hands together, she added gleefully, 'Right, lead me to that pompous oaf, Evans, I'll take the whole bloody world on now.'

Detective Inspector Roger Evans had spent two hours quietly studying all the case papers he had amassed on Sidney Grechen. In his career to date, he could not recall such a mess. In spite of his angry words with Jim Forsythe and in spite of the stupidity of that man's actions, he knew his own procedures had not been blameless. In leaping to the early connection between Claude Lines and the original murder, he had made an uncharacteristic but nevertheless basic mistake in good detective work. Just because the early clues had led easily to Lines, that had been no reason for discounting all other leads. If truth were known, part of his fury at Jim Forsythe's suppression of evidence, had really been aimed at himself. Further thought was interrupted by the impressive balancing act of Detective Sergeant MacDonald who, by turning the door knob with one hand, carrying two mugs of tea in the other and a small plate of dripping toast between his dentures, had finally managed to enter the room.

'That's clever of you, Mac,' grunted Evans as the sergeant managed to land both mugs and most of the toast on the edge of the desk.

'Oh, this is nothing, guv,' said MacDonald cheerily. 'You should see what I can hang from the end of me dick.'

'Spare me such details,' muttered Evans. 'In any case, I wasn't talking about your circus act, I was referring to your ability to know when I'm desperately in need of sustenance.' Reaching out for a mug, Evans then added, 'Sit down a minute, I'd like to talk.' Pulling the mug and the plate of toast towards him, he continued, 'If I can go over this case again, you agree our main need is now Grechen?'

'Uh huh,' agreed MacDonald through a mouthful of crumbs.

'Well, if he's done a runner to Ireland, it's not going to be easy to get him back. The Micks are not the most cooperative of people right now. Personally, I think we're in for a long wait. So what I need to do is get as much of the paperwork for this case filed away until such time as Grechen reemerges. After all, if the bastard's away for some years, it probably won't even be us dealing with it.'

MacDonald's customary twinkling eyes took on an unusual seriousness. 'I'm a big boy, guv,' he murmured. 'I know the routine, so you don't have to beat about the bush. How about coming straight to the point?'

Evans gave a wry grin. 'Yes, sorry, Mac, that was a bit patronising, I suppose. Anyway, what I'm saying is this. Jim Forsythe was certainly a class one idiot, but I'm sure it wasn't for any pecuniary gain that he agreed not to mention the blackmail to us and . . .'

'Deep down, I bet he still fancies her, guv.'

'Mac!' exploded Evans. 'Will you please forget that that woman was your first boyhood lust and let me continue? Good! What I'm saying is this. If I make a point of putting his omission into my report, then it's going to be in that report permanently and sooner or later some eagle-eyed bugger is going to pounce on it. Forsythe could then be ruined, but for what? What would be the gain for *anyone*? It would make no difference to Grechen one way or the other and a good man would be destroyed.'

MacDonald drained his cup and sucked at his teeth before replying. 'D'you know, I've had intermittent hearing problems for some time now, guv,' he said. 'It's really quite puzzling. For example, I didn't hear a word of what you just said and neither did I fully hear your conversation at Miss Bardell's house earlier today. I've been wondering what to do for the best and I've suddenly had an idea. You see, before I came here, the switchboard girl said Billie Bardell has been released from casualty and should soon be here with Forsythe to make their statements. As you said, that could take some time, yes?'

Evans nodded in agreement.

'Very well. Then while they're talking to you, why don't I pop to the chemist and have my ears syringed? It'd save me sitting around listening to them and I could be as good as new after you've finished. Of course it means I won't be able to hear what they say, but I can always read their statements later, can't I?'

Before Evans could reply, a taxi pulled up outside the front of the station.

'What chemist were you thinking of?' he asked, glancing out of the window. 'Only I hear the one at New Cross is good. O'course it's not the nearest and it'll take you some time to get there but they say he's absolutely brilliant with eyes.'

'Er— it's not eyes, guv, it's ears. *Ears*, remember?'

'Oh, yes,' nodded Evans, 'as you say, *ears*. Apparently he's even better with ears! That's fortunate isn't it?'

MacDonald who had finally dislodged a lurking crumb, nodded his head. 'Oh, I'd say that sounds just about as fortunate as anyone can get, guv, it really does.'

23

By the winter of 1934, it had been more than three-and-a-half years since Noel Grechen's younger half-brother, Sidney, had first come to stay in the little village of Kilideran on the rugged west coast of Ireland. The magic of the brothers' first acquaintance had faded before the week was out. Their mother, Kathleen Grechen, had fled the town in 1889 never to return. Her husband and Noel's father, Daniel Grechen, had been hanged for murder two years earlier when he had taken part in the 'moonlighting' protests of the period. During these protests, graves were dug late at night in front of the houses of the landowners as a means of instilling terror. Daniel Grechen and his lifelong friend, Thomas Gaulty, had argued over the depth of the grave they were digging and, as a result, Daniel had virtually severed Thomas's neck with his spade. Unfortunately he was then too drunk to escape from the grave and was found there asleep by the owner next morning. He was hanged three months later.

The charitable sympathy shown to the widow by the community did not stretch to forgiveness once her pregnancy, by an English soldier and barely six months after her husband's demise, became known. She was hounded from the town and subsequently from the country. Within a few weeks she had arrived penniless, alone and hungry at the Central Mission in Stepney where she remained until she died during her confinement with Sidney. Though Sidney proved naturally bright at school, his constant moves rendered his short education meaningless and, though the Mission furnished him with the family address in Kilideran, he had never considered visiting until Vic Wainwright's head had struck the asphalt yard of Queen's Buildings.

It was true to say that few members of the Grechen family fell joyously on Sid's neck when he had arrived in Kilideran in the late spring of 1931. For a start, there was the in-built, small-village suspicion of any new resident. Then there was the fact that he bore no resemblance to the average Irishman in either dress or speech. However, on the credit side, even the most cynical of the family doubters had noticed certain family characteristics, the most pronounced of these being an intimidating ugliness and a violent temper.

It had been Sidney's plan to return to London as soon as he thought it safe. The problem was, the only telephone was the call box near the crossroads a mile out of the village and, with London five hundred miles away, he had no means of assessing the situation. In addition, what little word that did reach him, indicated that London's problems seemed no better than Kilideran's. Having finally landed a job as a carrier's assistant on a daily trip to the town of Castlebar, twenty miles distant, there seemed little point in returning to the capital.

Meanwhile, Jim Forsythe had done his best to investigate Sid's whereabouts, usually by swapping favours with fellow private detectives in the west of Ireland, but with every inquiry he had drawn a blank.

Detective Inspector Evans had even less success. The request for Grechen's search, arrest and extradition had been filed by the Connaught constabulary somewhere beneath three trays marked SWINE FEVER, FOOT & MOUTH and WARBLE FLY and never saw the light of day.

In desperation as much as anything else, Billie Bardell had taken numerous holidays in those parts and, whilst optimistically going on every listed excursion, had neither seen nor learned anything of Sidney Grechen.

During a Christmas stay at the Forsythes with David,

Grace, Benjamin and Julia in attendance, Queenie had suggested to her mother that it might be time to put thoughts of Sid Grechen to rest.

'It's been nearly four years now, Mother,' she pointed out. 'He's no nearer being caught than the day he vanished and it's like a cancer eating away at you. You must be aware of the toll it is taking, surely?'

'I honestly do appreciate what you're saying,' replied Billie, 'but you couldn't be more wrong, really you couldn't.'

'It was my mother he murdered,' said Julia quietly. 'So I know how you must feel, but Queenie is right, Miss Bardell, you can't let it eat away at you for ever. There comes a time when you must pick up the pieces and get on with your life.'

'No,' said Billie emphatically. 'I know you mean well, but you are so wrong.'

'But why are you so determined about this?' asked Jim.

'Because it's my reason for continuing to live,' she said simply. 'Look, you must have known me and my earlier lifestyle, for what – twenty-five years now?' He nodded. 'Then would you agree I wasn't cut out for some genteel dotage in a retirement home? I mean, you can't see me knitting by the communal fireside and reminiscing about Queen Victoria, can you now? Be honest!'

'I still don't see what that's got to do with it, Mother!' cut in Queenie with a hint of irritability. 'We all know of your past, me more than most, I might point out! But that still doesn't make you unique. Julia has more reason to mourn the passing of Alice, but even she's come to terms with it. Why can't you?'

'Because Julia is a lovely girl and is *young*!' replied Billie sharply. 'Look, I assure you I am not being self-pitying. I have lived my life to the full and, if I died this minute, I could have no regrets. Other than my childhood, I have not known poverty or ill health and I've hardly regretted a minute and there's few can say that.' She looked across the room to where Benjamin was playing with a dozen lead soldiers in a little wooden fort. 'For most women of my age, just the hope of watching that young man grow up would be enough. Well, in my case, it isn't. There is still one more thing I must do, one more thing I must live for. It is vital to me to be in possession of all my faculties on the day they hang that maggot Grechen. I want to sit there every day in that court and just stare at him. Then, when the judge has the black cap dumped on his head, I want to cheer and shout to the murdering scum that at the exact second they hang him, I am going to sing with joy until my lungs burst. *That*'s why I can't put Sid Grechen at the back of my mind.' She looked around the now silent room.

'It's because it's only his death that keeps me alive, d'you understand now?'

The atmosphere in the room was so charged with emotion that even the child sensed it. Dropping his soldiers, he ran bewilderedly across to Grace and buried himself deep in her lap.

Julia then rose to her feet and walked across the room to where Billie sat with nostrils still flared. She stood legs astride in front of the older woman and pulled her head gently towards her. Laying her face against Julia's firm bosom, Billie Bardell wept as she had not done since childhood and the young girl quietly joined her.

Though Billie's emotions had put something of a damper on the yuletide celebrations, by the evening, with the reluctant Benjamin tucked firmly in bed, a thaw had taken place. Paper hats had been sensibly discarded. As Billie had tearfully stated, 'To cry with a paper hat on is as profane as buggering the King.' Queenie announced rather stuffily that personally she could not see the connection, but it was finally carried on a three-to-one vote and so four paper hats were tossed into the fireplace.

For Julia, the New Year was to be the start of her new career. She had completed her three years' training, plus most of a fourth year attached to a hospital, and now, from the 1st of January, she was to be released on the sick and lame of London.

'Where are you going to be nursing?' asked Queenie.

'Evalina Hospital in Southwark Bridge Road,' she replied proudly. 'It's a thirty-bed children's hospital and one of the best in the capital.'

'Evalina!' exclaimed Grace. 'Why, that's barely five minutes' walk from our flat.'

'I know,' nodded Julia. 'I've already had a look around there and I think half our customers come from your buildings.'

'And dare I ask about Duncan?' said Grace. 'Or do I take it you two don't see each other any more?'

'Well, our paths have been moving in different directions these last few years but we do keep in touch – nothing too serious, you understand,' she added hastily. 'But whenever he's due in town he writes to let me know and I try to get a couple of hours off.'

'You say "in town",' said Jim. 'So where is he now? Still at Windsor?'

'Good heavens, no!' replied Julia. 'He's not been there for years. He was in India up until a few months ago, but he's been in Malta for the last few weeks. He's a corporal now and the last time he wrote he said he might return to London for some course or other.'

'You still haven't really answered my question though, have you?' said Grace.

Julia gave a wry smile. 'Well, you know Duncan, don't you? I doubt if he's ever taken anything seriously in his life. Oh, I know I like the infuriating creature but I can't help feeling that he just strings me along. So many times now we have seemed to be on an even keel and then he does, or says, something totally insensitive or outrageous. Then I get angry, he laughs, and before I know where I am . . .' Her voice trailed off and she finished with a shrug.

'What surprises me most,' cut in Billie, 'is that I cannot recollect seeing you with anyone else. I've no wish to embarrass you, but you are quite a beautiful girl, you know. I can't believe you'd had no offers.'

'Well there is very little free time on the nurses' course you know and . . .'

'Come on,' chided Billie. 'You can't fob me off with that! They don't keep you in purdah in the Tower and there's always ways and means of getting out of any establishment if you want to see a good man – or even a wicked one, come to that.'

Julia chuckled before answering. 'I must confess that's right,' she muttered. 'My window was next to the dormitory drainpipe. Some nights more girls went over my sill than over the front doormat.'

'Were you one of them?'

'I have been,' she admitted. 'Oh, there's been the occasional bloke, I suppose, but perhaps I spent too long in Duncan's company. You have to remember I practically grew up with him. In my formative years we could hardly have been closer; he was everything to me. No matter how long it is since I've seen him, I always expect him suddenly to walk round the next corner, saying, "Hullo, kid, doing anything tonight?"'

'Meanwhile, I s'pose,' said Billie acidly, 'he's out turking half the dusky maidens of Bombay.'

'*Mother!*' snapped Queenie. 'What a thing to say to the girl!'

'Good God, woman!' replied Billie. 'She's a nurse! She's going to have to take such things in her stride. If she's nursing in south London, she'll probably find at least half her patients have the clap.'

'What! In a children's hospital!'

'She won't be in the damn hospital for ever, though, will she? Anyway, look at her. If you were a randy old consultant, wouldn't you like her in your clinic?'

'I definitely would!' Jim jumped in eagerly.

'Okay, okay,' said Queenie, 'I give in. But now your course is finished, are you going to look seriously for a mate or are

378

you going to dedicate yourself to your career?'

'Not forgetting to have some fun in the meantime,' added Billie quickly.

'It's not easy,' said the girl quietly. 'I've tried, really I have. But whoever I'm with, I can't help thinking to myself, I wonder what Duncan is doing now? Or what Duncan would have said at this moment.'

'And there,' said Billie, 'I think we should leave it. The girl's obviously a romantic idiot. Once I've shot that maggot, Grechen, I'll also do her a favour and shoot Corporal Forbes. How's that?'

There was a murmur of approval all round.

Julia Giles had certainly been right about one thing. Duncan Forbes was certainly on his way home. Though exactly why he should be was a cause of some mystery to him. After India, he had quite enjoyed Malta. Compared with the baking hundred-plus heat of Bombay, Malta had been practically cool.

As the liner eased from her anchorage in the Grand Harbour at Valletta, he stared out of the porthole as first the Fort then St Elmo's point and lighthouse slipped slowly by. Turning on a due west course, the point was gradually replaced by a vast expanse of empty sea dotted by the occasional fishing boat. It was now next stop Gibraltar and a few days later, home, though 'home' was going to be something of a problem. There was a cuddlesome fortyish widow in Battersea who was always pleased to see him and her cooking was good too. Then there was the Scots girl who had a room and worked in Harrods, or at least she *did* the last time he was in town. If all else failed, there was always the barracks at Windsor. But if he had to make a choice, he thought he would give Miss Bardell a call. Firstly he would like very much to see her again and secondly she almost certainly had plenty of room, providing, of course, she still resided in the same place. There was also the puzzling difficulty of the reason for his return. He had been instructed to call at an address above a shop in Whitehall two days after he docked at Southampton. This gave him two nights to fill in before his interview. He then had another ten days before reporting back, presumably to Valletta.

In the last few hours of their trip to Gibraltar, the Moroccan sun beat down so fiercely on the port side of the ship that below decks became a gigantic oven. The breeze-swept deck seemed the only sensible place to be, but access was barred by an enormous tattooed matelot.

'Sorry, corp,' he growled. 'Officers and their families only.'

'Do only officers and their families sweat then?' asked Duncan. 'If so, that's a surprise. I can't speak for their families, but I haven't seen an officer capable of working up a sweat yet.' In spite of the intimidating presence of the sailor, Duncan did not back off an inch. The matelot scratched his head for a moment.

'Tell yer what. Let's look at this sensibly shall we, corp?' he said quietly. 'They're up there, you're down 'ere. That's the way it works, I'm afraid. Yer see, until you're one of them, you're always goin' to be down 'ere. Now you may think that's unfair an' it probably is, but that's the way the British Empire's worked for two hundred years and no matter 'ow you feel about it, I bet yer all the tea in China, that in years to come, no bleedin' history book is goin' to say that one Wednesday afternoon, six hours from Gib, one bleedin' corporal in the Life Guards, changed it all.' He gave a great sniff before adding, 'What d'you reckon?'

A huge smile broke over Duncan's face. 'I reckon you're dead right and one day, sailor, you'll be a better bloody admiral than Nelson.'

When they finally docked at Gibraltar, Duncan had intended to take the sailor ashore for a drink or two, but the boat came and went on the same tide, staying just long enough for three red-ribboned brass hats to disembark.

380

Duncan was not too distressed about this, seeing as it meant he would reach London that much earlier. Once clear of the Mediterranean, the cooler south-westerlies of the north Atlantic made life much more comfortable and within three days they were docking at Southampton.

Though he had left for India barely fourteen months earlier, he felt he had been away for an eternity. Even the newspapers appeared different. When he had left, they had been full of political problems and industrial unrest, but now there was a vast coverage of an Italian attack on Abyssinia and a comical-looking German called Hitler who Duncan thought bore an astonishing resemblance to Charlie Chaplin. Within three hours of landing at Southampton, he was in Waterloo searching for a telephone box.

'Duncan!' exclaimed Billie Bardell. 'Of course, you can stay here! . . . For as long as you like, sweetie! . . . You'll find a few changes, though . . . Never mind about that now, I'll tell you when you arrive . . . Get a taxi, I can't wait to see you . . . Nonsense! . . . I tell you I'll pay the fare . . . Promise me now? Good, I'll get Elsie to run you a bath . . . Elsie? . . . Oh, she's my new maid. You're going to tie her in knots . . . It's wonderful to hear from you again. Be quick!'

Duncan watched as the shillings popped up regularly on the taximeter. He really did feel bad about Billie's gesture concerning the fare, but he knew if he paid it himself so soon after landing, it would devastate his budget. So, after a couple of miles, he ceased to stare at the meter and felt much better.

It was an hour, almost to the minute, before the taxi wheels crunched the old gravel drive. As he absorbed the scene, he was aware that part of the lawn he had once tended so lovingly had been turned into a gravelled car park with a sprinkling of small saloon cars scattered untidily around.

At the entrance to the house, he saw Billie Bardell standing in the doorway alongside a wisp of a girl in maid's uniform.

He tried quickly to calculate the last time he had seen Billie, but the taxi halted at the door before his calculations were complete. She had certainly changed, of that there was no doubt. He had noticed it as soon as the cab turned in at the gate. Though her figure had hardly altered, there were facial lines where none had been before. Yet, as he drew near and saw her features light up, she was indisputably the old Billie Bardell.

He had barely stepped from the taxi before she seized him and crushed him in an embrace that surprised him by its intensity. He happily reciprocated because he had always been fond of her and she had never once failed to be kind to him. Finally releasing her, he turned to the maid.

'Is it our turn now, Elsie, or do I wait until we have our bath together?' he asked solemnly. 'You see, when I was here before, it was always a perk that I slept with the maid. Still applies, I assume?'

Elsie hunched her shoulders, crossed herself quickly then clutched her hands tightly together in front of her.

'Oh, marm,' she pleaded. 'Listen to the heathen! And me having had me bath last Sunday! Is this the wicked one you told me about?'

Billie swung a powerful blow at the straight-faced Guardsman. 'Listen, you bugger,' she said sharply. 'It was you who lost me my last maid. As welcome as you are, if you lose me this one, I'll cut your throat.' Turning to Elsie she added, 'Take no notice of him, luv. He's nothing but a bloody torment. Just get us something to eat and I'll deal with him.'

It was obvious that Elsie was not placated in the slightest by Billie's assurances. However, in spite of her doubts, and within a few minutes, she presented a plate of sandwiches at the dining-room table.

Billie reached for the teapot and said, 'Right, now tell me all your news.'

'Never mind about my *news*,' said Duncan sharply. 'How

about my *lawn*? What vandal's turned it into a car park?'

'If you listen carefully,' explained Billie, 'you might just work it out for yourself.' Tilting her head, she cupped an ear. 'Hear it?'

Frowning, he listened. 'A piano?' he said. 'Where from?'

'From the new conservatory, of course,' she answered smugly. 'As from a year ago, I've lived in a music school. Sometimes you can hear a piano, sometimes a violin. Other times it's like the massed bands of the Brigade of Guards, but whatever it is and however loud it is, I love it! I absolutely bloody love it!'

'But why?' exclaimed Duncan.

'It was not my doing,' she said. 'It was the estate. They finally decided to eject me, so I contested it. My solicitor then dug up all sorts of twists and turns that no one knew existed. It was getting so confusing and expensive that all parties finally decided on a thirty-year lease to a residential music school. I came out of the deal with a good-sized ground-floor flat, access to the grounds and a maid for the duration of the lease.'

'And that suits you?' he asked.

'I should say it does!' she cried enthusiastically. 'I've rarely been happier. I have the run of the grounds, the music, the company and I even know how long I have left to live! Twenty-nine years,' she said, forestalling his obvious question. 'After all, there'd be no point in my moving house then. I mean, if I'm still around, I shall be too bloody old. So I'll probably go for a long walk into the sea. On a nice day, of course,' she added.

'So all Grechen's blackmailing would have been in vain, anyway?' he asked.

'That's the only black spot,' she agreed sadly. 'It wouldn't have made any difference to my poor Alice, but it would have saved me the second visit from the scum. Financially, he cleared me out for a year. Still . . .' she suddenly perked up brightly and raised her cup high. 'We shouldn't talk about him on such a happy day, should we? Here's to you, Duncan, and, dare I say, Julia?'

He laughed and also raised his cup. 'Well, to Julia, anyway.' He chuckled. 'Does anyone know where she is these days?'

'Oh, yes,' answered Billie. 'And if your next question relates to her marital status, then no, she's still single.'

'Julia is never likely to be anything else,' smiled Duncan. 'She's a great girl, she really is, but for the life of me, I don't know who could live with her.'

'Surely, *you* could?'

'Least of all me! I like to feel free to answer folk in whatever way they merit, but with Julia, I always feel I should run every word through a sieve first to ensure she can't possibly take offence. I've decided I couldn't live like that.'

'Yet you say you like her?'

'Oh, yes,' he agreed. 'And if I was really honest, I might even tell you I loved her. But that wouldn't make it better, would it? If anything, it'd make it a hundred times worse. This way we can see each other from time to time and enjoy ourselves without any ties. Afterwards, if she wishes, she can always have one of her predictable explosions. She can then storm out, a suitable time will then elapse and some day in the future we can do the whole thing again. But we couldn't possibly do that if we were to *love* each other. You see, when you actually love someone, a row is a very serious business indeed.'

'Duncan Forbes!' she cried. 'I've never heard such garbled nonsense in my life. It's just an excuse you've come up with for not making a long-term commitment.'

'Er—just a minute,' he said quietly. 'How about your own love life? I hate to say this, but you of all people are not in a position to preach to anyone. People who have conservatories shouldn't throw stones, you know.' By her immediate reaction he thought he would be having a fight on his hands, but within seconds she smiled and nodded an agreement.

'Truce?' she offered.

'Truce,' he echoed.

'So what are you going to do. Are you going to contact Julia? I have the address of both the hospital and the nurses' home.'

'No. Well not just yet anyway. Being away for some time, I wouldn't mind taking a day or so to get the feel of London again. Once I've had this interview, I have ten days before I report back. Perhaps I'll see her then.'

'Report back where? Malta?'

He responded with a puzzled frown. 'That's the point,' he said. 'I really don't know. I've been asked to see a—' he quickly opened a small pocket diary '—a Major Baker at an address in Whitehall. I can't think why I've had to come all this way to see him, but no one in Malta could help. They just shrugged and told me to treat it as a lucky break and enjoy myself while I'm here. So that's what I propose to do.'

'Would you care to stay here at my musical academy while you are in London? You're quite safe. I do have a spare room.'

'Curses, foiled again,' he chuckled, but then more seriously, 'well, certainly until I've seen the major. After that, who knows? But you're sure you don't mind?'

'Providing you cease frightening my maid, you can stay for ever. Can you drive?'

'After a fashion, yes.'

'Good, because I've got myself a little Morris Eight. If you've got tomorrow free, how about a drive and a picnic?'

'You're on.'

The picnic with Billie had been a perfect day. The sun had been warm, the traffic reasonable, the food excellent and the location, a riverside spot near Cookham, quite lovely. They had lain in the sun relaxed in each other's company. After an early conversation, they had felt no need for further talk and each just basked in the other's presence. It was a perfect friendship of an older woman and a younger man. As they lay, side by side staring idly up at the slow-moving clouds, Billie spoke the first words between them for almost a half-hour.

'I never thought I would hear myself say this,' she murmured, 'but now that I'm not trying any more, I'm finding a whole new peace of mind. If this is my future, I think I'm going to like it.'

'Not trying what?' mumbled the dozing Duncan. 'And what is it you're going to like?'

'The new me, of course,' she explained. 'Many years ago my daughter accused me of being an alley cat who collected scalps. Her metaphors may have been a bit mixed but the point was well made. I suppose you could say age has now caught up with me, though I'd prefer to say it's because I've become pleasantly serene. Anyway, I've slowly begun to realise I've got nothing to prove. D'you know, some men are actually nice blokes? You, for instance.'

Duncan turned towards her. 'Well, thanks, coming from you that's a rave review. Look,' he said glancing furtively around, 'as there's only you and me here, and as you think I'm a "nice bloke", and as you're "pleasantly serene" . . .' He turned and lightly kissed her shoulder. 'How about . . .' he paused to give another searching glance round, 'how about telling me your real age?'

'Duncan Forbes!' she exploded. 'Julia was right. You're a maddening, infuriating bastard!'

He roared with laughter before leaning forward and, lifting her chin, planting a warm kiss full on her lips. 'Billie Bardell,' he said, with all trace of laughter gone, 'nine years ago, when I was a very green and inexperienced young man, you taught me more about women in two weeks than most men learn in a lifetime. Not once during that period did I ever see you as a scalp-collecting alley cat, in fact I thought you were everything a real woman should be. So whatever happens, now or in the future, I will never see you as anything else. Now, if we've totally done with all this maudlin stuff, perhaps you'll shut up and let me doze. I've a big day ahead tomorrow.'

24

As the bus slowed to take the corner of Trafalgar Square and Whitehall, Duncan trailed a leg from the platform and jumped into the road. Miscalculating the speed, he staggered for some yards before righting himself by clutching a lamp-post. Feeling the gaze of a watching policeman, he felt obliged to give the constable a sheepish grin. A wave of relief surged through him as he realised how close he had come to attending his interview dabbing a bloodied nose every few seconds. Composing himself, he strode briskly past the shop fronts before coming to number 19. Appalled by its tattiness, he couldn't decide if the premises he sought were a mysterious secret abode, or if the major who was to interview him was so unimportant in the Whitehall hierarchy that he merited only a room above a derelict shop. Yet, if that was the case, why had they gone to the expense of shipping him two thousand miles for an interview?

In keeping with the anomalous address, the entrance was not in Whitehall at all but a few yards down a side street. It was a narrow green door badly in need of paint. There was nothing to distinguish it from a multitude of other doors of similar ilk except perhaps the nameplate BAKER situated high up on a bell push on the left of the doorframe.

He pushed the bell and, unable to hear a response, was about to repeat the exercise when he heard footsteps approaching. The door eventually opened to reveal an extremely tall beanpole of a woman of some forty years who, because of her stoop, appeared to view the world permanently across the top of her spectacles. Duncan thought she was the plainest woman he had ever seen, except for a glorious mass of jet-black hair that was gathered severely back into a bun.

'Can I help you?' she smiled.

'Er— I'm here to see a Major Baker,' began the young man. 'But I'm not sure if I've got the right . . .'

'Your details?' she asked, cutting into his explanation.

Noting she said 'details' and not 'name', he immediately decided he had the correct address and replied 'Corporal Duncan Forbes, Life Guards.'

'This way,' she replied, turning towards a long stairway and leaving him to follow.

Duncan had not noticed how high the premises were, but by the number of steps he climbed, he guessed their destination was near the top. Though they passed many doors, all were green in colour and tight shut without a chink of light showing beneath them. Finally they came to the top of the staircase and there, beside a sink and an ancient gas stove, was an opened door that led into a tiny windowed room littered with files, all of which were labelled COUNTRY HOLIDAY FUND and CHILDREN'S CHARITIES. In the centre of the room was a cluttered desk with a small typewriter and an old daffodil-type telephone.

'Go straight in,' said the woman, nodding to yet another green door in the far corner. 'Major Baker is expecting you.'

On entering the second room, Duncan's first thought was that if there was one thing that Major Baker did not resemble, it was an army major. A slumped, weary, fattish middle-aged figure, he bent over his desk studying one of the many newspapers that lay strewn across the top of it. He seemed to keep the pose until he was sure Duncan had absorbed every detail before he finally looked up. The major was not in uniform. For that matter, he did not look as if he had ever been in uniform. His grey trousers were crumpled and so was his white wing-collared shirt, or what one could see of it below a grimy and stained grey cardigan. He wore a skimpy knotted blue tie that sported an intricate striped pattern in the gaudy colours that could have been of some club, but its name was half buried under the cardigan. He had no hair on the top of his head but the two thick bushy tufts above his ears were flattened and greased sideways across the scalp.

'Sit down, Corporal,' the man said in a flat, Home Counties accent. 'Good journey?'

'Er – yes,' replied Duncan, unsure whether the scruffy figure in front of him merited the title of 'sir'.

'I'm Major Baker. I've sent for you because I'm sure you could be of use to us.'

Having had the rank of major confirmed, Duncan then decided to throw in a few 'sirs' just to let the major know he had not forgotten his discipline. 'Sir,' he acknowledged, before adding, 'in what way, sir?'

'Before I answer that, Corporal, I'd like to confirm that your personal details I have here are correct.' Baker glanced down at some papers for a few minutes then fired out the questions. 'You're single and unattached and have addresses in London you could give as your own if needed?'

'Sir!'

'You could, if the army required, take an extended break and earn your own living?'

'Er – yes, sir.'

'You're free of any convictions and you are not on records anywhere other than your army record?'

'Sir!'

'You could, if need be, return to your unit after a spell with another unit, and not tell anyone of the duties you had been recently undertaking?'

'Sir!'

'Very well. I will now outline all you'll need to know at this stage.' Baker slid three of the newspapers across the table to Duncan and the young man saw that a collection of items had been ringed with a red pencil. 'Read carefully and tell me what you think.'

There were about five or six pieces of varying lengths, each of which referred to an organisation known formerly as The New Party, but now as the British Union of Fascists. 'Basically,' said the major, 'I want you to join this organisation. You'll report to me when the need arises. I understand you're a gardener, correct?'

'Sir!' replied Duncan reaching for the newspapers.

'Good, sounds a perfect cover. Meantime, can I interest you in a cup of tea?'

Duncan was already deep in the first of the cuttings and barely grunted a reply.

'I'll take that as yes,' said Baker as he cupped a hand to his mouth and yelled towards the door, 'tea, Peg, please!'

A muffled female response was just audible.

Although much of the reportage was duplicated, Duncan took his time and devoured every word. 'I had no idea this new movement was so large, sir,' he murmured. 'How many members are there?'

'That's one of the things I shall be expecting you to discover. Now, as to identity. According to what I've discovered, your work as a gardener for a Miss Bardell in Hampstead ceased when you joined the Life Guards. In other words, you had no occupation between the time you left her employment and your joining the army.' He drummed his fingers for a moment. 'For our purposes, this is really ideal but, this Bardell woman – is she discreet?'

'She invented the word, sir,' said Duncan emphatically.

'Uh huh,' nodded the major. 'And if need be, d'you think she would be prepared to swear that you have never left her employment and, more importantly, agree to this without being given a reason?'

'If I ask her, she will.'

'You seem very sure of her,' said Baker, referring back to the papers in front of him. 'Why so positive?'

'I've known her through some pretty turbulent times and I'd trust her with my life,' Duncan said quietly.

'If I were you,' responded the major, 'I wouldn't say that lightly. You may well have to. Still, let's not be too pessimistic at this stage. Listen carefully. Not only will you use that address when you enrol for the BUF but you will also use your own name. There's less chance of a mistake that way. There is a recruiting office in Bethnal Green and I'd like you to attend there first thing Monday morning.'

'Can I ask a couple of questions, sir?'

Waving an arm, the major answered, 'The floor's yours.'

'Thank you,' replied Duncan. 'Of all the people you could have chosen for this task, why me?'

'You were only chosen after an exhaustive search of our records. I did not want to use a skilled intelligence officer because I have no idea how long this task might take. It could be three weeks, it could be four years. With the government cutting our estimates so savagely each month – well – to put it bluntly, as a corporal, you're less expensive and more expendable. But don't think I've chosen you lightly,' he added quickly. 'You have much in your favour. You're single, you don't panic easily and, according to records, you're a sensible chap who can handle himself.'

'What happens about my pay, sir?' asked Duncan. 'I'm almost skint as it is.'

'I must say this has presented quite a problem,' admitted Baker as his secretary carried in a loaded tea-tray. 'For a start you are going to need cash to tide you over. So what I've finally been able to manage is the temporary pay of a substantive staff sergeant plus five pounds a week expenses. It would be of assistance to me in maintaining this more than generous payment, if you did not claim the full expenses *every* week.'

'How much can I claim and how often?' asked the guardsman, reaching for a custard-cream biscuit.

Baker gave a loud guffaw. 'There, you see, that's one of the reasons for your selection. You summed up your priorities in some half-dozen words. I like that.'

'You may like it, sir, but you still haven't told me how much or how frequent?'

'Did you hear that, Peg?' asked the major looking up at the secretary. 'Impressed?'

She looked thoughtful as she poured the tea and replied, 'Just keep it a few pennies *under* five quid each week, Corporal. That'd convince pay branch of your integrity.'

'If I'm to submit a claim for a few pennies *under* to impress with my integrity, wouldn't they be even more impressed if I billed them for a few pennies *over* for roughly the same number of times?'

The woman did not reply until she had filled both cups with tea. Then, raising her eyes to the major, she replied, 'Yes, sir, I'm impressed.'

'Right, Corporal,' said the major. 'The first thing you'll need to learn is my telephone number. But rule one is do *not* write it down and, for the purposes of outsiders, we are a voluntary transport organisation dealing with outings for underprivileged children which you assist from time to time.' He paused long enough to drain his cup before continuing. 'A lot of your work for us cannot be planned, so you will need to make your own instant decisions. Don't be afraid to do so, that's why you've been chosen. Now, if you'd care to spend a few minutes with Miss Thornbury, she will give you most of the details that you'll need to know. I would like to hear from you, say,' he studied a calendar for a moment, 'a week from now. By the way, don't be in too much of a hurry. A gradual acceptance by these people would be ideal. You are not an agent as much as a listening post. So be discreet and don't take unnecessary risks. Good luck, Corporal, and I look forward to hearing from you.'

As he rose to his feet to shake hands, Duncan was amazed at just how huge the man was. He wasn't just fat he was also some six-and-a-half feet in height and probably some twenty stone in weight. In spite of himself, Duncan knew his surprise was apparent.

'Yes,' added the major, 'that's something else you'll need to learn – how to conceal surprise. You can see now why they made me a Whitehall Warrior.'

The subsequent interview with Peg Thornbury took far longer than Duncan had anticipated. He was surprised at just how thorough it had been but after some ninety minutes he finally emerged into a sunny Whitehall. His first instinct was to contact Julia but if she was nursing, he thought he might not get too friendly a reception, particularly if she was surrounded by sick screaming kids. The sight of the underground station at Charing Cross quickly reminded him he needed to visit Bethnal Green before he could even start on this new aspect of his career. It was true the major had suggested Monday morning as a good time to enrol but he had also implied that an ability to make decisions was also an asset. Well, there was no time like the present, so, quickly making his first decision he was soon on his way.

Some thirty minutes later, he had alighted from the Central Line train at Bethnal Green station, and was genuinely surprised how different he felt. In spite of the reminder that he was basically a listening post, he actually felt like a super spy, though whether a super spy would actually enrol at a place like Bethnal Green was arguable. One pet illusion that had certainly been shattered was the reputed glamour of the job. If he had thought Baker's office had been seedy, it was the Taj Mahal in comparison to the office of the British Union of Fascists. The main door to the premises had not seen a coat of paint since it was hung and had obviously been chosen for its solidity rather than its appearance. Neither did it take a genius to fathom that the pair of thickset scruffy loiterers near the front steps were security. As the first one made to challenge him, the second one moved round to Duncan's rear and out of his immediate sight. After being searched, Duncan was ushered into an outer office where an attractive but icy-looking blonde of some thirty-five years fired a barrage of questions at him across a heavily grilled counter.

'Wait here,' she finally instructed curtly and as she disappeared through a door at the rear, he could hear muffled voices. After a short time she reemerged to announce, 'Mr Stanton doesn't see people without an appointment but he has a brief gap in his schedule and will see you now.' She lifted the counter flap and snapped, 'You're lucky.'

Stanton? thought Duncan. Now where had he heard that name before? He was barely into the room when he knew exactly where he had heard it. It was the night Jim Forsythe had driven them back to Hampstead and a beer bottle had winged its way towards the car. David had claimed it was Lofty Stanton who had thrown it. So this is what he had progressed to?

'I understand you wish to enrol in our party,' said Stanton, leaning back in his chair and placing his fingertips together. 'I hope you know it's not as easy as that? We're not like the communists, you know, we're very selective and we don't want thugs. We'll need to know a great deal about you first. So, what can you tell me?'

That I'm a spy, thought Duncan before answering. He recounted his work as a gardener and of his voluntary work for children's charities.

'You'll be prepared to wear a uniform?' said Stanton.

'I'd be proud to wear a uniform!' replied Duncan fiercely.

'Uh huh,' nodded Stanton thoughtfully. 'And how about violence? You see, whilst we don't approve of it, we mustn't show weakness should it arise. Our policy is not to strike the first blow but, once that blow *is* struck, then we hit our opponents in every way possible – in self-defence of course,' he added hastily.

'Oh, of course,' echoed Duncan. 'And that sounds very fair to me. That way they can't complain.'

'Quite,' acknowledged Stanton. 'But our enemies must know from the first instant that we will retaliate and that we are the boss. Therefore, once we strike back, we must show no mercy.' He glanced down at a note. 'I shall need to send a deputy to confirm your address and to check out what you have told me. We can't enrol you until that happens, particularly as it's a fairly exclusive location. I take it that neither you nor your employer will have objections to that?'

'None at all.'

'Good.' Raising his head from his notes, Stanton stared straight into Duncan's eyes and held his gaze for some seconds. 'I take it you are a hundred per cent Anglo-Saxon?'

Duncan was puzzled and it showed. 'Well, I'm a quarter Scottish, if that's the same thing.'

'The movement will doubtless overlook that,' smiled Stanton. 'But what I'm really driving at is your address. I take it you are aware of the high proportion of Jews in that area? Your employer is not Jewish or has Jewish connections, by any chance?'

'She's never mentioned it and I've certainly never seen any.'

'Okay, I'll accept that for the time being. However, should anything to the contrary come to light, you will be dismissed from the organisation immediately. Understand?'

'Of course.'

'Do you have any questions you wish to ask?'

Duncan was about to say no when he had a sudden thought. 'There is one.'

Stanton nodded.

'I've only ever seen your actions reported in the press,' said Duncan. 'And in my experience the press is notoriously inaccurate. Do you have any meetings or demonstrations scheduled in the next week or so? You see, I would like to come along, just for experience, so to speak. I thought I might get a better idea of your philosophy that way.'

Stanton stretched across his desk and briefly studied a list. 'Until you've been fully accepted, you would of course be there unofficially,' he said, 'but you're most certainly welcome to come along as a spectator and sympathiser. We hold our weekly meetings in Victoria Park Square every Tuesday evening at 7.30 p.m. But we have a little protest meeting tonight in the Tower Bridge Road. Why don't you come to that? You'd probably be surprised how efficiently it's run.'

'Excellent!' said Duncan enthusiastically.

'Very well,' said Stanton, rising to his feet. 'You seem just the sort we're looking for. So, if your application passes muster, we'll be seeing each other quite soon. G'bye.'

It was with a great sense of accomplishment that Duncan made his way back to the underground station. It was barely four in the afternoon and he had already survived two interviews. He had been accepted by one organisation and was quietly confident of being accepted by the other. Considering that eight hours earlier he had had no idea of what the day had in store, he was justifiably pleased.

He decided to step out briskly for Hampstead to avoid the evening rush hour and it was therefore a little after 5 p.m. that he was crunching up the gravel drive to the distant accompaniment of Mozart's Horn Concerto.

'Ahah, Elsie!' Duncan exclaimed, catching sight of the maid as she made a vain attempt to conceal herself behind the kitchen door. 'Is it too late for afternoon tea or shall we settle for two hours of wild sex instead?'

'Duncan Forbes!' came Billie's voice from the dining room. 'If you frighten my maid once more – just *once* more – I shall circumcise you with a paving mallet. That's a promise!'

'Just the lady I want to see,' he replied cheerfully. 'I want to talk to you.'

'Seems everyone wants to talk to me today,' she sniffed. 'So what's *your* problem?'

'Everyone?' he echoed. 'Who's everyone?'

'Oh, I dunno,' she shrugged. 'Some woman rang me up an hour or so ago and said she was working for government security and she needed to speak to me urgently.'

'This woman, did she give her name?'

'No, and I got so annoyed I forgot to ask.'

'What was her voice like? Was it sharp and abrupt?'

'It was certainly that, the pompous cow. I hate being patronised, so I'm afraid I wasn't too responsive. That's probably why the second caller rang.'

'Second caller?'

'Yes. He said he was also from government security and he needed to speak to me. He's calling here tonight – in person, as a matter of fact.'

'Did he give his name?'

'Er – Stainton, or something like that, I think it was.'

'You don't think it was Stanton?'

'Yes, Stanton. Of course, that was it!'

'You've met Mr Stanton before,' he told her. 'He threw a beer bottle at us the night Jim Forsythe took us home. Remember?'

'Yes, of course! But he was just a thick oaf! How could he possibly be in government security?'

'He's not! But don't let that bother you because I have an important request to make of you.'

'Oh, good! Is it for those two hours of wild sex?' she asked hopefully.

'Er – no, I'm afraid it isn't,' he chuckled, 'but you'd have my eternal devotion in exchange for a cheese and pickle sandwich.'

'God, how boring,' she said raising her eyes. 'You can stuff your eternal devotion. Just tell me what it is you want me to do.'

Without disclosing too much, Duncan told her sufficient to get by.

'That's excellent!' she enthused. 'It'll be the first excitement I've had since I saw that flasher by the bowling green. Just think – as I'm reciting lie after lie to Mr Stanton, I shall inspire myself with memories of his beer bottle. Good enough?'

'Good enough, most certainly,' he echoed. 'To be on the safe side, I shall leave here about an hour before he's due. In the meantime, will you give me the telephone directory? I'll ring Julia.'

Duncan had guessed his day had to go wrong sometime and now was the moment.

'Nurse who?' snapped an angry voice at the end of the line.

'Nurse Giles,' he repeated. 'Er— I take it you *are* Evalina Children's Hospital?'

'That's *exactly* who we are!' said the voice. 'It's a children's hospital, not a paging service. If you think we have nothing better to do than run around searching for nurses, you have another think coming.'

'But how do I get in touch with her?' he pleaded.

'Write!' came back the angry reply.

'But I've come all the way from Malta just to see her,' he lied.

'Then you should have *written* from Malta, shouldn't you?'

'Who is this speaking?' he asked as his temper rose.

'Matron!' said the severe voice. 'Do you wish to impart *your* identity?'

'Good God, no!' he exclaimed. 'She hates me enough as it is. Just tell her I've developed amnesia and I don't know who I am, there's a sweetie.'

With a sigh of relief, he slammed down the telephone.

'I think I got the gist of that,' said Billie. 'I thought you were a bit optimistic speaking to the matron. Nevertheless, I think it'd be better if you weren't here when Stanton arrives. Why don't you try meeting the girl when she finishes duty at eight?' She glanced up at the clock. 'You've plenty of time.'

'But I'm not sure if she's working today, or for that matter, even what shift she's on,' he protested.

'Typical man,' she said. 'All you offer are excuses and there was I thinking you loved the girl.' She suddenly took him by the wrists. 'Look, you've very little to lose. You've got to be away from here before Stanton calls, so if you go to the Evalina and she's not there, it's no great loss. But if you go and she is there, think how impressive that'll be? What girl could resist devotion like that?'

'You're right!' he agreed. 'You can even have my cheese and pickle sandwich!'

Ten minutes later, as Duncan stood soaping himself beneath the cool shower, he suddenly became more and more convinced that he would see Julia that evening. It was only something he had built up in his own mind yet by the time he had reached Hampstead station, not a shadow of doubt remained. Finally alighting at the Elephant and Castle station, he strolled confidently along to the Evalina Hospital. With ten minutes to spare, he sat opposite the main door on the edge of the old granite horse trough and ran his fingers idly through its cloudy water.

It was a few minutes after eight o'clock when the first trio of cloaked nurses hurried out. 'Excuse me,' he called, 'is Julia Giles still inside?'

The question caused a giggle amongst the group but it was at least answered by a triple nod. A trickle of nurses then increased to a steady flow before fading to just an occasional one. Finally the heavy old studded door creaked open to reveal a trim figure who paused to look up at the darkening sky and the fine spots of rain.

'Julia?' he called as she began to open an umbrella.

'It's true! It *was* you!' she exclaimed. 'Oh, isn't that so bloody typical of you, Duncan Forbes? I don't see the skies over you for months on end, then when you graciously decide to show up, it's without warning – *and* you upset Matron!'

'I'm sorry, but I've been waiting here and . . .'

'And d'you know *why* you've been waiting there?' she cut in angrily. 'Well, I'll tell you. You've been waiting there because I've just spent fifteen minutes of my own valuable time in Matron's office being torn to shreds because my boyfriend – my *boyfriend*, mark you, and what a joke that is – tried to telephone me at work!'

Duncan abruptly shot up both hands in surrender. 'I've suddenly realised why I upset you so often,' he said, dramatically falling to his knees. 'It's because you look so damn beautiful when you're furious that it's instinctive.' Leaning forward a fraction, he placed his face almost level with the hem of her uniform. 'And, in addition, you have stunning legs.'

With his head now so accessible, she could not contain herself and promptly began to batter both sides of it with such fierceness that she knocked him sideways to the now wet pavement. 'You-you-bastard-you—' she began.

Suddenly the huge old door creaked open behind her and the vast cloaked figure of a woman emerged. Glancing disdainfully down at the protesting victim, she sniffed and said, 'Malta seems a deuced long way to come to have your ears boxed. I told you you should have written. Good night, Nurse.'

'Good night, Matron,' replied Julia respectfully as she pulled her admiring victim to his feet.

'Phew,' he said, rubbing at the wet patches on his trousers, 'now the usual formalities are over, do I get a big kiss?'

She stared at him briefly before shaking her head in resignation. Then, in the split second before she kissed him passionately, she hissed through clenched teeth, 'Yes, but I still hate you, you infuriating bastard!'

When they had finally come up for breath, he slipped his arm around her waist and said cheerfully, 'So where're we off to now?'

'I don't know where you're off to, soldier,' she said. 'But I've had a long day and I'm tired, so I'm off back to the nurses' home at Greenwich.'

'Sounds great to me,' he said enthusiastically.

'Er, I know you'll find this strange, but I do believe you've got the wrong impression. Now isn't that a surprise?'

'Oh, c'mon,' he protested. 'Where's your sense of romance? Here I am, a poor frustrated soldier seeing his young lady for the first time for over a year and I'm rebuffed, assaulted and misunderstood.'

'Believe me, Duncan Forbes,' she said determinedly, 'whatever else you are, it is certainly *not* misunderstood. I can read you like an open book and if you think you're going to breeze back into *my* life and leave dents in *my* mattress, you've got another think coming. You'd get into heaven easier.'

'But, sweetie,' he protested, 'I thought your bed *was* heaven?'

She smiled, and standing on her toes, whispered into his ear, 'NO! NO! NO! Get it?'

'Okay,' he sighed in resignation, 'I give in. But I've got some leave. Can you get any time off in the next few days? I thought we could catch up on all our news?'

'You serious?' she asked, 'or is this another of your little ploys?'

'Of course I'm serious,' he protested in a hurt tone. 'I'll meet you whenever you like and we'll spend a whole day together. Just think how much time you'll have to tell me what a bastard I am! Now you couldn't possibly resist an offer like that, could you?'

'All right,' she said suspiciously, 'if you'd like to escort me back to Greenwich and pay my tram fare, I may find someone to swop a leave day and I can let you know first thing in the morning. Any particular day in mind?'

'How about tomorrow?'

'Tomorrow? Why the urgency?'

'Well, when you suddenly realise that I'm the only man in your life and you can't do without me, we might repeat the operation on another day, or even several days!'

She shook her head in exasperation. 'Well, I suppose I should be grateful for one thing. You've obviously not been seeing many nurses. Else you'd know their days off are as thinly spread as your morals.' She tugged at his arm. 'C'mon, we've a tram to catch.'

It was a brisk ten-minute walk from the hospital to the tram terminus at London Bridge station and, though they had to run the last few yards, it was downhill and they caught the tram comfortably. As the vehicle began to gather momentum down Tooley Street, the conductor began his round with a loud announcement.

'We're runnin' a bit late, folks. There's a bit of a fight going on between the commies and fascists at the junction of Tower Bridge Road.'

'Blast!' exclaimed Duncan. 'I forgot all about that!'

Julia looked at him puzzledly. 'How did you even know? I thought politics was always the last thing on your mind?'

'Oh, er – you're right, of course,' he faltered. 'It's er – just that I heard some talk on the underground train. I meant to suggest we took a different route.'

'I'm pleased you didn't,' she said curtly. 'With any luck we might see some of those fascists get a duffing.' Her face suddenly lit up. 'Hey, I know! Why don't we get off and have a look for ourselves? We could add a bit of verbal support.'

'Oh, I don't know about that,' he began, before suddenly realising he might yet catch at least part of the skirmish. 'Well, all right,' he agreed grudgingly, 'but only if you promise not to get involved. We're just bystanders. Agreed?'

She pulled a face and appeared about to protest.

He seized her firmly by her arms and shook his head. 'Agreed?' he repeated.

'Agreed,' she nodded with an exaggerated sigh of acceptance.

As they neared the scene, the 'bit of a fight' promised by the conductor proved a serious understatement as the incident showed all the signs of a pitched battle. It had already crossed the rails and caused the tram to halt. The conductor was not the only one who had underestimated. Rodney Road police had despatched only two constables and the pair were in some danger of being swamped. 'Look!' cried Julia. 'That copper on the left. Isn't that David?'

'I wouldn't be surprised,' replied Duncan. 'It is his manor. Hey!' He pointed to the second constable. 'The other one is that big ox Reuben Drake.' Shaking his head he drew in his breath. 'I tell you what – I wouldn't like to be the one who upsets him. He'll be like a bear with the pox!'

'Come on, then!' she said, rising eagerly to her feet. 'There's now a new set of rules. We're off to rescue David. We're the goodies for law and order!'

In spite of his efforts, Duncan was already two yards behind the girl as she leaped from the tramcar platform into the mêlée of some hundred and fifty shouting, screaming, fighting people. To make matters worse, the first person he saw in a uniform was Stanton! Cursing his luck, he tried to duck out of sight, but then promptly lost trace of Julia. Perhaps the one blessing was that Stanton was so engrossed in his own battles that he had neither time nor inclination to seek out a casual observer.

Meanwhile, Reuben Drake was showing his complete impartiality by clouting everyone who came within range of either truncheon or fists. 'I ain't piggy-in-the-middle for no bastard!' was his bellowing reply to one protesting and bleeding participant.

A distant bell suddenly announced the arrival of a police van carrying six constables who promptly proceeded to thump and arrest as many demonstrators as possible, both guilty and innocent.

Duncan decided now was an opportune moment to seize Julia and escape from the scene. This was easier said than done, as many others were equally intent on putting as much distance as possible between themselves and the vengeful constables. His attention was finally caught by a scream away to his left. There, clearly illuminated beneath a street light, was Julia. The problem was that the powerful left arm of Lofty Stanton was gripping her throat. The tall fascist was holding her tightly up on her tiptoes, whilst he fought off a spotty youth with his other arm.

Cursing furiously, Duncan made the distance between them in seconds and delivered an almighty smash to Lofty's jaw. Turning to see who had hit him, Lofty lost consciousness before their eyes actually met. Before Duncan could comfort the distressed Julia, a vaguely familiar figure seized his arm and hissed, 'You bloody idiot! You're not supposed to be here! Get back on that tram quick!'

Duncan had not really needed Peg Thornbury's instruction to realise his plan had misfired. Sweeping up the protesting Julia, he quickly carried her over his shoulder onto the now moving tram. The dozen or so passengers buried themselves deep in their evening papers or looked stonily to the front as the couple fell exhausted onto the first two vacant seats. Once she had recovered her breath, Julia turned to Duncan and said in a loud voice, 'Okay, so that was my treat for today. So where do we go tomorrow?'

25

'C'mon, you dozy creature, time to get up,' said the voice. 'I don't know what you've done to my maid but she was too terrified to wake you, so I've done it meself.' With that there was a blast of chill air as the bed covers were whisked off him. 'And contrary to what you think, I've not stripped you to satisfy my mature feminine fantasies, it's just that the bloody phone has not stopped ringing for you this morning. So get up and put yourself about.'

Waking face down on his bed, Duncan did not feel any urgent need to cover his modesty, though he quickly clawed back the eiderdown to restore at least some of its cosy warmth.

'Ummm,' he groaned deep into his pillow, 'who was it? A rich oversexed widow who wanted my body?'

'No such luck, I'm afraid,' replied Billie. 'It was a bloke called Baker who didn't sound happy and said he wants to see you without fail at eleven this morning. The other was Stanton, the bloke who called here last night. He said he wants to speak to you urgently.'

'You said the phone's not stopped ringing. That's only two calls,' he protested.

'Well, there was a certain young lady who said she has managed to get the day off and she'll ring you back in an hour or so to see where you should meet. But I didn't think you'd want to know that.'

Duncan was suddenly very wide awake. 'Wait a minute!' he exclaimed. 'What d'you mean, Stanton called here last night? He couldn't have. I saw him at a meeting in Tower Bridge Road in the middle of the evening!'

'I tell you he called *here*!' she insisted. 'He came much earlier than he planned. In fact he only missed you by minutes. He said someone was sick or something and he could only stay for a short time because he had to take over control of a demonstration. Anyway, he wants you to ring him urgently.'

'And Baker? What did he say?'

'He said very little.' She pulled a wry face. 'If I were you, I'd eat up my spinach quickly. He sounded a very angry chappie indeed.'

Duncan fell back on his pillow in dismay and pulled the eiderdown over his face.

'Oh, Billie,' he moaned. 'What a pig's ear I've made of my first day in . . .' He stopped speaking as he realised the significance of his words.

'Duncan,' she said seriously, 'I'd like to ask you something. You don't have to answer, well not all of it anyway, and I have to make it completely clear to you it's not out of female curiosity but it certainly is out of concern.'

'Like you say,' he replied, 'I don't *have* to answer, so go ahead.'

'Well, I'll back you up in anything, you know that, but are you sure you're not out of your depth in whatever little game you're playing?'

He gave a laugh and reached for her hand. 'I'm never sure about you. I can never make up my mind if you're very perceptive or just a bloody witch. But perhaps I will tell you this. I've certainly taken on something that I cannot talk about. But don't worry, it's quite legal and, more importantly, I may need your unquestioning support from time to time. I certainly won't put you in any danger but you may have to recite the odd little fib.'

She stared at him anxiously for a moment before her customary saucy expression returned. 'Is that all? What a disappointment! I was hoping it would be something very lurid and I would have to wear a veil and spangles and slink about swinging my knockers all over the place. You're a real let-down, you are, Duncan Forbes. C'mon, you sod, get yourself up and out of my flat. Perhaps then my maid will stop hiding in the cupboard.'

Before he could reply, the telephone rang and the timid voice of Elsie could be heard answering. After a few seconds, there was a little knock on the bedroom door and a tiny voice squeaked, 'A Mr Stanton again, marm; it's for Mr Forbes.'

Clutching the eiderdown around him, Duncan ran out into the passageway, much to the consternation of the maid. 'Forbes here,' he said quietly. '. . . Yes, I'm sorry, I had a late night . . . Oh, you did? And how was it? . . . Oh, I'm sorry to hear that. Nothing serious, I hope? . . . Oh, good.' There was a long speech from the other end before Duncan finally replied, 'Well I'm very honoured indeed. Are you sure I can do it? . . . Oh, of course, I want to. Fact is, I'd be absolutely delighted! . . . Just a minute, I'll get some paper to take down the details.' For some moments Duncan scribbled frantically. 'Okay, I've got all that. Oh, this is what I've prayed for . . . Thanks, thanks a lot. I'll definitely be there and I'm very proud. Goodbye.' Replacing the telephone, a feeling of elation surged through him and as he punched the air in delight, the eiderdown fell away causing the maid to flee to the kitchen.

After a hasty shower and shave, Duncan sat down to a substantial breakfast to the accompaniment of Grieg's *Peer Gynt Suite*. 'You know,' said Billie wearily, 'we've got to find time for a truce between you and my maid. I'm fed up cooking your breakfast. Anyway, what are you going to do if Julia hasn't rung before you leave? You mustn't waste it, you know. The girl rarely gets a day off.'

'Oh, blast!' cried Duncan banging his knuckles on his forehead. 'I'd completely forgotten her!' He gave a wry smile. 'If she found *that* out, she'd kill me!'

'So she's still unaware of your plans?'

'Of course,' he said. 'You know yourself that these calls only came in since I left her.'

'So, what do you intend to do?' persisted Billie.

'I thought you could make up some excuse for me when she telephones.'

'Oh, I see,' said Billie softly. 'The girl is expecting to go out with you for the day and I'm to tell her she's unlucky? I've got that right, have I?'

'Sort of,' he said thoughtfully. 'Though put like that, it does sound a bit mean.'

'Oh, you've noticed!' she said tartly. 'How truly wonderful of you!'

'Right, listen carefully,' he said. 'Change of plan! I've got an appointment with Baker at eleven o'clock. That'll take, say an hour. Then another hour to get to Greenwich – there you are! Easy! I'll see Julia at one o'clock this afternoon. Perhaps you'd like to tell her that?'

'Oh, that's brilliant,' she snapped. 'I bet that'll please her no end! So I'm now to tell her that, although she's struggled to get a day off to spend with you, you can't collect her until this afternoon! Don't you realise that you two should have been out on the river or somewhere romantic about eight o'clock this morning?'

'We *could* have, but she wouldn't let me stay the night,' he protested. 'You can't blame all this on me this time.'

Billie put down her knife and fork and, with the tiniest shake of the head, just stared at him. 'You know, Duncan,' she said eventually, 'you're almost a nice lad. You have so many good traits it's unbelievable. BUT,' her voice increased in volume as each word was uttered, 'YOU ARE SO BLOODY THOUGHTLESS!'

'Yes, I know it seems a bit much,' he agreed, 'but I'll make it up to her. Honestly. I've done a lot of thinking about Julia these last couple of days and I have to admit that girl means a hell of a lot to me. I now realise I can't risk leaving her again without probably losing her.'

'I take it you are going to tell her that?' asked Billie hopefully.

'Well—' he faltered. 'Perhaps not today but if you just explain my current difficulty when she rings, I promise I'll be a new man from tonight. How's that?'

'I'm not sure I'm totally convinced,' she said. 'But I suppose it's the best anyone can hope for. Okay, you've got the benefit of the doubt – but only just.'

'Tell you what you could do,' he said, sliding back his chair and mumbling through the last mouthful of toast. 'You could ask that mob in your conservatory to give *Peer Gynt* a miss and give us a blast of "The Galloping Major". It might help me prepare for Major Baker.'

Thirty minutes later he had just made the Charing Cross train and flopped down into a seat. He had only been awake for a little over an hour and he felt exhausted. His first priority was to sort out his thoughts. Through none of his own doing, a great opportunity may just have fallen into his lap. If he was to make anything at all of this cloak-and-dagger work, the phone call from Stanton could well be the trigger. But first, there was the interview with Baker to be faced. He knew he was due a roasting if not a dismissal, but he felt the news he had to impart would be of the greatest help.

Peg Thornbury did not say a word as she opened the door and led him up the stairs to Baker's office. On entering, he noticed two chairs facing the major. The secretary sat in the first, but no word of invitation directed him to the other. He understood the message and remained standing at attention.

'I'm not sure who I'm more bloody angry with,' began Baker. 'Me or you! I must accept at least part of the responsibility because I was stupid enough to recruit you in the first place. This was in spite of my natural reservations due to your inexperience in this field. Unfortunately, I had no reservations about your bloody sanity! My biggest error was assuming you had at least a vestige of common sense. How was I to know you had your brain removed when you joined the Guards? If you remember, I said be discreet, subtle and don't take unnecessary risks. Didn't I say that? Well, you certainly listened carefully to that advice, I must say,' he hissed. 'You know, if I had to give an assessment of you on that basis, I'd say your discretion is that of a poxed ox and you're as subtle as a sack of prunes!' Pausing a second for breath, he continued, 'As for not taking unnecessary risks, what did you do?' he asked, rising to his feet then bending slightly to pound the desk as an accompaniment to each word. 'You knock out the area organiser for the BUF in front of half the newspapers in the country!'

'What!' exclaimed Duncan. 'Surely not, er – sir!'

'Oh! You didn't know?' replied the major sarcastically. 'In spite of the fact that there were at least a dozen reporters and photographers around, you thought you could flatten the BUF's head lad for the area and not be noticed? Good God, man, you're an even bigger blockhead than I took you for!'

Duncan stared down at the five or six pictures and perked up only slightly when he noticed that all the cameras had been to his rear. As a result, it was very clear who had been punched but it was by no means clear who had done the punching. There were at least three umbrellas that had partially hidden the assailant. 'But, sir,' he protested, 'surely no one could recognise me from those pictures?'

'And that's about your only saving grace,' agreed Baker. 'My feeling is, if Miss Thornbury hadn't blessedly been there as an observer, you'd have given interviews, handed out cigars and signed autographs with the words Duncan Forbes, master spy, available for lectures and masonics!'

There were several seconds of silence during which the major returned to his chair.

'Go into the outer office with Miss Thornbury,' he said calmly. 'She'll make you out a travel warrant to return to your unit. That'll be all.'

'Can I say something, sir?' asked Duncan.

'If you must,' said Baker without raising his head.

'I couldn't be more sorry about what happened and up until a couple of hours ago I would have had to agree with everything you said. But something has happened since last night that could change things. Can I tell you?'

Baker shot a quick glance at Peg Thornbury who in turn glanced quickly at Duncan before responding with the faintest of nods. 'Very well, go ahead.'

'I received a telephone call from Stanton this morning.' Both listeners sat up a little straighter at these words. 'He said because of sickness and now his own injury, his contingent for the fascist rally at Olympia tonight is desperately short. They were to provide part of the security. He said he wanted to take part and certainly felt fit enough to do so but because he has—' Duncan faltered a little at this stage, 'a black eye and a few facial bruises, it was decided he should not report in official uniform. There are certainly officers from other areas who would be only too delighted to take his place but, to be the security at a top rally like Olympia is considered a plum job within the party. Therefore, he has asked me to attend with him tonight where he will fit me out with a uniform and, as much as possible, be a mentor to me.'

'Stanton told you this?' asked an incredulous Baker.

'That's right,' agreed Duncan. 'I had to take a chance, so I agreed.'

'It's a trap!' exclaimed Peg Thornbury. 'It has to be. There's no way they would take such a chance with a new man so early. I bet they now know who Corporal Forbes is and they are planning their revenge on him. He should not attend. It could be suicidal.'

'I don't think so,' argued Duncan. 'If you could have heard Stanton's voice, you would realise how important this assignment is to him. Most of these area commanders would cut each other's throats for this job.'

'I think he's right,' said Baker. 'Anyway, the end could well justify the means. If we could get a trusted man within their security setup, it'd be invaluable. In any case, Forbes owes me this, don't you, Corporal?'

''Fraid I do, sir,' smiled Duncan.

'But I still don't like it,' protested the secretary. 'It's a needless risk and it's more or less saying this man is expendable.'

'Corporals *are* expendable, miss,' replied Duncan. 'It's their function, didn't you know?'

'What's your timetable, Corporal?' asked Baker sharply.

'For Olympia or for my return to Malta, sir?' queried Duncan cheekily.

'Touché, you saucy bastard. For Olympia, of course,' smiled the major. 'I've put you back in business, so for heaven's sake, don't bugger up this chance or you'll be found in an east-end alley with your throat cut – and I'll be the perpetrator!'

'Well, if I'm back in, sir, then the arrangement is that I'm to go to their district HQ at Victoria Park for a uniform fitting at six o'clock. Then they are taking us by bus to Olympia for a briefing immediately afterwards.'

'Okay. Now listen carefully. You will not be on your own in Olympia. We will have a dozen or so men and women scattered amongst the crowd but these will all be ordinary rank and file. We have no radio to connect you and none of them will be aware of your existence, so don't rely too much on them.'

'So, if you're saying they'll be no use to me, why are you telling me this, sir?'

'So that when you make your report tomorrow, you won't know how much we already know. Therefore, you won't be tempted to gild the lily,' replied Baker. 'You see, Corporal, if we're going to pay you a staff sergeant's wages, plus five pounds a week expenses, we want to know we're getting value for money.'

'How long do you propose to use him at the BUF, sir?' asked Peg Thornbury. 'After all, there is always the possibility that someone who was at the meeting in Tower Bridge Road could recognise him?'

'Yes, I had thought of that, but it's a risk we'll have to take.'

'*We'll* have to take, sir?' asked Duncan pointedly.

'Well, Forbes,' said the major, rising again to his feet. 'We are a *team*, aren't we?'

The young man gave a weak smile of acceptance.

On emerging into the busy lunchtime traffic of Whitehall, Duncan was dreading his next meeting as much as he had the previous one. Poor Julia had made great efforts to change her leave but, not only was he arriving late but he had to find the courage to tell her he was also leaving early.

As he jumped from the tramcar in front of the Miller hospital, he was still trying to think of a suitable excuse, or even more important, one she would believe. His confidence took an early blow when he saw her already sitting on the steps of the nurses' home with her chin deep in her hands. Even the fact that the pose enabled him to see the tops of her thighs did little to console him.

'Er – sorry I'm late, I was called to my unit's headquarters in Whitehall,' he said half-truthfully.

'Uh huh,' she replied as if she did not believe a single syllable.

'Er – anywhere particular you'd like to go?' he almost bleated.

'Yes, I'd like to see *Girl In Pawn* with Shirley Temple. It's at the Regent Street Plaza. That's if you don't mind?'

'Oh, er – no, I don't mind in the least. Er – Shirley *who* did you say?'

'No, not Shirley *Who*,' she corrected icily. 'The name is TEMPLE, Shirley Temple, she's a new American child star who's all the rage.'

'A *child* star, eh?' he replied with blatant lack of enthusiasm. 'Good, is she?'

'You probably won't agree because it's a woman's film,

but I'm sure you won't mind seeing it, especially if you thought I was enjoying it. That so?'

'Oh, er – of course,' he smiled painfully. 'If you like it, then I have no doubt I'll like it too. An *American* child, though, eh?' he added, as if the very word was a serious plague warning.

In truth, he had known at first sight that Julia was striking a wounded martyr's pose. He also knew he deserved it. But if she was like this because he arrived three hours late, what on earth would she say when he departed five hours early?

He sat through the film, the short comedy, the newsreel and the organ without really seeing or hearing any of them. He did put his arm round her shoulders for a few moments, but her stiff aloofness had the response of a dead tree. Finally, a little after five o'clock, they emerged into a sun-drenched Regent Street and walked towards Charing Cross.

'Er—' he began, 'er – I'm afraid I've got to leave early,' he said. 'You see, I've got to return to my old unit tonight. They've got some problems about— Malta, yes that's it – Malta and, well y'see, I'm the only Life Guard in London at the moment who's actually been there. I mean, I can see you again quite easily tomorrow morning, er – it's just tonight that's a bit difficult. Now you tell me when it's best for us to meet again and I'll promise we'll spend every minute together honestly. Just name the day.'

'The day?' she echoed. 'Oh, that's easy. That day is doomsday! That's the next day I would hope to see you again, Duncan Forbes. And if by that time we know whether we are going to heaven or hell, I would like to ensure, even if it means standing upside down in the flames of purgatory, that I am not in the same place as you. Understand?' Smiling sweetly, she strode off in the direction of the Greenwich and Dartford Line.

For a second, he considered pursuing her but he knew her well enough to realise that would never work in the street. He needed somewhere more intimate. Somewhere he could chat, coax, pet, whisper and finally win her over again. That moment could not come until she emerged from the silent rage in which she had enveloped herself. He glanced quickly up at the station clock. If he was going to Victoria Park, he was already cutting it fine. It had to be now or never. What the hell, he would see her again in a day or so and everything would be fine again. Hadn't it always been? Without as much as a glance behind, he ran quickly into the underground station.

Forty minutes later, the two thugs outside the BUF headquarters were checking him over before granting him permission to enter the building. On entering, Lofty Stanton called down from the top of an inside staircase.

'You've certainly cut it fine,' he said. 'Go into the snooker room, I'll be with you in a moment.'

The snooker room was a windowless room on the ground floor and the table top was partially covered by several BUF uniforms which consisted of little more than high-necked, heavy cotton shirts, black trousers and wide black leather belts. At first glance some shirts looked as if they might fit, but Duncan had misgivings about the trousers.

'I see you're already sizing up the situation,' said Stanton, entering the room.

Duncan was about to reply but his words faded at the sight of the injuries to the newcomer's face. If he ever finds out I did that, thought Duncan, he'll kill me!

'I see you're looking at my face,' said Stanton. 'Not very nice, is it? I got it in Tower Bridge Road last night.'

'Er – who did it?' asked Duncan in what he hoped passed for a casual inquiry.

'Well, there were several pictures in the newspapers this morning but I think they may have been misled by the angle. I'm pretty sure I know now exactly who did it.'

'You do? Oh, good,' he replied weakly.

'Yes, a tall woman with a slight stoop and spectacles has been seen a couple of times at our little dos of late and she was at the exact spot at the time of the assault. I'm almost sure she did it with a milk bottle – there was a fair bit of broken glass around. Anyway, we've got our eye on her, and if she turns up again at any of our meetings, believe me, she'll get more than she bargained for. Anyway, let's get down to work; we've little enough time as it is.' He glanced from the clothing to Duncan and swiftly back again. 'Shirts should be fine but trousers may be a problem. What size are you?'

'Thirty-two waist, thirty-four leg,' replied Duncan.

'Hmmn,' murmured Stanton sorting them over quickly. 'We have a few thirty-two waists and we have a couple of thirty-four leg, sadly not on the same trousers. Couldn't adapt could you?'

'In what way?'

'Well, you obviously can't wear them if they're too tight, so how about a pair that are the right length but are a forty-inch waist? You could always tighten your belt. After all, it is a fairly wide one.'

Of all the tribulations Duncan had suffered to date, wearing trousers that were eight inches too large round the waist appalled him most. He closed his eyes at the very thought.

'Look at it this way,' whispered Stanton seriously. 'As you put them on, remember it's for the cause!'

'Oh, of course,' replied Duncan in what he hoped passed for an enthusiastic tone, 'for the cause.'

Through the open door there was an increasing hubbub of voices from the entrance hall indicating departure time was due, and a distant cry of 'Bus is here!' caused even greater excitement.

'We change our clothes when we arrive there,' said Stanton. 'It's because bus companies insist that we drive through town incognito. It's in case their vehicles get damaged. That's certainly one of the first things we'll alter when we get into power, I can tell you!'

As far as Duncan was concerned, 'incognito' was the most blessed word he had heard for ages.

As the bus finally threaded its way into its allotted space in the Olympia vehicle park, Duncan had already learned much of the party's coming hopes and aspirations. They had deliberately planned this evening as a national showpiece and were hoping for plenty of opposition in the shape of communists, Jews, gypsies, anarchists and anyone else who felt threatened by fascism. The security was enormous. There were a score of athletic-looking women who were to deal with female hecklers. Then there was a group of milder individuals to deal with wheelchair protesters. Finally, there were the front-line storm troopers of whom Duncan was now one. These were an élite whose task it was to deal with any other contingency that might arise.

'We need confrontation to make the best impact,' Stanton confided. 'If it's a quiet rally, no one will take notice, but if we can provoke *them* to attack *us*, it'll be marvellous! The news coverage will be invaluable. Look there,' he pointed to a figure just visible on the roof. 'D'you know him?'

Duncan admitted his ignorance.

'That's the assistant commissioner of police. He's up there with a radio and he's in command of fifteen hundred coppers who are on duty here today. When you have that sort of attention, you know you've arrived! The maddening thing is, if my face wasn't in this state, I would be in the thick of it. I'll kill that bloody woman if I meet her, I really will!'

'All security guards to your post, please,' came a voice over the intercom. 'And remember, be fair but be firm, very, very firm. Good luck, all.'

'C'mon,' said Stanton. 'You're on the main entrance. You can see everything from there. If you're lucky you'll get your picture in tomorrow's papers.'

When Duncan discovered his exact role, he was at first concerned how he would carry it out. After all, he had no political leanings whatever. In fact, much to the disgust of Julia Giles, he had never even voted. Therefore, if he was indifferent, how could he possibly fight people with whom he had no dispute? This feeling remained with him until the crowd began to mass, then, just before eight o'clock, with thousands inside and another four thousand queuing outside, his problem was solved for him. The vast but orderly queue of fascists were suddenly charged by several hundred banner-carrying communists who had been assembling opposite. The resulting mayhem was in turn charged by some thirty mounted policemen. Many communists in this battle then found themselves much nearer the entrance than they had dared to hope a few minutes earlier. Unable to believe their luck, they made a concerted rush to the turnstiles where Duncan, and a few other blackshirts, stood between them and a quick entrance to the packed auditorium.

Suddenly Duncan's worries disappeared. He almost felt noble in his attack on these intruders. The political beliefs of these newcomers were of no interest to him whatever; he just took up position at a turnstile and defied anyone to enter. However, within minutes he knew he was in trouble and very much in danger of being overwhelmed. Suddenly help appeared in the unlikely shape of the battered Lofty Stanton whose nature could never restrain him from participating in such a brawl. In spite of the pair's spirited defence of the turnstile, any organised attack would still have trampled them into the ground, but mobs are rarely organised and instead the invaders moved to other turnstiles less adequately defended. Within minutes, however, the battle at the other turnstiles was also over and Lofty and Duncan sat for a breather.

'I can see you're going to be a real asset to the movement,' said Lofty admiringly. 'You did a great job for us just now.'

'Well, by the size of my trousers, they probably thought I was a giant. Anyway, as long as they couldn't get round the back of me, it was always going to be difficult for them,' replied Duncan modestly. 'But as it's now quiet here, is there any chance of a peek inside? After all, it's what I joined for.'

'Of course, come on!' cried Lofty, leading the way.

As they moved towards the staircase that led up to the arena, other blackshirts were continuing to drag out screaming protesters. Many were taken by the scruff of the neck, the hair, or any other part of their anatomy that would inflict maximum discomfort. As the vast auditorium opened up before them, Duncan was amazed at the sight. Huge spotlights swirled over the cheering packed crowd as the flags of the various regions were marched in.

Suddenly all the spotlights combined on a tall imposing figure who stood on a dais. He was clad in knee-high black boots and jodhpurs, a neatly ironed black shirt and tie topped by a close-fitting black tunic with a wide black belt and a peaked black cap. The figure raised his hands for silence. This seemed to be a signal for scattered groups of protesters, who had managed to secrete themselves among the mass of supporters, to begin various chants. These mainly consisted of 'Warmonger', 'Jew-Baiter' and 'Fascist Bastard'!

For some minutes, the speaker could not be heard, but wherever there was an outbreak of jeering or heckling, the blackshirted security piled in and within seconds they had dragged the protesters screaming from their seats. Lofty Stanton repeatedly pounded his right fist into the palm of his left hand and cursed the woman who had kept him from his duty-bound task.

Eventually, the dissenters were either ejected or silenced and the leader, Sir Oswald Mosley, began his speech. After such a build-up, Duncan was disappointed by Mosley's oration. The voice was overmelodramatic and, after each point made, the speaker would pause and glare around the auditorium as if preparing for the eventual adulation that would explode over him. As he and Stanton stood at the top of the aisle and faced down a long flight of steps, Duncan was vaguely aware of a struggle being played out half-way down. There, two of the female blackshirts were half dragging, half marching a young woman towards the exit. They were already close enough for both Lofty and Duncan to ease themselves back to facilitate their passage. Duncan was so fascinated by the response of the audience to the speaker that he paid no real attention to the struggling trio. At least he didn't until the girl suddenly spat straight into his face. 'You scum!' she screamed. 'You lying, deceitful, fascist scum! May you rot in hell! Get it?!'

There was no doubt about it, Julia Giles was not taking her ejection from Olympia at all well.

26

It was well after 1 a.m. before Duncan passed through the gates of Billie's house, having walked most of the way from Olympia. All he could think about on the journey was the expression on the face of Julia Giles as she spat obscenities. Fortunately, nothing she had said could have been interpreted as anything more than that he was an out and out fascist. He gathered, in subsequent conversation, that Lofty Stanton thought she had just been a pick-up to whom he had lied. Far from arousing suspicion, if anything, she had reinforced Lofty's trust in him which had increased steadily. Duncan had casually asked what happened to objectors and hecklers who were ejected and to his relief Lofty said most of the men 'got a few thumps' but the women, with the exception of the occasional bruise and the removal of one shoe, were released unscathed.

Once he had changed out of his dreaded trousers, Duncan did not return to BUF headquarters, saying he would find it easier to return to Hampstead direct from Olympia. The reason was accepted without question and as the bus left, he did an hour's tour of the locality in a fruitless search for Julia. In some respects, he had hoped he would not find her. He dreaded to think of her reaction if he stumbled upon her and she was not restrained in an arm lock.

Except for the lamp outside Billie's front door, the house was in darkness and he was thankful for that. The last thing he wanted was a lecture from Billie on his treatment of women in general and Julia in particular. Falling into bed, he suddenly wondered just what the hell he was doing. Although he had left Julia many times before, he was always confident he would see her again and they would resume easily their old love-hate relationship. This time was different and he knew it. He felt he would feel her venom until the day he died. When he slipped into a restless sleep, dreams and visions came and went in illogical sequence. Most featured the rally and all featured Julia.

Suddenly, forcing its way through a muted selection from *The Gondoliers* came a loud female voice.

'Duncan Forbes!' it yelled. 'Unless you cease scaring the shits out of my maid, you're out on your ear. I am not at me best this time in the morning, so either buy yourself an alarm clock or get your own sodding breakfast because you're fast wearing out your welcome. Get it?'

He knew from the first word it was Billie Bardell. There was really no mistaking her tones, but the phrase 'get it?' cut into him like a knife as he recalled they were the last words spoken to him by Julia Giles.

'Oh, hullo,' he mumbled. 'I'm sorry. Anyway, I don't want breakfast. Cup of tea'll do fine.'

'WOW!' she exploded. 'What a start to the day! An apology! You must go out with that girl more often, she's obviously making you considerate.'

'Well, make the most of it,' he growled. 'Because this is as considerate as I get.'

Sensing there was more in his tone than the usual banter, she ventured a 'why?'

If he had been awake a little longer or slept a little better, he may have been more reticent, but as it was, he left nothing out of his tale of lost love. 'Oh, I'm sure it'll be all right,' soothed Billie. 'This sort of thing happens between you two all the time.'

'No, it doesn't,' murmured Duncan. 'Never since I've known her have I seen such a look. I could taste the hatred.'

'Then it's time for a real humble-pie job,' she insisted. 'Go and see the girl, get on your knees, tell her everything you've told me and apologise.' Billie lowered herself onto the side of the bed and put a consoling arm round his shoulder.

'Look,' she whispered, 'arrange for her to come here, perhaps sometime at the weekend when the music school is closed. I'll take Elsie out and the two of you can spend the whole day making up. You know what she's like. Once you start to chat to her, she'll come round. You'll see.'

He shook his head. 'No, Billie, not this time she won't. Still, you're right about one thing. I must at least try to contact her. I'll write, but it will have to be to the nurses' home. I can't upset that bloody matron again; she's terrifying.'

Though Duncan's instinct was to drop everything and blindly search London for Julia, he knew he had learned so much about the BUF that he must report to Baker. He also knew, risky though it might be, his life would be far easier if he took Billie into his full confidence. Whatever her failings, she was good at secrets. With her history she had to be. He was just finishing his tea when Billie entered the dining room holding up a pair of large trousers.

'Elsie found these this morning. Did you come home with a circus last night?'

'Oh, I'm sorry, they're mine,' he said ruefully. 'I had them under my arm when I came in. I must have dropped them.'

'Dropped them?' she echoed. 'You could have dropped them over the house. They're much too big for you, surely?'

'They're certainly that,' he agreed. 'I must get them altered. D'you know a tailor?'

'No, but I know a dressmaker. What's more, she's right here. Elsie!' she called.

Within seconds the girl came running. 'Yes, marm?' she inquired nervously.

Billie held up the trousers. 'See this marquee? D'you think you could change it into a pair of trousers that would fit Mr Forbes?'

'Oooh, marm,' began the girl putting her knuckle to her mouth, 'I dunno.'

'It's all right,' Billie assured with a quick wink at Duncan. 'I'll do the intimate measuring. Can you do it or not?'

The girl gave a quick nod, then, bowing her head, scuttled rapidly from the room.

'There you are,' said Billie proudly. 'Another few weeks and she'll be eating out of your hand. So come here; I need to measure your inside leg.'

'I don't know who I'm in more danger from,' muttered Duncan. 'Those out there or you in here.'

'Just keeping me hand in,' she explained wistfully. 'My touch is so light you wouldn't know where I'd been.'

'And I'm not risking finding out,' he said, rising quickly from the table. 'If anyone wants me, I'm off to see the good guys. Then I'm searching for Julia.' He sped through his ablutions and dashed from the house. In spite of his gloom, he could not resist a little smile when he saw Elsie sitting at a window with his trousers on her lap. She was sewing busily to a bumpy version of *The Sorcerer's Apprentice*.

His greeting from Major Baker and Peg Thornbury, indicated to him just how much they now valued his work and he suffered none of the ridicule of the previous meeting. He was already able to give them numbers, intentions and dates and was quite touched when Baker twice showed concern for his safety.

'Certainly no worries at the moment, sir,' Duncan assured him. 'After last night, Stanton thinks I'm in line for an Iron Cross! There's one thing that does bother me, though.'

'Go ahead,' nodded Baker.

'Well, to be honest, I quite enjoyed that skirmish at the turnstiles. But it's not always going to be like that. What happens when it gets nasty in a public place, or if the police become involved? I mean, sooner or later someone could even be killed. Perhaps I could even be arrested. What then?'

'If that happens,' said Baker quietly, 'then you must go

along with it, even to the extent of appearing in court. When your work on this job ceases, I will get the record expunged and you'll be compensated. There's no other way to do it.'

'You will promise not to die in the meantime?' said Duncan. 'I'd really hate to cop seven years' hard once you were dead.'

'That's the risk all patriots must take, I'm afraid, Corporal,' smiled Baker. 'But I'm sure Miss Thornbury would put in a good word or two.'

'In that case,' said Duncan turning to the woman, 'I think you should know that Stanton is seeking your scalp to hang on his belt. He thinks it was you who clouted him the other night. So, whatever you do in future, please stay away from demonstrations. I daren't chance losing you both!'

With no fascist activity planned for some days, Duncan had time to start his search for Julia. To avoid delay, he wrote a letter and slipped it into the hospital letter box himself. He then travelled to Greenwich Nurses' Home intending to do much the same thing. However, having sat in Greenwich park and written out his thoughts, he recognised a passing young woman as being one of the nurses whom he had seen two evenings earlier.

'I'm sorry,' she replied curtly to his questions, 'but Julia is upset and has sworn us all to secrecy. Anyway, I don't know where she is, except she's not been at the hospital all day.'

'Would you leave this letter in her room?' he pleaded, offering the envelope.

Looking at him, she suddenly saw the sadness in his eyes. Without another word she took the letter and walked swiftly away.

As Duncan watched her disappear out of the park gates, he began to go over the sanctuaries that Julia might have sought. Billie Bardell's flat was obviously out, but how about Queenie's? She had taken refuge there before. Who knows, perhaps she had again? After checking his pocket diary he made for the nearest call box. He had already placed a coin in the slot before he suddenly realised Queenie could make up any tale on the telephone. No, this wasn't the way. He would call in person. If he was face to face, he would know instantly if she was protecting Julia.

Streatham from Greenwich is not an easy trip by public transport. One has to go into London before coming out again. With the approach of the evening rush hour, the journey time was further extended, and by the time Duncan approached the house he had gradually convinced himself that Julia would be there. On his approach, he even thought he saw her face at the window. As it was, he did not need to knock because Queenie was in the driveway cleaning her car.

'Duncan!' she exclaimed. 'How lovely to see you! What have you been doing? We haven't seen you for . . .' The expression on his face checked her in midflow. 'What is it, Duncan?' she asked anxiously. 'What on earth's the matter?'

'Don't you know?' he asked curtly.

'Know?' she echoed. 'Of course, I don't *know*. How could I? We haven't seen you for over a year.'

'But you've seen Julia,' he persisted.

'Julia? Of course we haven't. Whatever makes you think that? Look, come inside. You look as if you could do with a sit-down.'

He suddenly realised that was exactly what he needed. He allowed Queenie to take his hand and lead him into the house.

'She's not here then?' he asked almost childlike.

'Who's not here? D'you mean Julia? Is it her you're talking about?'

'Duncan, old son!' came Jim's cheery inquiry from the doorway. 'How you doing?'

Queenie turned anxiously to her husband. 'Look at him, Jim, something's wrong. He keeps saying Julia is here and I can't really understand him.'

'But we've not seen Julia for ages. I thought she lived in the nurses' home?'

'She's not there,' mumbled Duncan. 'I thought she was here. When I came up the road I was sure I could see her upstairs at the window.'

'Come on, old chap,' said Jim, pulling Duncan to his feet. 'You and I are going to search every room. Give me your arm.'

Queenie watched with concern as the pair ascended the stairs to the first of the rooms. She had never seen him like this before. As the footsteps went from room to room, she could not quite make out their muffled conversation. The footfalls finally ceased and she realised the pair were now deep in conversation. She had made a pot of tea but still the distant voices rumbled on.

'Your tea is stewing down here!' she called up the staircase.

'Okay, coming!' acknowledged Jim. Moments later, the pair entered the kitchen.

Queenie was somewhat surprised at the improvement in the younger man. 'Would you like something to eat?' she asked.

'No, not yet, he wouldn't,' said Jim, obviously trying to suppress a smile. 'He's having a whisky and he's staying for dinner because I've discovered his trouble,' he said smugly. 'What's more, the patient agrees and already feels better for my diagnosis. Top that!'

Queenie glanced quickly from one to the other. 'Jim, what are you talking about?'

Jim took hold of Duncan's right hand and lifted it high in salutation. 'For the first time in his life, this young man is actually in *love*! Ever since he was fourteen years old, he's been breaking female hearts. Well, now the biter's been bit and he's not used to it. Hence this wallowing self-pity. He's mucked that girl about for years but only now does he realise he loves her. Unfortunately, he's realised it twenty-four hours after she's spat in his eye and told him to piss off. Right, lad?'

Duncan nodded and gave Queenie an embarrassed smile. She tiptoed up to kiss his cheek.

'Well, I must admit I'm only half sorry for you,' she confessed. 'Because you tied that poor girl in so many knots over the years that at times she didn't know if she was coming or going. But I'm sure she'll come back. You two always looked right together.'

'I doubt it,' murmured Duncan. 'There was something about her this time that said finito. If that's so, then I admit it's no more than I deserve, but I'd like to know she's safe. If I can establish that, I'll not bother her again, I swear.'

'She'll get in touch when she's ready,' Queenie assured him. 'She's not a fool.'

Considering that Duncan's arrival had been unexpected, the meal Queenie prepared was excellent and it was a far more tranquil Duncan who returned to Hampstead than had left it. On his return, Elsie, who seemed to have gained confidence, gave him a message to ring Major Baker urgently. On doing so, Baker told him he had discovered that Mosley was planning a large Sunday march two weeks hence. The time and venue had been well known for days but the purpose of the march and the expected numbers were not. Though grateful for the renewed activity, Duncan dreaded the delay.

This proposed march was to prove more difficult for the BUF than was first thought. The original plan, to take it through Whitechapel into the east end of London, had faltered because of the opposition of many of the area's residents. Political pressure had been put on Mosley and he finally agreed the march would take place south of the river, winding its way through Bermondsey to a park at Surrey Docks. Although separated only by the width of the Thames, there was a vast difference in temperament between the average residents of these two areas. Whereas many east Londoners physically opposed the marchers, those south of the river showed more indifference and were content to view the street battles as an interesting diversion from their usual Sunday fare of winkle sellers, the Salvation Army and an afternoon doze.

Like most of London's constabulary, the personnel of Rodney Road station had had their share of fascist demonstrations, but this march was to be along the borders of their manor. This time they would be at the heart of proceedings.

'It's not that I mind these rumpuses,' complained Reuben Drake. 'Fact, sometimes I quite enjoys 'em. It's havin' that gutless bugger Marsh in charge that gits up my nose. When yer at the forefront, yer needs a guv'nor who'll back yer, not a fuckin' fairy who can't see past the next selection board. I told him he's here for ever. No board's goin' ter pass such a tosser but really I was wastin' me breath. He thinks he's a born leader.' Reuben shook his head in wonder. 'He couldn't lead a toy dog.'

'I do agree there are times when he's something of a liability,' said Poshie Porter, 'but I'm not sure he'll continue to fail promotion boards. I think he's approaching the stage when they'll promote him to get rid of him.'

'Well, I'll tell you this,' said Reuben. 'If he's standin' near me and a shower of bricks fly over, he'd better watch for mine, 'cos I don't miss from five yards.'

'Speak of the devil,' said David nodding at the doorway. 'Look who's coming.'

Just entering was Inspector Percival Marsh himself, accompanied by Station Sergeant Bill Barclay.

'Okay, lads,' said Barclay. 'All downstairs in the parade room; we've lots to discuss.' Cigarettes were stubbed and pipes were tapped as the twenty men filed downstairs into the large general-purpose room. Once there, they formed a double line and were inspected by Marsh.

'Right,' he said finally, 'you'll be on duty at the junction of Long Lane and Hankey Place. I don't expect any trouble at that spot because the march is headed for Southwark Park. Therefore I don't want to see truncheons drawn or anyone arrested. The last thing we need is a string of complaints. What's more . . .'

431

'How about if we 'as ter nick someone?' interrupted Drake.

'There's no such thing as "has to nick someone", Drake. They won't want to be arrested, so don't arrest them. That's simple enough, even for you surely?'

'So, if someone thumps me and, seein' as you say I shouldn't nick him,' persisted Reuben, 'can I wallop him back?'

'Good God, man, no! This is bordering on insubordination! Of course, you can't. It's these needless arrests that cause the trouble.'

'Okay, how about if 'e comes at me with a brick or a pole or such like. Can I draw me truncheon and whack him then?'

'Drake!' said the exasperated Marsh. 'Are you deliberately setting out to be disruptive. And the word "Sir" wouldn't come amiss from you either.'

'No, *sir*,' Drake emphasised. 'I simply want ter clear up for me own satisfaction and in front of witnesses, just what it is yer expect of us today.'

Marsh could feel the disapproving eyes of Station Sergeant Barclay on his back. Oh, why was it, of the twenty-two thousand coppers in the Metropolitan Police, he always seemed to be burdened with this obnoxious oaf? He was convinced that it was Drake more than anyone else who had caused his promotional deadlock.

'Your function is to keep Long Lane free of obstructions to the march and behave at all times in accordance with my instructions. Now Station Sergeant Barclay will have a word with you to explain what you should do if anyone complains.'

Whilst this briefing was taking place, the blackshirts were also assembling on Victoria Embankment. Once settled in line, they were addressed by Mosley himself, and as the band struck up, they marched proudly away. By now, most of Lofty Stanton's injuries had either healed or faded and, with Duncan in support, he was able to take up his role as area commander for his section. For the first time in his undercover work, Duncan was experiencing qualms as he realised he had to play his role in broad daylight. Everything he had attempted previously had been at night or in enclosed halls. He suddenly felt very vulnerable and exposed.

Meanwhile, a third but unsuspecting party to events, was just about to drive a truck loaded with all his worldly possessions from Queen's Buildings to his fiancée's bungalow in Maidstone.

'You're off then, Mr Lines?' said Grace sadly.

'Y-yes, mam,' acknowledged Wonky. 'I never th-thought I'd s-say it, but I'm not s-sorry to be leaving L-London. Besides, my Olive's a w-wonderful girl, so it ain't no great loss. S-She didn't w-want me to bring all my old f-furniture,' he shrugged, 'b-but it don't seem right s-somehow, does it? A man getting m-married and not f-furnishing the home?'

'Well, if she already has a nice home and she's happy for you to share it, why bother, Mr Lines?'

'S-s'pose you're right, r-really,' he agreed. 'Th-that's why I've arranged to p-pick up an old p-piano on my way. Saw it for sale for only f-five quid, I th-thought it'd be a nice s-surprise.'

'A piano?' queried Grace. 'Are you sure? I mean, if she doesn't want your furniture, she's hardly likely to want a second-hand piano! Where is it?'

'A l-lady had it for sale in a j-junk shop in L-Long L-Lane. It's in her yard. I've already p-paid for it and I'm c-collecting it on my w-way. I b-bet my Olive'll love it wh-when she sees it!'

'But Mr Lines!' cried Grace. 'The Mosley march is going down Long Lane. My Davy is on duty there. You'll never get through.'

'Oh, I m-must, Mrs Diamond, I m-must,' Wonky said anxiously. 'I've p-paid me f-fiver!'

'Well, you'd better hurry because most of the roads are closing.'

'I'm off n-now, anyway. Say goodbye to D-Davy for me, w-won't you? You've both been very g-good to me. Y-You must come d-down and v-visit us sometime. 'Bye!'

She gave him a vigorous wave and was genuinely sorry to see him leave.

Wary of the road closures, Wonky used his knowledge of local alleys and courtways, many barely the width of his truck, in order to reach Long Lane. As a result, he arrived at the junk shop to find it neatly between the approaching fascists and a communist barricade. The Rodney Road contingent also arrived at the same time and the first thing to catch their attention was the same street-wide barricade. Inspector Marsh stared in horror.

'We've got to move it,' said David, in an attempt to reactivate life into the inspector. 'If we don't, the march is going to stop just here and we'll be outnumbered in the thick of everything!'

'Er – yes, yes, you're right,' bleated Marsh. 'Er – okay, you men, clear the road.'

As the first of the obstructions was being cleared, a surge of demonstrators swarmed across and began attacking the police with whatever weapon came to hand. At first, the police were driven back, but the tide was eventually stemmed by the arrival of a ferocious man who complained that a piano, for which he had paid good money, was now the cornerstone of the barricade.

'I'm deuced glad he's on our side,' panted Poshie. 'Who is he? Hercules?'

David gasped. 'He's my neighbour, you remember? He was the driver in that fatal accident with the cab years ago in the Old Kent Road.'

'Good Heavens,' exclaimed Poshie. 'I remember him now. He was a placid chap!'

'That was before he lost his piano,' marvelled David. 'Just look at him!'

Within a few minutes, as the march approached, a

semblance of order was restored at the remains of the barricade. 'They'll just about get through now, thanks ter your mate,' said Reuben gratefully. 'I think we all owe him a drink. And I don't say that lightly,' he added needlessly.

David put a thankful arm around Wonky's shoulder. 'I still don't understand how you could lose a piano,' he said puzzledly. 'I mean, it's hardly an everyday item.'

Wonky, now devoid of stutter, fired out his sorry tale.

'So where's your lorry now?' asked David.

Wonky pointed down the road to a spot where the leaders of the march were about to reach. 'There, outside the junk shop.'

'Ye Gods!' cried David. 'How on earth did you get that through the road closures? Never mind, don't tell me. Just get it away before it joins your piano on another bloody barricade.'

'They can't do that,' protested Wonky, breaking into a run. 'Pieshop is in the cabin.' He had covered fifty yards before he turned his head as an afterthought, 'See you, Davy. 'Bye!' he yelled.

Even though Wonky was no longer looking, David raised an arm in a friendly wave of farewell.

Moments later, the first of the marchers reached the site of the barricade and inspired the protesters to renew their onslaught.

'I think we can sit this out for a bit,' said Reuben. 'Let the buggers fight each other this time.'

That they certainly did, with crowds of spectators in the nearby flats cheering vociferously. It was only when the enthusiasm of both parties had flagged that the police stepped in and slowly restored order. The march then resumed its momentum before finally fading out of sight towards Tower Bridge Road.

In its wake, the battle had left a kerbside littered with seated and prostrate figures, many bleeding profusely. The march having now passed out of sight, the police began to attend to the wounded. David was padding the eye of one young man when his attention was drawn by Reuben Drake.

'Davy!' he called. 'Who's this lad? We know him, don't we? Didn't he once buy us all a pint?'

In the gutter, bleeding and unconscious, with a large fragment of pavement resting against his skull, was the black-shirted figure of Duncan Forbes.

'Bloody hell!' exclaimed David. 'I didn't know he was a blackshirt!'

'Well, if he was,' observed Reuben, 'he might not be any longer. I don't like the look of him one bit.'

Of all the casualties that day, those at the Hankey Place barricade were arguably the most fortunate, being barely four hundred yards from the casualty door of Guy's Hospital. Yet another stroke of luck had been the nearby storage yard of one Jessie Trappitt. This lady had hired out carts and barrows to a generation of costermongers. Whilst these conveyances had made an ideal barricade, they also made excellent stretchers.

'He looks real poorly,' said Reuben, looking sadly down at Duncan. 'I hates ter see someone who's bought me a pint lookin' like that. If that prat Marsh wants ter know where I am, tell him I've taken a good man ter Guy's Hospital on a Jessie Trappitt barrer.'

27

In spite of first impressions, there was to be a slow recovery for Duncan, but recovery it eventually was, although as days became weeks and weeks became months, he felt it was never-ending. Billie, plus the Diamonds and Forsythes, had all visited regularly, but Major Baker and Peg Thornbury had made their visits out of hours so the two parties had never met. Duncan did wonder why he had not heard from Stanton until David told him Stanton had been arrested for stabbing a rival and was doing a stint of hard labour.

Finally, the long-awaited day of Duncan's discharge arrived and Billie came by taxi to take him back to Hampstead. In spite of the fact that he had been strolling around the corridors for some days, the trip from the ward to the taxi exhausted him and he fell wearily into the cab. To his surprise, Major Baker sat quietly in the corner puffing a pipe.

'Sorry about that, Duncan,' said Billie, as the taxi pulled away, 'but he insisted I shouldn't tell you.'

'Don't worry, Billie,' said Duncan, 'he loves all this cloak-and-dagger stuff.'

'Quite the contrary,' said Baker. 'I thought you'd like to hear some good news.'

'And that is?' asked Duncan with a hint of suspicion.

'You can throw away your blackshirt. You won't need it any more. We now have other sources. I have arranged for you to be transferred as an out-patient to the army hospital at Millbank and you can stay with Miss Bardell for the length of your treatment. Once you're totally discharged, you can have a spell of sick leave before rejoining your unit. There, that wasn't bad, was it?'

'Sorry I was a bit of a failure as a spy, though, sir,' apologised Duncan. 'I feel a bit of a let-down seeing as you shipped me all the way from Malta.'

'On the contrary. For a short time you were invaluable,' Baker assured him. 'But, as I said, we now have other sources. Anyway, I think you're a bit too open to make a long career as a good undercover man, but you do have other attributes. As such, once you're fit, I'm recommending you for an officers' selection board. Think you're up to it?'

'I've never known a senior rank who's bothered me yet,' replied Duncan with a tired smile. 'Though, on reflection, I'm not sure I should have said that.'

'Hmmmn,' muttered Baker thoughtfully. 'Probably not, but under the circumstances, we'll let it pass.' He glanced out of the cab window at Waterloo Bridge. 'Anyway, if you drop me here I'll be in touch when you're fit again. Good luck, Corporal.'

'Good luck, sir,' replied Duncan as the major slammed the door.

It was thirty minutes later that the taxi rolled along the gravel drive by Billie's front door. 'There's my Elsie looking in her usual panic when you're about,' said Billie nodding towards the maid who was hopping agitatedly from one foot to the other. 'Speak to her, Duncan, or she'll wet her knickers.'

'Hullo, Elsie,' he called, with false bonhomie. 'Are you well?'

'I am, sir,' said the maid. 'But I'm not sure about Mr and Mrs Forsythe. They're so excited they've been ringing all afternoon.'

'Why?' asked Duncan. 'They knew the time I was being discharged, didn't they?'

'Oh, no, sir, it's not you. It's Miss Julia, sir. They know where she is!'

'Julia!' he cried as the life surged back into him. 'Where? Where is she?'

'They didn't tell me, sir, but all you have to do is phone them, sir.'

With Billie and Elsie crowding his arm, he heard the warm tones of Queenie answer the telephone. 'It's Duncan here,' he began.

'Wait a minute,' interrupted Queenie. 'Let me get comfortable, because I know what you're about to ask. Julia is in a small town called Guernica.'

'Where's that, Scotland?' he asked naïvely.

'No, Spain,' she replied. 'We've just received a letter from her. She's nursing at a children's hospital. Most of them are civil war casualties.'

'Did she—' he began tentatively, 'did she say anything about me?'

'I'm afraid she did,' sighed Queenie. 'I doubt if you'll want to hear it though.'

'Try me.'

'She writes: "Thank Duncan Forbes for me, will you. If I hadn't found him out in his true colours, I'd still be chasing after him instead of here, where I'm desperately needed." I'm sorry, Duncan,' added Queenie softly, 'but you can understand her feelings, can't you?'

'Oh, yes,' sighed Duncan wearily. 'I can understand them now all right. Trouble is, I'm ten years too late.'

Although Julia had been at the children's hospital for many months now, the pangs of homesickness had not lessened. With thoughts of home also came thoughts of Duncan. No matter how many times she thought of him, she could still barely believe his betrayal. Lying in her tent, filling in her personal diary, she noticed it had been St George's Day. Lowering her pen, her thoughts flew back to those St George's Day morning assemblies in the school hall, singing 'Jerusalem'. It now seemed a hundred years ago. She was grateful the diary had room for barely three lines. Had there been four, she was sure she would have fallen asleep before their completion. Blowing out the candle, she slid down into the blankets and knew nothing more till morning.

Her motives for joining the civil war had been simple enough. She felt she had to distance herself from everything that Duncan now stood for. As a result, she could think of no better gesture than to serve the Republican cause against their Nationalist Fascist opponents. At least, that had been her intention, but what had seemed a noble cause from the safety of London, in reality had proved to be unparalleled, confused slaughter. The children's hospital was now in name only. How could a dying adult be turned away because the sign above the door said NINOS? The war would have been long over if the combined forces of Germany and Italy had not given massive support to the Nationalists, whilst the Russians did much the same with the Republicans. As a result, a poverty-wracked country became a killing field for three powerful nations experimenting with weapons of death. In keeping with many other volunteers, Julia's idealism had vanished and her main hope was simply to survive. In the town of Guernica, with the Fascists a few miles distant, even that hope was not easy to sustain.

The next morning she was due to travel by donkey cart eight miles to the port of Bermeo where two British destroyers were due to call to evacuate British civilians. Strangely, though she was frequently afraid, the idea of leaving Spain had not entered her head. Instead, she was hoping to use her nationality to beg medical supplies from the ships of her countrymen. Her knowledge of donkeys being nil, her escort for the journey was a small, fourteen-year-old slightly built orphan boy who, for convenience rather than accuracy, answered to the name of José.

The trip, though not long, was well within range of the Fascist guns that surrounded the nearby city of Bilbao. A lone donkey cart could hardly threaten an army, but if it was the only target in sight, could easily tempt a bored soldier with itchy fingers and an accurate weapon. As a result, the journey was constantly interrupted by the necessity to shelter by the roadside. It was during one of these interruptions that José tumbled from the cart and grazed his shoulder on the wheel. As the cart finally rolled its way down to the harbour, Julia could see the ships anchored out at sea. She discovered from newsmen on the quayside that negotiations with both sides were currently under way to ensure that any evacuation would not be fired upon.

'We'll be getting no supplies tonight, I'm afraid, José,' she said, squinting into the setting sun. 'We'd better find somewhere to sleep.'

Providing the couple weren't too fussy this did not present a problem, for much of the town was damaged beyond repair and had been hastily vacated. If windows and doors were not essential requirements then there was plenty of shelter, although food and drink was a different matter. Julia eventually found a room above an empty restaurant, and after attending to the donkey, did what she could to make the place comfortable. Leaving José in charge of the animal, she went out to scavenge.

Two streets from the harbour, she found a partially damaged café that still functioned, where several newsmen passed their time whilst awaiting the destroyers. Her arrival aroused no little interest amongst the reporters and they began to ask questions about the role of girls like herself, far from home, in a war that they barely understood. More importantly, and in exchange for her story, she was able to secure a few precious supplies which they purchased from the café owner at an exorbitant price.

Her happiness was short-lived, however, when Denis Watts, an old newsman, arrived with the news that docking negotiations had run into difficulties and no one now knew when, or if at all, the boats would dock. Julia was now in a dilemma. If she waited much longer, she would be sorely missed at the hospital. But if she cut short her trip and returned to Guernica next morning, the boats could easily put in within minutes of her departure.

'Well seeing as you're already here, love,' said Watts, 'I'd say the decision is made for you. You *must* stay, otherwise your whole journey is a complete waste of time.' Within a day she was to realise how fateful those words were.

'Yes, I suppose you're right,' she agreed, gathering bread, milk and fish into a bag. 'Anyway, the lad and I can catch up on our sleep, so the time won't be wasted.'

This plan for sleep was dashed an hour before daybreak when two of the correspondents broke into her slumbers to announce both ships had docked during the night. Though she had been unsure of obtaining medicines from the ships, the medical staff of both sick bays handed over most of their supplies in response to her pleadings. Soon after nine o'clock, Julia and José waved goodbye to the crews and newsmen and set off into the bright sunshine for the return to Guernica.

Because of the excitement of that morning, the pair had not eaten and the graze on José's shoulder was beginning to weep badly. Remembering the sniping on the journey out from Guernica, Julia looked for some degree of cover before stopping. She eventually found it beneath a group of trees set back a few yards from the roadside near the top of a hillock. As José tucked into a large piece of black bread, Julia examined his shoulder before grudgingly allowing him one of their precious dressings.

In the middle distance, the tall spires of Guernica could clearly be seen and Julia visualised how crowded the squares would be on that market day. She had just bitten into her first slice of bread when José tugged her sleeve and pointed towards the sun. At first she saw nothing, but through the glare she could hear a roar that increased by the second. By shielding her eyes and peering, she made out a series of huge black arrowheads. The arrows then dived out of the full glare of the sun, and she saw they were massed squadrons of dark

442

Junkers aircraft. Julia had seen attacking planes before but never on such a scale. The sky seemed black with them and all were heading in the same direction – straight for the heart of Guernica!

The pair watched in stunned horror but had no idea how long the attack lasted. It could have been minutes, it could have been hours. At first, several squadrons flew over the town and strafed it into oblivion. This was followed by a second attack that consisted of an equal number of planes dropping hundreds of incendiaries. These secondary bombs systematically ignited the ruin caused by the first wave. Almost before the secondary wave faded, a third followed. This last wave flew much lower as machine guns attacked everything in sight. Although the sounds of explosions and machine-gun fire carried clearly to the donkey cart, the screams and cries of the victims did not. As a result, once the planes had left, all that could be heard was an eerie silence. Even the birds had gone. As Julia and José stared at what had once been a town, the ruins gradually vanished beneath a massive pall of black smoke. José clutched in terror at Julia and, though she put a protecting arm around him, she could not drag her gaze from the horror in front of her. Mentally she tried to pinpoint the location of her hospital but all she could see was fire and smoke.

'Quickly, José,' she ordered. 'We must see if we can help.' Climbing into the cart she flicked the donkey's reins. Creaking and groaning, the old cart gathered momentum and began rumbling its way towards the flattened town. They had almost reached the outskirts when they heard a car approaching from the rear. Tugging on the reins to let it pass, Julia glanced curiously over her shoulder. To her surprise it contained most of the newspapermen who had bade her farewell barely three hours earlier and sported a union jack on its bonnet.

'Where the hell are you going?' called the driver as the car skidded to a halt.

'To my hospital – if it's still there,' she answered.

'And if it's not, what will you do?' he persisted.

She nodded towards the burning town. 'I'd have thought you're capable of seeing that for yourself,' she replied acidly. 'I *am* a nurse, you know.'

The older newsman quickly alighted from the rear of the car. 'But you can't go in there, love,' he said anxiously.

'You're going, aren't you?' she argued.

'But you're a *girl*,' he cried. 'Look, see over that hill yonder. There are some twenty thousand Nationalist troops who've been flown in by the Germans and most of them are Franco's Moors. We've seen their handiwork. They kill all wounded, cut rings from fingers and tear out gold teeth. They're barbarians of the worst kind! Now the town is smashed, they'll be here within hours. You can't possibly stay. You must go now!'

'So why aren't you going?' she countered.

'Because they know we're newsmen. They love the publicity. They don't seem to realise the civilised world is sickened by their actions.'

'Thanks for your concern,' she said quietly, 'but I came to Spain to nurse and nursing's what I'll do.'

The newsman turned helplessly to his colleagues. 'I did my best,' he shrugged, before turning once more to Julia. 'Look, miss, the two destroyers are already leaving Bermeo, so we've decided to cover the attack on Guernica before heading north for the French border. If you get into town and find it's more than you can take, look for us. It'll be a privilege to get you out.'

The girl made no reply but nodded her head slightly and jerked the animal's reins. The newsman, still shaking his head, climbed back into the car and called, 'Remember, don't be too proud. If you want to change your mind, just look for us. We'll be around for a while. Don't forget now.'

'I won't be leaving,' she replied, 'but it's sweet of you to offer.'

He gave a final wave and within seconds, the vehicle and its occupants faded into a cloud of distant dust.

Julia had no real idea of what she would find in Guernica but she still wasn't prepared for the carnage that awaited her. The stench of burnt flesh pervaded everything and buildings that should have stood sixty feet up from pavements, now lay ten feet high across streets. Nothing appeared to be standing and everything blazed fiercely. Bodies and bits of bodies of all ages lay scattered in every conceivable position. The occasional citizen who appeared uninjured was mainly in a zombie-like daze or cradling some deformed dead figure whilst rocking to and fro in silent grief. The cart could no longer negotiate the streets and Julia left José once more in charge of the animal as she picked her way over the ruins towards her hospital. As she turned what should have been the last corner, the entire street looked like a gigantic and unfinished mausoleum. A feeling of total helplessness overcame her. She felt like the sole survivor of a planet collision and began to wonder what one little nurse on her own could accomplish. Perhaps it was time to look for the newsmen, after all? Suddenly she heard the sound of small explosions. Though no expert, she guessed this was riflefire rather than anything heavier. If it *was* riflefire, it could only mean one thing. The Nationalist troops were already attacking the town. But why did they need to attack? The town was dead; there could be no resistance. Surely they could see that?

She suddenly began to fear for José. Having lost both parents, she thought the least she could do was remove him from the nightmare of this shattered town. As each pile of rubble looked like every other pile, she soon lost her bearings and it was another thirty minutes before she stumbled on the spot where she had left him. At first, all she could see was the cart. As she moved nearer she saw that the donkey was lying dead across its shafts. Before she could fully take in the scene, she heard a scream and saw a movement behind a collapsed wall. José was now lying motionless with a Moorish soldier, bloodied knife in hand, sitting across his chest. All her fear now left her and she ran screaming at the man. The ferocity of her attack momentarily surprised the soldier but then, with one violent swipe, he knocked her to the ground.

She was soon on her feet, however, and cried out loud when she saw the boy was virtually decapitated.

'WHY! WHY! WHY!' she screamed at the soldier.

Suddenly, his expression changed as he saw her for the attractive young woman she was. Sheathing his bloodstained knife, he ran his gaze quickly over her body. Instantly, she was aware of terrible danger. If he had cut the throat of an innocent boy, there was no doubt what he had in store for her. She made to run, but the street was too cluttered to cover much ground and, before she had gone twenty yards, he was upon her.

Seizing her like a child, he glanced quickly around before his attention was drawn to the remains of a doorless garden shed which had been only partially destroyed. Carrying his rifle in one hand and dragging her with the other, he entered the shed and, after propping his rifle against the wall, threw her onto a rubble-strewn table. As his hand tore at her collar, she could feel the small pieces of masonry beneath her pressing into her spine. He then pulled her forward so that her legs hung down from the table before ripping most of the clothing from her. Raising one knee, he forced her thighs apart and tugged his trousers open. The pain was intense as he entered her dryness and she instinctively put all her energy into one final struggle. For a brief moment she wriggled free and moved around the table but there was only one exit from the shed and he more than covered it. She scrambled frantically but he caught her by the foot and laughed loudly as his trousers fell to his ankles. Though she struggled as violently as ever, she could feel her strength ebbing and suddenly thought it was an appalling place to die because die she certainly would once he had finished with her.

'PEDRO! Or whatever your fucking name is, leave her be!' She was as surprised as her attacker to see two of the newsmen she had met earlier, standing at the doorway aiming the soldier's own rifle at his head.

The Moor raised one hand defensively. '*Non,*' he cried. '*Non dispara! Non dispara!*'

Julia wanted to cry with relief. But the Moor was not yet done with her. She could feel his hand drop to his side, but she carelessly thought it was to tug up the trousers over his still erect penis. Instead his hand whipped up with the same curved knife that had killed poor José. Tugging her backwards he held the knife so tight against her throat that she felt it would sever her windpipe. For the briefest of moments there was total stalemate. The rifle was still aimed at his head and the knife was tight to her throat. However, because of the table, her assailant had not been able to stand immediately behind her and the lower part of his body was still exposed to the newsmen.

The second newsman suddenly pointed at the soldier's exposed genitalia. 'Tell him you'll shoot the lot off. He won't be so keen to chance that!'

The old correspondent instantly saw the possibilities of the situation and slowly and deliberately dropped his aim to the soldier's groin. '*Non! Non!*' screamed the Moor, shaking his head vigorously and dropping the knife to the floor.

'Okay, love,' said Denis Watts. 'Get dressed quickly. We must get out of here before his friends show up.'

Snatching at her clothing, she panted, 'Ask him why he killed the boy.'

Denis Watts, who seemed to know some Spanish, spoke briefly to the now sullen Moor and received a mumbled reply.

'He said it was the boy's shoulder. Apparently these Moors have been shot at so many times by civilians that they now examine everyone's shoulder. If it's bruised they kill them. He reckons the boy's shoulder proved he was a sniper.'

'But I don't understand,' cried Julia. 'How can a bruised shoulder prove anything?'

'Some of the rifles used in this war are old and heavy and have a hell of a recoil,' he explained. 'If you're not used to handling them, they'll bruise like a kick from a mule.'

'But he hurt his shoulder falling from a donkey cart!' she screamed at the Moor. 'A bloody donkey cart! Don't you understand, you bastard? He was trying to get supplies to help the wounded. He was just a boy! A young and innocent BOY!'

'C'mon quickly,' urged Watts. 'He doesn't understand a word you say. We must get away as soon as possible. Once he tells his mates what's happened here, they'll kill us as easy as they killed your little lad. Newsmen aren't supposed to take sides in a war you know.'

'So what do you propose?' she said. 'Because I'm not leaving here until I've buried José.'

'If we do that, we're dead,' he said. 'It's as simple as that. What we have to do, is to tie this fellow up, gag him so he can't attract attention and leave his rifle well out of reach. We then have to put as much space as possible between us and the rest of his army.'

'Well, I can't tie knots to save my life,' said Julia. 'He'd have it undone in seconds. You two tie him. I'll hold the gun.'

'Okay,' agreed the newsman, 'but for Pete's sake, let's hurry!'

It was all over in seconds. She had no sooner been given the rifle than she put a single bullet straight into the brain of the Moor.

'There,' she said, ignoring the blood that had spattered onto what was left of her clothing. 'Now, we don't have to worry about him telling anyone anything, do we?'

'My God!' cried the younger newsman brushing brains from his coat. 'What the fuck have you *done*?'

'She's given us an outside chance of getting out of here.

That's what she's done,' retorted Denis. 'Quick, shove him under that table, sling some rubble over him, and let's go!'

'Not until I've buried José,' she insisted.

'Look,' snapped Watts. 'José is dead, together with this town. If you stop to bury him, you'll be joining him. If we stop with you and they discover that Moor under the table, we'll all be dead – not very pleasantly and not very quick. For little more than the time it'll take to bury José, we can all be at the French border. This is no time for histrionics, so can you tell me how risking all our lives is going to help that little lad's path to heaven?'

'You're right,' she agreed. 'I've had one scare and I'm not yet ready for another. Let's go!'

Pausing long enough for her to touch the dead lips of poor José, the trio dashed across the rubble to a crater-strewn municipal garden where three other reporters waited impatiently.

'Are you all going back to England?' she asked as the car gathered speed.

'Yes, we've each done our stint out here,' said Denis. 'It's time someone else held the torch for a while. We'll all be back again for the real thing in a year or so anyway.'

'What "real thing"?' asked the girl curiously.

'The real thing with Germany,' explained the newsman. 'There's not another country in Europe that could currently wipe out a town like we've just seen done to Guernica. And these are only their toys! You wait till they field their first team! Still, perhaps the government might now listen to people like Churchill.'

'They'd better,' said the younger man. 'Or "Guernicas" will be a daily occurrence with matinées Wednesday and Saturday. Thank God, we're out of it for a while.'

'I wouldn't speak too soon about that,' said Denis quietly. 'Look what's up ahead.'

At a curve in the road, a truck appeared to have been recently ambushed. There were several dead men on the road and at least a dozen Moorish soldiers stripping the bodies together with what seemed to be a Spanish officer.

'We correspondents should be all right,' Denis muttered quickly to Julia. 'But we may have a problem with you. D'you have a passport or any papers giving you permission to travel?'

'No,' she replied. 'Everything I had is beneath the rubble of the hospital.'

'Right. Then listen carefully,' he snapped. 'We are English reporters heading for home via the French border and you're an English nurse we've picked up because you've been injured in a road accident and robbed. They won't know the blood on your clothing is actually Moorish. You'll need to be conscious because we may need you to speak to prove you're English. On the other hand, you'll need to appear groggy. Get it?'

'I can see why you're a newspaperman,' she whispered before she dropped her jaw and lay back motionless in her seat.

With three rifles now trained on their windscreen, the reporters' car came to a halt.

'Papers!' snapped the officer.

The collective passports and papers were handed over. After a careful scrutiny, the officer then pointed at the dazed Julia.

'Who?' he demanded.

Denis then recounted a tale in halting Spanish in which the villains of the piece were wicked Republicans. This seemed to reinforce the officer's general opinion of all Republicans as thieves and murderers and with a gracious nod, he waved them on their way.

'Phew,' exclaimed Denis as he watched the roadblock fade into the distance, 'I'm beginning to think I'm getting too old for this job.' He was only slightly miffed when no one contradicted him.

Conversation then petered out for the next twenty miles

until the town of Zarauz came into view.

Leaning forward, Julia announced, 'There's a temporary field hospital on the outskirts of this town. If you drop me off here, it'll do me fine. Thank you all for your help.'

'What d'you mean, drop you off here? You said you were coming with us to France,' said Denis.

'No,' she corrected. '*You* said I was going to France. *I* never mentioned it. I'm a nurse, remember? This is where I belong. I'll be seeing you, fellows. And I'll tell you this. I'll never say another rude word about reporters.'

28

'How much longer will you be attending Millbank out-patients department?' asked Billie over breakfast.

'Two weeks, they say,' replied Duncan without looking up from his newspaper.

'And how much sick leave will you be due then?' she continued.

'Eh?' he mumbled with his head still buried into the sports' pages. 'Oh, I dunno. Twenty-eight days or thereabouts.'

'And do you have anything planned for those twenty-eight days?' she persisted.

He slowly raised his head and carefully folded the paper. 'Okay, I give in. I'm obviously not going to be allowed to finish the paper. Why the sudden interest?'

'Well,' she announced, 'if you had read the newspaper correctly, and not from back to front like you usually do, by now you'd have seen it for yourself. Try the feature article next to the editorial. You may find it of interest.'

There was something in her tone that made him open the paper quickly at that page. His eyes raced over the article without really absorbing any of its content. He knew he was looking for something, yet he had no idea what it was. Yes, he did! It was there in front of him! It was Julia Giles, or rather *Nurse* Julia Giles! Flitting back to the beginning of the article, he found it related to the bravery of young nurses in the Spanish Civil War. After reading it through twice, he dashed to the bookcase in a vain attempt to find an atlas.

'It's on the settee. I looked it up when you were still in bed,' said Billie smugly. 'Zarauz Field Hospital is twenty miles from the port of Hendaye, which has a British consulate on the French-Spanish border. I thought you might be interested.'

His initial enthusiasm faded slightly when he suddenly remembered it was almost impossible for a lone traveller to enter Spain because of the war.

'There's also the small matter of your out-patient treatment,' pointed out Billie.

'Yes,' he agreed. 'And that really *is* a problem. If I don't finish my treatment, I won't get my leave. It's as simple as that.'

'But that's no bad thing, is it?' she said brightly. 'If you were to use the spare time between appointments sensibly, you never know what ideas you might come up with in the space of two weeks. If you're successful, you could leave the instant your leave starts. By the way, I take it the army will let you go to Spain?'

'Good God, no!' he exclaimed. 'They'd have a fit! It'll have to be a secret. You know, change of name and that sort of thing. I suppose you've no idea where I should start first, bearing in mind I can do nothing officially?'

'As a matter of fact I do have an idea,' she murmured quietly. 'Why don't you get in touch with Denis Watts? He's the one who wrote the article in the newspaper. He'll certainly know Spain better than anyone you're likely to meet. You could say that if you're able to find Julia and chat her into coming home, he'd have sole rights to your story. There's not a reporter in the world who could refuse that sort of sequel. It'll cost him nothing and he'll make a few bob.'

'Billie Bardell,' he said rising swiftly to his feet. 'If I wasn't already in love with my Julia, I'd kiss you all over.'

'Hmmn. That is a problem, I suppose,' she said thoughtfully. 'Perhaps you could just settle for a few bits?'

* * *

Denis Watts did indeed think such a love story would be a journalistic scoop, but he also pointed out to Duncan the futility of the idea.

'You'll never get into the country for such a reason,' he said. 'At the moment, I'm afraid Spain is not heavily into romance. However . . .' his voice trailed away.

Duncan suddenly became very alert. 'However' to him meant that all was not lost.

'Yes?' he said. 'Tell me more about this "However" bit.'

'Currently, there is one sure way for a determined young man to enter Spain. It's arduous, dangerous and could possibly be fatal, but I'm sure someone like you could manage it.'

'Go on,' encouraged Duncan.

'You could join the International Brigade,' said Watts. 'That would certainly get you to Spain.' He gave a quick shrug. 'Of course, you could be dead by the first morning, but that would be governed by either the luck of the draw or your ability to stay alive. Once there, you would need to desert. When you do that, of course, *both* sides would be trying to kill you. Still fancy it?'

'Where can I join?'

'You could try the Communist Party offices in the Ball's Pond Road. They'd welcome a fine big chap like you. If you survive, come and see me when you get back. It'll be worth twenty-five quid from the paper for your story. Fetch the girl back with you and they'd probably make it a hundred. Oh, and by the way, do you smoke?'

'Smoke?' queried Duncan, puzzled. 'No, I never have.'

'Good,' said Watts. 'Then go out now and buy as many tins of cigarettes as you can afford. You'll find them priceless when it comes to bartering because they're worth more than currency and you don't have to keep changing them at borders.'

'Thanks for the advice,' said Duncan, offering a quick

handshake of farewell. 'And you can tell your newspaper to start saving their cash because I'm due a hundred quid the next time you see me.'

The next two weeks could not pass quickly enough for Duncan and after a quick call to Major Baker, his leave was confirmed. 'Doing anything special?' asked the major out of polite curiosity.

'Not really,' lied Duncan. 'Just a little change of scene perhaps.'

As Watts had suggested, Duncan's little change of scene began in the Communist offices, Ball's Pond Road where, after a ten-minute interview, six questions and no hint of a medical, he was given a three-day return rail ticket to Paris via Victoria and Calais.

'I'm afraid I have no passport,' he said to the frumpish, sharply spoken, middle-aged woman who interviewed him.

'Not needed for Paris,' she grunted. 'That's why we go that way. When you arrive, you'll need a taxi to this hall in the Rue de la Convention.' She handed him a small printed card. 'All you'll need are your personal toiletries, some Spanish currency and a change of under clothing. Any questions?'

'When do I leave?'

She glanced down at a heavily inked list. 'Thursday, 10 a.m. from Victoria and don't miss the train. Unused tickets are expensive. Good luck, comrade.'

When he recounted his day to Billie, she exploded. 'It's quite the most idiotic thing you've ever done,' she cried, clapping her hand to her forehead. 'And for you, that really is saying something! You know what's going to happen, don't you? Julia's going to come back thriving and married to some dago with six sherry groves and a beard and you're going to be spread all over some bloody Barcelona boulevard like marmalade. You're stupid! You're absolutely bloody stupid!'

'They don't have boulevards in Spain,' he grinned. 'They have avenidas.'

'And *that*, old clever dick, is about all you know about the bloody country!'

He slipped a friendly arm round her shoulder. 'Aw, come on, Billie,' he pleaded. 'At least be on my side to start with, eh?'

She looked at him for a few seconds before her face broke finally into a smile. 'It's still a stupid idea, y'know,' she murmured. 'But I suppose you could just be lucky enough to carry it off.'

'That's unless she's married some dago with a beard, of course. Then I'll shoot them both and come back and really will kiss you all over. How's that suit?'

To his surprise, she suddenly looked anxious. 'It's no time for jokes, Duncan. I've lost Alice and Julia. I don't want to lose you too. Tell me what you *really* know of this International Brigade? I'm worried sick.'

'Not a lot,' he conceded. 'I think they're mainly a bunch of idealists who mean well and have decided they must fight fascism. They've been flocking to Spain for over a year now and they're badly trained, badly armed, can't speak the language and taking a hell of a pasting. That's about all I know really.'

'And that's going to be you in a few days time?'

'No, of course not,' he assured her. 'For several months I was a small-arms instructor in India. If nothing else, I'm at least capable of foot soldiering.'

'This foot soldiering you speak of,' she queried. 'Does it cater for shooting down aeroplanes and fighting tanks?'

'You know, Billie,' he said, kissing her forehead lightly, 'I've never thought of you as a pessimist before. In any case, I've got to return to England because Major Baker said we'll be having a war of our own soon. Now, seeing as the new king has spent an awful lot of money training me, the least I can do is come back and give him a hand. So, how about you and Elsie coming down to Victoria station on Thursday morning and seeing me off? It'll make my incentive to return that much greater, eh?'

'Well, you may yet regret inviting Elsie, but we'll both be there.'

If he had been honest, Duncan would have admitted he had not been too impressed by the frumpish woman in the Balls Pond Road. Yet the itinerary she had given him had been exact in every detail and, other than some emotion from Elsie at Victoria station, the entire journey from Hampstead to the Rue de la Convention had been smoothness itself. In fact it had been so smooth he felt it could not last and he was certainly correct about that. Firstly, the hall was in chaos and, because there were so many languages and dialects, few of the officials understood the mass of volunteers. The whole communal principle of a combined international force was soon in tatters. One of the few things Duncan was able to discover was that early next morning, they were to catch a train for the town of Perpignan which was some twenty miles from the Spanish border. After picking at a dreadful meal, he found a quiet corner and curled up on the floor for the night. To his surprise he slept very soundly and it took him some time to work out where he was next morning. Breakfast turned out to be no more exciting than dinner had been and, in common with most of the volunteers, he found himself aching to leave Paris and start his share of the war.

The long train ride to Perpignan was as uncomfortable as Duncan had expected. The train was packed, the carriages claustrophobic and no food was provided. His one consolation was the peaceful countryside outside. He found it almost impossible to look out of the window and think of going to war. At least that was the case until, in the far distance, he saw his first glimpse of the Pyrenees. For him and thousands before him, the barrier of rugged mountains that separated France from Spain was like a massive safety curtain. On one side was peace and tranquillity, on the other, fire and chaos.

It was late at night when the volunteers disembarked into

lorries that waited to take them to a camp two miles out of town. Duncan was beginning to think that subjecting them to all the miseries of this journey was a deliberate ploy to make them forget their hunger. He had hardly eaten since he left Victoria and for the second consecutive night, he was to sleep on the floor. In addition, he suspected that he, together with several of his new acquaintances, had acquired a generous helping of lice.

Next morning's breakfast, being the fourth dreadful meal in a row, aroused the first mutterings from the men. The meal had been taken in the open air in the shelter of conifers and shrubs.

Suddenly complaints were stifled as a rotund bespectacled figure in a stained uniform and torn beret climbed onto a tree stump and held up his hands for silence. To his credit, he quietened the babble immediately and as the voices faded, he proceeded to make several announcements in English, French, Spanish and at least two other languages that Duncan could not place. Each attempt was greeted by ironic cheers from the nationality addressed.

The text of the English announcement seemed to be that they were to leave in a few minutes for their training camp at the small town of San Durrin just over the Spanish border. The contingent would consist solely of English speakers, who, besides the British, included a fair sprinkling of Australians, Canadians, New Zealanders, Americans and one Indian.

'Can we wash there?' asked Duncan hopefully.

'Of course, meester, they 'ave river! You'll see plenty soon.'

'Thank God for that!' exclaimed an American voice from somewhere nearby.

Though the journey to San Durrin was not long, the rugged terrain did not make for speed and it took the best part of three hours to cover the twenty-five miles to the remote camp in the foothills of the Pyrenees. All that could be said in favour of this latest camp, was that there was a slight hint of order. By now, it was clear that everyone was so lousy that heads were shaved and clothing baked. However, any improvement to clothing was so marginal that the American claimed the only difference was warm nits. The close proximity of sleeping spaces in the tents did little to help this infestation, but some ferocious red powder at least gave the illusion of something being done.

Though Duncan had decided not to mention his army background, it became increasingly difficult not to do so when faced with the paucity of army skills.

By the third day they were issued with what passed for a uniform. This consisted of a thin jacket and trousers plus beret and personal bedding. This clothing was totally unsuited for such an elevation and most men wore their civilian clothing beneath their uniforms in a vain attempt to keep warm. Whilst this improved their temperature, it did nothing to combat their lice.

Once these uniforms were issued, their three-week training began. Yet, in spite of this development, there was general apathy because of the absence of a single real weapon. There certainly appeared no shortage of home-made and obsolete explosives but as yet, not even a hint of a rifle. Early morning runs were made in the hills whilst foot drill and lectures were carried on well into the day, but without weapons it did not feel like being in an army. This atmosphere was not helped by the absence of badges of rank and the practice of calling everyone 'Comrade'.

Duncan began to find himself intrigued by a small, wiry, one-eyed instructor with a badly disfigured face who claimed his name was Cornelius. No one knew if this was a surname or Christian name and he certainly never volunteered explanations. The story around the camp was that he was wanted in England for a number of serious offences though this was never confirmed. Duncan guessed that Cornelius had spent at least part of his life in the army, because even without weapons, his knowledge of explosives was good and no matter how futile the training, he could always retain the recruits' attention with humour. This had been particularly true one morning when he was instructing a class how best to disable a tank.

'Yer finds a suitable bush,' said Cornelius, 'in which yer 'ides yerself until yer enemy tank appears. On 'is approach, yer scuttles out from yer bush wiv' ten feet o' lethal copper wire which yer ties to a bush opposite. Then, when the tank touches the wire, yer explosive is fired out this old water pipe an' it strikes the tank a ferocious wallop on its trackin'.'

'Er – these bushes, comrade,' said a cynical Australian. 'Are we issued with them? I mean, the chances of finding *two* bushes in the centre of the tank's path is remote, wouldn't you say? Meantime, what's the tank's gunner going to be doing while we're scuttling underneath his nose with ten feet of copper wiring?'

'Ah!' said Cornelius, 'that's a very pertinent question an' I'm pleased yer asked it. Yer see these bushes are probably of the collapsible variety an' the theory is, that the gunner will be so intrigued to know what yer doin', that 'e'll fergit ter shoot yer. It's a recognised military tactic, that is. It's called psychological warfare and our side's very good at it.'

'This explosive,' asked Duncan. 'How penetrating is it?'

'Oh, it's extremely penetrating, an' it's top secret,' said Cornelius glancing confidentially from side to side. 'At a range of four yards,' he rubbed his chin thoughtfully, 'I'd say it'd make a hell of a dent in a zinc bath.'

At this point the American stood up and understandably pointed out that, having travelled three thousand miles at his own expense to fight in the war, he felt he should at least have access to decent equipment.

'If we 'ad decent equipment, comrade,' said Cornelius quietly, 'I'd be able ter teach some of yer 'ow ter be soldiers. But as we ain't, I can't. So I'm just teachin' yer ter stay alive. Believe it or not, this anti-tank joke is listed as a suitable weapon fer infantry and I'm supposed to teach you how to use it. Now, after this little lecture, 'ow many of yer will be daft enough ter do so?' There was total silence, as they all looked anxiously at each other. 'Good,' he said. 'Because personally I think you're all bleedin' 'eroes ter be 'ere in the first place. But just because you're 'eroes don't mean yer should chuck away yer lives uselessly. Do yer know, on some fronts o' this war, the International Brigade kill more of themselves than they do the enemy? If I can prevent that 'appening to just one o' yer, then me time ain't been wasted.' He glanced at his watch. 'Okay, comrades, five-minute smoke break.'

The afternoon sun had burnt off some of the mountain cloud and the valley was now quite warm. Duncan used the opportunity to flop down in the long grass and close his eyes. He was vaguely aware of someone dropping beside him but felt no inclination to speak.

'Why 'aven't yer let on about yer army background?' whispered Cornelius. 'I'm not pryin' but we could do with all the 'elp we can get when we're trainin' recruits like these.'

'How'd you know I've an army background?' asked Duncan curiously.

'It's written all over yer. I don't wanna know yer motives; I just need yer 'elp.'

'As far as I can see,' said Duncan, 'these lads are earmarked for nothing more than cannon fodder. If that's the case, they'd at least be better off learning fieldcraft and rifle work. But as we don't seem to *have* any rifles, there's not much point even to that.'

'Rumour has it we'll be getting twenty-five Lee Enfields in three days,' said Cornelius. 'Now, d'you fancy givin' a hand?'

'Twenty-five rifles for thirty men?' queried Duncan. 'For your sake, I hope you find five blokes who aren't easily offended.'

'No problem at all,' said Cornelius. 'In nearly every intake there are six men who're as blind as bats, four who can't walk

462

properly and one who's got about a week to live. Did they give *you* a medical when yer joined?'

'No,' admitted Duncan. 'I must say I'd forgotten that.'

'There yer are then, so what d'yer say?'

Although he would have never admitted it, Duncan was secretly relieved at being given the opportunity to help. Since arriving in Spain he had acquired a guilt complex about his plan to desert and it had nagged at him continuously. Perhaps this was his chance to placate his conscience.

'Okay, I'll do it.'

''Ow about staying on 'ere for the whole duration of the war and 'elpin' train each intake?' said Cornelius hopefully. 'We could certainly do with it.'

'I don't have that sort of time,' replied Duncan. 'Anyway, don't push your luck, you've got one result. As soon as I've got twenty-five blokes who can fire a rifle in the general direction of their enemy, I'm in the clear. Agreed?'

Cornelius nodded reluctantly and held out his hand. 'Agreed.'

Whether Cornelius had been responsible for spreading the rifle rumour among the intake, Duncan had no means of knowing, but from that day the men's attitude changed considerably. Perhaps no one wanted to be one of the luckless five, but whatever the reason, there was a definite surge of enthusiasm as Duncan instructed them in their first lessons in fieldcraft. Before the morning was out, men were already assessing landscapes, camouflaging themselves and responding to basic signals. In fact, with rifles, they might even have passed for soldiers.

There was not long to wait, however, as, true to Cornelius's rumour, a truck rumbled into camp on the third day with a wooden case of well-greased, brand-new, Lee Enfield rifles.

'I've been in Spain nigh on three years an' this is the first time I've seen a *new* rifle!' marvelled Cornelius. 'Perhaps you're a good omen!'

Each day, Duncan found his conscience weighing the

improvement in his colleagues against the guilt of his impending departure, until, on the twenty-first night, Cornelius held a meeting to announce the postings. Next morning they were all to march twenty-five miles to Figueres to join up with five hundred assorted members of the International Brigade. From there they were to travel to Madrid to take over the trenches at the south of the city.

'I suggest yer all get an early night,' advised Cornelius, 'because from now on, yer'll need every second of sleep yer can get.'

'That be pretty safe advice,' moaned an East Anglian voice, 'seeing as there be nuthin' here for a man's passion but squirrels and a cold river.'

It was the cold river that was bothering Duncan most. If he was to leave the camp it had to be tonight while he was still close to the border. The trouble was, he was on the wrong side of the river. To start an overnight eight-mile hike across the Pyrenees soaking wet was asking for disaster. He decided to set an example by wriggling deep into his sleeping bag in the hope that the rest of the group would take the hint. As usual, there was always one contrary individual who seemed far removed from sleep and it was practically midnight before he felt the camp was finally quiet. His plan, such as it was, was to return to France then follow the border westward until he reached the Atlantic coast. Originally, he had not intended to pack his blanket but if he was going to wade the river, he would need its warmth until he dried. Tiptoeing from the tent, his movements were unhurried and it was with quiet confidence that he left the camp and reached the water's edge.

'Are yer sure yer thought all this through?' whispered a familiar voice from the darkness, 'because it don't look like good fieldcraft ter me.'

Duncan's finger tightened instinctively on the rifle trigger. 'I hope you don't intend standing in my way, Cornelius,' he replied quietly.

'Certainly not! I'm just pointin' out that yer fieldcraft is crap, that's all,' explained the instructor. 'You're taking on the Pyrenees at night and yer goin' ter be soaking wet from the first minute of yer trip. Surely yer remember yer fieldcraft? Yer've been spoutin' on about it enough times the last three weeks.'

'Come to the point, Cornelius,' snapped Duncan curtly. 'I've got a long way to go.'

'Just a little advice, son, that's all. If yer take a detour upstream fer a couple o' miles, the water's quite shallow and yer can cross it by stepping stones.'

'Why are you telling me this? You could have justifiably shot me.'

'Oh, I knew from the start yer were never a political idealist. I've seen 'undreds, if not thousands, of them and yer not like a single one of 'em. So yer 'ad ter 'ave some other reason fer comin' ter Spain. I s'pose joinin' the Brigade is the only way ter do it while the war's on. Well, yer've been very 'elpful ter me and I quite like yer as a bloke, so, if yer wants ter piss off it's not my business.' Pointing his rifle at a gap between trees, he added, 'Just follow that path an' that'll take yer to the stones. Oh, by the way, I'll have ter relieve yer of that rifle, I'm afraid. It's bad enough losin' you, but a rifle is far more valuable than any man, so put it down gently please.'

Duncan knew the hard truth of those words and nodded a reluctant agreement.

'Where yer bound fer?'

'Zarauz Field Hospital, it's near San Sebastian.'

'Bloody 'ell, man!' exclaimed Cornelius, 'that must be two 'undred miles away. I 'ope yer've got plenty o' money, 'cos yer'll certainly need it!'

Duncan was not sure how best to answer. After all, it was dark and he could not see Cornelius clearly. In addition, if the man shot him as a deserter, who would care if he also robbed him? In such situations it was almost expected. 'I do have cigarettes,' he replied. 'A lot of them.'

'Sensible lad,' nodded Cornelius. 'Much better than money, but you'll get the best deal on this side of the border. Once you cross it, the French will rob you blind.' The old instructor rubbed his chin thoughtfully. 'Y'know what I'd do, if I was you? While I was still in Spain I'd trade some of those fags fer an old bike. There's always one lyin' around these villages. Then, once yer across the border, yer can always be makin' at least some progress instead of just sittin' on yer arse waitin' fer somethin' ter turn up. I mean, if the worst comes to the worst, yer could even bike the whole way in about ten days.'

'It's a great idea,' said Duncan, 'except I'd need to go into a Spanish town to buy the bike. I'd then be fair game for anyone to shoot me – of either side.'

'Well,' said Cornelius slowly, 'it so happens . . .'

Duncan stared at him for a second. 'You old crook!' he finally exclaimed. 'You knew all along what I was up to, didn't you?' He shook his head in disbelief before adding, 'How about three hundred Player's cigarettes for a deal?'

'What's the matter with five hundred?'

'Four hundred; not a fag-end more.'

'Done!' The instructor bent down into the shadows and lifted a sturdy old cycle from the wet grass. 'Take my word fer it, it's a good runner, as they say.'

'If it's not,' said Duncan, rummaging in his rucksack, 'I'll report you to both sides for treason.'

Cradling the eight tins of cigarettes in his arms, Cornelius said, 'Yer must put as much distance between yerself an' this camp as possible. Because if anyone wakes early an' finds you gone, I'd be expected ter search fer an' shoot yer. So, on yer way, soldier, an' the best of luck in whatever you're looking fer.'

Hoisting the cycle onto his shoulder, Duncan, now a fugitive, set off along the river assessing his situation as he went. He was cold, tired, hungry and in a foreign country at the dead of night with a probable stolen bike and, for the first time, beginning to wonder just what the hell he was doing there.

29

Duncan's planning to reach Julia Giles had hardly been meticulously thought out. He had done little more than head off in the general direction of Spain – the wrong side of Spain as it happened – and hope for the best. The best, as it turned out, had happened in the shape of Cornelius's cycle. It was a pity though that the instructor's two-hundred miles estimate to Zarauz had been so wildly inaccurate. Cornelius had cheerfully assumed that all Duncan needed to do was cross the French border and turn left. But Duncan was riding a cycle not a crow and soon discovered there was no such thing as a straight road in the Pyrenees. Some days the only road headed north, some days south, but as long as it didn't wander back into Spain, Duncan stuck to it doggedly. If the best blessing was the cycle, then the cigarettes proved to be runners-up. Hugging the border as closely as possible, he usually managed to barter for a meal. The uniform of the International Brigade was at first a worry, but by reversing it with his civilian clothes, it was mostly hidden. In remote farms, where he usually spent the night, deserters from either army were not entirely unknown and, though conversation might be scant, so at least were questions.

The ten-day journey estimated by Cornelius had run into two weeks before Duncan free-wheeled down the steep hill that led into the French port of Hendaye. With his total lack of French, he had thought he might have had difficulty finding the British Consulate but the cluster of tired wretches who gathered outside the grey-stone building flying the Union

Jack indicated differently. Until he laid eyes on them, Duncan had deluded himself into thinking he was fairly nondescript, but seeing them, he realised that a deserter is a deserter the world over. Propping his cycle against a tree, he took his place in one of the two queues.

'I'd not leave the bike there if I were you, mate,' said a voice behind him. Duncan turned to see a young, slightly built man with eyes twenty years older than his face and wearing a grimy bloodstained head bandage. 'If it can be sold it can be nicked,' continued the youth. 'And if it can be nicked,' he shrugged, 'then it will be.'

'Thanks for the advice,' said Duncan. 'But I don't really know where I can leave . . .'

'Take it with you. No one's going to mind – except whoever was planning to nick it, I suppose,' he said wearily.

Realising the advice made good sense, Duncan collected the cycle and rejoined the youth in the queue. They fell into conversation and Duncan discovered that the Republican front was crumbling fast.

'It's nearly all over now,' said the youth. 'We just don't have the weapons. What good is a rifle against aircraft?' he asked bitterly. 'It's like pissing against the wind. There's not a piece of equipment on the Republic side that remotely compares with the Fascists'. We came out here with the best of intentions, but it was a slaughter – just a slaughter,' he repeated, his voice trailing away.

Up until that moment, Duncan had been afraid he was going to be asked about his own experiences. Riding a nicked bike across France for a fortnight was hardly the stuff of heroes, but the youth had returned to his shell and was now staring vacantly into the distance.

After more than two hours, Duncan finally reached the head of the queue where a plump, surly-looking, middle-aged blonde sat with a black cigarette in her mouth that gave off so much smoke that one eye seemed permanently shut. He had heard her tone with several in the queue and had taken an instant dislike to her manner. However, in spite of this, he found himself compulsively staring down her neckline. He wasn't sure if it was a trick of the light, a fold in her dress, or if he really could see the top of a large left nipple.

'Yes?' she asked acidly.

'I wonder if you can help me. I'm trying to reach Zarauz Field Hospital,' he said, still undecided as to the nipple. 'I understand it's about twenty miles over the border. I want to fetch out a British nurse who's working there.'

'Is she being held against her will?' asked the woman.

'Well, not that I'm aware of, no. She's just nursing.'

'Is she injured or mentally ill?'

'Well, I don't . . .'

'Has she requested your assistance to leave Spain?'

'Well, no, but . . .'

'Do you have a passport and the necessary papers to get her through the Spanish border control?'

'No, of course not!' he snapped irritably. 'Look, all I'm doing . . .'

'Oh, I know exactly what you're doing,' she snapped. 'You're looking down my dress, you beast!'

For the first time in his adult life Duncan knew he had reddened. It was true he had been looking down her dress and he was now desperately wishing he hadn't.

'Is it worth looking down, mate?' said an unhelpful voice from further down the queue. 'Only we ain't seen a lot of tit lately. If you hurry up we can all have a look.'

The words provoked a burst of cheering from those nearest the head of the queue and a great deal of rubber-necking from those further away. The commotion was enough to draw the attention of the assistant consul from an inner office. 'Just what *is* going on here, Miss Vincent?' he asked in a superior drawl.

'It's this applicant, Mr Wedgewood. He's being coarse and vulgar and staring down my dress.'

'Now wait a minute!' protested Duncan. 'All I'm doing is

trying to trace a nurse from Zarauz hospital.'

'It's gone,' droned Mr Wedgewood. 'Closed weeks ago.'

'You mean it's moved?' asked Duncan.

'I mean it's *closed*,' repeated Mr Wedgewood sharply. 'It closed because of a typhus outbreak. Those who died are buried there. Anyone well enough to travel was shipped back to their own country.'

'Do you have a list of the British nurses who survived?' asked Duncan anxiously.

'No, but the son of our cashier was in the quarantined group. He'll know where they were transferred. Wait, I'll find out.'

True to his word, he returned within seconds. 'Apparently he doesn't know the address but it was somewhere in Kent.'

'Do you mean to say that I've come all this . . .' began Duncan closing his eyes in self-pity. 'No, cancel that. How do I get back to England?'

'Same as everyone else,' said Mr Wedgewood, as if speaking to a particularly backward child. 'One resumes one's place in one's queue. One presents one's passport politely to Miss Vincent. Then one ceases to peek at her bosom. That way, one gets home. Easy, isn't it?'

There were precious few British applicants to the Hendaye consul who had *any* means of identification, let alone a passport. But at least they were in France. France did not want them and therefore made every means available to speed them on their way. Once documented, the applicants were directed to a local hall where soup, bread and clean wound dressings were freely available. Then, every hour or so, a messenger would arrive with a list of names to report back to the consul. There they would be given a time and place of departure. It seemed by the differing locations allocated, there was no overall plan and that men were directed to fill whatever vacancy could be found. To Duncan's relief, he missed the truck journey to Le Havre by two places but made the steamer to Falmouth by the same number.

Having received that blessed news, he decided it was time to abandon the old cycle in the hope that whoever next acquired it would inherit his good fortune.

'You'd better pray for calm weather crossing the Bay of Biscay tomorrow,' said the clerk at the consulate, 'because the wounded will be below deck but the rest of you will be in blankets on top.'

'I doan't care if they skewer me arse to the flagpole,' said a Welsh voice. 'Just as long as we git there. Hi've seen enough foreigners for a lifetime.'

'I'm afraid you'll be seeing a whole lot more very soon,' said another voice. 'And you won't have to leave home to meet them either.'

Duncan was surprised at the agreement that greeted this prediction and realised it was one that was universally accepted amongst all who had fought in Spain.

Wednesday morning dawned with an early mist that caused the sailor on the gangplank to assure the refugees of a smooth trip.

'I trust we're straight to Falmouth?' said the Welshman worriedly, 'and not calling at Norway first.'

'No,' chuckled the matelot as he ticked their names off his list. 'It's definitely straight to Falmouth. You'll be home afore you know it.'

Duncan had lost track of the time he had been away, though he suspected his sick leave had probably overrun. He was also in a quandary as to his best course of action on landing, because if Julia *was* still alive, he would need further time to search.

Having stuck to his real name throughout his journey he saw no reason to change. After all, if he *had* been classified as an absentee, the army was unlikely to look for him amongst the tattered remnants from Spain. His fears on that score proved groundless as the ragged contingent were waved with surprising speed through the dockside control at Falmouth.

'It's because you're an embarrassment,' whispered a

sympathetic custom's officer. 'The government didn't want your lot to go in the first place and now you're back it's easier to pretend you never existed. Especially as the other side's going to win!'

Whilst this news of their anonymity was welcome, it did present one great difficulty for Duncan. He was now in Cornwall, dressed like a vagrant, with ten francs and forty-five fags to his name. As he stood on the pavement, the red telephone box at the dock gates was looking particularly inviting. He was just wondering if his pride would allow him a reverse charge call to Billie Bardell, when his thoughts were interrupted by running footsteps and a soft Cornish voice.

'Have 'e any money, soldjur?' it said breathlessly. He turned, half expecting a dockside whore. Instead a smiling, pleasant-faced, fiftyish woman stood, shoulders heaving, before him. ''E were out o' the gates so fast, we never 'ad time to ask 'e.' She pointed back to a small shed where a collection of his travelling companions were queuing for tea. 'None o' you young men seem to 'ave any English money.'

'I don't understand?' said Duncan suspiciously.

'Nuthin' *to* understand, me darlin',' she smiled. 'It's just a voluntary charity o' local mums. We carn't let you all go 'ome as ye are. You're welcome to a cup o' tea and a sandwich, and, if you really 'ave no money, there be two-and-sixpence to start you on your way. It's nothin' special, I'm afraid.'

'Nothing special?' he echoed. 'It's bloody salvation!'

As he returned with the woman, she told him the local church had organised a jumble counter where an assortment of old clothes had been left by its parishioners. 'Gets better by the minute,' replied Duncan. 'I'll get home looking like the Prince of Wales.'

''E ain't seen many of our parishioners then,' laughed the woman. 'Still,' she said, glancing him up and down. 'Four tatter sacks an' a pair o' skates 'ud be an improvement on what you're wearin' at the moment, luvvy.'

Once in the shed, Duncan realised that the majority of the

men present were in much the same situation as himself, namely, miles from home with little or no finances. He further guessed most of them would eventually be heading the same way, which was to the main Exeter road in the hope of thumbing a lift. He certainly could do with a change of clothes, whilst a sandwich and a mug of tea would not come amiss either but he felt his first priority was to get onto a decent lorry route. As he pondered, he once more noticed the telephone box in the distance and felt his eyes as irresistibly drawn to it as they had been to Miss Vincent's nipple. Feeling in his pocket for his ten-franc piece, he decided to toss for it. Heads he would eat, drink and ring Billie; tails he would be first onto the Exeter Road. He tossed it high and it came down tails. It should have been the Exeter Road, but overruling his own decision, he would telephone Billie Bardell.

One by one, it dawned on the men in the shed that the open road was really the place to be. As each tried to steal a minute on his neighbour, the room emptied like water from a holed bucket. If Duncan was going to throw himself on Billie Bardell's charity, he had first to find a place to stay. He decided to seek out the woman who had fetched him to the hut.

'There be a workin' man's 'ostel round from t'harbour,' she said, pointing beyond the dock gates. 'That's why we decided on two-shillin'-an'-six,' she explained. ''Cos fer that, a man can get breakfast, blankets an' a bed of sorts there.'

Duncan thanked her politely and, as he left the hut, her wistful gaze followed him until he was out of sight. Because it was barely noon, there were still several vacancies in the hostel and, though spartan, it appeared clean with only the faintest aroma of unwashed bodies. The proprietor was a tall, skinny individual with a heavy moustache and a permanent dewdrop hanging from his nose, but he seemed friendly enough and, after collecting Duncan's two shillings and sixpence he handed over a box key, two blankets and willingly exchanged Duncan's remaining cigarettes for a very welcome shilling.

The unsheeted bed was one of twenty-five in a long barrack-style room. Each bed had a tightly rolled mattress lying across its springs, and underneath stood a white-enamel chamber pot and a padlocked box. A large, yellowing notice on the wall displayed a list of house rules. These mainly consisted of an alcohol ban, a request to rinse the chamber pot, a threat of violence to anyone singing and a warning not to leave boots under beds as management accepted no responsibility for their loss.

'I've seen worse,' sighed Duncan. 'Where's the nearest public telephone?'

'Dock gates,' replied the surprised proprietor. 'Don't usually get much call for telephones here, though.'

Duncan found himself running towards the dock gates, trying to put the thought out of his mind that Billie might not be at home. At the moment she seemed his only salvation and he knew he needed her before he could resume his quest for Julia. Having given the operator the number for the transfer call, it seemed an eternity before the girl replied with, 'You're through now, caller. Go ahead.'

'Duncan Forbes!' came the blessed tones of Billie Bardell. 'What the bloody hell are you doing in Cornwall? You've not started a civil war down *there*, have you, you aggravating sod?'

'I'm afraid it's a long, sad story, Billie,' he said, 'but at the moment I'm marooned in Falmouth with just a shilling to my name. Can you send me a money order for ten quid? I'll settle up with you directly I get back to town. If you *could* get it in the post today, I may have it by morning.'

'Well, I have a million questions but they'll keep. I'll get to the post office right away. Give me your address.'

'Oh, you beauty!' he exclaimed before quickly reciting the details.

'This hostel?' she queried. 'I assume it's safe? I mean, you won't wake up in the morning with your throat cut and my letter nicked?'

'I never thought of that,' he said anxiously. 'Look, don't

worry, I'll find out what time the post comes and I'll be waiting for it. Bless you, Billie, I'll ring you directly it arrives. Goodbye!'

He walked away from the call box a considerably happier man. After all, he now had a warm jumper, a bed for the night, a shilling in his pocket and a promise of ten quid tomorrow. If he only knew Julia's whereabouts he would have been halfway to contentment. Never mind, he would soon be in London and picking up his life again.

If he had been asked next morning if he had slept, he would have denied it, primarily because he woke so often that the night seemed to consist of nothing but men snoring, coughing and farting. Nevertheless, he missed seeing the dawn break. One moment he woke and it was dark, the next a climbing sun was seeking out every stain on the window. He searched instinctively for the clock on his bedside locker, but all he saw was an open-mouthed, snoring drunk in the next bed. He realised there never had been clock nor locker. There was only a box, a chipped chamber pot and the occasional flea. He felt under the blankets for his clothes, under the mattress for his shoes and in the box for his rucksack. Once attired, he clattered quickly to the ablutions.

A smell of burnt toast led him to a partially open door in reception. The proprietor looked up, startled, as Duncan entered.

'What're you doing up so early?' he greeted. 'You won't be popular if you've woken them up at this time . . . Want some toast?'

Duncan gave a grateful nod and quickly asked if the mail had arrived.

'Good God, no,' replied the man. 'It'll be seven thirty at the earliest. Why? You expecting something good?'

Duncan realised that his concern had possibly betrayed him and he now dared not leave reception until the postman called. 'Aw, go back to bed,' coaxed the proprietor. 'It'll be an hour yet. I'll fetch it up as soon as it arrives.'

'Er – no,' said Duncan. 'Thanks very much, but now I'm up I think I'll stay up.'

'Please yourself,' said the man indifferently. 'But you'll have to make yourself useful if you want breakfast.'

'Try me,' replied Duncan.

The man nodded to a large walk-in pantry. 'Slice up four loaves, shove three saucepans of water on the gas stove and make sure there are no cockroaches in the margarine. Think you can manage?'

'You're talking to a cordon-bleu,' said Duncan. 'Stand aside.' He was halfway into the fourth loaf when the doorbell rang. 'That the post?' he called.

'No,' said the proprietor. 'Far too early. Probably some drunk who's just woken up. Ignore it.'

Not only did the bell ring again but it rang again *and* yet again. The noise was further compounded when a woman's voice yelled through the letter box.

'Duncan Forbes! Get your arse out this very minute, d'you hear me? This very minute!'

'Sorry!' called Duncan to the proprietor. 'Sounds like my letter's arrived!'

Running to the door, he threw it open and sweeping up Billie Bardell in his arms he swung her around a full circuit. 'How the hell did you get here, you witch?'

'Night train from Paddington, then cab from the station. Knowing you, I thought you'd be bound to lose the bloody money order, so I fetched it myself. Christ, don't you stink!'

Holding her nose with one hand, she pushed him down the steps with the other to the open taxi door. 'Take us to a decent hotel, mate,' she ordered the cabbie. 'I'm not speaking to him again until he's been boiled in lysol.'

Duncan's laughter as he fell into the cab vanished the instant he saw Julia Giles sitting quietly in the corner. 'But – I thought you were . . .' he began.

'I know!' she cut in. 'And I thought you were too!'

'Look, you pair,' said Billie. 'You're not only a pain in the arse to yourselves but you're also bloody expensive to me! We're going to find a decent hotel, he's going to have a bath and once the shops are open, he's going to buy himself some new clothes. Then tomorrow we're all going back to London and then, YOU'RE ON YOUR BLOODY OWN!'

30

That night in the lounge bar of the hotel, Julia was finding it more and more difficult to hide her frustration as Duncan recounted the tale of his fascist deception.

'But this comes of not trusting me!' she muttered, drumming angrily on a chair arm.

'Me not trusting *you*!' he laughed. 'I like that! Who was it that distrusted me so much that they buggered off to Spain and almost died of the pox?'

'It wasn't the pox!' she hissed, trying to keep her voice down. 'It was typhus, and anyway,' she dropped her tone to a mumble, 'I didn't get it.'

'No, but you could have done,' he reproved. 'And none of this need have happened if you hadn't jumped to so many wrong conclusions.'

Billie, who was just returning from the ladies, heard this exchange of views and stood open-mouthed. 'I don't believe I'm hearing this! I'm away for five minutes and you two are at it like a pair of bleeding jackals! What is it about you? Are you mad or something?'

'Well, he makes me so angry,' complained Julia. 'I'm sure he does it purposely.'

Duncan's intended reply was stifled by Billie who, spinning round on him, pushed an intimidating finger under his nose.

'Don't you *dare* say another word! D'you understand? Don't you dare! This is what always happens with you two. You're a lovely couple but you are so bloody pig-headed. He's right, though, Julia, you did bugger off to Spain to spite him and she's also right, Duncan, you went to search like some medieval knight who was going to take her to his castle and hoist up the drawbridge. Instead of that, you wind up looking like Jack Rags and she's bloody lucky not to have had her throat cut. By rights I should be banging your stupid heads together.'

Duncan rose to his feet and crossed to Julia's chair. Bending forward he slipped his arm over her shoulder and kissed the top of her head. 'I'm sorry, kid, it's just relief, that's all. To be honest I never thought I'd see you again, and I thought, "Bloody stupid cow, why did she want to go to Spain when I love her so much?"'

Julia stared at him for some time before replying. 'I tell you what I'm going to do Duncan Forbes,' she said finally. 'I'm going to settle for that, because that's about as close as I'm likely to get to a declaration of your undying love.' She tilted her head. 'Give me a proper kiss, you aggravating bastard, because I think it's time you started to spoil me.'

'Okay,' agreed Duncan. 'How about we spend our first week back in London making up? Suit you?'

'Suits me an absolute treat,' she agreed in pleased surprise.

'Well I'll believe *that* when I see it,' muttered Billie, raising an outsized gin. 'Perhaps you should both give it to me in writing?'

'I'm so pleased to be going back to London that I'd even do that for you, Billie,' Duncan said. 'Cheers to you both!'

Duncan's delight about returning to London was not a feeling shared by everyone. There was one man who viewed his own return to the city with more dread than most. He had been very lucky to escape from it when last there and his long absence had not made his heart any fonder. But then Sidney Grechen was in something of a dilemma. Since being domiciled in Kilideran, the local Gardia had shown no interest in the warrant for his arrest issued by the British police nine years earlier. So, his life had settled and he had become pleasantly rural.

However, the situation was changing fast. It was not the Gardia that had decided to lean on him, but the IRA. With war between Britain and Germany looking more imminent each day, a busy terrorist cell could cause havoc in London at such a worrying time. The main problem with this was that the IRA had no one currently trained for such a venture. They needed a violent criminal with a good working knowledge of both London and its underworld and they did not have one. At least that was their assumption until someone remembered Sid Grechen.

'But I've 'ad no experience,' wailed Sidney. 'An' I'm wanted fer murder and GBH there anyway. I'm really too old fer this caper. I'd only be a liability to yer.'

It was then quietly pointed out to Sidney that, if the Gardia was told of his whereabouts, he could be swinging on a Pentonville rope inside six months. On the other hand, after a few weeks of blowing arms and legs off innocent civilians in London, he could have a hero's retirement in Connaught and free Guinness for the rest of his natural.

Whatever else Sidney was, he was no fool and it was with a resigned shrug that he found himself, together with three other men, once more on the Rosslare to Fishguard ferry. Their instructions were not to go into action immediately but settle in and wait for the war either to commence or to be so close that a few bombs could cause serious disquiet. Sidney was therefore instructed to stay away from his old haunts and perversions and keep his head down in Kilburn until the signal to maim was received. By chance, both he and Duncan arrived in London on the same afternoon – Sidney at Euston and Duncan at Paddington.

Duncan was amazed how much the capital had changed during his short absence. Although officially at peace, London was on a war footing. There were air-raid shelters in the parks, adverts for chemical toilets, stirrup-pumps and sandbags everywhere, plus a definite increase in military personnel.

'Whatever's going on?' he asked, staring in amazement out of the taxi window.

'Of course,' exclaimed Billie, 'you wouldn't know, would you? We've been placed on a virtual war footing. If that little private slaughter in Spain brought no other benefit, it at least seems to have opened the government's eyes to what bombers can do to big cities.'

'I can vouch for that,' murmured Julia with a shudder. 'I saw Guernica, or rather the hole where Guernica used to be.' She huddled closer to Duncan. 'I shall never get it out of my mind.'

'Even my music school may have to move,' said Billie. 'I shall miss that if it has to go. I *do* so like waking up to violins.'

'Your music school?' echoed Duncan incredulously. 'How can closing a music school help a war effort?'

'The house, being so large, is to be requisitioned,' she explained. 'It won't affect me, really. I'd still have my flat, but they are thinking of using the grounds as an army vehicle depot and the building itself as their living quarters and offices.' She leaned forward in her seat, hunched her shoulders and rubbed her hands eagerly together. 'I think me and my Elsie might quite like that – all those sex-starved young men wandering about. Sounds quite exciting.'

'And how about you, Julia?' asked Duncan. 'What's your next step? No more foreign wars, I trust?'

She shrugged. 'Well, God forbid it should happen, but after what I've seen in Spain, I think there'll be more than enough for me to do here. Bombs don't differentiate between big soldiers and tiny babies, you know.'

As the taxi rolled into the driveway, Elsie could be seen staring anxiously from a window.

'There she is, bless her,' said Billie. 'I bet she's been popping backwards and forwards for hours. Y'know, when Grechen killed your mum, I thought I'd never find anyone so kind and considerate again. But I tell you what – this lass runs her damn close.'

'Yes,' agreed Julia. 'I once thought I would never be able to return to this house but, between you and Elsie, you've made me feel I belong again.'

As Billie paid off the taxi, the front door was thrown open and the eager face of the maid flushed the instant she saw Duncan.

'Excuse me, marm,' she said, glancing down at a written note, 'but a Major Baker has telephoned twice this morning to Mr Duncan. He said he'll be at the War Office all day.'

'Well, that's all right, Elsie,' replied Billie. 'You can tell Mr Duncan yourself. He won't bite you.'

'Well, perhaps just your bum!' cut in Duncan quickly.

'Oh, marm!' cried the girl, immediately flustered. 'What a thing to say!'

'Take no notice of him,' said Billie. 'I'm brave. I'll volunteer in your place.'

'Look,' said Duncan. 'I don't wish to interrupt this noble gesture, but will you kindly give me Baker's number? I'm so late back from leave that right now, he's just about the last person in the world I want to upset.'

Collecting the note from Elsie, Duncan ran to the hall telephone and was soon speaking to the major.

'Well, it's rather a long story, sir,' said Duncan, 'but you see, I went to the continent and lost my pass . . . Yessir . . . I see, sir . . . Uhhuh . . . As soon as that, sir? . . . Good, I'll be there.' He glanced at his watch. 'At least a half-hour before then. What will I need to take? . . . I see. Thank you. Goodbye, sir.'

Replacing the receiver he was suddenly aware that all three females were sitting on the stairs with their chins in their hands staring straight at him.

'Well?' they chorused.

'I've got to report with as much of my army kit as I can find by eight o'clock this evening at the latest.' He gave an approving nod before adding, 'Seems England has been waiting for me to return before they can really swing into top gear.'

'Hope you have more success in England than you did in Spain, then,' observed Julia cattily. 'If not, give us a ring and we'll come and rescue you.'

'Touché,' acknowledged Duncan. 'I admit I deserved that.'

'So, come on,' said Billie impatiently. 'Exactly what's happening? If I'd known the army wanted you before we went to bloody Cornwall, I'd have said, sod him, collect him yourself!'

'It's my selection board for a commission,' he explained. 'They're speeding everything up and I have to report to Sandhurst for three days of interviews and tests. Seems a bit like panic stations to me, but who am I to argue?'

Whilst Elsie prepared a meal, Duncan and the two women tore around cleaning, pressing or polishing every bit of his equipment they could find.

Later as he sat on the staircase shining his boots, Julia came and sat down beside him.

'If it's okay, I'd like to wave you goodbye at the station. Which one do you leave from?'

'Waterloo,' he replied. 'But why see me off? I'll probably be back in four days.'

'I know,' she replied quietly. 'But though you and I have known each other for years, we hardly ever seem to have had any time together. Perhaps I'm getting to the stage where I like to treasure the moments that we do have. Don't mind, do you?'

'Mind?' he laughed. 'I should think not but if you want to cab it to the station, I'll need to toss you for who pays.' He looked at her for a moment and suddenly thought how lovely she was. 'Tell you what,' he said pulling out his ten-franc piece. 'We'll toss now. Your call. Okay?'

'Okay,' she nodded. 'Heads!'

He rubbed the coin vigorously on his sleeve as he closed his eyes and muttered silently beneath his breath. 'Heads, I pay the cab fare and tails . . .' He spun the coin high in the air. 'Tails, you marry me.'

As the coin descended, it bounced against the banister rail then, tumbling to the floor, it squiggled its way across the hall before finally disappearing beneath the old settee.

It would have been scant consolation to Julia to have known she was not the only one who felt her life was being traumatised by the threat of war. Police constable Reuben Drake was also of the same mind, the only difference being that Julia was taking hers with dignity whilst Reuben was close to psychotic murder. For almost all of his service, Reuben had the date of September 1939 engraved deeply on his brain as the month he would leave the constabulary in receipt of his thirty-year pension. Whereas once it had been like a spot on a faraway planet, it was now so close he could almost touch it. All those plans, all those ventures, all those opinions he could vent on all those senior officers were now but a few tantalising weeks away. At least they *were*, but that was before the emergency was declared. He was then to discover that no police officer could retire for the duration of the war except through illness or disability. It was as if Hitler, Chamberlain, the Commissioner of Police and every senior officer he had served under plus every villain he had arrested had formed a pact to carry out some personal vendetta against him. Reuben Drake therefore, was not a happy man.

This was not, of course, a situation that applied solely to Reuben. There were many other police officers equally frustrated and their numbers would increase as the emergency continued, but it was only Reuben who took it as a personal affront. As such, he would pursue any avenue to contest the ruling and in that late summer of 1939, he approached his local council, his MP, his doctor, the London evening papers and the Police Federation, all to no avail.

It was while returning from the Federation offices on a forty-two bus, that the vehicle was stuck in traffic just north of Tower Bridge. The young constable on point duty had let his concentration lapse and within moments every vehicle in every direction had ground to a halt. Reuben mentally added this unknown pointsman to his list of people he currently hated and sat and seethed as he waited for the traffic to move again. Peering from the upstairs window of the bus, he tried to see if he recognised this idiot who was snarling up London, but he found his view obscured by another bus inching its way in the opposite direction. There was only one passenger on its top deck and the fool was also impairing Reuben's vision of the pointsman by wriggling impatiently to see the cause of the delay.

There was no doubt that the world was against Reuben that morning and he was about to announce this fact to his fellow passengers, when the bell of recognition rang in the back of his mind. That person, the one on the other bus, surely it wasn't, was it? He leaned forward and, peering intently, cursed himself for leaving his spectacles at home. As he squinted, the man suddenly turned and for a moment their eyes met. If Reuben had had doubts, Sidney Grechen had none. Before the old copper could exclaim, 'It's him!' Sidney was out of his seat and halfway down the gangway. To be fair to Reuben he did his best, but by the time he alighted from the bus, Sidney Grechen was already racing down the steps of the nearby underground station.

'I tell yer it *was* 'im!' Reuben later yelled at the detective inspector. 'There's got to be a warrant in the files somewhere. It was a murder, a rape an' Gawd knows what else. I tell yer 'e's back in town.'

'Who was dealing with it at the time?' asked the detective inspector.

'DI Evans from Hampstead CID,' replied Reuben, 'though he wasn't dealing very well if yer asks me.'

'I wasn't looking for a character reference, thanks very

much,' responded the inspector acidly. 'Just some more useful information would do fine. You see, if this really was Grechen, then I should pull out all the stops to find him. But at the moment we are on a war footing and the very last . . .'

'Oh, don't I *know* we're on a bloody war footing!' exploded Reuben. 'D'you know what the buggers have done? I'll tell you! They've suspended my retirement until . . .'

'DRAKE! Will you shut up about your retirement. PLEASE? Everyone at this station knows about your bloody retirement! In fact, we're all sick to *death* of it. I'm sick, the superintendent's sick, the local MP's sick, even Hitler himself is sick. D'you know,' he said, leaning forward confidentially, 'so many people are sick that the sanitary inspector thinks it's a recurrence of the Black Death? Did you know *that*?' Pausing for breath, the inspector resumed, 'Now, as I was about to say before you interrupted, the last thing I want to do is use a large number of men on a wild-goose chase. So, are you absolutely sure this bloke you saw was Grechen and not some poor demented sod you bored into screaming desperation about your bloody retirement?'

In twenty-nine years and eleven months no one had ever spoken to Reuben Drake like that. As a result, a stunned and expectant silence hung over the Rodney Road CID office. Suddenly, and to everyone's total surprise, Reuben rose to his feet and walked from the office without saying another word, except, that is, for an undecipherable mumble.

'I think he's finally gone off his head,' said a voice.

'Not totally unexpected, though,' said another.

'I'm not so sure,' said the DI thoughtfully. 'With all his faults, he's been a bloody good copper. He might be paranoid, bad-tempered, surly and bloody nigh schizophrenic, but he can smell a crook in the next county and if he claims to have seen Grechen in town, then I for one won't dismiss it lightly.'

The door burst open to reveal an excited young detective with a teleprinter message in his hand. He read most of it aloud to the office. 'A bomb's gone off at Blackfriars. First accounts say at least one killed and many injured. Other devices are expected in the area. Says here, that because it was aimed at civilians without warning, the IRA are suspected.'

'Oh, well,' sighed the DI. 'It's so close to our manor that we'll just have to leave Sid Grechen to simmer for a while. Can't say I'm happy, though. The more I think of it, the more uncomfortable I feel.'

31

It was with great embarrassment that Duncan wrote to Julia to explain why his four-day absence was to stretch to three months and to assure her he really wasn't personally responsible for the outbreak of war and that furthermore his marriage proposal still stood.

Apparently his secondment to Major Baker's department, plus long months in hospital, followed by his extended sick leave had not endeared him to his own regiment. Neither did the fact that he had passed the Sandhurst interview – which would involve future absences – help his cause overmuch. 'Seldom-Seen Forbes', his CO called him when he finally returned to his regimental headquarters at Windsor. As for Julia, while she accepted these absences, she did feel going to Sandhurst for three days in August and still being absent thirteen weeks later was tiresome to say the least.

'Watch him, girl,' advised Billie. 'Just because that coin came down tails, he could be having a touch of the seconds. Blokes, do you know, they go out with the lads, down three pints of beer, grope a busty barmaid and think they're playboys.'

'My Duncan's not like that,' replied Julia slipping into her coat. 'Well, anyway, not by the letter I received today. He's got permission from his CO to marry and says can we do it next Monday because he has to report to Sandhurst on Tuesday. Of course, it's very short notice but I've managed to book most things provisionally.'

'When is he due back from France?'

'Friday evening. Queenie has offered to put everyone up for the weekend, so we'll all be ready for the wedding at Streatham on Monday morning. Jim has said he'll collect you and Elsie, and Duncan and I will also be meeting there.' She glanced quickly at her watch. 'Surely that's not the time! I must fly. If there's any change in developments, I'll give you a ring.'

'Chances are,' said Billie pessimistically, 'you'll do all this tearing about then they'll post you to Singapore four hours before he arrives.'

'Not this time,' smiled Julia as she kissed the older woman goodbye. 'If nothing else, what happened in Spain has ensured that the government is keeping a full nursing staff in our big cities. In fact, at the moment, we're falling over each other. We've had a dozen children admitted because of IRA attacks but even that has stopped now the bombers have all been arrested.'

'All except one, according to the radio,' corrected Billie. 'Pity that. It would have been nice if they could have hanged the lot together. So much tidier.'

Sidney Grechen, of course, would not have seen it that way. Contrary to the strict instruction given him before he left Ireland, he had departed from the sanctuary of the terrorists' 'safe' flat in Kilburn to visit a local prostitute as her first client of the morning.

'How much?' and 'You're early, darlin',' had been about the sum total of conversation that had passed between them before Sid got down to the purpose of his visit. Sid, being Sid, had left the whorehouse complaining bitterly that he had not had value for money. Yet as he turned the corner of Brondesbury Road, instead of being short-changed, he suddenly realised it was the best thirty bob he had spent in his life. For there, only yards in front of him, all his colleagues were being led handcuffed to a waiting Black Maria.

Whilst this was indeed a lucky escape, the problem now

arose as to where to hide next. To a certain extent, he had allowed himself to be carried along on this terrorist venture. It wasn't really his scene and he had been given small choice in the matter anyway. If the cell leader had said 'jump' Sid had jumped. It had suited him and enabled him to put his brain in neutral and think of little else but the promised early retirement in Kilideran.

Now all that had changed. He would now be a very wanted man indeed. His first instinct was to flee back to Ireland as quickly as possible, but first he must wait until the evening edition of the London newspapers to discover what had happened that morning. Next he needed a crowd to hide in until he had time to assemble his thoughts and plan his next move. The approach of a bus prodded him into action and he quickly made the two miles to Oxford Street where he was soon lost amongst the thronging lunchtime shoppers. Meanwhile, two young detectives were bagging up everything they could find at the flat and a fingerprint expert was dusting every inch of surface. Sidney Grechen's new career as a terrorist bomber looked to be in severe jeopardy.

'You know, Elsie,' said Billie, as she stood peeling potatoes later that afternoon, 'I must say the pleasure of having all these young men about the place is ruined by the bloody noise they make. Even the music-school drum practice was never like this. What on earth are they doing out there? They're shaking this kitchen to pieces.'

Elsie licked a finger and tested the heat of the flatiron before responding.

'They had a problem with a tank track this afternoon, marm,' she replied as she began ironing a sheet with long smoothing sweeps. 'Apparently it broke as they were removing the tank from its carrier. Unfortunately, it's right outside this door and the tank is stuck halfway down the ramp and they're trying to ease it down the rest of the way.'

'You are bloody knowledgable, girl,' said Billie admiringly.

'How do you know all these terms? Is it that staff sergeant I keep seeing you sneaking little goodies out to by any chance?'

'Oh marm! How could you think that?' protested Elsie with a crimson face.

'Hmmn,' said Billie, 'I noticed you didn't deny it, though. Anyway, what d'you think about the wedding? Personally I shan't believe it until I see it. It looks to me like it's going to be one of those typical here-today-and-gone-tomorrow wartime weddings. Trouble is, it's impossible to plan anything.'

'I think they'll make a lovely couple, marm. Where do they intend to hold it?'

'It will have to be at the Streatham register office because of the short notice, but Queenie said she will hold a reception of sorts at her place but there won't be time to invite anyone other than the immediate family, plus yourself, of course.' Elsie shook her head in sympathy. 'I really don't know how youngsters cope nowadays. Some actually manage to marry with only twenty-four hours' notice and . . .' Her voice stopped so suddenly that the abruptness of its cutoff caused Elsie to look up sharply.

'Whatever's the matter, marm?' she began, as her eyes followed Billie's stare.

'Oh, no!' exclaimed Elsie as she swayed and almost fainted.

'Git that dopey cow out of the way,' snarled Sid Grechen as he sidled in from the hallway, revolver in hand. 'I'm in no mood for dramatics.'

'Oh, we've got a gun this time, have we?' jeered Billie. 'My, my, we are becoming an important little shit, aren't we?'

'Listen ter me,' snapped Sid. 'I've only got minutes ter spare and I want money! Now I've put one stripe down this dopey cow's face an' I'll match the ovver side if yer give trouble. I'm already goin' ter swing if they catch me, so I've nuffin' ter lose. I want at least fifty quid an' I want it qui— who's that?' He pointed with his revolver to the kitchen door where the outline of a man could be seen through the thick frosted glass.

'It's one of the soldiers; they've got some problem with a tank track or something,' explained Billie. 'You should have asked her. She's an authority on tanks.'

Grechen looked disdainfully at Elsie. 'Yer just git on wiv' what yer doin' an' yer'll come to no 'arm. Understand?'

'Yes, sir,' whimpered Elsie. 'Shall I carry on ironing, sir?'

'Eh?' he grunted. 'Oh, yer, but be quiet abhat it or I'll rip yer throat out.'

Sidney moved over to peep from the kitchen window whilst Elsie prepared to swop over her flatirons. Laying the cooler iron on top of the stove, she wrapped a thick cloth holder round the handle of the second iron that had gas flames licking angrily at its base. Sidney, once satisfied the soldiers were more than fully occupied, turned and faced back into the room. He had barely focused before Elsie's red-hot flatiron was thrust sizzling into his right eye-socket. It was debatable which was the loudest noise, the shot he fired blindly into the floor or his screams. Both women raced for the door and, with his hands covering his face, Sidney sightlessly followed suit. Before they cleared the doorstep, the urgent yells from the tank-transporter crew drew their attention to the broken track that lay on the ground. After colliding with the doorframe, Sidney Grechen had no such advantage and tripped and fell sprawling over the ramp. Probably the only advantage that Sidney now had, was to be spared the anguish of seeing a thirty-ton tank slipping slowly down the transporter ramp three feet from his chest.

The nearest soldier was up on the vehicle and could only yell a warning. Billie was undoubtedly the closest and she found herself reaching instinctively for the still screaming Sid. She was amazed at Elsie's strength as the maid seized her around the waist and bodily swung her away from the path of the tank. Within the space of little more than a second, the scream was replaced by a sickening squelch that, in turn, was replaced by total silence.

'WHATEVER YOU DO DON'T LOOK AT HIM!' cried the soldier, jumping from the transporter.

'We've no intention of doing so,' Elsie assured him, fingering the scar on her cheek. 'Not ever again.'

Duncan Forbes had not found the journey from Amiens to Streatham all that easy. It was one thing to have an official pass in wartime, it was quite another to have the transportation. But, by a series of threats, promises, bribes and bare-faced deceptions, he finally jumped from the platform of a 133 bus in Streatham late on Friday afternoon. Within seconds of his knocking at the door, Queenie promptly fell on him before leading him into the house.

'Jim is not back from work yet,' she said. 'But, more importantly for you, Julia is in the bathroom. Shall I warn her you're here?'

'I'd sooner you didn't,' replied Duncan. 'I'd like to see her exactly how I've imagined her for the last three months – you know – with that surprised look on her face.'

'Well, I think you're about to get just that because the bathroom door's just opened. Would you like me to do a roll of drums?'

'Oh, Queenie!' called Julia, descending the staircase. 'Could I borrow your perfume? I'd like to knock that bastard sideways if at all possible and . . .' Her jaw suddenly dropped. Duncan was sitting on the bottom step wearing one of his most impish grins.

'How about that!' he exclaimed. 'I don't see you for three months and when I do it's right up your bathrobe! D'you know what? I feel I've been knocked sideways!'

'Duncan Forbes!' she exploded. 'Isn't that just typical of you? You leave me cold since August and when you do arrive, you're too bloody early! Come and kiss me, you blighter!'

Queenie decided it would be diplomatic to leave the

couple to their reunion and tiptoed quietly into the kitchen and closed the door.

After an hour, having contemplated the volume of work in store for the weekend, she wondered when it would be diplomatic to emerge. The problem was solved for her by a ringing telephone. On answering, her apologetic husband told her he was going to be at least two hours late and he suggested that Duncan might care to drive to Hampstead to collect Billie and her maid.

'Well, I think he's heavily engaged right at this moment,' she replied, glancing over her shoulder. 'But if I put it to him nicely, perhaps he'll oblige. 'Bye, Jim.'

'We'd love to go. Wouldn't we, girl?' said Duncan in response to the request. 'It'd be lovely to drive a car again, I'm getting a bit sick of army horses.'

'Bless you,' said Queenie gratefully. 'I'll ring Billie and say her lift will be a little delayed, shall I?'

'No need,' said Duncan. 'Once Julia dresses, we're ready to go. Aren't we, girl?'

Julia agreed and within minutes he had reversed out the car and they were on their way to Hampstead.

Although the night was reasonably clear, Duncan soon began to realise the difficulty of driving in the London blackout. The masked traffic lights and the tiny torches of road-crossing pedestrians were just one more additional hazard to the lorries and buses that were all but invisible in the darkness. On their approach to Southwark Bridge, Julia said anxiously, 'Why don't you pull off the road for a little break? After all, you're not used to driving in this blackout. If nothing else it'd give your eyes a rest.'

In truth, by this time, Duncan had adjusted fairly well to the conditions, but for some while now his desire to look again at his Julia had been mounting. A short off-the-road break sounded more than ideal to him. Nodding wearily, he put on a tired countenance and turned the car off the main road and drove through the maze of little streets and alleys that led down to the river. Driving through one such street, he caught a momentary glimpse of a tall man in a long black mackintosh weaving across the cobbled road on an unlit cycle.

'Bloody fool!' yelled Duncan, swerving sharply. But the man faded into the darkness as quickly as he had appeared. In any case, there were far more important matters to concern a fine healthy lad. Within a few minutes, the car bumped noisily over the Victorian cobbles of the narrow Bankside thoroughfare and Duncan parked tidily by the river wall.

'Well,' said Julia, looking at the black river on one side and the sinister warehouses on the other, 'it's not quite what I had in mind, but . . .' Her voice was stifled as he swamped her face with kisses. She did not even offer token resistance but counterattacked with kiss for kiss and bite for bite. Within a few minutes, she was lying back moaning with passion on the rear seat with her eyes closed and her lover deep inside her. After climaxing, she dreamily opened one eye and reality came crashing back when she saw not one, but two faces, absorbed in her now bare breasts. There was firstly her lover but beyond him, his face pressed flat against the window, was a horrible, leering individual. She gasped and stiffened. Duncan turned his head instantly over his shoulder. The face disappeared in a trice and, after a pause to button up, Duncan was in hot pursuit, screaming murderous threats.

He was gaining fast when his foot caught against the wheel of an old cycle that had lain propped up against the river wall. He was sent sprawling and by the time he was on his feet again, the peeper had reached a barbed-wire fence which sheer terror enabled him to scale at the cost only of his mackintosh. By this time Duncan had lost a shoe and a fair bit of enthusiasm. However, he did have the mackintosh on which he gleefully pounced before venting his fury by shredding it into strips. Pausing to brush himself, he again saw the old cycle lying flat on it side with the wheels still revolving. Without further ado, he picked it up and after a couple of practice heaves, cast it as far into the river as his strength would allow.

'Feel better for that?' smiled Julia as he returned.

'I'd have felt a whole lot better if I'd caught the bastard,' he panted. 'I would have ribboned him like his coat and slung him in the river with his bloody bike.'

'I doubt it,' she said.

'Why d'you say that?' he asked irritably.

'Because that wasn't his bike,' she replied quietly. 'If you remember, we saw that bloke when he swerved across your path ten minutes ago, and he didn't have any cycle lights. That bike did. The back one was still shining when it sank in the water.'

'What!' cried Duncan, glancing frantically around him. 'Let's get out of here quick. We've had enough bother as it is!'

After straightening his clothes, Duncan began a three-point turn and having completed it, was just about to move away when a figure appeared out of the dark of an alley opposite. 'It's him!' cried Duncan slamming on the brakes. 'It's definitely . . . Er, wait a minute, no, I'm afraid it's *not* him,' he whispered as the dark figure slowly took shape as a burly policeman.

'Oy, there, just a minute, guv,' called the constable.

'Oh, hell!' Duncan muttered to Julia. 'I know this bloke. Let's keep our heads down and hope he doesn't recognise me . . . Er – yes, officer,' he said, winding down the car window a bare inch.

The policeman pointed to the river wall. 'You seen anything of a bike that was left there?'

'Er – no, I'm afraid not,' lied Duncan. 'My er – wife and I got lost in the blackout. We're trying to get back to Southwark Bridge. If we continue this way will we be all right?'

'Will you be all right? Will you be all right?' the constable repeated furiously. 'I don't give a shit if yer all right. D'yer know, I've 'ad that bike fer nigh on thirty years and now it's gorn, so *I'm* 'ardly *all right*! D'you also know I shouldn't even 'ave been 'ere ter lose it? I've done my service already,' he snarled, rapidly prodding his huge chest with a fat forefinger. 'By rights I should be retired. And d'yer know *why* I'm not retired? No? Well just you listen to this . . .'